Barbara Toner is an acclaimed author and columnist who has written extensively about the lot of women in all its manifestations, with all its glorious and less glorious intricacies, both in fiction and non-fiction. She is married and has three daughters, and divides her time between England and the far south coast of New South Wales.

FOUR Respectable LADIES SEEK Part-time HUSBAND

BARBARA TONER

BANTAM
SYDNEY AUCKLAND TORONTO NEW YORK LONDON

A Bantam book
Published by Penguin Random House Australia Pty Ltd
Level 3, 100 Pacific Highway, North Sydney NSW 2060
www.penguin.com.au

First published by Bantam in 2018

Copyright © Barbara Toner 2018

The moral right of the author has been asserted.

All rights reserved. No part of this book may be reproduced or transmitted by any person or entity, including internet search engines or retailers, in any form or by any means, electronic or mechanical, including photocopying (except under the statutory exceptions provisions of the Australian *Copyright Act 1968*), recording, scanning or by any information storage and retrieval system without the prior written permission of Penguin Random House Australia.

Addresses for the Penguin Random House group of companies can be found at global.penguinrandomhouse.com/offices.

 A catalogue record for this book is available from the National Library of Australia

ISBN 978 0 14378 755 6

Cover design by www.blacksheep-uk.com
Cover illustrations from Depositphotos
Typeset in 12.5/17 pt Adobe Garamond by Midland Typesetters, Australia
Printed in Australia by Griffin Press, an accredited ISO AS/NZS 14001:2004 Environmental Management System printer

Penguin Random House Australia uses papers that are natural, renewable and recyclable products and made from wood grown in sustainable forests. The logging and manufacturing processes are expected to conform to the environmental regulations of the country of origin.

*With much love to my excellent sisters,
Carolyn and Grette, and to sisters everywhere*

Prologue

When Adelaide Nightingale, Louisa Worthington, Maggie O'Connell and Pearl McCleary threw caution to the winds, disgrace was bound to follow. They lived in a time and place peculiar in history on the matter of sex versus gender.

The time was September 1919. The war was over. Everyone who was going to die from the flu had done so.

The place was Prospect, a bustling rural town in southern New South Wales known abroad for its sheep and awful weather but distinguished in its own eyes by the imminent arrival of the railway and the excellence of its general store, Nightingales.

It sounds harmless enough. It wasn't.

Nightingales was pivotal to the ladies' fate, although right-thinking people argued the mess was of their own making and could be traced directly to the arrival in Prospect of Pearl McCleary. The shop, these decent people insisted, had nothing to do with it. But it did, because Nightingales was equally at odds with the time and place, just the oddness was never mentioned.

This might have been because it was owned by the upright family Adelaide had married into, but more likely it was because of the comfort the town had taken in its luxury all war long. Nightingales was uniquely well stocked. Customers came from hundreds of miles just to breathe in the heady scent of indulgence and smallgoods that whacked them in the face as they crossed the threshold.

For maintaining such extraordinary standards, which it was generally believed reflected Prospect's own, the town gave thanks to Archie Stokes. There was no finer shopkeeper in the whole of Australia than this large, white-haired, purple-faced, steely-eyed beacon of respectful service with his infallible grasp of all things grocery and his cunning understanding of ways and means. He was the shop's – and so the town's – heart and soul.

Which was one way of looking at it.

Chapter One

There are always dissenters, especially silent ones. Adelaide Nightingale née Bluett was dissenting her heart out as she hurried along Prospect's main thoroughfare, Hope Street, on a bitterly cold spring day when no one could have foreseen the outrage that would bring horror and delight to the town in equal measure. Her blonde head was bent against the wind, her large grey eyes were watering from cold and despair, and two bright pink patches of remorse coloured her faintly freckled cheeks.

She clutched a thin poplin coat about her to ward off the weather but it no longer met across her chest. It failed in every way to ward off anything, least of all the bitter knowledge that while she'd been in charge of the shop, Archie Stokes had wormed his way from its perimeter into its precious centre where he'd become sole procurer of merchandise and sole keeper of the books. He wasn't the last word in honesty everyone believed him to be. He was a liar. He was a thief. She knew it. She knew he knew she knew it. She knew they both knew there wasn't a thing she could do about it.

'Now, Mrs Nightingale,' he'd said just ten minutes ago, 'you pay me to do the books, so leave the books to me.' He'd smiled and winked at her. They both knew that every night he cooked those books and took from the till whatever amount he guessed wouldn't be challenged by a woman famous for being as silly as a duck since she'd had her noisy baby. He was famous for his excellent business brain. He could, within seconds of clapping eyes on a customer, tell you how much they owed and how quickly but politely he would refuse them further credit. No one doubted him for a minute. Except Adelaide, who'd yet again failed to confront him out of cowardice. And exhaustion. And uncertainty.

Adelaide was as certain about Archie Stokes as she could be, but she was blessed with a sweetness of nature that suggested second thoughts on everything. She thought she was sure, but who would believe her? Not her husband. Not his mother. No one she could think of, since she'd never been sure about anything.

The uncertainty raging in her poor, tired brain played on her face for the entire world to see. There were deep blue circles under the grey eyes that were blank from lack of sleep. There was misery about her mouth and something unkempt about her hair, which was a poor show in an eminent businesswoman. Not that anyone considered her to be a businesswoman any more than they believed her husband to be all there. She knew what everyone thought. Captain Nightingale had been back for more than a year but there was still no sign of the bit of his mind he'd left in France. She sometimes wondered if he hadn't mislaid it locally in his youth but in her eagerness to marry him she'd failed to notice.

In its absence, Archie Stokes had consolidated his position as young Mrs Nightingale's trusted right-hand man on whom she relied for everything because she was a bit of an idiot. This was how she was seen, Adelaide was sure of it. She looked like a woman who was failing to manage, who would never be able to manage because she had no idea how to run a household, let alone a store famous for the joy it brought to harsh, rural wartime living. She looked like a woman with a bawling baby she couldn't calm, a raging husband she couldn't pacify and a life far more complicated than anything she'd been prepared for.

Poor Adelaide, walking so fast along Hope Street that she could have been running, stifled a sob. Did she care that women running in broad daylight look mad however sane they think they are? She did not. She was stupid and cowardly and also ugly, so what did it matter? That's how she looked so that's what she would become. She had gone to the store in her capacity as the owner's wife and, yet again, she'd failed to exert herself.

She broke into a trot as she passed through the large sandstone Coronation Arch that announced to travellers that they were arriving or leaving Prospect, even though the town, strictly speaking, began a quarter of a mile along the road where the plain gave way to bush. The bush turned into scrub, which was barely distinguishable from the first property you came to on the right if you approached from the east.

This was the O'Connells' rundown farm. Between the O'Connells' and Adelaide's own large house was a dusty lane leading to the vast acres of Somerset Station, fifty years the Bluett family seat, currently owned by Adelaide's brother, Angus, but let to an antisocial man called Fletcher. Across the road was the Worthington place, once as smart as Adelaide's but now reduced and neglected. All those properties were as entitled to have been included within the town's boundaries as anything further up Hope Street, but they'd been overlooked in the siting of The Arch, and so somehow the residents of the enclave known as Beyond The Arch had come to be regarded as separate. It mattered. In the long run, it mattered.

Close to home, Adelaide began to run. It was well after lunch, milk from the two o'clock feed was drenching her bodice and she could hear the baby screaming from 200 yards away. She thought she could hear Marcus yelling at the new housekeeper to make that baby go to sleep and she pictured Pearl McCleary cooing and rocking and clapping and singing and skipping about the room, banging a pan with a wooden spoon as the child grew ever more frantic.

She didn't see Louisa Worthington backing out of her front gate, and because she was leaving backwards, Louisa didn't see her. They crashed to the ground, each grabbing the other, though whether to save herself or her neighbour no one could have told. Adelaide, the taller by a good four inches and heavier by several stone, fell on top of Louisa, who blinked at her in disbelief.

'Heavens, Louisa, watch where you're going,' the now not-so-gentle Adelaide snapped. She pushed herself to her feet and yanked at Louisa's arm to help her up but dropped it when Louisa didn't budge. 'You're not hurt, are you?'

'Your baby's crying,' Louisa said. 'Screaming.' She hauled herself upright and brushed down her skirt. 'I'm on my way to the shop. Do you know if my tea has arrived?' But Adelaide had already crossed the road, hurried down her path without looking back and closed her front door behind her. Her house suggested wealth with its many asymmetrical gables but it needed paint, and here and there, nails.

Louisa stared after her, then back at her own house, equally large but with fewer gables and in need of not just paint and nails. It could also have done with a new roof, a new path to the front door and the total demolition of the crumbling brick wall to which a once lovely gate was only half attached. She asked herself if she should go back into the house to check that the doors and windows were locked. She'd been glancing back for possible points of illegal entry when she'd reversed into Adelaide. If she returned to the house she could examine her clothes for dirt and holes. She thought about it. But she didn't. She wouldn't let herself. Punctuality was more important than a tiny rip in a lace blouse or a silk skirt and she was darned if she'd let nerves get the better of her. She stopped thinking about Adelaide as quickly as Adelaide had stopped thinking about her. Like Adelaide, she had so much more to worry about.

She didn't run, or even walk unusually fast, back the way Adelaide had come along Hope Street and into the town. She strolled, in the composed manner of a calm widow from an important local family on her way to interview a bank manager who would certainly be from something less. Her plan was very definitely that she should interview him and not the other way round. She was a client with a substantial property and clever moneymaking schemes that couldn't fail to appeal to anyone with an eye for a sound investment from an attractive woman.

Louisa knew from constant assessment that grief had, if anything, improved her looks. She was just that bit slimmer in the face and more delicate in her carriage. She knew very well how to drop her disturbingly blue eyes in the face of men's brilliance. She knew how to tantalise by wrapping a long dark tendril around her index finger as she gave men's opinions respectful due. So stately was her pace along Hope Street that she could easily have been taken for the woman she hoped the world believed her to be: slightly bored and rich, with no more on her mind than tea. She clung to the confidence she'd spent days marshalling even as it began to slither away from her.

Ahead of her was the horror of the bank. Behind her was the horror of home. She wished she'd worn a coat. Lace and silk were no match for the wind. She shivered but she didn't falter. She squared her shoulders and took a deep breath, turning her attention to the speech she had prepared. She had a house. She had many horses. Surely a moneyman could see the possibilities, and if not the possibilities, then the obligation to a widow whose husband had sacrificed his life so that the nation's banks could prosper.

She passed St Benedict's, she passed The Irish Rover, she passed the offices of *The Prospect Gazette*, the town hall, and on the other side of the road wide enough to accommodate stampeding cattle, she passed the chemist, the newsagents, Elsie's Teashop, the baker, the butcher, Browns the fabric shop, and Furlongs, which sold ugly clothes. She saw but didn't acknowledge Theresa Fellows carrying flowers into St Benedict's and Charlie Saunders overseeing the unloading of beer barrels at the pub. She didn't register the sheep being herded into the stockyard down Endeavour Road.

What stopped her in her tracks was a staggeringly large sign so poorly fixed to the noticeboard outside the Arts and Crafts Hall that, had she not jumped out of its way, it would have slapped her hard across the chest. 'This is ridiculous,' she said to no one in particular. And it was ridiculous. Nothing could have been more ridiculous.

The sign announced 'A Very Special Evening with Florence Mayberry', who was to speak at seven o'clock sharp that night on 'A Matter of Huge Importance to The Nation'. Mrs Mayberry was to impart information of the Utmost Significance to Each and Every Household but most especially to Prospect's Womenfolk. Louisa would have laughed out loud had she not been so upset by the sign's near miss with her bosom.

Florence Mayberry had never uttered a single important word in living memory. Florence Mayberry was a ludicrous woman who had devoted herself to being the Mayor's wife for as long as Louisa could remember, so constantly at his side that she could easily have been mistaken for his plump, fretful shadow. What on earth could she have to say on behalf of the nation that she hadn't so much as murmured during the war or in the face of the flu? Not even 'Help make masks' when families were breathing their last twenty miles away, or 'Knit more socks' even though her son would have benefited from them as well as any other Prospect man who'd signed up for King and Country.

Louisa gave the sign a tug, releasing it even further from its moorings so that now it dangled pointlessly and even more precariously. She hurried on, her pace quickening with her heart at the sudden and welcome thought of William Mayberry. Handsome William Mayberry who had called to offer his condolences. 'Your efforts on the home front were very much appreciated, Louisa, I want you to know that,' he'd said, because she had been a keen if spasmodic knitter. She'd given him a playful push in the chest and poured him more gin. She could recall even now the feeling of that firm chest under her hand. How mad that silly Mrs Mayberry was his mother. And oh Lord, here was the bank already.

Louisa paused to moisten her lips with a tongue that was suddenly parched. She'd completely forgotten the details of breeding or possibly racing quite thin horses or maybe re-inventing a carriage that looked and sounded like a car but still required horses to pull it. And now she was walking past the teller and here was Mr Thomas, the manager, ushering her into his office and, so quickly did the time pass, there turned out to be none at all for any interviewing or proposing on her side, let alone tantalising.

Mr Thomas asked some very short questions concerning income, which she answered untruthfully as best she could, and then he offered a series of explanations that brooked no argument. She had the house, but the house was in need of repair. Even if it hadn't been, until she could prove some way of repaying any loan he might make, she was a very poor investment. He was sorry, he had the greatest respect for her late father and late husband – her mother wasn't late as well, was she; so many people had gone – but he could make no advance against her house or her horses.

'I have forty-three,' she said.

'Get rid of them,' was his unhelpful advice. And she could. She could shoot the lot and what would that make her in the eyes of the world? A horse murderer, when at the moment she was their saviour, accommodating them in a large paddock with plenty of grass. She was now, like it or not, potty Mrs Worthington, widow of the apparently not-rich-after-all Lieutenant Worthington, in her grief collecting horses and with hare-brained schemes about what she could do with them.

If the general view was humiliating, the truth was even more so. The late Lieutenant had been so far from rich that despite being up to his eyes in mud and combat, he'd entered into an insane arrangement with unknown creditors to ensure her future comfort. There was to be no comfort, only poverty. Unpaid for and now unwanted horses, destined for the Front at his instigation, would continue to be delivered to her paddock in the dead of night until she found the money he'd agreed to pay for them. But there was no money and never would be.

The air was so chilly when she was shown out of the bank that she began to shiver. Her whole body shook. Her brain seemed to be shaking, unable to control itself in its panic. No brave soldier husband to help her. No Daddy. Only her mother who, in widowhood, had removed herself to the south of France from where she had written, 'Louisa, you were warned.' Ahead of her lay ruin.

Across the road to taunt her was Nightingales, where possibly her tea was waiting but what did it matter when she couldn't pay for it, when all it represented was everything she no longer had or would ever have again? How dare Adelaide treat her so rudely, knocking her to the ground and stalking off without a word of comfort? How dare great galumphing Adelaide, never as beautiful or clever or graceful as she was, now have everything she didn't have, like a husband, a baby and money to burn.

Poor Louisa, walking so slowly back along Hope Street that other pedestrians trod on her heels, wondered what would become of her. She didn't know how to be poor.

Maggie O'Connell, on the other hand, with only vague memories of being anything else, rarely fretted about what would become of her. 'Hello, Maggie,' Louisa said dully when she reached the Arts and Crafts Hall to find the third resident from Beyond the Arch reattaching the sign by weaving bits of wire around hooks and nails. 'Heading home?' It was less the question than the way it was asked that startled them both. It was full of need and melancholy that suggested, what? They walk together? They had never walked together even though they had lived within coo-ee of each other for five years.

'I'm going to work, Mrs Worthington,' said Maggie.

'Of course,' said Louisa. 'The Mayberrys.' She lingered as Maggie gave the main wire a final twist. 'What do you think she has to tell us?'

Maggie picked up her basket. 'Search me. She's been to Melbourne, that's all I know. She's been to Melbourne and seen the light.'

'Surely not God.'

'Wouldn't know,' said Maggie. 'She's very pleased with herself.'

They faced each other awkwardly, buffeted by the wind but no longer threatened by the sign. 'What do you make of the Nightingales' new housekeeper? Not very friendly, is she?' Louisa said, so clearly wanting company that Maggie edged away.

'Theresa Fellows says she's got airs and graces.'

'Does she? Not that Mrs Fellows would know.' The neighbours stared at each other, one dark, the other fair, one elegant, the other making-do, one parading as rich, the other quite plainly poor. How little they had in common.

'I'd better get a move on,' said Maggie, and off she headed to clean the Mayberrys' rambling house, leaving Louisa shuddering at the possibility that, any day now, she too might be reduced to drudgery.

Maggie, just eighteen and as fair and fresh-faced as a newly bloomed tea rose, though less fashionable, rarely shuddered at her lot. She worked at the Mayberrys' every day for five hours and although that house never grew any cleaner, it didn't bother her a bit. Maggie's thoughts turned mostly on pleasant things. Today these included the serial she was reading in Mrs Mayberry's latest copy of *A Lady's Leisure*, some cheese she would buy from Nightingales on the way home, her brothers having stayed at school all morning, and the possibility she might come back into town after tea to listen to her employer speak.

Hers were simple pleasures. She accepted that she had no money and that her house was so dilapidated her neighbours would cheerfully have kicked it down had ever they mustered that degree of civic pride and cruelty in the one breath. The farm had had gone to rack and ruin but it was still hers; her twin brothers were a trial but she loved them, not just for themselves but also for the mother who'd died the minute they'd left her womb and she'd understood there were two of them. She loved them more than she loved their father who'd seen the war as his best chance to run off with the redhead being trained in the telegraph at the Post Office saying, 'My country needs me' and not been heard of since. She loved Ed and Al more than anyone else on earth, which was just as well when everyone else on earth struggled to tolerate them. That anyone did even a little bit was a credit to the way she'd raised them for the past three years. Now they were ten, they very nearly had some manners.

Florence Mayberry let it be known that she employed Maggie out of the goodness of her heart because Maggie was The World's Worst Cleaner. Theresa Fellows, who had a son the same age and fed the boys once a week, laughed her head off about that. Everyone knew Mrs Mayberry paid poor Maggie a pittance. And she knew in her heart that her own kindness to the boys was self-interest. If Maggie slit her throat from desperation, Father Kelly would expect her to take them in.

It goes to show how little she knew. Maggie might have had just cause to be an own-throat-slitter, but nothing was less likely. She could make the most of simple pleasures because her dreams were as large and starlit as the Prospect sky on a clear December night. Her faith in glorious outcomes was so glowing and shiny and uplifting that it held her aloft through the very bleakest of times.

Her most brilliant dream was that any day now, with the railway on their doorstep, a handsome stranger would seek her out and transform her life, as well as the lives of her wretched brothers, forever. He'd arrive without ceremony, and without ceremony he would restore to her the wealth and property that had been wrenched from her family by her neighbours, the wicked Bluetts. True love, she was certain, would triumph over the injustice that stained her past. True love, along with the passion, the riches and the muscular care she knew was in her future. And no one would have guessed any of this because Maggie's demeanour suggested only that she was a tough little blighter, taking life on the chin, a blessing when it had so very little to offer.

It was only now and again that things got the better of her and today wasn't such a day. Today, she knew that Florence Mayberry would be so distracted by the enormity of her first public appearance as a solo performer that she wouldn't care less whether her daily help scrubbed or ironed or plonked herself down in the scullery to smear polish over the family silver while reading her magazines from England. Maggie had no qualms about shirking. The magazines compensated for the very low wages and the long hours she spent working her fingers to the bone. She told herself as she passed Nightingales, *I'm better off than Adelaide Bluett, in any case*, and she found that heartening.

Where Louisa looked into the world and saw only horses and darkness, Maggie showed a lively interest. She had no love for any Bluett, even one who was now a Nightingale, but she'd heard Adelaide's baby screaming, seen her husband's madness and beadily diagnosed her as a woman about to crack from nerves.

Adelaide might not have swapped places with Maggie – who in their right mind would clean for Florence Mayberry or raise two criminal boys single-handed unless they had to? – but if they were talking about getting enough sleep, then everyone was better off than she was. As Maggie decided she would buy not only cheese but also pickles on the way home, Adelaide was asking herself where she would be without Pearl McCleary and how on earth she'd ever managed without her.

Thanks to the new housekeeper she'd suffered just the single minute of panic when she'd marched away from Louisa, slammed the front door and found each successive room so empty of babies that the only possible explanation was infanticide. Panic mixed with elation, if she were honest. But the baby had been far from dead, and now that he was no longer hungry he slept in his pram by the open kitchen door and the house was calm.

The house was calm because Pearl McCleary was calm. Everything about her conveyed calm. Her low and measured tone, her even moods, her ready smile, her gentle laugh, her pleasant looks, her intelligent gaze, not to mention the sure and certain manner so easily mistaken by Theresa Fellows for airs and graces. 'Tea?' she suggested to Adelaide once the baby was fed. 'And what about a sandwich?'

You'd have thought she was born to restore order to a troubled household, but no such thing. Pearl McCleary was in that household under false pretences, fooling everyone with her calm. She might have been valued for her quick solutions and decisive planning, but beneath that calm exterior was a skittish interior.

She was no more calm than the next woman struggling to track down the newly returned but vanished soldier she no longer loved even though she had promised to marry him. She was no less jumpy than anyone else hunting a man so determined to avenge an unspecified wrong done to a barely known fallen comrade that he had placed himself in mortal danger with no thought whatsoever for the ailing sister who was pining for him.

Pearl McCleary betrayed nothing of this, and it was easy; a housekeeper is required to have no past of any consequence. The only bit of it that mattered, in any case, was very recent, so she had no qualms about concealing the crisis that had overtaken it.

She might have tolerated a longer parting from her missing fiancé, but his frail sister, Beattie, could not. Little Beattie's sixteen-year-old heart was so exhausted from flu and waiting for her brother to return unscathed from war it now threatened to stop beating altogether. 'Please find him, Pearl,' she'd begged when Pearl had explained he wouldn't be coming home as planned. 'Promise me you'll find him. If anyone can, you can.'

Pearl had cradled the little thing and promised. And now here she was, doing her best to find him but her best was turning out to be so useless that every nerve in her outwardly unruffled body jangled. She feared for the hearts of both sister and brother. Daniel Flannagan had certainly lost touch with the proper demands on his. The fallen soldier wasn't even a proper comrade. His dying moments were the only ones they'd shared. In her pocket, as she fussed about the Nightingale kitchen, was the letter that proved it.

I went to war to make you proud of me, Pearl, he'd written not two weeks before. *But I'm not proud of myself. Heroes fell when I didn't fall and one of them died for me. He died in my arms, Pearl, from the sniper's bullet that should have killed me. He was a Catholic man and he died, not with a prayer on his lips, but cursing a villain whose cruelty has deprived his children of their birthright.*

Kneeling in the blood-soaked mud of Ypres, Daniel had pledged to right the terrible wrong done to that man even though he didn't know him from Adam and the wrong had been done many years ago in a place even less accessible than Woop Woop. Worse, by the sound of it, the mission was no less dangerous than Ypres. The wretched soldier had made that clear. His enemy was ruthless. But Daniel had sworn before God he would see the family right and now, he said, he must square himself in the eyes of God.

'Who cares about God, Annie? What about his own sister?' Pearl had said bitterly on reading the letter. And Annie McGuire, as good as a mother to Pearl for twenty-three years and Beattie for the past eight, had ordered her not to blaspheme. 'I'm going to find him,' Pearl had vowed, 'and I'm going to shake some sense into the idiot. He's not even that religious.'

Annie had urged restraint. 'You don't know what passes between a man and his Maker,' she'd said. 'Read the letter again,' she'd advised. 'He says, "Don't try to find me." He has his reasons, Pearl. Please, think before you act.' But it wasn't in Pearl's nature.

The most significant part of the letter, as far as she was concerned, had been its postmark. 'Where is Prospect?'

The journey had been slow and tiring, via train to Cooma, then by coach across the Monaro, but Pearl had been rewarded for her trouble by the Divine Providence Annie had prayed for. On Annie's advice – 'The man is struggling with his immortal soul' – she'd made her way directly to the presbytery attached to St Benedict's where, miraculously, Father Kelly had agreed he had heard the confession of a man resembling her missing friend. Then Providence, for reasons best known to itself, had shot through. The man had left the day he arrived. Going where? Pearl had wanted to know, but the priest had said even if he knew, he couldn't reveal what had been said in the confessional.

'He wouldn't have told you this, I bet,' Pearl had said angrily. 'He's looking for a wronged family who has nothing to do with him and he's turned his back on his own sister who is dying.'

The priest had shaken his head. He was sorry, he'd said, but he couldn't help. He could only advise caution and patience. Daniel wouldn't be the first returning soldier to need time to himself before facing his loved ones.

'He needs to face them,' Pearl had snapped, 'while they live and breathe.'

And the priest had sighed. He'd stared for a few minutes at the statue of The Sacred Heart on the mantelpiece and then he'd said as if the Sacred Heart had told him to, 'Have you thought about the railway?' She'd asked what railway and he'd said the one connecting Cooma to Prospect due for completion within the year. It was hiding all sorts of misfits and desperate men.

Pearl might have said, *He's not a misfit*, but it had seemed to her that the priest was giving her the most helpful information he could, so she'd gathered her gloves and bag. 'I'll go at once.'

'You can't!' Father Kelly had cried in alarm. It wasn't safe for a woman to go alone to such a place. No one would countenance it. He most certainly wouldn't. Why didn't she hire a man to find her friend? It would be so much simpler.

A lesser woman might have wept. The priest had plainly expected tears. He'd offered her tea and a copy of *The Gazette* to console her, and here Providence had relented and come up with a suggestion. In *The Gazette* under a heading in bold that read **Very Urgent**, Pearl had found Adelaide's plea for a desperately needed housekeeper, a sign if ever there was one that Prospect was where she should station herself.

Adelaide had interviewed her that afternoon and given her the job on the spot, to start immediately. 'Of course it's a good idea,' Pearl had insisted impatiently to Annie in a phone call from the Post Office mainly concerned with the trunk she needed to be packed and sent at once. 'Think about it, Annie. Who cares about a housekeeper?'

On this score, at least, she'd turned out to be right. She'd no sooner unpacked the meagre contents of her overnight bag in the small room assigned to her than who she was or had ever been disappeared from public view. Within minutes, Adelaide had sat her at the kitchen table to talk and talk and talk at her, and she'd showed positively no interest in the whys and wherefores of her new employee's existence. She now knew only as much as was required by protocol.

Miss McCleary was a woman whose fiancé was missing in action, who'd been raised in Sydney by an Irishwoman, not her mother, called Mrs McGuire who took in unwanted children. She had no brothers or sisters that she knew of and she was a Catholic. 'We are Church of England,' had been her only comment and Pearl had waited for the implications but there hadn't been any. That was it. That was enough. It suited them both down to the ground.

Pearl, dark-haired, dark-eyed, pale-skinned and slender, might have been better looking than Adelaide, younger than Adelaide, as educated as Adelaide and in many respects as well dressed, well mannered and cultured as Adelaide but, in the very few days they'd lived under the one roof, Adelaide had appeared neither to notice nor care so they were a perfect match. Adelaide needed kindness, her housekeeper was happy to provide it.

'Why don't you put your feet up while I get on with dinner?' Pearl suggested now that order had been thoroughly restored. But Adelaide didn't feel like putting her feet anywhere except under the table opposite an adult who would listen to her with interest.

'Let's not worry about dinner for a minute. Sit down and have a cup of tea with me,' she said. 'The shop was full of gossip this morning. The Mayor's wife has done something extraordinary but I still have no idea what.'

Pearl sat and handed Adelaide a copy of *The Gazette*, which she'd scoured for descriptions of random strangers and wronged families. 'Was it this?' she asked.

Adelaide scanned the article without understanding it. 'What on earth is she talking about? Addressing the nation. Florence Mayberry is the most ridiculous woman on earth.'

'I thought I might go,' Pearl said.

'Don't be so silly,' Adelaide replied. Then they looked at each other in silence, equally puzzled because Adelaide's opinion hadn't been sought and Pearl wasn't sure why it had been offered.

'Rabbit pie?' she suggested, getting to her feet.

'Why not?' Adelaide poured herself more tea. Nothing in Pearl's manner suggested injured feelings or impending scandal. Just unflappable composure. 'I ran into Mrs Worthington on the way home.'

Pearl chose potatoes from a basket. 'Did you ask about her horses?'

'I forgot. I ran right into her. Smack! She landed flat on her back. It wasn't funny. Well, it *was* funny. She's such a vain little thing. There she was staring up at me like, well, I don't know, an underdressed baby rabbit I'd shot in the head. It was funny.'

Adelaide continued to prattle as Pearl peeled the potatoes then chopped onions and carrots and meat. 'You wouldn't believe the tickets she has on herself. Like Mrs Mayberry. The pride of that woman!'

'I'd like to hear what she has to say,' Pearl said, smiling to show she meant it.

'She's so dull,' said Adelaide. 'It'd be such a waste of time.'

Pearl laughed. 'But I haven't had a night off since I got here. It might be an outing.'

Adelaide clapped her hand to her mouth. 'Of course you need a night off. By all means have a night off. If we can get the baby to sleep before we go, Marcus can mind him and we can both have an outing.' She pushed herself to her feet. 'In that case I'd better do the books while I can. Oh Lord, I hate sums.'

Maggie O'Connell did not hate sums because her life depended on them and she, hurrying down Hope Street after a not very gruelling day at work, calculated and recalculated and came to the very conclusion Adelaide had reached months ago.

What Adelaide thought she knew for sure, Maggie now definitely suspected. She'd bought the pickles as well as the cheese. She could afford neither but shopping at Nightingales gave her as much pleasure as a heartbreaking novel. Mr Stokes had totted up the bill. One and threepence, he'd said, and Maggie had handed him two shillings. He'd given her change, not the nine pence she'd been expecting but threepence, and when she'd smiled and told him he owed her sixpence, he'd said, 'No, girlie, don't argue with Mr Stokes. He never makes a mistake.' So she'd left the store, counted her change and after a few minutes' deliberation gone back in to confront him.

'I know what was in my purse,' she'd said.

He'd sighed. 'I suppose you want me to take everything from the till and count it and check the whole day's dockets to see which of us is handier with numbers.' He'd winked at Theresa Fellows next to Maggie at the counter. That *was* what she'd wanted but Theresa Fellows had said shame on her, Mr Stokes was as honest as the day was long. Maggie had been tempted to ask, would that be any old day in bush week? But she'd thought better of it because she needed Theresa Fellows to feed Al and Ed once a week.

Now she stopped outside the Arts and Crafts Hall to examine the meagre contents of her purse one more time in case he had given her the right change after all. She tipped the coins into her hand and counted them again. But there had been no mistake. She knew how much money she had to the farthing. Florence Mayberry staring down at her from her poster wore an expression that said louder than any words she might have uttered, *Beggars can't be choosers*. This was the trouble. All of those ladies were light on for choice, not because they were feeble but because times were against them. And they were a little bit feeble.

Chapter Two

The entire country was enfeebled, having emptied its coffers defending the King. Australia was so stony broke that people were asking if the stupid war had actually been worth it. Traitors, obviously. Of course it had been worth it. The King was safe and so was his Empire, which was all that mattered. This was the view of right-thinking people, and even as valiant ships disgorged sung and unsung heroes to their native shore and families counted their losses, these very people were shaking their heads in rural towns right across New South Wales.

As towns went, Prospect might have been lucky to have escaped the flu that had despatched so many but it was, in other respects, no luckier than anywhere else. Men who'd disappeared from the landscape for four years were coming home without the foggiest notion of what was in store for them. Letters to the Front had been brave and optimistic, in recognition of their own bravery and optimism. *We're doing fine,* they'd said. *The Murphys sold their pigs. We have loads of pumpkins.*

The returning soldiers had no way of knowing that home had changed forever and the women at home were in no way prepared for the horrors their brave men brought back with them. There were exceptions, of course, but by and large nothing was what it had been. Everything was in a state of flux. Not chaos, flux, and amid the flux, subversive elements were suspected of taking advantage, which scared the living daylights out of the right-thinking people. In the general clamour to fend them off, unexpected voices rose with astonishing vehemence. In Prospect, Florence Mayberry's. Florence Mayberry!

How extraordinary that this mouse of a quite large woman should find passion so close to her voice box. She'd been silent so long she'd occasionally been mistaken for a mute. But as Maggie had explained to Louisa, she'd been to Melbourne the minute quarantine was lifted and come back transformed. The light she'd seen shone not only on The Threat Within as described by powerful city voices, but on her hitherto unsuspected gift for oratory.

So inspired had she been by the horror as described by a marvellous woman from a convention in South Yarra, she'd known it was her Bounden Duty to bring the message to the masses, to speak out as that woman had done. And this is what she was doing to the packed Arts and Crafts Hall on the freezing September evening that followed our heroines' nerve-racking day. She was speaking out to such great effect that Pearl and Adelaide, sitting together, and Louisa and Maggie in different rows on opposite sides of the hall, found themselves transfixed. Everyone was transfixed.

Who was this unrecognisable and faintly insane-looking firebrand on the stage? They marvelled at her voice, so unbelievably penetrating with its exceptionally high-pitched nasal quality and occasionally remembered lisp. What kind of woman, Louisa asked herself, who was fifty if she was a day, had a voice like that? It wasn't even a voice Maggie recognised, though in fairness, Florence Mayberry communicated with her mostly in writing and the lisp was newly acquired. Mrs Mayberry was intrigued by its potential to command attention.

Tonight, it was only too clear she was determined to be heard. Not just in the Arts and Crafts Hall but by the whole of the shire. Her message was as bewildering to some as it was beguiling to others, punctuated by many, many words with Capital Letters, which she indicated with the crafty employment of extra volume. She was undeniably and staggeringly fluent, as well she might have been when most of what she had to say was word for word what the inspirational Melbourne woman had said. Not entirely, but as best she could remember, and she'd practised her delivery for long hours in front of the bedroom mirror Maggie polished when she felt like it. She had timed every gesture for maximum impact.

'I'm talking to you, you, you and you,' she advised loudly from the podium, aiming a plump index finger at individual women in the front rows who, startled, looked behind them to see who could possibly have merited the attention. 'I'm addressing the entire female population of this great town because it ith,' she lisped, 'My Duty. My Duty is,' she didn't lisp, 'to remind you of your Patriotic Obligation To Our Noble Nation.' She might have been the vicar's wife with a speech impediment.

What she was urging was that Australia's Men Should Be Men and Australia's Women Should Be Women. 'Dear Lord,' muttered Adelaide to Pearl. It was their great nation's only chance of survival. Women, Mrs Mayberry insisted, must return to the hearth and allow their menfolk to run the community in the time-honoured way. If they didn't, the natural order upon which All Of Human Life Depended would collapse, and from the rubble God alone knew what kind of socialist terror would arise. She spoke, she thought they should know, on behalf of The Country Women's Campaign For The Restoration of Family Life, an unofficial branch of something similar which was famous in Melbourne

'Our nation, our state, our cities, our towns, *this* town, is threatened by Subversive Elements whose Fearful Aim is no less than the Destruction of Tho-ciety. Sothiety,' she cried, though her voice was giving out, 'has been fractured by Unnatural Circumstances dictated by Foreign Malevolence and so we must rebuild it along the lines ordained by God the Father in Heaven and Mother Nature here on Earth.'

Mrs Mayberry was beside herself at the notion of the creeping socialism Melbourne had said would be the nation's ruin. 'I will Not Allow Ruin, and I'll say it one more time, *Not Allow Ruin*, to enter Prospect, which it might well do with the arrival of the railway next month and those bushrangers murdering families in Myrtle Grove.'

'What bushrangers?' Maggie asked those about her, but no one answered.

'Men must be given back the jobs to which they are entitled and women must man the domestic barricades against the –' Florence couldn't remember how best to describe what was on the other side of the barricades. 'The train line and the bushrangers.'

'Which bushrangers?' Maggie asked her neighbour again but the neighbour put a finger to her lips impatiently.

'Men must Protect and Provide. Women must be Protected and Provided For. It is their Entitlement.' Mrs Mayberry dropped her voice. She wanted every woman there tonight, and those who were not, to grasp to their bosoms – she grasped her own quite substantial bosom – the horror on their doorsteps so they might recognise and repel it. She was improvising now because it was going so well. 'It is your Duty and your Entitlement. Every woman here tonight must accept her responsibility to become a loyal wife and a devoted mother.' She paused. 'Or a caring spinster.' She paused again. 'Or a widow. I have two words for our widows. Grace and Humility. The same goes for our brave spinsters.' She smiled at Adelaide and Pearl on whom her gaze had fallen and the applause was rapturous, shocking them to the core.

Maybe it was what the hall wanted to hear. Maybe the women of the town loved the idea of entitlement to anything that meant freedom from worry. But more than likely they clapped so long and hard because Mrs Mayberry was a novelty act and her unusual delivery utterly compelling. She sounded holy.

To Pearl and Louisa, who as far as they were concerned had only ever done their best by womanhood, she sounded demented. Worse. Dangerous. If the whole town thought she was right, then their predicaments were dire. They were Un-provided For and Unprotected and so, they inferred from the Mayor's wife, dependent entirely on grace and humility.

Adelaide, who, on the one hand, could hear sense in the notion of men being men and women being women, was, on the other, as discomforted as Louisa and Pearl. She might have had a husband in residence but what kind of man was he? She was as vulnerable as they when it came to lack of protection and provision, and who knew what that meant for the path her life was taking? It was so silly it should have meant nothing. But something in the rapture suggested that the silliness had taken root and that there would be consequences.

Adelaide guessed it meant she could never take on Archie Stokes, who wasn't a returned soldier but was a man beloved of the entire town. He'd held the fort and kept them all in Worcestershire sauce and nutmeg, even the families who neither wanted it nor could afford it. More importantly, he was revered by her husband's family and she wasn't.

Louisa guessed that there could be no going back to Thomas at the bank for another interview in nicer clothes, no one would stop the arrival of the horses and she truly was destined for poverty. Pearl understood at once that a town full of Florence Mayberrys could complicate matters horribly for a woman on a desperate foray into the local underworld with nothing to assist her but a cloak of invisibility.

All Maggie could think was that she didn't have a gun. She didn't have a gun because the boys couldn't shoot straight, and now there were bushrangers on the doorstep. She was completely Unprotected and only as Provided For as Mrs Mayberry deemed reasonable. Mostly she was provided for by her chooks and her vegetables and anything neighbours were kind enough to give her from their table. Still, she said to herself, at least she wasn't a widow and also far too young to be called a spinster. At least she wouldn't have to have grace and humility.

As the crowd spilled from the hall and headed in different directions, the four respectable women found themselves walking together because it would have been odd not to. None of them asked aloud what Mrs Mayberry could possibly know about Real Life when she'd only ever been well provided for by men with status if not looks.

As they parted company at the turn-off to Maisie Jenkins' place where baby Freddie was safely asleep (Marcus having made it clear he had no interest in minding him), Pearl did enquire, 'Was the Mayor in the audience?' And although Maggie replied, 'I suppose he was,' Louisa called over her shoulder, 'Of course he wasn't. All that limelight not on him.'

'What did she mean about the bushrangers?' Maggie asked before walking on. 'No one's told me about any family murdered in Myrtle Grove.'

'Because there wasn't one,' Pearl said. 'Someone took a shot at the driver of an army goods cart.'

'And he lived,' said Louisa.

'Then why did she say a family?'

'Because not everything she said was true,' Pearl pointed out with magnificent calm and everyone breathed a sigh of relief, which turned out to be premature.

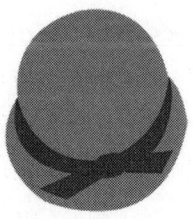

Chapter Three

In the days that followed, Florence Mayberry's plea to the nation bounced off Prospect's surrounding hills and swooped down Hope Street, up the side streets and into the outlying districts, fuelled by general amazement and frank admiration. If she'd taken a few liberties with the truth no one seemed to care much. She'd made sense, hadn't she? Men needed jobs; women needed a break. Order needed to be restored.

That was certainly the view of *The Gazette*, which thanked Mrs Mayberry the next day for her insight. Immediately alongside the jubilant headline 'Railway Work Full Steam Ahead', it announced 'Common Sense Comes To Town'. The paper congratulated employers who'd already relieved exhausted females of jobs to which men were better suited. *Womenfolk*, it exhorted joyfully, *we welcome you back to the hearth. Enter our exciting quest for the town's most sparkling kitchen.*

There were people who laughed up their sleeves and a couple who didn't even bother with sleeves. Baby Worthington, for instance – Louisa's sister-in-law, properly called Mrs Larry Murdoch when anyone remembered – had never heard anything as comical as Mrs Mayberry addressing the nation. She'd announced as much as she stomped from the hall well before the bitter end. 'There goes Baby,' Louisa had mumbled to no one in particular. Another was Joe Fletcher, the grumpy tenant at Somerset Station, so rarely seen that almost no one recognised him and those who noticed him at all only did because he was heard to laugh out loud more often than anyone had ever heard him speak. Who cared about them? These were people unaffected by the message and of no real consequence to the town.

Nearly everyone else took the message to heart one way or another, Adelaide, Louisa, Maggie and Pearl included. Had they been less burdened by circumstance, what Mrs Mayberry thought and said might not have made a scrap of difference to their wellbeing, but as things stood, what she thought and said somehow served only to underline the depth of their loneliness and the enormity of their plights. None could admit publicly what troubled them privately, let alone to each other, and so their predicaments ate away at them.

Not two days after the speech, while Baby Worthington and Joe Fletcher continued to chuckle to themselves, the ladies floundered in their isolation. Adelaide might have become immediately dependent on Pearl, but she would never in her wildest dreams have given the slightest indication to her housekeeper that she was struggling financially, emotionally, intellectually, spiritually, marital-ly – you name a 'ly' and it was in her struggle – because the store manager she'd been trusted to oversee was sending the family broke and the head of her household didn't give a fig.

She couldn't admit it to anyone, least of all Louisa, who might have comforted her about the actual and metaphorical implications of a lost husband, because the past was against them. In a small community where the tide of friendship ebbs and flows according to acknowledged favours and perceived slights, you can be alienated from the very person with whom you have most in common because something happened or didn't happen years ago.

Because they didn't trust each other, Adelaide had no idea Louisa was being driven to the brink of madness, not by widowhood but by a ruthless creditor. She could never have guessed from the appearance of forty-three horses in the home paddock that Louisa was so short of funds she'd thrown herself one more time on the mercy of the cold-hearted mother she'd married Jimmy Worthington to escape, and that mother had once again turned her back. Would Adelaide have been surprised? Not by the mother. Louisa had never been the daughter that mother had wanted, or that any other mother would have wanted, was the general view.

As Adelaide steeled herself to confront the once loving husband who now terrified the life out of her, Louisa was watching herself cry in her bedroom mirror. In her hand she held her mother's heartless reply. *You made your bed, Louisa, so now you can lie on it.* Huge tears rolled down her face and every so often a dreadful sob escaped from her pretty mouth. If she'd believed there was any slight consolation to be had from across the road, nothing in her reflection encouraged her to think it was worth pursuing. Her beauty had come between them and there it had stayed. Jealousy, never pure and simple, sticks and with time hardens like boiled sugar. Louisa sighed noisily at the memory.

She'd taken a shine to William Mayberry when he was supposed to have taken a shine to Adelaide. His own shine for Adelaide had been a very small one and had been wiped from his inclination the minute Louisa had informed him of hers to him. Unluckily, hers had faded to nothing when she'd met Jimmy Worthington weeks later. The alienation of young Mayberry's affection had scandalised the town but the friendship with Adelaide might have been salvaged. All it had required was for everyone to pretend nothing had happened. In Prospect, the same as anywhere else, friendships that are knocked to the canvas one day can shake themselves off and recover the next, left to their own devices. But gossip's prickly tentacles can poison the buds of any recovering friendship. Even within families, confidences that should be valued as highly as rubies are traded as cheaply as gravel in passing conversation. Adelaide's mother had told Baby Worthington at the cricket that Adelaide thought Louisa was no better than a tramp and Baby Worthington had told her brother who had told Louisa and then Louisa had married the brother.

Had the past not been the past, had they been closer, Louisa might not have said when Adelaide had hurried across the road with soup the day the awful telegram had arrived, 'Soup! Thank you, Adelaide. I now have enough to fill a dam.' She might have thrown herself into her former friend's arms and sobbed her heart out for the loss of her lovely boy. Then again, that might have led to an admission that she and the lovely boy had quarrelled every day they were under the one roof and the only thing they had in common was a passion for the bodies that had attracted them in the first place. Who are you going to tell that to when your reputation is for using your considerable looks to get what you want, then deciding in retrospect that you never much wanted it after all? Not the woman whose boyfriend you stole. Louisa, struggling with nausea and hunger in equal measure, consoled herself only with the thought that her beauty was intact and that she should take it for a walk because the house was suffocating her.

The possibility of confiding in anyone, let alone either of her neighbours or anyone in their employ, was as far from Maggie's thoughts as it was from Adelaide's. Unprotected and unprovided for she most certainly was, but she was strong, she told herself. She could stand on her own two feet, which, tiny as they might be, were the only two feet she trusted. This left her in as splendid an isolation as Adelaide's and Louisa's, as she penned a letter to L Murdoch Esquire, husband of Baby Worthington. It was he who had advised her father in his claim against the Bluetts, representing them in court although he wasn't a lawyer but an accountant. 'It's a money matter,' he had counselled.

Their feud had come to a head over who owned cattle on the 400 acres each family claimed to own. Shouting had led to threatening, and threatening had led to Adelaide's father shooting Maggie's father. Against all advice, Maggie's father had insisted that a civil case be brought against Adelaide's father for shooting him as well as for stealing land he could prove was his. He had tended the paperwork in court. It was Mr Murdoch who had recommended that Frank O'Connell accept the generous settlement on offer, and years later it was Mr Murdoch who had written to her father denying any knowledge of the paperwork's whereabouts. All documents attached to its ownership should be in the town's municipal offices, he'd explained. He had no idea why it might not be there, because he didn't have it. In any case, he'd written, surely the matter had been settled to everyone's satisfaction. Payment had been made, hadn't it? But payment had only ever been made for the shooting.

Maggie picked up her pen. *Dear Mr Murdoch*, she wrote. *I have been alerted to the weakness of my position in the world by Mrs Mayberry at the Arts and Crafts Hall the day before yesterday.*

I would be grateful if you could see me to explain why there is no record of our ownership of the land that was agreed in 1913, because you must have had it when you represented my father in court. Yours sincerely, Maggie O'Connell (Miss). She blotted her letter and read it again. Then she stood and listened in alarm to the silence in the house. 'Boys!' she bellowed. 'Get up. Get up right now! You're going to school whether you like it or not.'

Louisa didn't hear her, although she was heading in her direction. What she heard was Marcus declaiming heatedly to his wife. The words were muffled but their thrust was clear. Had she stopped by the gate she would have heard them exactly. 'If you're going to tell me the bloody shop's losing money, I don't care. You work it out. You're in charge.'

She could not have heard Adelaide reply because there was no reply. Adelaide had retreated in despair, no closer to restoring her husband to the kind if dull protector and provider she'd believed him to be when she married him than she was to accusing Archie Stokes of theft. She had withdrawn to her own lonely room where she lay on the bed to contemplate her hopelessness.

Pearl contemplated hers as she walked baby Freddie along the river path that led to a bench where she could sit and fret in peace. As difficulties went for a woman in September 1919, her own was on the brink of insurmountable. A second visit to Father Kelly had been short and useless. He hadn't even admitted her into the presbytery but spoken to her through its half-opened door. 'I am very busy, Miss McCleary.'

'But I can't wait until Confession, Father, I need to know. He was looking for the family of a dead soldier. Please, please tell me if he mentioned their name to you.'

The priest had said, 'Miss McCleary, you must stop this. It's not your business and it's not mine.'

'But did he?' she'd insisted. 'He did. What was it?'

'I'm sorry,' Father Kelly had said, closing the door on her. He'd turned from her – the door was almost shut – when he mumbled, 'If there was a name, it didn't belong to anyone in this town.'

So there it was. There she was. Stuck in Prospect with positively nothing to go on apart from the fact that Daniel had passed through weeks ago and there was a railway she couldn't get to where he might or might not have headed to be a misfit. She was no closer to him, or the wronged family, or the wicked person who had done the wrong than she had been when she'd left Sydney.

In her mind's eye she could see Beattie gasping her last breath, Daniel collapsing in a hail of bullets and Annie inconsolable at their gravesides. In her heart all she felt was the enormity of her own folly. There was a baby in the pram, there was sunshine dappling the town's famous river nicknamed Chatterbox (motto 'never dries up'), but did she see them? She was aware that the huge gums smelled of early morning, but only dimly. On the bench she took from her pocket the small leather-bound diary attached to its very own pencil given to her by Beattie last Christmas.

She turned to the back pages designated *Notes*, ready to record any that might clear her brain of recklessness and stupidity, any that could form the basis of a plan on which she could act. The wronged family could just as easily live in Bondi. There was no point in looking for them. Would she be any better placed to look for Daniel in Sydney when surely he'd come all the way to Prospect for a very good reason?

Her pencil was poised over the notebook but she made no notes because the information she had was as sparse as it had always been. She had a missing returned soldier (alive, as far as anyone knew), a cruelly wronged soldier (dead, definitely dead), his family (unknown) and the thug who had wronged them (unknown and possibly dead). The only one she stood any chance of finding was the one whose name she knew. But where? Would Daniel work on a railway?

She didn't hear the crunch of twigs under Louisa's delicate foot any sooner than Louisa spotted the pram and someone not Adelaide in charge of it.

'Hello,' said Louisa once a greeting became inevitable.

'Hello,' Pearl agreed. 'Lovely morning.' They eyed each other without warmth, since neither had good cheer at their disposal.

'Cold,' said Louisa. 'Don't stand. I'll sit.' It hadn't been her intention but, having sat, she felt a little better. Pearl, she remembered from the night of the speech, sounded surprisingly cultured for a housekeeper. She must be very poor. 'Recovered from the Mayberry onslaught? Grace and humility! I ask you!'

Pearl frowned. 'She was hard on widows, I thought. The pension isn't going to provide and who's going to protect?'

Louisa frowned back. Was the housekeeper intending to discuss money? Surely not. 'Are you a widow?' she asked. Pearl was jiggling the pram without appearing to know that she was.

'A spinster,' Pearl replied.

'But not unprotected. Or un-provided for. Captain Nightingale protects and provides for his entire household.'

'I have a fiancé,' said Pearl, surprising herself. Her mouth had simply rejected the notion of dependence on a job in a household that had Captain Nightingale at its head. 'He's missing.'

'Oh,' said Louisa. 'Missing is horrible. My husband was never missing, just dead. I think dead is probably easier. Not that your fiancé will end up dead. Just, ending up dead having been missing is horrible.'

Pearl said nothing. She wondered if Louisa wanted her to show an interest in her grief. Would a housekeeper show an interest in her employer's neighbour's grief? It didn't matter. Mrs Worthington couldn't stop talking.

'I'm sure your fiancé isn't dead,' she was gabbling. 'In any case, he might be missing, but you mightn't necessarily miss him.' *Good God*, thought Louisa. *Shut up!* The woman would think she was raving. 'I'm sorry. That wasn't what I meant to say.' She waited for offence to be taken but Pearl nodded.

'No, it's true. He's been gone so long, I've forgotten how to miss him. It's so much worse for you, having lost the man you married.'

'It is,' said Louisa softly. 'And it isn't. I miss having someone to talk to. Mrs Nightingale is lucky.'

'I'm sure you could join us for morning tea.'

'I meant Captain Nightingale. She has her husband to talk to.' The remark created a silence and in the silence Louisa reminded herself she'd rather talk to no one than to priggish Adelaide who'd grown even more pleased with herself after her marriage.

'Of course she has. But female company is different,' Pearl finally said.

'I wouldn't trouble her,' Louisa replied. 'She's looked so miserable since she had the baby.'

'Just tired. As you must be, with so many horses.'

'Not so many,' Louisa said. 'Do you ride?'

'No,' said Pearl. It left them stranded, as baby Freddie duly noted with a loud roar for which they were both grateful.

'I'll leave you to it,' Louisa said and she hurried away, none the wiser about the depth or cause or even existence of Adelaide's misery. As far as she was concerned Adelaide was lucky, even if Marcus had returned from the war odd and jittery when he'd gone away so solid and proud. Adelaide was lucky because there was a man in her life between her and trouble. She strolled back along the river, dawdling because home was horrible, and diverted because the housekeeper's admission had been so peculiar.

It had been very bold to say out loud to a grieving widow she'd met just the once that she no longer cared for her poor fiancé missing in action. She should have asked if she still wrote anyway. William Mayberry had taken her hand and said how important it was to hear from the girls back home, even the girls who weren't your girls but your friends' girls. He'd told her how Jimmy had thought of Louisa every time a biscuit had turned up, or a sock. How they'd all thought of Louisa because Jimmy had produced her photo at every opportunity.

Probably he was dead or she'd have heard, Louisa decided of the fiancé. It was unlikely he'd be missing so long after the armistice, even with the flu and the quarantine. On the other hand, loved ones were being traced to hospitals all over the world so he could be in one of them but just not yet traced owing to terrible burns or a head encased in bandages. Poor man, in a foreign hospital pining for the girl back home who couldn't care less about him. Louisa took in a deep breath and exhaled easily. A whole half-hour had passed without her heart racing and her breath failing. But now she'd arrived back at her gate and there was Adelaide staring across at her paddock.

'Louisa, surely you don't have more. I'd swear there are more than there were yesterday. Where on earth are they coming from?' Louisa cast a very quick look at the land beyond her house, which stretched all the way up the hill to bushland, and thought, *Oh God, there are.* But rather than flee to her bed, which is what her heart instructed her to do, she smiled bravely at Adelaide.

'Almost certainly,' she said. 'It's very gratifying. I met your Miss McCleary and Freddie down by the river. She's a treasure, isn't she?'

'A treasure,' agreed Adelaide. 'I hope Freddie wasn't disturbing the peace.'

'He was as good as gold. She really works miracles with him. Will you keep her, do you think?'

Adelaide continued to smile. 'He's not that bad,' she lied. 'And Pearl's just learning . . .' The thought trailed away as she peered down the street. Louisa also peered. 'Is that smoke?' They both moved towards the white spiral coming from the O'Connells' house, the white spiral that was, they now saw, engulfing Pearl who was running towards them, pram in front of her.

'Fire!' she was calling as if they hadn't noticed or heard the dreadful boys yelling.

'Look what you've done, you stupid galoot!'

'You lit it, you bloody bastard!'

And over their noise, and the awful racket of incinerating chickens, they could hear Maggie O'Connell crying, 'What did I tell you! What did I tell you? This is what happens when you don't go to school. Al, take the bucket and get water from the creek. Hurry up! Ed, get sacks. Look for them. Under the house.' Her voice was loud and impatient but not hysterical.

'Come out of the flames, Maggie, come out of the flames!' shrieked one of the boys.

Pearl wasted no time on words. With twenty yards to go, she pushed the pram towards Adelaide and if Freddie protested she didn't take time to apologise or soothe him. She dashed back towards the O'Connells', closely followed by Louisa for whom any distraction was a godsend.

'She'll need more buckets,' Pearl called. 'Go back and get buckets.' But Louisa was interested only in running towards the excitement not away from it and, in any case, saw no reason to take orders from someone to whom she should have been giving them.

'You run back to Adelaide's and get hers,' she said. But Pearl didn't, because out of habit she trusted herself over anyone else in a crisis.

This one was short-lived. There was more smoke than fire and though the chook house was beyond help, no one was hurt or even looked as if they might have been hurt, just a few measly chooks. 'Well done, Maggie,' Pearl said.

'What, for losing three good layers? For letting the boys stay home from school?' said Maggie angrily. 'It's not well done. One day they'll kill us all.'

'You should send them away,' said Louisa sharply.

The boys stopped shoving each other. They looked from Louisa to Maggie, then from Pearl to Louisa, then from Louisa back to Maggie, faces smeared with ash, eyes wide with shock, still in their pyjamas since they had refused to go to school. 'Where would we go, Maggie?' Al finally asked. 'Who'd want us?'

'I want you,' said Maggie furiously, before turning on her rescuers. 'And you two can bugger off.'

Chapter Four

Louisa and Pearl might have been mistaken for old friends as they hurried home together, despite Louisa knowing that her mother would never have spoken so freely and for so long to a housekeeper. Yet here she was undeniably comfortable in the company of Adelaide's, which must account for it. Adelaide employed her, therefore she, Louisa, had no obligation to distance herself. As logic went it was rum, but who cares about rum in the face of unremitting loneliness? 'It was unbelievably rude, even for an ignorant girl. All I said was the boys were out of control, which everyone knows they are.'

'It was rude,' Pearl agreed. 'But she'd had a fright.'

'No excuse,' said Louisa. 'The family's a disgrace. Always has been.'

'Heavens, that's Freddie,' Pearl said. 'I'd better run.'

'What's wrong with him?' Louisa asked, keeping up. 'Crying so much can't be normal.'

'It's normal,' Pearl said. 'The morning's upset him, that's all.'

'He's always upset,' said Louisa. 'I've never known a baby be so upset, morning, noon and night.'

'How many babies have you known?' Pearl smiled at Louisa, a teasing, confident smile.

Louisa smiled back. 'Not many.'

'Well then,' said Pearl. 'Probably no more unusual than the O'Connell boys playing with fire.'

But it was unusual. Freddie had been so upset by the morning there really was no consoling him. In Pearl's absence, Adelaide had jiggled, sung, jumped, skipped, shushed, rocked, shouted, pirouetted and taken the baby into the garden to point out leaves on bushes, but he'd screwed up his face at everything and bellowed. 'Block your ears,' she'd muttered when Marcus had complained from the bedroom.

As Louisa was asking Pearl if she fancied a cup of tea later that afternoon and Pearl was politely declining, Adelaide was reaching the end of her tether and at the end of that tether was resentment. Pearl McCleary was paid to be here and not with Louisa Worthington at Maggie O'Connell's, especially when the O'Connells were no friends of the family and nor was Louisa Worthington. Saving the O'Connells' house was of no concern to anyone in this household when the very best thing that could happen to that miserable place was its total destruction. The O'Connells would move and that would be the end of it. The Bluetts would have won because there would be no O'Connells left to argue about stupid land they said her father had stolen.

She bounced the baby on her lap vigorously and the baby yelled vigorously. The ten o'clock feed hadn't been offered until half-past ten, and only yesterday Nurse Fairweather had said, 'Every four hours, Mrs Nightingale, no more, no less. A baby needs a routine.' But this baby didn't know the meaning of the word, Adelaide had tried to explain, and Nurse Fairweather had said it was up to her to teach him. 'You're making a rod for your own back,' she'd said. And look at this morning. No routine at all because Pearl McCleary, who might have calmed the baby, was showing greater concern for households other than the one employing her. Freddie shrieked and spat milk onto her skirt.

'She's making a rod for her own back,' Louisa was saying to Pearl.

'Must fly, Mrs Worthington,' Pearl replied. 'Thanks for your help.'

'No,' said Louisa curtly, 'thank you for yours.' She marched angrily up her path, overwhelmed by the rejection of her generously offered tea and the uppity tone of someone who was so far from being her social equal. She closed the front door behind her, leaned against it and was, without warning, overwhelmed by trembling because if anyone was scared to death, if anyone felt alone and abandoned and friendless, she did. Her mother was right. She had no one to blame but herself.

Louisa slowly removed her smart brown coat and her jaunty cream hat, sent by her mother from Paris, and hung them with her bag over the coat stand. Then she walked with purpose down the no longer highly polished floorboards into the dining room where she took from the dresser a pile of papers.

She held them without looking at them. She crumpled them in her fist. Then she took them to the table where she smoothed them and spread them so she could study the horror in the clear light of day. One at a time, most recent first, delivered the night before with the stallion and the colt. It was the most alarming of all on the one hand, but no worse than the first on the other.

Two hundred was agreed, so two hundred you're getting, it said. *Pay up or we'll break you.* She knew they could and she knew as well that her choice was this: private crime or public ruin. She went into the kitchen and vomited into the sink.

Across the road, where peace had been quickly restored by Pearl singing 'Too-ra-loo-ra-loo-ral', Adelaide was eating a scone. 'Maggie does her best, but they aren't a nice family, I don't care what anyone says. The mother was pleasant enough. I forgive her, may she rest in peace, but I can never forgive him. Not after what he did.'

'What did he do?' Pearl asked, rocking the baby gently, placing a soft finger over eyes that flickered in barely achieved sleep.

'He provoked my father into shooting him.' It should have been damning enough but Pearl's silence seemed to require a reason for the shooting, which might have annoyed Adelaide had she not been enjoying her scone. 'By making ridiculous accusations about cattle and land. You'd have thought the stupid man was sitting on a gold mine.'

'Look, he's asleep,' said Pearl. 'Would you like me to get on with lunch so you can get back to the ledgers?'

It was the last thing Adelaide wanted to get back to. She said, 'Excellent idea, thank you, Miss McCleary.' She watched as Pearl carried Freddie to his room and she went into the office where the ledgers were laid out on the desk that had been her father-in-law's, then her mother-in-law's, then her husband's, and should now by rights be hers. She yawned. How warm and soft and welcoming the desk looked. If she could just rest her head on that desk, as she had done at school when Miss Valiant had ordered them to sleep after lunch, she would feel so much better. She placed her head on her folded hands and closed her eyes, but she didn't feel better.

She thought how cruel it was that she'd inherited her father's head for figures. Had the gift for arithmetic travelled down the female line, the hateful bookkeeping would have been a piece of cake. And how unsettling of Pearl to say only, 'Look, he's asleep,' when the question of loyalty to her family was hovering quite obviously between them and needed addressing. Surely a housekeeper with even the slightest inkling of her place should have sided unequivocally with the household that employed her, but somehow she hadn't. Why hadn't she? And why was Marcus so cruel? Why was he so unaware of the pain she was in? The war was one thing. His temper was another thing altogether. Her sunny nature was being tested to the limit.

She raised her head to stare uselessly at the ledgers, struggling with net and gross as she always did, and outrage with her lot filled her famously mild breast. Women had babies and the men who fathered those babies were obliged by virtue of their manhood to stride into the world and deal with its horrors from which women should be shielded, especially women who were useless at sums.

'I'm going out,' Marcus said from the doorway, startling her and causing her to knock a pile of receipts to the floor.

In the silence that followed they considered each other without love. Adelaide decided that her husband was no longer handsome. He was too thin, too pale and somehow too tall and too stooped. His once friendly eyes were dull. What she saw in them was an interest in her no greater than he might have had for a broken chair he wasn't inclined to fix.

'Where to?' she asked, dropping to her knees to retrieve the dockets.

'Just out.'

'And when will you be back?'

'Later,' he said, heading out the door.

'Marcus? Marcus!' she called after him. 'How do you carry twelve?'

Chapter Five

So there was Adelaide distraught over figures that made no sense, and there was Louisa clutching the abominable letters, and here is Maggie, equally troubled by the columns in front of her though sums were the least of her worries. Maggie could have told Adelaide in a trice that if you are adding you never carry twelve, you save the two and carry the ten although if you're multiplying you carry by adding – but who knew that Maggie was cleverer at sums than even Adelaide's mother?

Maggie could add a column of ten items in under ten seconds. She could divide 243 into 17926 and tell you how much was over, which she sometimes did for fun. It was a lucky knack because had she not been able to add her means to her ways and subtract them from her needs in order to make mismatching ends meet, her family would certainly have starved to death. She might have been sixteen when her father had left home but she'd been holding that family together since the twins were born.

The house stank. Smoke from charred bits of chook pen continued to drift accusingly around the backyard and over the vegetable patch where Ed and Al were burying the hens and hoping to find potatoes. Maggie stared at the page in front of her, which she'd carefully ruled and divided into two columns called Income and Expenditure.

A month ago, the Income column had contained two entries: one from Mrs Mayberry, the other from Mrs Quirk at The Irish Rover where she'd washed dishes four mornings a week for three years. But that job had gone. Mrs Quirk had said she should be happy to give it to a returning soldier, and there was no doubt that the Foley lad had returned from somewhere, but was his need greater? Maggie had asked Mrs Mayberry for more hours to make up the shortfall but Mrs Mayberry had declined adding if Maggie had been better at washing up, Mrs Quirk would never have entertained the idea of the soldier.

The page opposite Income and Expenditure was headed Weekly Budget, which began with the now single figure from the Income column and then listed, by day of the week, how much was spent on what and how significantly it reduced the starting figure. The tally as it currently stood was worse than it should have been mid-week. It stood at precisely empty. The next entry in the Income column wasn't due until Friday, which was when Mrs Mayberry would pay her for thirty-five hours of housework undertaken five hours seven days a week.

She should never have bought the cheese, let alone the pickles. She should have bought flour. She shouldn't have gone to Nightingales. But why shouldn't she? Why couldn't she be a chooser when being able to choose was in the family line? The answer was clear enough. Yesterday's choice of cheese had made today's choice between eating and begging.

Maggie turned away from the troubling sums to stare out the window imagining, as she often did, a lush garden with a well-tended orchard and rows of vegetables and a pig pen and a proper chook house and ducks and geese and a couple of cows and goats and everything else you could grow to eat on a couple of acres of excellent soil. But it had never been that. Her father's heart had never been in it. He'd married a landowner's daughter without having ever been on the land, he'd gone into battle with neighbours who'd cheated him out of acres he knew he'd honestly purchased, and then he'd gone to rack and ruin, just like the acres.

She looked with bitterness to the great wide paddocks of Somerset Station, still in the Bluett family even if they had installed a manager, and she thought of the income she should have had. She thought of the man who'd come on the train who'd fight for the land, who'd stock the paddocks and make everything grow in the gardens with his magic touch. She thought of his magic touch and how she would tingle to it. He'd be tanned and broad and gruff and loving, with arms so shapely she would long to be in them day and night. He'd do the work while she spent his money in Nightingales, where she'd order a pound of this and a pound of that and five pounds of this and six dozen that.

It wasn't far from that thought to the next, which was that Nightingales owed her sixpence worth of something and she meant to have it. She thought it so quickly that she was on her feet with her hat and shawl on before she had time to consider the wisdom of it. It was justice and the Nightingales owed her justice. The Bluetts *and* the Nightingales owed her justice. As well as sixpence. Captain Nightingale might own the shop but Adelaide Nightingale was in charge and she was a Bluett. He might have been back from the Front but he wasn't all there, so Theresa Fellows said. Therefore her argument was with the Bluetts, as it always had been. Too bad about the horrible baby.

She paused at the gate. Wisdom piped up. *Take only what you need and take something you can hide.* She removed the shawl, went back to the house and took from the wardrobe a moth-eaten coat which had been her mother's. 'Alec, Edward,' she called, 'I'm going into town. Any mischief while I'm away and I'll thrash the living daylights out of you.'

She walked very quickly up Hope Street, staring straight ahead, having no wish to speak to any neighbour about any fire or any badly behaved boys or any strange-looking coat that didn't fit and plainly wasn't hers. That coat had deep, deep pockets which she intended to fill with dinner.

The store was busy and as alluring as it always was to a girl for whom its every item was a reckless indulgence. As usual, the smell was of food so fresh and expensive that wellbeing could be the only outcome of eating it. There was a queue. Of course there was a queue. Returned soldiers might have been desperate for work but Mr Stokes made do with kindly Mrs Lambert, wife of Bert who ran the stables, and Ginger Albright, her nephew. Customers were taking their time as they always did because there was just so much to choose from and because they loved to discuss the pros and cons of every purchase.

As far as Maggie was concerned, the throng couldn't have been better, but oh how it could have been! Mrs Mayberry being somewhere else would have been miles better. As it was, the newly acclaimed oracle was causing much of the congestion around the smallgoods. An admiring group had gathered about her, wanting to be amazed at what she was ordering because now she was an oracle, what she was ordering was surely what they should be ordering.

'Hello, Mrs Mayberry,' Maggie said pointedly, having wandered the full length of the counter while she decided whether drawing attention to herself was better or worse than being noticed while trying not to be. Mrs Mayberry acknowledged her with a blink because she was in full flow.

'It was the Bolsheviks, of course it was. We never had a flu like it before. Did I say bacon? I meant black pudding.'

Maggie moved on, weaving in and out of people with money, noticing that there weren't many possibilities worth sixpence.

'You come back for your tuppence, missy?' called Archie Stokes with a loud laugh. 'She accused me of robbing her yesterday.' And while Maggie wanted to unmask him by shouting back, *He is a thief!* she smiled and positioned herself by the display closest to the door and least occupied.

She tried not to look at anything in particular, or anyone in particular, but to study instead, as if it were an everyday shopping list, the ancient note she'd found in the lining of her mother's coat pocket in which was folded a very small key. She didn't recognise the key or the recipe scrawled on the note for Drought Buns. She put the key back in her pocket and thought if she wanted anything it would be a bun, but a bun was out of the question. More to the point would have been a pie, and just slightly out of reach was a selection of family-sized savoury pies on a stand, each worth nine pence at least.

If you're not a criminal, if you have no experience of petty theft, but if you are absolutely determined on a course of stealing food and you're hungry, then it simply isn't easy to act with forbearance. You don't even pause to consider how you might execute the sleight of hand required to secrete a pie about your body in a shop crowded with people who have been wary of you from birth and who are staring at your coat. A pie is the one thing you crave beyond liberty. Common sense tells you to walk away, but can you? Maggie was hungry, her brothers were hungry, Archie Stokes had cheated her, Mrs Mayberry was starving them, and this was a shop related by marriage to the family that had brought her family to its knees.

Maggie walked up to that pie tray and, as casually as you like, she knocked a single pie to the ground. She picked it up and attempted to cram it into her pocket, but it crumbled. Five people saw it happen. Ten people formed a circle around her accusing her of theft in tones that ranged from disgusted to overjoyed. Someone demanded that Bob McDermott, the policeman newly installed from Bowral, should be fetched so poor Maggie could be cast into jail.

'Seize her!' cried Oracle Mayberry as Maggie made a futile lunge for the door. There were so many people in the way milling and pointing and wondering what they were missing that she had no clear path. They made room only for Archie Stokes, who had Maggie firmly by the neck before anyone could say, *Urk, black pudding.*

'Seize who?' asked Adelaide from the doorway. 'Mr Stokes, what on earth are you doing? Let the girl go.'

Chapter Six

What is a woman plagued by uncertainty to do? There were fixed points in Adelaide's life from which she took comfort, stanchions which had provided the parameters for her slim sense of purpose. These included love for her mother, devotion to her father, affection for her brother, a fondness for Church, relief in her marriage and an assumption that she was known to be a lovely person, all of which were well and good. Less in keeping with her reputation for loveliness was the hatred she felt for Maggie's father. Frank O'Connell had brought upon her family's head the terrible humiliation of a court-ordered settlement from which her own father had never recovered, and as a consequence, neither had she. You nurse hatred like that in your heart, however soft, then forgiveness will never be easy to summon.

'Good Lord! Mrs Nightingale!' Archie Stokes panted, releasing Maggie's head but maintaining a firm grip on her upper arm. 'Lucky thing, too. This might need a woman's touch.'

'What's happened?'

'The child is a thies,' lisped Florence Mayberry. 'After all I've done for her.' It was a remark that as recently as a week ago would have brought the house down, but Mrs Mayberry's stock had grown so high that the offence she was taking at Maggie's pilfering seemed infinitely more to the point than any small loss to the shop.

Someone cried, 'Thack her!' because a popular lisp is a contagious thing but Mrs Mayberry smiled beatifically, though her brain was racing. She knew that the quality of mercy droppethed like a something or other and could flatter a woman newly acclaimed as The Voice of the People. On the other hand, the people had spoken. She raised her hand and nodded to indicate she had heard it.

Adelaide looked from Mrs Mayberry to Maggie, from Maggie to Archie Stokes and then back to Maggie, whose expression bore none of the hallmarks of shame but hovered somewhere between defiance, shock and anger. It was the expression of someone who hadn't realised she was out of a job. 'He robbed me of sixpence yesterday,' she said. 'He wouldn't pay me back so I took what was owed.'

'The pies are a shilling,' said Archie acidly. 'And I have witnesses who can prove I robbed her of nothing. I've worked for your family, Mrs Nightingale, since before she was born and I know how to add up.'

'I think I'll deal with this in the office,' said Adelaide.

Oh God, the turmoil in her heart and in her head, in her past and in this awful present. Who is the greater villain? A two-faced employee you know is robbing you blind or a pilfering child on whom revenge for the sins of her father could now so justifiably be taken? 'Mr Stokes, you can return to the counter. We have so many customers waiting. I'm sorry, everyone, for the inconvenience. Maggie, follow me.'

It sounded decisive, definitely, and as long as it took them to reach the office door, she could be decisive. She would be fair to both of them. Everyone had seen Maggie take the pie. No one had seen Archie Stokes steal Maggie's sixpence. But she knew he was capable of such an act because he stole from her every day, sixpence here, a shilling there. Maggie's father was a thief and Maggie might well be a thief. Archie Stokes was a liar. One of them was in the wrong. Justice must be done. But in the office, behind the closed door, the facts of the case deserted her. 'Sit down, Maggie,' she said as she took off her gloves. 'Did you lose many chooks in the fire? Is it completely out? Why do boys love fire?'

'I lost three good layers,' said Maggie cautiously, not sitting down. 'What do you care?'

Adelaide's heart hardened at the insolence. 'I don't care, especially. What bothers me is that you stole from me. I deserve an explanation.' She didn't need an explanation. It was in the girl's blood.

'I've given you one,' said Maggie wearily. 'And you don't believe me. No one will believe me. They'll say, "She's an O'Connell, what can you expect?" I'll go to jail, the boys will go to an orphanage and that will be the end of us, which is what you've always wanted.' In her head she went on to think, *Then the man who runs the orphanage will fall in love with me and he will burn your house down.*

Adelaide's heart softened. 'That won't happen if you tell me the truth. Now sit down as I've asked.' Fairness was so hard to achieve in the face of impudence and history.

'I took what I was owed,' said Maggie coolly, not sitting. 'Yesterday I bought cheese for nine pence and pickles for sixpence. Total cost one and three. I gave Mr Stokes a two-shilling piece. He gave me threepence. He owed me sixpence. I told him he owed me sixpence. He said he didn't. I went outside, I counted my money, I went back in and told him he'd made a mistake. He said I was a stupid girl and he refused to pay. You stole from me. Again.' There! Gauntlet slung! Implications only too clear!

'I am not a dishonest person, Maggie,' said Adelaide, and Maggie, staring at the troubled eyes with the tragic dark circles, granted she might not be. Her father was, but possibly she wasn't.

'But Mr Stokes is,' said Maggie. 'And you will take his side because it's me.'

Through Adelaide's head rampaged sixpences and threepences and ninepences and cheeses and pickles, which meant nothing to her, and through her heart charged devotion to her father and suspicion of the O'Connells, which she strove to set aside. In the way was fear of her own cowardice and her very poor ability at arithmetic. 'It might have been a genuine mistake,' she said.

'It wasn't,' said Maggie. And Adelaide knew she was right. She stared back at the neighbour whom she'd hated by association and neglected out of loyalty and she saw someone young and outraged and tired and her heart suddenly ached for her. The poor little mite had troubled brothers, but why wouldn't those boys be troubled? They had no mother, no money and a wicked father who had abandoned them. She was a girl doing her best, and now she was the one person in the world who knew, as she did, that Archie Stokes was a thief.

'You know what I think, Maggie,' she began. But whatever she thought was lost in such a fierce drumming at the door that it quaked in its frame and might have fallen in had it not been opened without invitation by Archie Stokes, announcing the arrival of the Constable McDermott.

'You can hand her over now, Mrs Nightingale,' said Mr Stokes. 'I bet that baby of yours is wondering where you got to.'

Adelaide ignored the shop manager. 'I'm sorry you've been troubled, Constable,' she said. 'As far as I'm concerned the matter is now closed. Mr Stokes, please wrap a pie for Miss O'Connell. There will be no charge. Maggie, if you'd like to walk home with me, I know Miss McCleary is baking and we'll have far too much to eat ourselves.'

Chapter Seven

The cakes were cooling as the neighbours walked in silence down Hope Street, each as confused as the other by the turn of events. Pearl herself was, at that moment, sitting at the small table in her bedroom, reading and re-reading a letter freshly received from Annie McGuire. *Dear girl*, it said, *I can't sleep for thinking how foolhardy you can be when you imagine you are in the right. Please, please be careful. I beg you not to make any direct approach but to find an intermediary who can handle his fists.* She sighed at both the criticism, and the absurdity of it. She was no closer to making a direct approach to anyone than she was likely to find a physically fit intermediary. Father Kelly wasn't an option. *Also,* Annie had written, *Dr Spencer paid a visit. He says Beattie needs no more worries. I think you should come home.*

She took up the pen in front of her, dipped it in ink and wrote. *Dear Annie, I can't come home. Father Kelly is a kind man and helping with my enquiries but progress is necessarily slow. The situation isn't* . . . At the sound of a key in the front door, she put down her pen and hurried into the hall just in time to be brushed aside by Marcus, head down, ploughing past her like a bull through a herd of repulsive cows. 'Can I get you anything, Captain Nightingale?' she enquired.

He turned to her, puzzled. 'Why?' he asked in bewilderment. And there being no obvious reply, Pearl went to the baby's room because Freddie had woken at the sound of the door and was now as unhappy as his father.

'Where's Mrs Nightingale?' Marcus appeared in the nursery doorway, glass in hand. 'In her absence can I offer you a drink, Miss McCleary?'

'She's at the shop. She'll be home soon,' said Pearl. 'The baby's due to be fed. I think I might take him to meet her.'

'So you don't want a drink?'

'I don't want a drink, thank you.' She lifted young Freddie from his crib and carried him past his father and into the hall. She settled the baby in his pram, piled it high with blankets of all weights and sizes and headed for the door, hearing Adelaide addressing an unknown companion before she opened it.

'My husband will take care of everything.' She wanted to warn her with all her might that in his current mood he almost certainly wouldn't, but too late. Adelaide, and Maggie of all people, were in the house and removing hats and coats before Pearl could even say, 'The baby's getting hungry.' And Captain Nightingale was already at the drawing-room door looking for trouble.

'Your son's going to forget who his mother is. I want to talk to you in here at your convenience. No, at my convenience, if you don't mind.'

Maggie, whose quickness wasn't confined to figures, reached at once for her outer-garments but Adelaide was doing what she believed she did best, which was making the most of a desperate situation by pretending it was normal. 'Hello Freddie,' she cooed into the pram. 'He can wait a couple of minutes, can't he, Miss McCleary? It's only a quarter past two. And Marcus, I'd like to see you as well. You can spare a minute for Maggie and me, can't you?' She led Maggie into the drawing room where Marcus was adding whisky to his whisky. 'A lemon cordial for us,' Adelaide said. 'Surely you'll sit down now, Maggie,' but Maggie wouldn't, sensing only too well that at any minute running might be required. Adelaide closed the door on Pearl and confronted her husband.

'You must sack Mr Stokes,' she said. 'He steals from us every day and yesterday he stole from Maggie.'

Marcus stared, then laughed unnaturally long and loud. 'I'm sorry,' he gasped, 'but is this the Maggie who tried to steal from me yesterday and would have stolen again from me today except Archie Stokes grabbed her as she ran? It's all over town. Mrs Mayberry saw it all. You don't need to concoct some ridiculous story to keep the girl out of jail.'

'I have my own evidence against Mr Stokes. It's in the ledgers.'

Marcus laughed again. 'Adelaide, please! This, if I'm not mistaken, is also the Maggie whose family stole your cattle.' Maggie inched towards the door but Adelaide grabbed her hand.

'This is Maggie O'Connell who's struggling to raise two motherless boys on almost no money and who can't afford to be robbed of sixpence.'

Marcus put his glass down in order to confront his wife unencumbered. 'Archie Stokes has served my family since I was a boy. This girl has bad blood in her veins, you've told me so yourself, and Archie Stokes is a man of impeccable reputation with a brilliant head for business.' He turned to Maggie. 'I suggest you run along home and be very grateful I have such a sentimental wife. Anyone else would have had you arrested.'

Maggie snatched her hand from Adelaide's grasp and Adelaide stared in horror at the man who would never have been so heartless had he not gone to war. 'She has no job. She has no money. Our employee robbed her.'

'That's enough,' said Captain Nightingale and it might have been except, from across the road, they all heard quite clearly the sound of gunshots as Louisa, thinking she had a human target, unloaded a couple of rounds into the horses. Then they heard her scream, a quite horrible scream that drained whatever colour there was from his face.

He fell back into his chair, knocking over his glass in the process and covering his head with his hands.

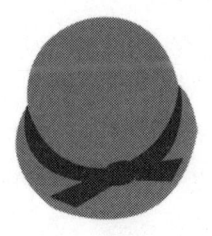

Chapter Eight

Maggie and Adelaide ran for the door, across the road and through Louisa's front gate only inches behind Pearl who, having heard enough from outside the drawing-room door, had decided to take the baby out for as long as possible, feeding routine notwithstanding. 'Gunshots,' Adelaide called.

'Take the baby home, Mrs Nightingale,' said Pearl. 'It's well after two. Maggie, come if you want to but stay well behind me and be prepared to drop.'

'Drop what?' asked Maggie.

'To the ground,' said Pearl. Adelaide took charge of the pram but she didn't go home. Home was as hideous to her as the notion of a dead body riddled with her neighbour's bullets.

'Did they come from the house?' she called.

'From the paddock,' said Pearl. So Adelaide and the baby headed to the house and Pearl ran towards the paddock, closely followed by Maggie, who could not have been more astonished to find herself secondary to the excitement. They saw Louisa soon enough owing to the billowing whiteness of the nightie she was wearing. She was on the ground, cradling the horse she had shot and crying as if her heart had finally exploded from sorrow.

'Mrs Worthington?' Pearl called gently.

'She's gone mad,' Maggie observed sensibly. Louisa did look mad when she turned to face them, possibly not as mad as Marcus had looked only minutes before, but where he was out of his mind, she was most profoundly within hers and it was full of terror.

They helped her inside and arranged her on the daybed in the sunroom, opposite Adelaide, now feeding the baby, who, out of some unearthly understanding of the generalised horror, didn't fuss. Pearl would have made tea but there was no fire and, as it turned out, no tea. There was, however, a bottle of gin on the sideboard in the kitchen, so she poured each of them a small cupful and although manners and breeding required them to refuse it, they each accepted and sipped it on their empty stomachs. Even Maggie, who'd never had a drink in her life. A surprising calm settled on the room.

'What happened, Louisa?' Adelaide asked.

Louisa, as white and fragile as the nightgown she was wrapping around herself, closed her eyes and rested her head on the back of the bed. 'I thought I saw someone in the paddock and I fired over his head to warn him but there wasn't anyone. I shot the poor horse.' She took a deep breath. 'Oh God!' she gasped. 'I have to tell someone.' They waited. The prayer suggested a nightmare. 'I'm being blackmailed,' she finally whispered. 'I don't want the stupid horses. But they won't let up. They'll send me more and more until I find two thousand pounds.'

'Holy hell,' Maggie cried.

'You must go to the police,' said Adelaide.

Louisa shook her head. 'Jimmy ordered the horses. He said the Army would buy them from him. It would make us a mint, he reckoned.' Louisa put her hands to her forehead. 'I don't know how he thought he could pull it off, but that was Jimmy. He knew the officer who did the buying and he knew a man with horses to sell. Then he was killed, the war ended, no one wanted the horses. I can't pay for them so they're starving them and delivering them to me a few at a time. In the end they'll be bringing me piles of corpses.'

'But they know you have no money,' said Pearl.

'They want the house.' She looked at the faces opposite, wide-eyed and slightly tipsy, settling on Adelaide's, which she scrutinised for signs of condemnation or mirth.

'Who is they?' asked Adelaide.

'*Are* they,' Maggie corrected her. Her smug laugh hung in the air alone and unwanted.

'If I tell you that, it'll be around town before dinner and *I'll* be the corpse.' There was no escaping the bitterness.

'Louisa, it wouldn't. I said you were a tramp *to my own mother, years ago*. And this is different. You've nothing to blame yourself for.'

'But I do,' said Louisa. 'I do blame myself. I told Jimmy I had no money. I told him he'd left me destitute. I said I might never eat again and the house was falling down and he said I wasn't to worry, he'd get me money, but how could he, from a trench?' The faces struggled with such poor behaviour and Louisa noticed. 'I've been such a greedy, ridiculous person and now I've shot a horse and I don't even know how to bury it.' Tears rolled down her slim little face. A single violent sob caused her shoulders to heave.

'We'll burn it,' said Pearl, 'won't we?'

'Will we?' Adelaide frowned. 'I don't think we can.'

'You need to get Mr Lambert to take it away,' said Maggie. 'It'll stink if you don't. It was a shame you shot it.'

'I thought I heard someone,' Louisa protested. 'I aimed at the sound.' She rubbed her eyes so hard that for a minute it seemed that she might blind herself. 'I can't pay Bert Lambert. I don't have the money. At present.'

'We can take care of it,' Adelaide said. 'Can't we, Miss McCleary?'

'He'll do it as a favour to me. Ginger's a friend,' said Maggie. And if this felt all wrong to Adelaide, who wasn't sure why Maggie should have more sway than she over Ginger's Uncle Bert, from whom her own family had bought sulkies for as long as she could remember and when she employed Ginger himself in her very own shop, she said nothing. Louisa had started to cry all over again and what was needed immediately was sweetness of nature.

'Don't cry, Louisa,' she said. 'Please don't cry.' She took the tiniest sip of her gin. 'Even I make mistakes.' All eyes turned to her. 'I'm so stupid at sums that I've let Archie Stokes rob me blind year in, year out but Marcus won't let me sack him because he says I'm stupider than Mr Stokes and the mistakes in the books are all mine.'

'Heavens above,' Louisa said through her tears. 'That's awful.' It was awful and she was grateful.

'But she isn't stupid,' said Maggie. 'Because he tried to rob me.'

'And then you tried to steal from him,' Pearl sympathised. 'And I can't say I blame you.'

'There is blame though,' said Louisa. 'Theft is against the law.' It was a harsh judgement from a woman who'd just shot a horse.

'But there will be retribution,' said Adelaide. 'Maggie has lost her job.'

'She didn't sack me,' cried Maggie in alarm. 'Did she?' She leapt to her feet. 'Oh no! I need to go. I have to work or we'll have no money. I need to ask her to forgive me, and now I've been drinking.'

'Dear, she won't give you your job back and you mustn't beg from her. She's a ridiculous woman. We won't let you starve,' said Adelaide. 'We can give her one of our cakes, can't we, Miss McCleary?'

Maggie fell back into her chair. 'We're sunk,' she said. 'What will I do? I can't protect and provide and dig and build and make the boys into normal men, it doesn't matter how many cakes you give me. I don't know how.' She stared blindly at the faces turned towards her. She put her head in her hands, as Marcus had done. 'It's just too hard.'

And it seemed to the room that she spoke for them all. They sat in ghastly contemplation of the mountains they were being asked to climb and finally Pearl spoke so softly they had to strain to hear her.

'I think we could all do with a bit of help.' It was either recklessness or the gin, loosening her grip on the need for secrecy.

The others thought she must have said *you* not *we*, because quite clearly she wasn't in need, and it wouldn't have surprised any of them had she come up with answers to all of their problems on the spot. She looked and sounded so sensible.

But then she said, 'We need help and we're going to have to find it,' which couldn't have been clearer. They couldn't take their eyes off her. Nothing in her face resembled desperation or poverty. She had a good job in a respectable household and she was secure as could be.

'You only have a missing fiancé to worry about,' Louisa pointed out.

Pearl took a short, sharp breath. 'He's only missing because he doesn't want anyone to know where he is.'

'Does *he* know where he is?' Louisa had clung all day to the idea of a puzzled man swathed from head to toe in dressings.

'Of course he does,' said Pearl. 'He doesn't want anyone to know where he is because he's hunting for someone he wants to bring to justice and he has to look for him in secret. If the man he's hunting knew he was being hunted he'd try to kill the man hunting him. Who is my fiancé. Do you follow?' They sort of did. It wasn't easy.

'So why *are* you looking for him?' Louisa asked.

'Because his sister is so ill and he's been away so long. She might die without seeing him again.'

'Dear Lord,' said Adelaide.

'Strewth,' said Maggie. 'Is he a hired gun?'

Louisa giggled through her tears, delighted that she wasn't alone in functioning so close to the edge of the law.

'Not a hired gun.' Pearl's treacherous smile showed positively no consideration for her extreme need to keep matters to herself.

'And the man he's hunting is in Prospect,' cried Maggie. 'It's why you're here. Is it Charlie Saunders?'

'Maggie, that's silly talk,' said Louisa. 'Is it Charlie Saunders, Miss McCleary?'

'You're not really a housekeeper, are you?' Gin had bestowed on Adelaide the gift of insight.

'I'm a teacher,' Pearl admitted and even as she did, she heard her folly. The fear she had contained through fire and gunshots surged from its moorings, flooding her heart then her brain. What had she done? In revealing so much, *what had she done?* Her brain, as adept at raising alternatives as Maggie's was at calculating sums, fought with the gin for a clear way forward. Her heart throbbed in agony at such a terrible lapse. It pleaded with her to go back to her tiny room, but she'd had the germ of an idea that was rapidly contaminating her whole being so she wasn't going anywhere.

'I knew it,' said Louisa. 'It's why she dresses so well. And why she's so bossy. And why she knows so much about children. Surely you smelled a rat, Adelaide.'

Adelaide put her hand to her brow. So many rats in a single afternoon. It was too much. Where did it leave her on cooking and cleaning? She couldn't fault the teacher on cooking and cleaning but she couldn't forgive the deception either. She was sick to death of deception. 'You said you were a housekeeper.' There was pain as well as accusation in her tone.

'You asked me if I'd kept house and I said yes. I have, for Mrs McGuire. I stopped teaching when we all caught the flu and Mrs McGuire needed me at home. If you've any complaints, I'll leave.' Pearl heard assurance in her voice and was thankful, but Adelaide wasn't thankful.

It was shocking to find herself saddled with a housekeeper who wasn't a housekeeper and who had a fiancé who consorted with killers. She needed to consider the implications for her household and her baby son. 'Why must there be any killing?' she asked.

'I didn't say must. I said he could get killed himself.' Pearl paused to calculate the impact of any possible killing on her germ of an idea. 'But he probably won't.'

'You said kill.'

Pearl recalculated. 'Maybe kill. I don't know.'

'Then tell me what you do know,' said Adelaide. 'I have a child to consider.'

Pearl sighed. 'I must ask you all to keep what I'm going to tell you to yourselves, because lives are at stake. Though not Freddie's.'

'Why on earth would Freddie's be at stake?' said Louisa.

'You'd know if you had children,' snapped Adelaide.

Pearl spoke up quickly. She reported the facts as simply and coolly as she could but the nub of it was clear. Her fiancé was on a wild goose chase to help a dead mate. Pearl didn't know who the dead mate was. The fiancé was needed at home. 'I'm here because he posted a letter from here but I'm no nearer to finding him now than when I arrived.'

'You need help,' Louisa confirmed.

'I do.'

'Well I need a husband,' Maggie interrupted loudly. Louisa had topped up her cup without thinking. 'I'm sick of doing this on my own. I want to marry someone who can shoot straight, make me a garden, build me a chook run, fix up the farm, look after the animals, love the boys and keep me warm in bed at night with big strong arms and lips that search for mine.' She didn't say resume war with the Bluetts. How could she? It hardly mattered. Her need was already dreadful. All their needs were dreadful.

'I need someone to get rid of the horses, get rid of the people sending me the horses, find me an income, fix my house and give me a future.' Louisa stared longingly out the window in case such a person was hovering by the gate.

'I'd like someone to unmask Mr Stokes. Definitely I'd like that,' said Adelaide.

'We all need someone,' Pearl said. 'We each need a man who can take on our problems as only a man can and do all the things we can't do because we are women.' She paused for the briefest of moments while she decided that as plans went, this one was excellent. 'I think we should employ someone and share him.'

'What on earth do you mean?' Louisa's eyes glinted.

'Someone to protect but not provide, to speak on our behalf, to fight with his fists if needed.' The line between need and hysteria was a fine one. Pearl saw it in the six eyes pinned to hers.

'I want to be provided for as well.' Maggie was adamant. 'I don't want to share.'

'We're not talking about a husband exactly,' said Pearl.

'Of course not a husband,' said Adelaide. 'I have a perfectly good one.' To contradict her would have been cruel.

'I wasn't thinking of anyone we'd be stuck with.' Pearl's idea was mushrooming even as she explained it. 'I was thinking of a man we could pay to do all we required and then we could send him on his way, as if he were a carpenter or a shearer. A part-time husband.'

Adelaide gasped. 'Don't be ridiculous, Miss McCleary. What would people think? Or are you joking?'

'She isn't joking,' said Maggie.

'I'm not,' agreed Pearl.

'Then you *are* being ridiculous. How would we find him? What would my husband say?'

'Your husband need never know,' Maggie smirked.

'I like the idea.' Louisa was positively buoyant.

'We could advertise,' said Pearl, then sensing luck being pushed, rose to her feet and suggested they sleep on it. If any of them thought she'd gone too far only Adelaide took a firm grasp of the wrong end of the stick.

'If you're suggesting for a single minute that I betray my husband with any other man then I must warn you I take my marriage vows very seriously and I suggest you examine your own conscience for . . .' She couldn't remember what for.

'For heaven's sake, Adelaide, it's not about sex,' Louisa said.

'But it *could* be,' Maggie said quickly. She might have winked at Louisa had she had a sip more gin.

Adelaide flushed so deeply and Maggie and Louisa laughed so delightedly that Pearl had to remind everyone that sex had positively nothing to do with it. She was using the word husband loosely because such a man would need access to their private affairs in order to solve their problems.

'I don't want anything to do with it,' Adelaide insisted loudly, and she left the house in high dudgeon, colliding with the side table by the sunroom door. Pearl followed with the pram, wondering if her plan was the work of the devil or pure genius.

Chapter Nine

As Pearl and Adelaide departed and Louisa and Maggie continued to delight in the unexpected turn the conversation had taken, Florence Mayberry, at the other end of town, was enjoying a small joke of her own. The joke was her husband. The Mayor was sitting opposite her at the dining table, so consumed by rage that his face looked suddenly piggy. Pink, fat and pig-like.

How very funny, Mrs Mayberry was thinking. As recently as a month ago she would have called it manly. She would have said his slightly larger than usual mouth was sensual and his slightly smaller than usual nose, refined. How blind she had been. How very funny she had been so blind. All those years playing second fiddle to a man who looked like a pig when her natural position all along was first fiddle.

As she watched her husband's quite large mouth open and close, she dimly acknowledged the contents that spewed from it. She waited for it to close just long enough for her to interject and then she said, 'But, George, why shouldn't I stand? And I wish you wouldn't shout. It's giving me a headache.'

'There, you see?' snorted George. 'Men shout. What do you think goes on in Parliament? Men shout. They will shout at you because frankly, Florence, you will annoy them beyond endurance, then you will cry and then you will say you have a headache and everyone will laugh at you and the newspapers will say that's what you get for letting women into politics. That's why we haven't let women into politics.'

'But the law says I can. The law lets women stand,' Florence insisted, even though she knew he wasn't listening because he never did. When he was speaking, all that mattered was what he was going to say next.

'It's a new law and it hasn't worked, you silly woman. How many females are there in Parliament in the state of New South Wales? None. And they're not there for a reason. It's a man's forum and I will not allow any wife of mine to be part of it. I forbid it. For-bid-it. Do you hear? Do you understand?' He was spitting. Then he stopped spitting to wheedle. 'Please, Florrie, you're my wife. I'm on the brink of the greatest achievement of my life and in that I include the butter factory. This railway is the greatest achievement any mayor of this town has ever' – he groped for the right word – 'achieved. There would be no railway without me, and if I take my eye off the ball, or if I become a laughing stock, there still might not be a railway. Do you know how difficult a time this is for me?'

'For *you*, George. This is my point.' There was no trace of a lisp but her tone was undeniably nasal. 'I have no time for your precious railway. I hate your railway. You've never once discussed with me how I feel about it, and if we are speaking frankly, George, I feel it is A Threat To Our Peace of Mind. You don't know who it might bring to town. What pollutants. What Bolsheviks.'

The Mayor looked puzzled. 'What do you mean, Bolsheviks? What do you know about Bolsheviks?'

Only what she'd heard in Melbourne but it was the cornerstone of her platform, as any decent husband would have known had he been in the audience to support her maiden speech. 'I have struck a chord with the nation. I owe it to the people who have such faith in me to represent their interests. The railway is not in their interests.'

George thumped the table. The cruet bounced along it. 'Baloney!' he yelled. 'Baloney, Florence, and you know it. You made a speech that wasn't yours and you had an audience because you are married to me. They went to hear you because you are my wife. You know nothing about the railway and even less about Russia. Do you even know what they drink in Russia? You do not.'

A month ago she would have seen his point and apologised. But now there was no regret in her heart, no small voice admitting he was a brilliant man who had always been kind to her. She had hardened. Universal adulation had coated her in confidence and now it clung to her like a new and tight-fitting armour. Florence felt ready for battle. She said, 'Had you been there you would have seen how well I was received.'

'What? Women back to the kitchen was well received? Men's jobs for men? Do you hear yourself, Florence? Do you hear how you're preaching one thing for everyone else but demanding a special exemption for you? You should practise what you preach. You should lead by example. Parliament is for men. You should go back to the kitchen, though Christ alone knows you're useless even there.'

George glowered at his wife and through the mist of rage saw what he thought was malice in her eyes. Surely not malice. She was his greatest champion. 'Let's not fall out, Florrie. I need you now more than ever. I've worked so hard. Please will you listen to reason?'

But what a peculiar thing reason is. There was his and there was his wife's and neither bore any resemblance to the other. There was Pearl's and there was Adelaide's, which was no less awkward given the similarly great need each had of the other.

Chapter Ten

Dinner was no sooner eaten, and Captain Nightingale no sooner departed for his bottle, than bottomless stores of frustration, misery, loneliness and resentment welled in Adelaide's heart and hurled themselves at her housekeeper. 'Are you out of your mind?' she hissed. Who knew how much a very drunk man could hear a room away? 'I don't know what you imagine my husband is but I can assure you, although he isn't himself at the moment, he both protects and provides. He's more than a husband. He is head of our household. He protects and provides for you as well, yet here you are suggesting – well, I don't know what you're suggesting, but I've never heard anything so ungrateful or so un-Christian. To be honest, Miss McCleary, I thought you had more sense. What's more, I resent the fact that I'm being lumped together with the rest of you, who I don't doubt for a minute need help from somewhere.' She was tired.

Pearl was tired. The gin had worn off and she too was less confident of the sense she'd seemed to make just a few hours before. She stood with as much dignity as she could muster and excused herself saying it had been a long day and she'd certainly no wish to offend.

'Can I have your assurance that you won't proceed with such a stupid idea?' Adelaide demanded. But Pearl would give no such thing. She retired to her room, leaving ambivalence to hang around in the kitchen. The certainty she took with her was this: although Adelaide alone was respectably married to a protector and provider, which the rest of them were not, her protector and provider was Marcus and only a very deluded wife would be foolish enough to rely on him.

By morning, this same certainty had revived her confidence and the plan it had formed was ready to be acted upon. All that had changed was its contents. It no longer included any other wives, part-time, full-time, widowed or hopeful. Just a man handy with his fists, as recommended by Annie, who could go into battle a step ahead of her. And to the railway.

She had no idea where Adelaide would stand on the matter after a good night's sleep but she would insist on clarity from her employer because her own intentions were perfectly plain and she wanted to proceed with them honestly. 'I think we need to be clear about my position,' she said as she hung nappies on the line after breakfast and Adelaide rocked Freddie in his pram parked in the small shaft of sunlight by the peg basket.

She spoke without rancour. She sounded as reasonable as could be. But she didn't look at Adelaide. She looked only at her pegs. 'I will abandon my plan to find someone to act for all of us but I intend to look for my fiancé. I won't work any less hard but I'll need reasonable time off. You might like to think about it a little longer.' She picked up the clothesbasket and headed back to the house. 'Can you spare me for an hour later today? I have a couple of errands to run.'

Poor Adelaide. She hated gauntlets and now she shivered. She trembled. It was another bitterly cold day and although the sun shone on the kitchen door, there was no heat in it. Not even warmth. She desperately wanted to ask what errands but settled for, 'Once the jobs are done.' And with that, she went to her books feeling even more out in the cold than she had by the washing line. The arm's length between her and Miss McCleary had grown to a very long leg and she regretted it. Repugnant though the idea of a part-time husband had been to her, she could see a mad kind of logic to it. Sensible, calm, dependable Miss McCleary had made it sound like the right thing to do. If it was the right thing to do, then surely she should be included in it. But how, when it was also, quite clearly, the wrong thing to do?

In the office, at the desk on which the treacherous ledgers were neatly stacked, she tried to make sense of the situation by converting the pros and cons into lists. Something on paper that didn't involve numbers would surely reveal the truth. She tore a page from the current ledger, ruled it down the middle and under Why We Are All In Trouble, she itemised individual needs, which included thoughts such as *thieving store manager, untrustworthy housekeeper, unnaturally hungry baby, look ugly, future bleak*; then: *no money, no job, out-of-control brothers, future bleak*; and *too many horses, too much make-up, never enough clothes on, future bleak*. As an afterthought she considered her housekeeper: *blind to danger to self and others, no other cares or responsibilities, future secure.*

On the other side of the page she labelled a list of Possible Solutions. She stared at it long and hard, but it remained steadfastly empty. When she heard Pearl tiptoe into the nursery, deposit the baby in his crib, then tiptoe out again, she accosted her in the hall and beckoned her into the kitchen, where her authoritative tone wavered in the face of Pearl's gaze, which was never anything but steady. 'I wonder . . . if your errand includes conversations with Mrs Worthington and Maggie O'Connell on the subject of last night's . . . subject?'

Pearl hesitated but only fractionally. 'It does,' she agreed.

'Then I would thank you to have it in your own time,' she said.

So, only three ladies gathered in Louisa's dining room during Freddie's six o'clock feed, and without benefit of alcohol Pearl wasted no time. 'I've had second thoughts,' she said.

'No!' cried the others before she could continue, but continue she did.

'Mrs Nightingale is thoroughly opposed to the idea and I don't think I can work around her or even if I should work around her. It would be irresponsible and none of us would benefit. I will continue to deal with my problem as best I can and leave you all to manage yours as best you can. I'm sorry.'

'You can't. You can't,' said Louisa. 'You're our only hope. Our lives depend on you to fix them.' She clung to Pearl's arm. Her dark tendrils fell about her beautiful pale face. 'Promise you won't abandon us. Please promise.' Such fear rose in her eyes.

'Promise,' whispered Maggie. 'Please promise.'

'I can't,' said Pearl and she left at once, taking every drop of hope from that house, leaving it as bleak as a bleak house could be.

Chapter Eleven

The house she returned to was even more miserable. Freddie was crying as lustily as he always did when woken by cold air, warm air, a mother, no mother or discovering he was where he didn't want to be. 'Hello,' said Captain Nightingale emerging stark naked from his office. 'Been for a walk?'

'Just coming, Mrs Nightingale,' Pearl called. 'I'm sorry, Captain Nightingale, the baby. And you seem to have no clothes on.' She spoke loudly so her words would carry to the nursery.

Adelaide, bouncing young Freddie for all he was worth to shut him up and to soothe her own shattered nerves, heard them and was sickened. They required action but what action? She threw open the nursery door and yelled, 'For God's sake, Marcus, get some clothes on! Get some stupid clothes on or go back into the office and stay there. Miss McCleary, get dinner.

We'll discuss your position once we've eaten.' It was as decisive as a dithering woman could be.

Pearl gathered strength for the confrontation but there was none. Dinner – leftover rabbit pie with mashed potato followed by lemon jelly – was eaten by each of them separately, and nothing of consequence followed. Pearl took Adelaide's on a tray to the nursery where it was received with a curt, 'Leave it there, thank you.' She deposited an identical tray on the bookcase in the office where Marcus, in his dressing gown, mumbled that he wasn't hungry.

She ate at the kitchen table, she washed the dishes, cleaned the kitchen then knocked on both office and nursery doors to ask if anything more was needed. Adelaide said, 'Nothing, thank you.' There was no reply from the office and so the day appeared to be over.

Pearl took a jug of water to her room, lit the lamp, closed the door, then argued with herself over the wisdom of leaving lamps ablaze in the kitchen and the doors unbolted. The doors were Captain Nightingale's duty, possibly his only duty, so she'd left them for him as a respectful housekeeper might. She would abide by the protocols of the household, however slapdash, hostile or naked they were, however disconcerting the idea of bushrangers on the prowl nearby. Did bushrangers hold up respectable households? What if they attacked the houses of Maggie and Louisa, which were even less protected than this one? She hoped their doors were bolted. Their lives depended on her, they had said. She wondered if she should hurry across and along to check on their safety. God, what had she done?

She knew what she had done. It was what she always did. She made plans that sounded plausible, she sucked people in, then she lost interest in them just as everyone else prepared to act on them. She picked up her pen to finish the interrupted letter.

'. . . nearly as clear as I might have hoped. Discretion and long hours at work are large stumbling blocks, so even if I wanted to, I could take no drastic action and certainly wouldn't without warning you in advance so you could alert the Light Horse. I'm sure, with nothing better to do, they will gallop to my rescue with all speed. Please give Beattie a hug from me and tell her to keep her chin up. Doctor Spencer's advice makes me even more resolved to do what I came here to do. I am in no danger and don't intend to become so. The weather here is much colder than I expected but the town is pretty, and walks by the river are lovely. We are also very lucky in our access to an extraordinary choice of provisions from Nightingales. I can't imagine how such an elegant store in such a small town did so well during the war and the quarantine.

The more she wrote about trivialities, the more normal her descriptions of the life she was leading sounded, the saner her thoughts became. They informed her that life with the Nightingales was far from normal. Theirs was a household at war with itself, consisting of an exhausted woman with no experience of, or stomach for, fighting battles on her own behalf and a man so exhausted by bloody battles that the only fight left in him was the one he waged with his wife.

It was hardly the safe haven she'd thought it might be when she'd accepted Adelaide's offer. The choice, Pearl decided as she tucked her letter to Annie into an envelope, to leave or to stay, might not be hers alone. Adelaide might order her to leave, which would settle the matter. If it were up to her, then the argument for staying was only that she was already here. The arguments for leaving were she'd be no less unprotected and un-provided for than she currently was, she'd no longer be at the mercy of an employer whose whims would almost certainly clash with her own, and she would no longer have to answer for the implications of a problem she should never have mentioned. Leaving won hands down. She would hand in her notice in the morning, advertise for a man to help her and begin her search in earnest.

Adelaide, curled up in the large lonely bed from which her husband had fled the minute she'd announced she was pregnant with Freddie, tried not to think of the morning. She blocked her ears with her fists, desperate for sleep. She could hear the baby grizzling in the next room, and she thought she could hear her demented husband prowling about the office. Worse, she couldn't hear a thing from Miss McCleary's room and Miss McCleary, the rock on whom she'd been depending for clarity and order, had turned out to be made of clay and gone to bed without bolting the doors.

How could she sleep when in the morning she might be without help again and still no closer to sacking Archie Stokes? Unless . . . unless . . . his petty theft could be endured for the sake of respectability. Unless she could simply put it aside and allow life to go on. No more fights; no more dread of the shop. It was the only pleasant thought she'd had in days. But in the nursery, Freddie's grizzling found some momentum. 'Mwaaa,' he bawled. 'Mwaa, mwaa, mwaa!' Louder and louder. She would let him cry. He would cry himself to sleep. She would go to sleep. 'Mwaa, mwaa!' Fury swelled in the baby's lungs as he strove for greater volume. On the other hand, it had been three pounds last week, five the week before. The shop couldn't afford it. That's why he had to go. All those horses! All those bushrangers! Those criminal boys not a hundred yards away threatening to burn the whole town down. Who would save her?

Pearl knocked at Adelaide's door. 'Would you like me to soothe him?'

'Yes, please,' said Adelaide. And within minutes Pearl had.

Chapter Twelve

Louisa, sitting on her verandah with a gun on her lap, stared at the house opposite, willing Pearl to emerge and say she'd help one way or another. Through the window above the sturdy front door she could see lights being carried from room to room. Then, unexpectedly, the door did open and she saw not Pearl but Marcus, wearing only a pair of trousers and carrying a bottle, walk unsteadily down the path. His gaze, she thought, was fixed on her and, sure enough, he crossed the road. But though he stared at her house, he appeared not to see her. She thought that if she stayed very still, he wouldn't notice her. She held her breath. She cursed the breeze that lifted her skirt.

'Hello, Louisa,' he said. 'May I come in?'

It was late, she was in her nightclothes, she was carrying a gun. He was scarcely dressed, he was carrying a bottle, he sounded sad and lonely and drunk. She felt sad and lonely. 'Of course,' she said.

She stood. She squared her shoulders. She adjusted her neckline. A tiny hope, not even articulated by any voice her brain heard, was that if she allowed Adelaide Nightingale's very dull and steady, though less steady than he had been, husband into her empty house in the dead of night, he would fall in love with her, leave his family for her and she would have no need of a part-time husband. As he tottered unsteadily up her path, the hope found voice and from it a gigantic future leapt. Were she in Adelaide's shoes, she'd soon sort out Archie Stokes. She'd soon restore happiness and order to the Captain's life. Louisa hadn't eaten in days. She'd polished off the gin and another note had arrived. *Fifty more coming your way, you slut*, it had said. And 'slut' had cut her to the quick. Now she said to herself, *I'll give them slut!*

She looked quickly up and down the street, then admitted Marcus into the house. She led him into her drawing room, where a single lamp flickered and the gin bottle stood empty on the sideboard. She found two unused glasses, took the bottle from her guest, who seemed to be shivering, and poured two generous whiskies. 'This will warm you up,' she said. 'I'd say sit by the fire but as you see, there is no fire.' She took a blanket from the sofa and threw it to him. He made a broad sweep with his arm to catch it but missed it by miles so he left it where it fell at his feet. He dropped into one of the matching armchairs, which had once held promise of a marriage for life. Louisa arranged herself on the sofa, where the flickering light from the lamp on the corner table flattered her lovely, sad face.

'That's very kind of you,' Marcus said. He stared at her with eyes so moist and red and confused that Louisa wondered what was up with him. She wished it was nothing. She wanted him to be steadfast and powerful and rich and hers. And he seemed to know it because he said, 'You really are a very attractive woman, Louisa. You always have been. So small, so dainty . . . I don't imagine you'll stay a widow for long.' The words were indistinct but his intention was clear. 'Poor Jimmy.'

Louisa wiped her eyes, not crying but with an instinct for the right gesture. Marcus rose unsteadily and, tripping over the blanket, lurched towards her. She stood as well, alert to the danger of imminent injury if he fell on her, but he didn't fall. He put his arms around her, he rested his head against hers and suddenly, he sobbed. He sobbed because his heart was broken, crushed by the awful loss of some mind he couldn't locate no matter how long he slept or how much he drank.

Louisa held him and patted him but she hated the noise, she hated the sorrow, she hated the weakness. Her husband had gone to war and died. Marcus was alive and drunk. 'You'd better go home,' she said. 'Take this.' She handed him the blanket then she took his hand because he seemed to be lost, and led him back down the very dark corridor. She closed the front door behind him and heard him stumbling down the path. When a terrible shriek shattered the night air, she thought that surely it couldn't have come from him. It must be a horse, and she froze. Then she heard footsteps running and she heard Adelaide say, 'Maggie, for goodness sake,' followed by, 'Marcus, go inside. You've frightened her.' When she opened the door a fraction she saw Maggie wearing what appeared to be a ball gown, holding hard to her fence gasping, 'I thought he was a bushranger.'

Adelaide laughed more from anxiety than amusement. 'It's just silly Captain Nightingale, bolting the door and enjoying the night air.'

'What on earth are you doing out this time of night and wearing so little?' Pearl asked, emerging briskly from the shadows to assume control in case her loss of it had been the cause of the shock.

'I was sewing and I suddenly remembered I had no job.' Maggie was trembling so violently that words tumbled from her mouth incomprehensibly. Pearl wrapped her own shawl about the girl's slender bare shoulders. 'I found a key to my mother's trunk with her beautiful clothes in it . . .'

'But dear, it's so late,' said Pearl, tightening the shawl and rubbing Maggie's freezing hands between her own. 'Where were you going?'

'To Mrs Mayberry. To give her a letter. I need her to forgive me.' Poor Maggie clung to Pearl as she had clung to no other in years. 'I'm sorry I called out. I didn't recognise him.' To which both Adelaide and Louisa might have added, *Me neither.*

Louisa quietly closed her front door and disappeared back into her cold, friendless house. Adelaide attempted to take her husband's arm as he headed towards theirs but he shook her off. They entered their house in silence and disappeared into their separate rooms, each swamped by their own misery, ever the natural outcome of unnatural silence.

Pearl, gripping Maggie's arm, walked with her along the boundary of Louisa's paddocks before they crossed the road and hurried past the grand entrance to Somerset Station, without so much as glancing at it. An icy wind ripped down Hope Street from the mountains. 'I need a job,' Maggie was babbling. 'I don't think anyone understands how much I need a job. If I don't work, we don't eat. And I've ruined this dress by cutting it too short. Do you know how to sew?'

'Let's talk about it in the morning,' Pearl said. 'No one's going to let you starve.'

'I need a husband, that's what I need,' Maggie said. 'A man who'll get me back my land. Please, Miss McCleary. We all need a husband.' How sad she sounded. How sad is hope when it's been doused in cold water and drowned.

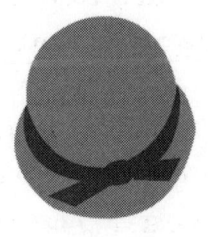

Chapter Thirteen

Next morning, comfortless Maggie woke fraught and anxious, but pluck had arrived in the nick of time to help her. Pluck and defiance. She ordered her two grumpy brothers from their beds, gave them porridge, packed lunch for them and took each firmly by an arm as she marched them to school. 'I don't care,' she said when they complained that she would make them a laughing stock. 'From now on you're doing what I tell you, because if you don't I'll lock you in the woodshed and you'll die there.' Al and Ed scoured her face for a joke but it was no joke.

From the school, Maggie headed to the Mayberrys'. In the pocket of the very big coat was the letter she had penned. *Dear Mrs Mayberry*, it read. *I know you think I am wicked for having taken the pie but Mrs Nightingale understands why I did it and she has forgiven me. I hope you will forgive me too. I am very grateful to you for the work you give me and I will try even harder to do a good job if you will give me another chance. Yours respectfully, Maggie O'Connell (Miss).* She had copied the letter three times, checking and re-checking the spelling and the punctuation.

The morning was grey and dreary but less cold than the one before. The Mayberry house, built three years previously in deep purple brick, sat square and gloomy in a garden the Mayor's wife liked to call 'pure Surrey'. Or pure 'Thurry', if she remembered. She meant it had roses in it, and magnolias, camellias and rhododendron. She had planted it with a view to the kind of grandeur that befitted a mayor and his wife. She imagined garden parties where she would move among the townspeople nodding and smiling, possibly waving.

Maggie knocked on the door, intent on delivering the letter in person. A living soul, she had persuaded herself, clearly in need of a job, had to be harder to resist than a letter whose handwriting might be illegible. She waited. Surely it wasn't too early. School was in. Surely someone was up. How long should she stand on the Mayberrys' doorstep looking suspicious and feeling this anxious? She was halfway to the gate when the Mayor himself opened the door.

'Yes?' he said to her back.

'I was hoping to find Mrs Mayberry at home.' Maggie returned to the door. The Mayor's face, she noted, was blotchy.

'Why?' asked the Mayor.

'Because I wanted to give her a letter.'

'Give me the letter.'

'And I'd hoped to speak to her.'

'What about?'

'About my job.'

'What about your job?'

What could Maggie do, short of run? 'I would like to keep it.'

'The letter?'

'The job.'

'And why wouldn't you keep it?'

'Because yesterday Mrs Mayberry sacked me for taking a pie she believed I had stolen from Nightingales, but Mrs Nightingale was giving it to me. She told Mr Stokes she was giving it to me but I'm not sure Mrs Mayberry knows.'

The explanation was truthful as far as it went, if you were prepared to ignore the crime's *mens rea* and see only the *actus reus*, but neither seemed to concern the Mayor even though he had a sprinkling of law in his repertoire. He had no idea that Maggie's sacking was reckoned by the entire town, on whose good opinion he was relying, to be the Right Thing. Not a single part of his understanding acknowledged that his wife's popularity was, as of last week, considerably greater than his own. What he saw before him, tiny and anxious and quite pretty now he looked at her, was an opportunity to remind his wife who was boss. So he smiled and said, 'Well, I think Mrs Mayberry might have been a bit hasty. I'll speak to her and you can consider your job restored.'

'Thank you, thank you very much, Mr Mayor,' Maggie said, flashing him a smile that was, he thought, really very lovely. He told her to run along and not give it another thought, then he went in to a hearty breakfast, prepared by Mrs O'Reilly, the mother of Mrs Quirk from The Irish Rover, while his wife still slept, and he felt very pleased with himself.

The further she hurried from the Mayberry house, the less elated Maggie felt. It was all very well for the Mayor to give her back her job. She had still to confront his wife. She wished she'd insisted. She wished she'd left the letter. By the time she reached the bridge, she wished she'd spoken to Miss McCleary first. She would speak to her now. Which was odd because precisely the same thought was occurring to Adelaide and Louisa.

Louisa had woken knowing she would beg if she had to. Miss McCleary was her only hope. She would talk to her as soon as she had the strength to dress and comb her hair. Adelaide had woken knowing that, however un-Christian Pearl McCleary might be, she couldn't do without her. She was the only person who could relieve her of the baby, the only person who could keep the house orderly and clean, the only person she could ever imagine so unfazed by her husband naked and drunk she didn't even mention it. She'd speak to her the minute breakfast was over. She'd suggest a stroll in the garden where Marcus wouldn't hear the baby screaming, so they could reach an agreement of the new conditions of her employment.

But Pearl got in first. As Louisa was sticking pins in her hair and Maggie was trotting through the Arch, she said to Adelaide, 'I wonder if I could speak frankly.' And before Adelaide could take steps to avoid 'frankly', Pearl added, 'I'd like to hand in my notice to be effective immediately.'

'No,' Adelaide said. 'Please no,' and she'd certainly have said more but Maggie banged very loudly on the door. Knowing that any minute the head of the household might appear in any stage of undress or anger, Pearl flew to let her in and guided the girl into the kitchen where Adelaide was hovering by the sink in no mood for visitors.

'I have my job back,' Maggie reported breathlessly, regardless of any conversation she might have been interrupting. 'But I don't feel right about it.'

'Why ever not?' snapped Adelaide. 'How astonishing of Mrs Mayberry to see reason.'

'She didn't,' Maggie said. 'The Mayor did. And she won't be pleased. I know she won't be pleased. She won't be pleased because he seemed to be so pleased.'

Amazing insight though this was for such a young girl, it meant very little to Adelaide and Pearl, and there was no chance for her to explain further because Louisa strolled into the kitchen, remarking casually, 'The front door was open. How is Captain Nightingale this morning?'

'I wish people would close the door when they enter my house,' said Adelaide but no one cared.

'He was out so late and wearing so little,' Louisa said, then realising her mistake added quickly, 'I saw through the window.'

'I didn't see you,' said Adelaide.

'He gave me such a fright,' said Maggie. 'I thought he was a bushranger. But guess what? I have my job back.'

'Wonderful,' said Louisa, then immediately turned her back on the wonder. 'What I've come to say is this. I think Miss McCleary should come and live with me.' If it sounded blunt, it was only because the point needed to be reached quickly.

'I thought she could come and live with me,' said Maggie.

'Don't be ridiculous, she works for me,' said Adelaide. 'She's staying where she is.'

Pearl looked from one to the other in astonishment. 'Thank you for the offers,' she said, 'but I'm planning to move on. I need to do what I came here to do and I now see that involving anyone else is irresponsible. We each have our own way of seeing things.'

'You're wrong,' said Louisa. 'I see things exactly as you do. If we all act together we'll have one another and if we advertise for a man to help, we'll have a team. That's what I've been thinking. We can help each other. Then none of us will feel so . . . useless.'

'Me too,' said Maggie. 'That's what I've been thinking.'

'I don't see why you should go.' Adelaide addressed Pearl crossly. 'You might as well stay where you are. At least you'll be paid.' She flushed at the lie. 'At least there's food in the house.'

'We have food in our house,' said Maggie. 'Of course we do. Or we'd be dead.'

'But you have to steal it,' said Adelaide spitefully. It was horrible, but she was so tired and so angry that the woman she'd intended to sack had resigned before she'd had a chance to sack her then reinstate her because she'd have had second thoughts which might have been kind or selfish but who would have been able to spot the difference? And she felt so betrayed that Louisa, who only the day before yesterday she'd rushed to comfort, was undermining her, and that silly little Maggie, who only the day before yesterday she'd saved from jail, was sitting there looking as if she had a better claim to her housekeeper than she did. 'Of course you must do what you think best,' she said, which was impressive given what she was thinking. 'But please think of baby Freddie who loves you so much and the routine you've established, which is so important to him and to me when I'm trying to resolve a crisis in the shop, which may I remind everyone is a secret. I can depend on you all to respect that, can't I?'

'Of course,' said Pearl, and the others nodded without interest, disinclined to cooperate with anyone so reluctant to cooperate with them.

'Please stay, Miss McCleary,' Adelaide said. 'Please, please stay. I don't think I can manage without you,' and because she began to cry, an unprecedented move, neither Louisa nor Maggie felt they could insist her own need was greater. Louisa even wondered if she should cross the room to give her former friend a pat on the hand.

No coats had been removed. No seats had been taken. No one had thoughts beyond their own urgent need to speak. But it seemed to Pearl that if anything was to be achieved by this conversation it should be conducted in a civilised manner.

'I'll make tea,' she said, planning, revising, planning and revising. Why and how, why and how.

'But will you stay?' Adelaide insisted.

'And what about cake? I made a butter cake yesterday. Should we have some cake?' Pros and cons, this or that.

'Of course have cake if anyone wants it,' Adelaide said.

'Then let's all sit,' said Pearl, which was not her place but since no one seemed to know exactly what her place was, they accepted she was in charge and so did she. When everyone was sitting and everyone had tea and cake, she said, 'I think we can avoid the use of the word husband which so upset Mrs Nightingale.'

'But not me,' said Maggie.

'Or me,' said Louisa, struck suddenly by the allegiance she was forming with a girl so far beneath her in social graces that some form of correction was required. 'Not that we are in any way comparable. I, for instance, do not steal.'

'And nor does Maggie, except in the criminal sense of the word,' said Pearl. 'If we're going to act together and draw strength from each other, then we can't judge each other. We're all responsible for our predicaments to a greater or lesser degree and my feeling is that Maggie's degree, as she is the youngest by far, is the least.'

Louisa picked up her cup, which obscured most of her face, and blinked. *That was uncalled for,* she thought.

'So where will you live?' Adelaide asked.

'I'll continue to live and work here if that still suits you,' Pearl said. 'I will work my hardest to help you in any way I can. But the condition is that, regardless of what you think of the way I handle my own problems, you don't involve yourself.'

'That seems reasonable,' said Adelaide.

'What about our problems?' Maggie wanted to know. 'What's your plan for us?'

'Well,' said Pearl, 'this is how I see it.'

And how she saw it was exactly as she had seen it originally. The man they needed had to have skills, which included bravery, common sense, knowledge of the law, ability to his use fists, tracking, shooting, building, banking, horses, retail and also wholesale.

'Also good with figures,' said Adelaide. 'And prepared to listen.'

'Not frightened of anyone. Did we say that?' said Louisa. 'Not dependent on me for everything.'

'And who might be a good husband for one of us,' Maggie added. 'So, strong and affectionate and helpful.' She was ignored.

'There won't be any such person,' Adelaide said. But the others insisted there would be in times of such awful unemployment and in any case, Pearl pointed out, that was the least of the immediate hurdles. They needed to agree where he might live and how he could be paid. Louisa said he could live with her in the guest bedroom. She could say he was her cousin. Adelaide said it would draw gossip. Everyone knew that Louisa didn't have a cousin.

'Then he could be my cousin,' said Pearl. 'We will need to offer him payment. I have some money but not much. Maggie has none and Louisa has none.'

'I have a little,' Adelaide said, but only because she didn't want to admit to none. She did have a little in a bank account. It was for the rainy day her father had said dampened all married life sooner or later.

'A little is plenty to start with,' Pearl said. And so it was agreed. Pearl and Adelaide would put up enough to cover a month's wage subject to their approval once they had met him. Louisa would prepare her guest room. Maggie would help with the cleaning. The advertisement would be placed in the *Sydney*

Morning Herald because Sydney was far enough away to ensure anonymity, and Annie McGuire would interview the applicants because her very sound judgement could be trusted.

And so the notice appeared:

> Four respectable ladies in friendly country town seek part-time husband. Must have knowledge of the law, banking, horses and bush skills as well as a grasp of boxing, farming and retail. Salary by agreement. Contact PO Box 293, Sydney.

Oh Lord. The term 'part-time husband' had crept into the advertisement after all. Adelaide and Pearl had despatched Louisa to Myrtle Grove to place it confidentially, and exhilarated by the change of scene she hadn't been able to help herself. She laughed and laughed at the wickedness of it.

She'd have laughed on the other side of her face had she guessed the fury, full of flame and smouldering ember, her mischief would raise in the breast of Annie McGuire. Had Annie known that silly, reckless, thoughtless Louisa was to blame for the folly, she'd have been on the earliest coach to Prospect and brought Pearl home in an instant.

As it was, the advertisement appeared just two days after the letter Pearl had sent asking Annie to interview applicants for a job that in no way had caused her to think 'shared husband'. On reading it she could only imagine that Pearl had lost all reason and that her foolish scheming was out of control. She blamed herself. She should have seen it coming. She'd driven the wretched girl clear out of her mind.

While awful responses to the disgusting invitation gathered in the Post Office box, the full horror of their possibilities played havoc with Mrs McGuire's conscience. On her knees by the side of her bed with her rosary wrapped around her fist she agonised, as well she might. What was the wilful girl thinking? In the name of Jesus, Mary and Joseph, *what was she thinking?* Who were these other women and how could they possibly imagine they were respectable? Brazen barely touched it.

Pearl's letter hadn't so much as hinted at brazen. *I know, dear Annie, that this will sound peculiar, advertising for a man to help four respectable ladies but we are all in dire need with manifold problems (ha ha!). It would be a big help if you could sort through the replies and interview the most likely candidates. I've considered the sort of man who might reply to our advertisement and devised a way that might weed out any with unsavoury intentions. You must pretend to be one of us and you must suggest that the other three are older than you and even poorer.*

Annie called upon the Blessed Virgin to guide her through the mire and the Blessed Virgin, who could only have been a loving woman with a practical nature, elected not to appear to her supplicant in a dream but to let her reach her own conclusion, which by morning she had. She would collect the applications. She would sort through them. She would interview any who sounded sane. She would give one of them the job and she would place her faith in God the Father, repellent though the whole sorry thing would be to Him.

As early light broke through clouds over Bondi Junction the next morning, a hopeful ray pinpointed Annie's exit from the modest house in Limerick Street: a short, dumpy woman wearing a squashy brown hat pulled down hard over her ears, striding in a grey, shapeless gown towards the tram that would take her to the General Post Office in town, and thence to Gomorrah.

Chapter Fourteen

The Mayor of Prospect greeted the day with less conviction and even greater trepidation than Annie McGuire's. He'd gone to sleep knowing that his wife was spoiling for a fight. He'd woken with a dreadful foreboding, which abated only slightly when he saw that she slept still and with luck would continue to sleep until well after he'd made his escape. He crept from the bedroom carrying clothes discarded from the night before to save time and he cursed as he crashed into the washstand. 'Wait in the breakfast room,' his wife ordered from her sleep. 'I have something to say to you.'

Such a chill gripped his innards. It was ice-cold acid, spewing from the mouth of a woman he no longer recognised as his wife and entering his body just below the heart, striking him in his guts over which he placed a protective hand. 'I can give you five minutes,' he said. 'But you must be quick. I have a meeting.'

He had no meeting. His wife seemed to know he had no meeting. She dawdled from the bedroom a good half-hour later, during which time he told himself more than once to run. Leave. Disappear. Let her get on with it. He'd given her due warning. But he didn't dare and not daring caused even greater pain to his poor stomach.

'What is it, Florrie?' he asked when she appeared. 'I'm in a hurry.'

'I have a proposal to make,' she said, taking a seat opposite him and pouring herself some tea. She sipped and studied him over the cup. It was true. He had taken on a piggy aspect and she no longer cared much for him. 'It's perfectly straightforward. You've formed an attachment to the O'Connell girl and –'

He blustered at once, knowing that he must. 'I have done no such thing! I merely said her job was safe because she needs a job and it behoves a Mayor to bestow kindness on his less fortunate citizenry.'

'When she has a nice bust and when there's an underfunded railway on our doorstep with your name on it,' Florence observed calmly.

Her calm was unnerving. Why wasn't she jealous? Why wasn't she insisting he tell her he loved her? She'd always been so compliant. Her opinions had always been his and yet here she was exercising judgement she had no business to exercise. 'I don't for a minute think this whatever-she's-called has a nice whatever-you-call-it. I can't even place her. She's just a blur.'

'I don't care about her bust. It matters not a jot to me. What I care about is that you promised her a job no one believes she's entitled to keep, and by no one I mean In The Whole Town. You don't seem to understand, George, that I have Right and The Whole Town on my side, so if you go against me you will be in The Wrong and The Whole Town will be against you. I think you'd find that very inconvenient. Given the way things are with the railway.'

George Mayberry blinked slowly, watching his wife's mouth in disbelief, filtering its weird and unfamiliar emanations through his eyes as if they could help. Had he put in some kind of appearance at her maiden speech the style would have been less foreign. But he hadn't, so now he had to make of it what he could. What he made of it was bad. The railway was indeed on the brink of stalling yet again. Money had dried up. He was hard at work applying pressure on the money source to release enough funds to finish the bloody thing before the next Mayoral election, 'to give work to our returning boys'. And now here was his wife about to ruin everything. He'd spent enough gruelling years in local council to recognise a threat in the offing.

'If I tell Mr Stokes that you restored the girl to her job against my wishes, then make no mistake, George, The Whole Town will soon believe you've Formed An Attachment even though you're married to me, and the very least thing you would become is a Laughing Stock but more than likely people will think of you as An Adulterer. I might even be forced to consider Divorce.'

'Florrie, that's ridiculous,' said the Mayor, knowing it wasn't, no longer prepared to underestimate the silly creature across the table from him. 'I have no intentions towards the girl and we are happily married.'

'Unless, of course, I choose to save you.'

'And how might you do that?' Despite his revulsion, the Mayor was fascinated.

'By reaching an agreement. If you support me, I will support you.'

'I do support you. I provide for you. I care for you.'

Florence laughed. 'You are mithing the point, George. I want you to change your position on the matter of me and Parliament, then I will reconsider mine with regard to you and the girl.' Mrs Mayberry had never before used her lisp in married life but in view of its success with the public she was inclined to test it in private.

The Mayor was floored beyond endurance. Who was she? Where had the lisp come from? Surely not Melbourne. She had gone to Melbourne to visit her sister and buy a hat. It could only be the sister, Minnie Forrester of South Yarra. Had Minnie Forrester encouraged the lisp along with ideas so beyond his wife's normal capacity they reeked of madness? He would stop the rot at its root. He would write to Minnie Forrester and get her to make her sister see sense. No he wouldn't. He would talk to Archie Stokes. He was one hundred per cent sure that he held more sway with the grocer than his wife did. This was the Mayor's foolhardy decision.

Chapter Fifteen

Louisa bustled into Nightingales to collect her tea. She had no money for tea, or for anything else that might bring comfort to her unfed body, but she was confident she had a healthy line of credit. It was a family line and untouchable by dint of her standing in the community and the heroism of her late husband. She hurried straight past Ginger and Mrs Lambert behind the counter although Mrs Lambert was smiling at her in expectation. She made her way right to the back of the store where the manager was slicing ham from a large, pink, immaculately glazed and studded leg, each slow cut a loving caress. There was no finer ham to be had between Prospect and Goulburn. It was a fact. Apart from the excellence of the pig, no one else could lay their hands on cloves.

'Good morning, Mr Stokes,' Louisa said. She smiled at him more enthusiastically than was required but Archie Stokes was familiar with such enthusiasm, just as he was quick to notice that the beautiful Mrs Worthington was very slender these days and very pale.

'Lovely day, Mrs Worthington,' he said. 'How are those horses of yours?'

'As well as can be expected for such sorry animals.' Louisa sighed. 'I'm only too pleased to be giving them a home.'

Archie Stokes carefully placed a muslin cloth over the tray of delicately smoked succulence and addressed his customer with a smile. 'And what can I do for you this morning?' he said, knowing full well what he could, but might choose not to, do.

'I've come for my tea. Has it arrived?'

'It has.' He didn't declare its provenance as he usually might with something like: 'On the Boronia direct from Ceylon to be carried by rail from Sydney to Goulburn and Cooma then on to Prospect courtesy of Mr Cobb.' He went directly to: 'And I expect you'd also like to settle your bill.' He slowly wiped his beefy hands on his apron. 'Would you like to come into the office?'

Louisa most definitely did not want to go into the office. Mr Stokes' manner, generally so fatherly and unstinting, held a suggestion of stint. Fatherly still, she could hear, but no longer completely respectful. She followed him, trying to hear resolve above the pounding of her heart. He'd never sounded so much as firm with her before, but today there was flint in his tone. He'd been talking to Thomas at the bank, who must have told him she had no money nor any likelihood of money. She should never have exposed herself to the bank when no one in this flaming town could keep a confidence if their own life didn't depend on it. But what else could she have done?

'Take a seat,' he said as he eased himself into the comfortable chair reserved for managers or owners behind the large desk. She took the less comfortable chair opposite, reserved for thieves and debtors and hard-pressed sellers believing they could negotiate. She arranged her face to be both solvent and contrite.

'Just the tea, is it, this morning?' Mr Stokes was flicking through his large debit and credit book, looking for the Ws.

'And one or two other things, but just the tea would do.' Louisa winced. She either wanted more than tea or she didn't want more than tea and clearly she did want more than tea so she shouldn't have said just the tea would do.

'As of close of business last night, you owe us fifteen pounds, seven shillings and eight pence,' Mr Stokes said. His eyes rolled up and down the list of figures, clearly giving him cause for thought. 'No payment for four months, which is longer than we'd like but an oversight I'm sure. And how would you like to pay that this morning?'

The choice was clear. Burst into tears. Promise payment later. Throw herself into his arms. Laugh. The choice was not clear. 'I won't be paying anything this morning, Mr Stokes, though thank you for enquiring. I have an arrangement with Mrs Nightingale so I'll settle my bill directly with her.'

Last traces of fatherliness left the expression of Mr Stokes. 'Of course,' he said. 'I gather little Maggie O'Connell has something similar. I'll take it up with Mrs Nightingale so we can keep our books neat and tidy.' He stood. He opened the door to show her out. He closed the door before she could pass through it and lowered his voice. 'Just a thought, though, Mrs Worthington, about those horses. They're a sickly bunch, but should you need them taken off your hands I know a man who could turn them into meat, no questions asked.' He opened the door for her and leered into her face. 'Total discretion,' he said. 'Think about it. He might do the lot for something in the order of fifteen pounds, seven shillings and eight pence less a little for interest.'

He followed her into the shop. 'Mrs Lambert, could you wrap Mrs Worthington's tea for her?'

Louisa hardly noticed the tea being handed to her or the sympathetic look on Mrs Lambert's face as she passed it across the counter. She prayed only that she'd find Adelaide at home and alone. Poor Louisa. No one listening. Not even God.

Adelaide was as at home as could be, but so was her mother-in-law, Phyllis Nightingale of Toorak, who'd arrived out of the blue from Melbourne, summoned by her trusted delivery man turned miraculous manager, buyer and profit maker, Archie Stokes. She was in the office with her son and the door was firmly closed against the rest of the household, much good it did them if it was privacy they wanted. Phyllis knew no pitch other than forte.

'Marcus,' she was bellowing, 'your wife is a very stupid woman. I'm sorry you have headaches but you must step in. She's making life miserable for poor Stokes and if he goes, we're sunk.' She could be heard comfortably in the street and uncomfortably in the hall where Adelaide was lingering not three feet from Pearl who was preparing Freddie for the morning air.

Pearl kept her eyes firmly fixed on Freddie, who wisely kept his eyes on her, smiling at her as she smiled at him so that between them there was only joy. Adelaide's gaze, directed at her feet, contained only despair as she waited for her husband to defend her. But Marcus's pitch favoured the sotto in his mother's presence, so all she heard clearly were the final few sentences, which contained nothing in the way of chivalry.

'I know exactly what's going on and I'm sorting it out. You have nothing to worry about, Mother. Now, if you're staying for a few days I'll get McCleary to prepare you a room.' Adelaide's gaze shifted to Pearl in alarm but Pearl had her back to her as she steered the pram through the front door, and her back gave nothing away.

'Miss McCleary, Miss McCleary,' Louisa called, spotting her as she passed through the Arch. 'Hang on a minute.' Pearl waited as Louisa hurried towards her. 'Is Mrs Nightingale in? I really need to speak to her. Is she free, do you think?'

'She's in but not free at this very minute. Her mother-in-law has arrived.' Pearl dropped her own voice to pianissimo.

'Good God. Phyllis. I thought she was in Italy.' Louisa stared at the house for some kind of explanation.

'I'm off for a walk,' Pearl said, moving towards the river. 'Do you want to walk? Or are you going to try your luck?'

It was such a shocking day for luck. Louisa might have called on her neighbour and paid her respects to her mother-in-law, she might have walked with Pearl and discussed the likely outcome of the advertisement, which had appeared two days before, but she chose to do neither. She chose to go home, where there was no food, no warmth, no comfort, just a note on the door announcing *WHORE!* And now fifty-two horses, which Archie Stokes might have persuaded a less nauseated woman were mouth-watering.

This was luck if ever there was luck. Had she opted for the walk, she'd have found that Pearl wasn't heading to the river, but into town to collect her ordered copy of the *Sydney Morning Herald* with its significant entry. Pearl would have discovered Louisa's folly, she would certainly have known the fury in Annie's heart and she would certainly have turned on Louisa for her thoughtlessness, her stupidity, her rotten moral fibre and her breathtaking arrogance. *WHORE!* by comparison, if Louisa had only known it, was better.

Chapter Sixteen

Happily, there was no one at Pearl's side when she read the offending insertion, apart from little Freddie, who was sleeping peacefully so didn't hear her choke. 'Oh no, oh help, oh Annie,' she muttered to herself as she wheeled him at a furious pace to the Post Office to make good the damage. She calmed herself before approaching Mrs Quirk's daughter Norah, who'd replaced the redhead as the town's transmitter of confidential information to anyone who cared to listen. Her telegram read: *Mistake in job description. Sorry. Please press on*, causing Norah to wonder about a long-distance ironing accident.

Annie, reading it several hours later, grasped its intent, despite its lack of explanation. If she felt comforted, it was only slightly. There was nothing good about any of it. In her sitting room, on the table by the fire, was a shockingly large pile of rapid respondents, twenty-six in all, who'd made haste to suggest themselves as ideal for a job so honestly advertised. Honest. That's what seven of them called it when it was no more honest than it was respectable. An invitation to hell and damnation was what it was.

She glared at the pile. She asked herself if the Virgin Mary was directing her to throw the lot onto the fire and report to Pearl that none had been suitable. She looked out the window and said a decade of the rosary recalling The Agony in the Garden. She went to the kitchen to pour herself a glass of water, then returned to the sitting room where she could keep an eye on Beattie Flannagan in the backyard listlessly sketching the lemon tree as instructed 'to keep her mind off things'. She gingerly took up the first reply and held it close to her face so she could properly decipher it. *Dear Respectable Ladies (I bet)*, she read. *I am a widower and quite capable of satisfying ALL your requirements. I may be older than others who apply but, believe me, my stamina is undiminished.* Holy Mother of God, help me, she prayed.

It echoed all the way to the Nightingale household though it changed direction en route. 'Help me, Mother,' a desperate Adelaide sobbed silently to her dead parent. She hadn't lingered outside the office after Pearl's departure. She'd taken herself to her room where she'd decided to remain all morning, allowing self-pity, impotence and fury to overwhelm her. She'd made an enemy of Archie Stokes, she looked a fool in the eyes of her husband and mother-in-law, and the only hope she had was in an advertisement for a non-existent man who would almost certainly arrive and fall in love with Louisa.

She heard the front door open, the murmur of voices in the hall and then the office door pulled shut as she might were she in someone else's house and of little consequence when it came to comings and goings. It was such an insult. She'd been in charge of Nightingales all war long and Nightingales had thrived all war long. She hadn't given up when the war had ended as everyone had expected. She'd kept going despite a horrible pregnancy, a demanding baby and a husband incapable of a rational opinion. Her mother-in-law had removed herself to Melbourne the minute war was declared and accepted without acknowledgement the generous allowance the shop made to her, which appeared without fail in the monthly accounts. Now here she was, sticking her oar in when she'd never exerted any effort.

Adelaide couldn't stand it a minute longer. She might be a fool but she wasn't a coward. She splashed water on her face, she brushed her hair, she straightened her clothes, she slipped on brown shoes with a small heel that indicated common sense and she paused for just a second to listen at the door for any hint of ridicule.

She should have paused a fraction longer. She would then have known that the front door had opened to admit Archie Stokes, who was enjoying a vast joke with Marcus and his mother, infinitely more comfortable in their company than she had ever been. She might have prepared herself. He stood as she entered but made no attempt to temper his amusement. 'Mrs Nightingale,' he said. 'Junior. The very person I've come to see.'

'And here I am,' Adelaide said, when she might have told him she had no wish to see him.

'We decided you were asleep,' lied Phyllis. Her gaze was fixed on her son, ordering complicity, which was given without question.

'I was changing my shoes,' said Adelaide. 'What was it you wanted to say, Mr Stokes?'

'The books, Mrs Nightingale, the books.' He too looked not at her but at his allies. 'Some small question marks.'

'I gather you've had some trouble adding up and subtracting.' Phyllis smirked.

Adelaide flushed. 'But I've mastered both.' She would hold her ground even if it was giving way beneath her feet like dirt down a hill in a storm.

'Be that as it may,' said Mr Stokes. 'What I need you to clarify for me is the matter of special favours to friends.'

'If you mean Maggie O'Connell then I think we decided, didn't we, that there had been a genuine mistake I was happy to correct as a matter of good will.'

'Not only the O'Connell girl but Mrs Worthington, who has a large unsettled bill she says you've agreed she needn't pay.' If it wasn't quite what she'd said, who was Adelaide to argue.

'I've made no agreement with Mrs Worthington.'

'Louisa Gibson that was,' Phyllis reminded herself. 'Pretty girl. Bit of a tart.'

'Now a widow,' Adelaide forced herself to say.

'A very pretty widow,' agreed Mr Stokes. 'Wouldn't you say, Captain?' And when the Captain failed to say anything Mr Stokes added, 'But apparently not very honest. Widow or no widow, pretty or plain.'

How kind-hearted Adelaide was tested. The look on the face of Mr Stokes was as unendurable as the faint grin from her husband, which had nothing to do with neighbourliness. This was how men reacted to Louisa. Louisa who had stolen William Mayberry but not wanted William Mayberry, then had not really wanted Jimmy Worthington but had married Jimmy Worthington and was now mourning Jimmy Worthington, while possibly starving herself to death owing to the folly of Jimmy Worthington and also, by her own admission, her own folly. Poor Louisa, claiming an arrangement she hadn't made but perhaps would have tried to make had Adelaide shown her any kindness, despite the past and the likelihood of the debt ever being repaid, which was nil.

Just how these trains of thought were ever going to arrive at a helpful station was anyone's guess. They might have kept on chuffing about Adelaide's tired old brain all day had Mr Stokes not said, 'Why don't you just leave her to me?' And had not Phyllis replied, 'Just what I was saying to Marcus.' And had Archie Stokes not nodded and beamed. But each gesture conspired to bring the useless agonising to a stop and suddenly Adelaide had clarity of purpose as well as firmness of voice.

She addressed only her husband. 'I would like to make an arrangement with Louisa because I know she's currently in a hole. You're fond of her, Marcus, so I think you'll agree with me. Her husband was killed fighting for our country. You were fortunate.' She chose her words deliberately knowing they would create a confusion in Marcus's breast no less complicated than the jumble in her own.

'That's an outrageous thing to say, Adelaide!' his mother bellowed. 'Jimmy Worthington was a reckless boy who grew into a reckless man. If Marcus survived, it was because he was more cautious and not because he was fortunate.' She saw her mistake too late. Her son first lost all colour then found a violent pink.

'Shut up, Mother!' he cried. 'Shut up. You know nothing about it.' He left his position by the fireplace. He rounded on the others with an expression of wild incomprehension. 'Jimmy Worthington died for his King, His God and His Country. I wish I had.' Then he strode from the room, the house and, for all anyone knew, their company forever, leaving them to a silence so alive with possibilities that for a good minute no one could address any of them.

Adelaide was, unexpectedly, the first to recover. 'Thank you for coming, Mr Stokes. I think for the time being you can leave the matter of Mrs Worthington to me, don't you agree, Mrs Nightingale?' Mrs Nightingale did not but she said nothing, struck dumb as she was by the fearful anger of the only person in the world she loved nearly as much as she loved herself.

Chapter Seventeen

Archie Stokes did the correct thing and left the Nightingale household within minutes, appalled by the turn of events, furious that he had lost control of them when it had been going so well. He examined the conversation to the finest nuance to see where it had gone wrong but could find no fault in himself.

He hurried, head thrust forward like a giant melon on his thick stalk of a neck, back along Hope Street, nodding here and there to people who greeted him with love and respect, and slowly his annoyance abated. Abated but hovered, unhappily for the Mayor with whom he collided at the store's entrance. The Mayor was looking to Mr Stokes for a little of the subservience that had disappeared from his home.

'Mr Mayor,' Mr Stokes acknowledged, intending to pass without being waylaid but at the last minute changing his mind because you never knew. You stopped, you passed the time of day and how often did the time of day yield an unforeseen opportunity even when you weren't in the mood? 'Lovely day for it.'

'For what, Mr Stokes? For a gutful of domestic annoyance?' The Mayor felt he could speak freely when his plan was, pure and simple, to belittle his wife in the eyes of the town.

'You sound like a man who could do with a beer.' Mr Stokes looked at his watch. 'It's lunchtime. Mrs Quirk's?'

'I don't know,' said the Mayor. 'I could do with the beer but not Mrs Quirk's.'

'Then come into my office. Mrs Lambert will sort us out.' The move was unusual. Mostly they did not lunch together but today each was drawn to the other in the expectation that the other would restore normality to their place in the world.

'Had a good morning?' the Mayor enquired resentfully. He couldn't have cared less.

'Mrs Nightingale Senior is in town,' observed Mr Stokes. 'That woman has a brain on her.'

'I'm not very fond of a brain in a woman,' the Mayor said and Mr Stokes, who'd intended to work his way round to the stupidity of Mrs Nightingale Junior and the erratic behaviour of her husband, sensed a more rewarding path so kept his trap shut. 'My wife seems to believe hers is as good as any man's and intends to prove it. Against my wishes.' The Mayor sounded not only mystified but petulant.

'She spoke very well at her meeting though,' Mr Stokes remarked. 'You can't take that away from her. People were impressed.'

'By what?' said the Mayor. 'It's bunkum. It's all second-hand thinking. The woman's never had an original thought in all the years I've known her which, by God, have been long.' He paused for the merest second while Mr Stokes took a loud, thoughtful slurp of his beer. 'And now she wants to go into Parliament.

I won't have it. I won't support her even if she does decide to spread it about that I've taken a fancy to the maid, which I certainly have not. No one in their right mind would believe I'd done anything so ridiculous.'

'If you mean the O'Connell girl, I think they would,' teased Mr Stokes. 'She has a lovely chest. No one would blame you.'

'That is not what Mrs Mayberry thinks. Mrs Mayberry says if word gets out, I'd be branded an adulterer and bang would go the railway and me getting credit for all my efforts.' The Mayor had never before taken the grocer so dangerously into his confidence. They'd done business, naturally, but the footing had always been as it should. He was the Mayor and Mr Stokes was the grocer, more or less. Slightly less than more, possibly. 'She's expecting you to go along with her,' the Mayor said now, with a look of Great Significance, as his wife might have described it.

'Is she?' said the grocer. And through his despondency the Mayor heard in his tone something disrespectful, something mocking, something that suggested a wrong turn in the conversation.

'I assured her you most definitely wouldn't. You wouldn't, would you?' the Mayor asked in alarm.

The effect of beer on a man's empty stomach is as random as gin on a woman's. Where it induced in the Mayor deep despondency, it imbued the grocer with a curious elation. Mr Stokes bit into his ham sandwich and rejoiced in its wonder. He considered it for a moment, as if it might have an opinion. 'It depends,' he finally said.

'On what?' asked the Mayor, whose own sandwich had been set aside with just the single bite taken from it.

'Well, you have my sympathy,' said Mr Stokes. 'Obviously. Man to man. But I'm not just a man. I'm a Business Man and I can see a transaction here that might profit us both.' He held the Mayor's wary gaze for just a little longer than was comfortable. 'I will save your reputation if you help me out on the small matter of the Bluett land, which an interested third party has asked me to revisit, as it were.'

The Mayor's jaw crashed to his neck. The Bluett land was surely history. Unpleasant history. Ancient and upsetting. All that remained of it was the sour taste of corruption and injustice plus some highly sensitive documents in his safe. What was the fellow up to? What third party? He was blackmailing him. Man to man counted for nothing. Past favours counted for nothing. The grocer was without loyalty or conscience and now he was holding a loaded gun to his head. His, the Mayor's head. Surely he wouldn't dare pull the trigger. If it came to power and influence the name of Mayberry surely trumped the name of Stokes. He smiled at the grocer. 'What about the Bluett land? It's dead and buried. Settled ages ago.'

'Not quite,' said Mr Stokes, smiling back. 'I know you'll appreciate this, Mr Mayor. You were magistrate, so you'll remember the case. Pegs in the ground but no papers to prove it, so a question mark. There's always money to be made from a question mark where land is concerned and someone has contacted me with a view to making it.'

'Who?' asked the Mayor. But the grocer simply grinned and raised his hands in a gesture of surprise at such a dumb question. 'Well, it's impossible, anyway,' said the Mayor. 'You and I know why the papers are missing. No one else does. But we do.'

'I don't know that we do, Mr Mayor,' said Mr Stokes winking. 'This town knows you to be an honest and upright man and if they don't, I'll tell them. They'll listen to me. Your wife knows that.'

The insult wasn't lost on the Mayor. As he made his way home it stuck in his throat along with the sandwich. How dare the grocer! How dare his wife! Well they could all go hang. He'd have none of it. He wouldn't be bullied. He wouldn't be blackmailed. He was his own man. He was clever, wasn't he, smarter than all of them, wasn't he, so why wasn't he using his brain? He had an excellent brain and he should use it. He would. He'd apply himself.

His brain, when consulted, said of his beloved, *Let her stew in her own juice*, as she surely would if she stood for Parliament. His brain went on furthermore. *Why shouldn't the stupid girl keep her job?* He'd given it back to her and he was not only Mayor, he was king of his own castle. His brain asked what kind of hot water he'd be getting into if he agreed to shady back-room dealings over land that had already caused him trouble enough, and his brain replied, *She is pretty*, because there she was, in his hallway, polishing the mirror. She smiled at him with such warmth he completely forgot the lack of respect he must have imagined in his wife's eyes over breakfast. 'Your job is quite safe,' he said to her.

'I know,' she'd replied. 'Mrs Mayberry told me.' Which obliged him to acknowledge that lack of respect all over again. And now where was he? No further ahead of the game than he'd been when he'd sought out Mr Stokes with every intention of putting his wife in her place. His wife was not in her place and he wasn't at all sure how he was going to cram her back into it. The Mayor went directly to his office to examine ancient documents he'd been paid good money to keep well out of harm's way.

Chapter Eighteen

There is a world of difference between sounding like a woman who can move mountains and actually being one. Pearl, having agreed to lead the charge against all mountains confronting the respectable ladies Beyond The Arch, found herself flailing in the face of her own. Her fiercest charge took her back once again to the presbytery and Father Kelly, who this time allowed her through the front door but only briefly. Was there a known criminal in the town, she asked him this time. A man famous for extortion, say, or theft, or anything else that might bring a family to its knees?

The priest considered her sadly. He said there was no one with any such reputation. 'Have you tried the police?' he asked hopelessly. But of course she hadn't. Where would they look, in any case, if not in Prospect, last known point of contact? 'The railway?' he priest suggested again. 'Why don't you get a big, strong fellow to go to the railway with you? A man on the road meets other men on the road and someone might have heard of him.'

All she could do, all any of them could do, was pin their hopes on the big, strong fellow Annie McGuire would certainly send them. But it was with a faint heart that Annie, on a dismal Sydney morning, went to meet the prospective part-time husbands. She'd prayed all night that none would turn up because, Lord alone knew, she'd done her best to put them off. 'We are four elderly women of limited means,' she'd explained as instructed. 'But we need a capable man who can help us with tasks we are increasingly failing to manage. None of them intimate.' Now she sat in the dimmest corner of an almost empty tea room with the brown squashy hat pulled as far down her face as it could fit so no one passing would immediately take her for the kind of woman who might be interviewing men for the personal use of brazen hussies.

In the event, neither Sergeant Harold Fletcher at two o'clock nor Mr Martin Duffy at half-past two had any trouble finding her. Mr Smith didn't turn up at three o'clock, or if he did it was after Annie had made her decision and left.

Sergeant Fletcher was a man in his late thirties, well built with an unsmiling weather-beaten face, one eye concealed by a patch, and a manner that suggested a tough but successful war as clearly as the medals he wore on his chest. He asked sensible questions, such as, 'Have you decided what tasks will take priority or will you leave that to me?'

'I'm not one of the ladies, Sergeant Fletcher,' Annie confessed. 'I'm acting on behalf of them because they live so far away. Will you mind living that far away?' He said he wouldn't, which struck Annie as odd when he couldn't have known how far, since she hadn't mentioned it. She thought she hadn't mentioned it.

Maybe she had. When she asked further if he was familiar with that part of the world, he said he was, so she must have. And since the lapse was obviously hers, she let it pass. He understood horses, could build a shed, was capable of adding a column of figures and after what he'd been through, he feared no man. He was neither handsome nor frivolous. His manner, while not rude exactly, was abrupt; a private man, Annie guessed. He was, by any reckoning, the perfect candidate. 'And what religion are you, Sergeant Fletcher?' she enquired as he was leaving.

She gave the job to Martin Duffy because she wanted to. The poor boy hadn't fought for the King because he had brothers fighting against him in Ireland. 'I know you understand me,' he'd said and of course she had. He'd had a difficult war, being young and fit and failing to fight, and not much had improved with the peace. Work was even harder to come by for a man who hadn't served.

He was tall, slender, pale skinned, softly spoken, with a lovely voice, Annie thought. If she failed to notice his long-lashed blue eyes sparkling with mischief, or the extreme handsomeness of his face, it could only have been because she deemed them unimportant. His arithmetic was rough and ready and his chief knowledge of horses was that they could run very fast and the fastest were the safest to bet on. He wasn't a big man with his fists, but he could argue pretty well, he told her, and he could sing if that was any use. All in all, when taken as a whole, weighing one thing against another, such admissions did the trick. Annie was delighted with his candour. Honesty and simplicity were great virtues. She was looking for a good-hearted man who wouldn't bully or throw his weight around, and here was a fellow countryman in great need. 'Do you drink?' she'd asked. Now and then, he'd said. 'Do you go to Mass?' Now and then, he'd said. So they'd agreed the wage Pearl had suggested of one pound a week plus board and lodging.

She'd given him the train ticket to Cooma, the fare for the coach to Prospect and instructions to present himself as the cousin of Miss Pearl McCleary care of the Nightingales, to Mrs Quirk at The Irish Rover. Mrs Quirk would give him further directions. *Martin Duffy arrives Tuesday 4 o'clock coach. Best I could do*, read the telegram she sent to Pearl.

Between its receipt and his arrival a scant three days later, the ladies made what preparations they decided on their own account needed to be made. Adelaide's astonishing resistance to the combined force of Mr Stokes, her mother-in-law and her husband had resulted in a molten atmosphere from which, the entire household knew, nothing good could come if you excluded Adelaide's unprecedented concern for Louisa. Within hours of Mrs Nightingale Senior's hasty return to Melbourne, Adelaide marched into Nightingales and demanded of her manager that he not only give Mrs Worthington more time to settle her bill, but that the shop provide a hamper of essentials for which there would be no charge at all. It had so taken Louisa by surprise that she'd forgotten to be grateful, but it hardly mattered. The concern was as much for the lodger as it was for his landlady, who might otherwise have failed to provide board along with the lodging.

The quality of the lodging similarly concerned Maggie. She arrived on Monday afternoon to inspect the room designated for him, a filthy tip as she later described it, and she spent the next four hours scrubbing, polishing, sweeping and washing down not just that room but the kitchen, the drawing room and the dining room as well. She might have spent another three had she not been desperate to get home to attend to herself. Had the room been in her house, she'd have made it perfection, but it wasn't, and so it was more important that she made herself perfection.

Maggie's wardrobe was improving by the day. She found that the more she applied herself, the cleverer she became, and because she was her mother's size and shape, she needed to make just enough adjustments to turn a twenty-year-old trousseau into a wardrobe fit for the town's most alluring catch of 1919. She would turn herself into the kind of woman with whom a part-time husband might fall in love at first sight. Her model was Mrs Worthington less ten years.

She washed and put her hair into rags so she could have tendrils. She applied oatmeal to her face and polish to her nails. She examined herself in the mirror, looking for defects that might be disguised and assets that might be accentuated, then she tried on one last time the skirt and blouse so similar to ones Louisa had been wearing they could have been bought from the same shop. Had they said he would be good-looking? She couldn't remember. She knew he would be.

Louisa was equally hopeful. She too had prepared her wardrobe, but where Maggie was dressing to flatter her figure and her rosy complexion, the wiser, older, more experienced Louisa was dressing for sympathy. Her intention was to present to the part-time husband the understated, fragile beauty of a widow who needed the strength and protection of a burly, loving man.

Pearl and Adelaide entertained no such thoughts. Pearl hoped only that Annie had chosen wisely and Adelaide prayed that Marcus would stay too drunk to query the propriety of their housekeeper's cousin living under the same roof as Louisa when Louisa had never suggested that she was cut out to be a landlady. His looks, as far as they were concerned, were immaterial.

Norah Quirk, on the other hand, noticed them at once.

'Mrs Quirk?' Martin Duffy asked on finding her sipping tea behind the bar of The Irish Rover even though she was being paid by the Post Office.

'Do I look old enough to be my mother?' she replied boldly. She directed him to Nightingales, counted to thirty then hot-footed it up Hope Street arriving just in time to hear him introduce himself as Martin Something, ask Mr Stokes if he were Mr Nightingale and further could he possibly have a word with Miss McCleary who was his cousin.

He was the handsomest man to come to town since Joe Fletcher, she announced to Theresa Fellows whom she met in the street minutes later. Mrs Fellows hoped that he'd be friendlier and Norah said how could he not be? 'But what do you make of this? He's not staying with the Nightingales. He's staying at Mrs Worthington's.'

It was a bombshell. If there was nowhere for him to sleep at the Nightingales then surely he should have booked into her mother's pub with its excellent reputation. Mrs Worthington's own reputation was . . . not excellent. 'Something's funny,' said Miss Quirk. 'Mark my words!'

Pearl, on the other hand, took one look at Martin Duffy and wanted to scream in disappointment. No! she might have screamed. He was so profoundly not what she'd had in mind, not what she wanted, not what she needed, not what any of them needed, that it was all she could do not to punch him. 'Follow me,' was all she could bring herself to say by way of greeting at the Nightingales' gate. Instead of a capable, well-put-together man, Annie had sent a ridiculously weedy Irish boy who looked as if he'd never done a day's hard work in the whole of his life and would expect breakfast in bed and nights on the tiles. In terms of brawn, in terms of muscle, in terms of fearsomeness and out-and-out manliness, he might just as well have been a woman.

Worse, the minute she saw the look on the faces of Maggie and Louisa she knew their hearts had melted. She regretted beyond measure that she had trusted Louisa to send the advertisement and that the others, when apprised of it, had decided to forgive her and allow the man to come.

The minute he opened his mouth and said how pleased he was to meet them all, the minute he smiled and said what a delight it was to find them in such robust and youthful health if they didn't mind him saying so, he had Maggie and Louisa eating from the palm of his hand, regardless of how pale and soft it was. Good humour shone from his very blue eyes. His fine head of black hair, slightly wavy and swept back, revealed a perfectly proportioned brow, which may or may not have suggested intelligence but definitely invited longing. How well Pearl knew the type. They were two a penny at St Canice's, arriving for ten o'clock Mass during The Offertory and leaving during Communion, pink eyed and bleary from the night before.

As the four respectable ladies gathered about the table that had conjured him into existence, she looked from them to him and back again and she wanted to yell. Even Louisa might have been handier with her fists than he was. What did it matter that he had excellent teeth?

Martin Duffy dragged his gaze to the end of the table where Pearl sat, arms folded, eyes flashing and he took command of the moment with grace and ease. 'My name is Martin Duffy and I would like to thank you for your kind proposal of a part-time marriage.' He fished about in his jacket pocket and produced a small bag, the contents of which he tipped into his open hand. Four curtain rings. 'I would like to offer each of you a token of my commitment to our arrangement. If you could just introduce yourselves I would be most grateful. It's always handy to know a wife's name I find, for when we are out and about.'

Louisa and Maggie giggled to show their delight. Adelaide, whose hopes and dreads were being met all at the same time, flinched. It was so poorly judged in Pearl's eyes that she made up her mind to cancel the 'arrangement' before it began. 'Mr Duffy,' she said, 'be under no illusion. The reference to any kind of matrimony should never have been included in the advertisement and if this is what has brought you here then we will pay for your immediate return.'

'It has not. Certainly it hasn't,' began Martin Duffy, clearly alarmed, but Pearl hadn't finished.

'It's true that we each have urgent and hair-raising problems that we find ourselves unable to address on our own because we are women, but they are not to be diminished by any foolishness from you. This is not a lighthearted experiment and we won't hesitate to let you go if you fail us.' She placed her ring on the sideboard next to the decanter, which was full of rum ordered by Louisa on credit to supplement the hamper. 'This does not represent seriousness to me,' she said.

It was embarrassing. What kind of person with any proper manners spoke so angrily to a newly employed right-hand man who was to live among them as an equal? *A housekeeper*, Louisa told herself. 'Oh, Miss McCleary,' she chortled. 'The man has just arrived. There's plenty of time for us to be serious.'

But Pearl would have none of it. It was a business agreement, she said again. Mr Duffy must be tired and hungry – she gave him no time to contradict her – and as it was very nearly tea time, Louisa must give him something to eat, show him his room, then leave him in peace until morning. They would meet again at eight o'clock, assuming that suited everyone.

'She's awfully bossy,' Maggie whispered to Mr Duffy, placing a gentle hand on his elbow.

'But always right,' said Martin. 'I can tell from looking at her.' Which he was doing so steadily that Pearl was obliged to pick up the baby even though he wasn't crying.

Adelaide, halfway to the door, said, 'Remember, Louisa, the food only needs half an hour in a slow oven. I think you'll find Miss McCleary's rabbit casserole excellent, Mr Duffy. Come on, Maggie.'

Chapter Nineteen

Three respectable ladies stood in the street and, as one, saw only too clearly the folly of leaving the fourth in sole charge of a man she had labelled, against their wishes, husband. If there was a circumstance in which Louisa Worthington could not be trusted, it was alone in the company of a good-looking man with a gallon of rum on the sideboard. They could almost hear her say as the door closed on them, 'I can't stand stew on an empty stomach.'

Maggie said, 'She'll get her claws into him before bedtime.'

'Maggie!' Pearl snapped but it was what they were all thinking. 'I should go back and chaperone.'

'You can't,' said Adelaide. 'I need you.'

'He should be staying with me,' Maggie said. 'At least I don't live alone.'

'He shouldn't,' said Pearl. 'And I can't imagine Captain Nightingale being happy to have him in his house. We'll have to trust her.' That was how they left it, at odds with their better judgement, which overcame Maggie so early the next morning that she knocked on the Worthington door a full hour before she was expected. She was wearing a freshly restored floral frock that revealed her much admired chest and an expression that suggested she was a match for any temptress.

As a puzzled Martin Duffy admitted her to the house she asked breathlessly if he needed any help with the horses. 'Do I?' he replied. 'Mrs Worthington's still in bed. What am I supposed to do with the horses?' He lowered his voice. 'To be honest, I'm not much good with them.'

Maggie flushed at the confidence and at his closeness as he leaned towards her to draw her into it, shocking though it was, dreadful though he didn't seem to realise it might be. 'You'll still need breakfast,' she said. 'What would you like? Eggs?' She turned herself to finding and cooking them so delightfully that he would immediately love her. She hunted out pans and bread and butter and tea and soon she was chatting so comfortably about her life and his that it was easy for her to imagine that this was how it would be when they were married. She was in the process of correcting him, 'No, Somerset Station is the Bluetts' land and it runs behind ours and the Nightingales',' when Louisa appeared, fully dressed and properly groomed even if her face was the colour of cucumber.

'Good Lord, Maggie, surely it's not eight,' she said.

'She thought I might need help with the horses,' said Martin Duffy smoothly.

'What's wrong with the horses?' Louisa asked.

'I thought they wanted moving. I thought that's what you said.' Maggie stirred eggs, head bent low over the pan, hearing the anger in Louisa's voice without having to see it in her eyes.

'I didn't.'

'Well someone did. I'm sure you said . . . Oh no, it was Mrs Fellows. She said she'd heard that you'd sold them to someone and they'd need rounding up and moving and who was going to do it.'

'Well I haven't and they don't,' said Louisa. 'You can tell stupid Theresa Fellows that if Mr Stokes thinks I'm selling them for meat, he's barking up the wrong tree. I now have a man to help me manage them and we won't appreciate or tolerate any further interference from him. Isn't that right, Martin?'

Martin! They were on Christian-name terms already. God, what had they been up to when no one was looking? Maggie laughed loudly. 'I wouldn't be so sure about that, Mrs Worthington. Martin was just saying he isn't much of a man for –'

'I think I could move a few,' he said quickly. 'I can't imagine having any trouble with that.'

'Of course you wouldn't,' murmured Louisa. 'But they're not being moved, so it won't come up. I can do the eggs, thank you, Maggie.' She nudged the younger girl out of the way and took the wooden spoon from her. She handed it back almost at once as the very sight of a yellow, runny, oozing mess made her heave. 'Excuse me,' she said. 'Too hot.' She stepped outside, breathing deeply, checking whatever she'd eaten that was rising in her throat, which included humble pie as well as rabbit.

Martin Duffy had turned out not to have a fondness for drink, despite his jolly appearance. He hadn't been jollied into rum, he hadn't wanted to sit with her while she had rum and he hadn't wanted a second helping of casserole. He'd done exactly as Pearl had instructed: unpacked, joined her to eat and spoken only of the delicious food and the chilly weather. Then he'd gone to his room, almost as if he really were dull Miss McCleary's cousin.

She had exactly the same thought an hour later when Pearl addressed him as she might a very annoying and stupid younger brother. 'I hope you have your wits about you this morning, Mr Duffy,' she said as she produced a large notebook in which there was much written even though there had been no consultation.

She was as cool as ice, Louisa noted, even though the baby was fussing in his pram and Adelaide was wondering aloud whether he needed to be taken outside for a minute. 'He'll settle,' Pearl assured her.

'I assume you intend to lead this discussion, Miss McCleary?' It was her house, Louisa told herself, so any leading should be hers.

'Of course she does,' smiled Maggie, mostly so she could show how white and even her own teeth were.

'I thought I'd outline the basics,' Pearl said. 'I've simplified them as best as I can so we can arrange them in order of urgency and ease of managing. Is that all right by everyone?'

Martin Duffy said, 'Suits me.'

'But before we do,' Pearl said, glancing up at him, 'I'm sure we'd like to hear about you. I know Mrs McGuire approved of you but she hasn't been able to tell us why.' This was less than cousinly, Louisa admitted to herself.

'There isn't much to tell,' he began. Either there really wasn't much or he was keeping himself to himself but the bones, laid bare, were sparse. He'd come from Cork with his mother in 1913, taken a job in a boiling-down works, taken a job in a pub, taken a job on a building site, then taken another job at the Sydney City Council moving papers around, which he enjoyed. 'More sitting about,' he smiled. 'But I left to give way to a returning soldier.'

'And why didn't you go to war?' Louisa asked. It was provocative. Of course it was, but his own fault. He should at least have agreed not to let her drink on her own.

'You know why,' Maggie answered for him. 'So I don't think it's fair of you to ask.'

'Well he has the Archbishop to thank for his safety,' Louisa said tartly. 'Lucky him.' Then, suspecting she was doing herself no good, added, 'Not of course that I have anything against Catholics. Anyway, you gave up your job to a serving man and now here you are.' She smiled at him and he smiled back, so the heart that had hardened, softened and the confidence that had ebbed, once again flowed.

'I'm as loyal an Australian as the next man,' Martin Duffy said. 'I struggle with loyalty to the King of England.'

The words hovered over the table, darting tiny arrows into Adelaide's heart where they landed like treason to which she had no proper response. How could she employ a traitor when her own husband had come back from saving the King a changed man and Jimmy Worthington hadn't come back at all? On the other hand, he had a pleasant manner, he spoke beautifully and she was guessing from the glint in his eye that he had a great head for numbers. There was no point in looking to anyone else for reassurance. Every eye was fixed on the table as each woman searched her heart.

Martin Duffy broke the silence. 'I know it isn't comfortable. No one's been less comfortable than I have. A third of the men in this country chose not to go to war and they all had their reasons. You mightn't agree with mine but the fact that I'm a man of principle must carry some weight with you. If it doesn't . . .'

Pearl scanned the faces for a consensus but found none. 'Please leave the room, Mr Duffy. We'll vote. It will need to be unanimous.' As the door closed behind him, she said, 'Hands up he stays.' She raised her own hand as Maggie raised hers.

Louisa said, 'Of course he must stay. He's only just arrived.'

His fate rested with Adelaide, who asked herself, *Man of principle, or coward?* How could she tell? Did she need to vote for King and Country or could she vote for her own salvation? 'I would like to abstain,' she said cleverly. So, Pearl called him back into the room and proceeded to outline the problems that beset the ladies as she understood them, knowing, without admitting it to herself, that she had allowed her heart to rule her head exactly as Annie McGuire had. She supported him for reasons that had nothing to do with competence, manliness or a way with horses, so her plan was this: to keep him under her thumb.

'There,' she said in conclusion. 'We're all in strife and we're relying on you to get us out of it.' He nodded. 'I suggest that you make a friend of Mr Stokes because he is at the root of Mrs Nightingale's problem. Also that you visit Maggie at home so you can meet her boys. But first of all, I'm going to ask you to come with me to the railway because I have very urgent business there and I have been advised I won't be safe going by myself.'

'The railway?' he repeated dumbly and Louisa cried, 'Just a minute. What about me?'

'Blackmail is beyond my area of competence,' Pearl said. 'I'm sure Mr Duffy will come up with something.' She turned to Mr Duffy. 'If you're trying to find a missing returned soldier, the railway is the most obvious place to look. Men come from all over the country looking for work and I bet there are men on the run and men wanting to hide among them. If you drive, we can take a car.' He didn't drive. 'Then we can ride. I'm not much of a horsewoman but I'm game.' He was less game.

'You can take our sulky,' said Adelaide.

'Can you handle a sulky, Mr Duffy?' He could, which was a huge relief even to those who were thinking that Pearl was putting her own needs before everyone else's in a way that wasn't acceptable and what did she know about the railway when she had never discussed it with any of them as far as they could recall?

Pearl tore a page from her book and handed it to him. 'All the jobs we need you to do are urgent but we have to start somewhere. Read this and when you've thought it over, we can talk about the best way to proceed.' She looked to the others. 'Agreed?' And what could they do but agree? She was so sure of herself.

Martin Duffy stood. 'That's clear enough. I'll go to my room and then I think I'll have my dinner at the pub if no one minds. I'll be tossing it all over the whole time I'm there, don't you worry about that.'

Chapter Twenty

They waited for the door to close on his room then Pearl suggested a quick walk. Beyond that, not a single word was uttered until they were clear of the house and beyond the paddock with heaven only knew how many horses in it. They all had opinions and complaints spilling from their brains into their mouths but there was no way of knowing if the man had miraculous hearing and an ill-considered remark might cause him to pack and leave before they had time to decide what they thought.

It wasn't until they were accosted by Maisie Jenkins, who appeared to be counting the horses, that they were obliged to make some kind of noise. Even then, Mrs Jenkins required less in the way of responsive noises than she did of sympathetic nodding. She needed to tell them in as many words as possible that she was craving fresh air because the air in her house was thick with her husband's snoring and the smell of last night's beer on his breath. She needed to admire baby Freddie, who was as good as gold this morning, wasn't he, but most of the time, she knew Adelaide wouldn't mind her saying, he did have a pair of lungs on him, didn't he? When she eventually did move on, it was only inches. She stopped almost at once to remark to Pearl, 'Must be nice having your cousin visit. Where's he from?'

'Sydney,' said Pearl.

'No, I meant in Ireland. Where's he from in Ireland?'

'Dublin,' said Pearl. 'My family is from Tipperary but most of them are from Dublin.'

'And Cork,' Maggie reminded her. 'Some of you are from Cork.' It was an odd exchange, odd enough to make Mrs Jenkins' morning anyway.

The ladies were obliged to contain themselves until they were squashed tightly on the bench by the river. Then the tensions that had been simmering rose to boiling and were given voice. Mostly by Louisa. 'I don't know what prompted you to arrive so early, Maggie. It was ridiculous. And what on earth are you wearing?'

'Just wanted to be on the safe side,' Maggie replied uncomfortably.

'What safe side?' Louisa asked hotly. 'Be very careful, Miss, with your insinuations.'

'No insinuation,' Adelaide said quickly. 'She just wanted to be on time.'

'So you left your brothers alone for a good hour when they could have been setting fire to your house?' Louisa smirked at Pearl, who pretended she hadn't. 'And why did you abstain, Adelaide? Because he's a Catholic? Maggie's Catholic and so, I believe, is Miss McCleary. You are a Catholic, aren't you, Miss McCleary? If the question is do we want a Catholic coward for a part-time husband, then only Adelaide can answer it. No one else has no problem with it.'

134

The challenge hung above the river like a very fat duck, unsure of its fate. If it dropped would it sink or just create an almighty splash? Why on earth Louisa should decide to pick a fight with a neighbour who had offered her kindness was beyond them. It was even beyond Louisa, who could hear her voice but seemed unable to stop it because it was giving vent to sorrow and anger and heartbreak and rejection.

'I don't care that he's Catholic,' Adelaide said sharply. 'I care that he might be a shirker. It's cold here. I'm really cold. Is Freddie well rugged up, Miss McCleary?' Sink without trace, went the fat duck. 'The point is do we think he's going to be up to the job? Does he have a head for figures? He didn't answer that.'

'Anyone's will be better than yours,' said Louisa. 'No offence. I'm sure we can trust him.' She was both remembering and putting aside his caution of the night before. It showed respect. It hardly meant he didn't find her attractive. She knew he did. He had a way of smiling at her that was common to all men who found her attractive, which was all men.

Pearl sighed, troubled by her conscience. 'Let's give him two weeks. Let's see how much headway he can make in two weeks.'

'That's ridiculous,' said Louisa. 'You want him to find your fiancé, I need him to catch some blackmailers, Adelaide wants him to prove Mr Stokes is a thief and Maggie needs him to be a father to her brothers. We all need him to fix up our houses. Not even a man twice his size could manage it.' And they might have debated all morning the importance of muscle plus manliness, the meaning of urgent and the nature of time, but the breeze from the mountain was far too sharp and, really, what would it have achieved? 'Let's see how he gets on with Mr Stokes,' Pearl suggested.

'And the hen house,' Maggie agreed, which was the very conclusion Martin Duffy might have reached himself had he been paying proper attention to Pearl's list. He was staring at it in the privacy of his room, not absorbing its contents but getting the drift. Because it was cold and there was no fire in his grate, he was lying fully clothed on the bed, definitely a slender man, definitely a man used to being admired, possibly a vain man, but not a mean man. There was no meanness in his face.

From appearances, you might have imagined him being able to master a bit of house painting and possibly summon a few polite questions, but could he pass for a man who would chase down blackmailers and missing persons? A sensible observer, eyeing him on his bed, would have said, forget it. That observer would have watched as he roused himself, brushed himself down, examined himself in the mirror provided for shaving, and cringed as he winked at himself. Was it a sly wink, a cunning wink or just the usual wink of a man alone with his reflection? He looked at his watch, straightened his tie and left the house, jaunty as you like, untroubled apparently by the demands, preoccupied by thoughts no more complicated than lunch at the pub and the cheeky girl behind the bar.

Chapter Twenty-one

Louisa breathed in his smell when she unlocked the door to let herself in and her heart leapt. It wasn't a large smell. It was a coat smell, an unfamiliar-soap smell and possibly a something-for-his-hair smell, a man smell. How different the house felt. How much better than it had when Martin Duffy was only expected. It had a more occupied air, a greater sense of purpose and it hummed with heady possibilities. This is what a man in your life can do. A good-looking man too. A man at ease with himself.

Any wonder silly little Maggie was throwing herself at him. Louisa didn't doubt that Adelaide and even Pearl were as aware of his charms as she was. But he was living under her roof and, frankly, if it came to a contest, she by far had the most to offer. It was to his credit that he hadn't wanted to drink himself silly on the night he arrived. He wasn't unduly boastful or optimistic. He had the stoic manner of someone prepared to try and fail, the opposite when she thought about it of poor dead Jimmy, who'd embraced every day with unwarranted confidence. What's more, Mr Duffy's gaze contained the lively interest of a man who understood things, women in particular.

It was a pleasant reverie and one she might have continued to enjoy had she not heard her gate open and close. She looked out of the window and saw only the fleeting shape of someone running for all they were worth back towards town. She walked slowly to the front door and even more slowly to the gate. The figure had vanished but it didn't matter. She could think of no one's it resembled more than Ginger Albright's.

A note had been crammed hastily into the letterbox. *Buyer willing to proceed. Seven shillings and sixpence per item less costs*, it said. She hurried back into the house to the kitchen sink and vomited into it. Oh Lord, her poor stomach. Nerves were getting the better of her. If they didn't improve with Martin in residence, she'd need to take something for them.

Across the road, where Pearl and Adelaide folded bed linen, the reveries were less reassuring. Mrs Nightingale Junior was feeling increasingly tricked and anxious and fearful. The part-time husband she'd hoped would be her saviour might well be pleasant but what use was pleasant? Any minute now, Marcus would ask what the housekeeper's cousin was doing at Louisa's. Any minute someone would think it odd that he wasn't staying at the pub. What on earth was she doing in such a hair-brained scheme with an O'Connell and a lying, scheming Louisa Worthington who'd been astonishingly rude this morning? She shot Pearl, who'd plainly misled her, a look so loaded with suspicion a lesser housekeeper might have buckled.

Pearl continued to fold and smooth as if folding and smoothing were her joy, but she was as full of regret as was Adelaide. What on earth was she doing in a Protestant household so riddled with bigotry? And why on earth did she imagine she could rely on women she barely knew to keep secret the mission she was on, to save the life of a Catholic, when their own Protestant concerns were overwhelming them? Any minute Adelaide might ruin everything by denouncing Martin Duffy as an Irish traitor, brought to the community by a housekeeper with criminal connections. What was Annie doing sending her Martin Duffy, a fool of a boy from Cork or Dublin who'd never tried very hard at anything and who'd survived on the goodwill of others? A lesser orphan would have cursed the woman who'd raised her but Pearl loved Annie with all her heart. The nuns had said, 'No one wants her.' But Annie had taken her in just as she'd taken in other children, some for a few weeks, others for months. Beattie had been with Annie for two years now. Pearl loved Beattie like a sister and she loved Annie like a mother and so she would soldier on for them. She placed the final sheet onto a pile she would shortly iron and said, 'We have to remind ourselves why he's here. We need him, or if not him, someone like him.'

'What if he does more harm than good?' said Adelaide.

'We'll get rid of him before he does. For the time being, he's here and we need to stick together and make the best of it.'

Which, at that very moment, is what the Mayor was saying to his wife, who replied, 'I've always stuck with you, George. Now it's your turn to stick with me. I gave Maggie O'Connell her job back. You know what you have to do for me.' She left the house without explanation, to meet who knew whom, to say to them God alone knew what, and for what hideous outcome Christ only knew.

It took the Mayor to his bureau drawer, from which he withdrew a map of the district. He laid it out on the floor so he could examine it more thoroughly. He needed reminding. He found his spectacles in his pocket, he put them on and he dropped to all fours for the best possible view of the matter. He studied the part of town Beyond the Arch, which had once been grand of course but was now badly neglected or he'd have bought into it himself.

He traced his finger along the right-hand side of the road as you travelled out of town, to the Worthingtons', a shabby rambling house on six acres, which included paddocks on either side and a substantial garden behind. It had been a great house for high jinks when the Worthington Seniors had paid the rates. On the left-hand side his finger stopped at the Nightingales', an even larger house with an excellent billiard room, built by Ernest Bluett, grandfather of Mrs Nightingale Junior, as a wedding present to her father, his son Arthur, who'd sold it to the Nightingales when he'd inherited Somerset. The Mayor remembered Phyllis Nightingale's glee on moving in and up in the world. A handsome woman, but mean. She'd spoken meanly to him on more than one occasion. He thought about Phyllis Nightingale's meanness for a full minute before returning to the map.

Between that house and the O'Connells', a track led from the main road to Somerset Station. Before the gates to the estate were reached, the land bordering it to its left belonged to the Nightingale property and to its right the O'Connells', previously the Careys', left to Cissie Carey who'd married Frank O'Connell. This was where discomfort began, where the Mayor's conscience collided with his sense of entitlement.

He bent low over the map. He swung his weight onto his substantial bottom to relieve the pain in his knees and he considered not only the map but his own position. There, beyond the gate on the right hand side, were the 400 acres in question butting onto the O'Connells', pegged – everyone agreed – by Ernest Bluett but, in a disastrous oversight, never bought by him. Who knows why he hadn't spotted the anomaly when the Crown had released the lots? But he hadn't and in the fullness of time, Frank O'Connell had.

There had been paperwork to show that the plot wasn't part of the original Bluett acreage, and paperwork had been tendered to the court to show that Frank O'Connell had legitimately purchased it. Then all the documentation had vanished into thin air, if you could call the air inside the Mayor's safe thin, because he'd reached an agreement, brokered by Larry Murdoch with Arthur Bluett, and as a result he had been Mayor ever since.

The Mayor sighed. Why resurrect a dispute that had been laid to rest? Who was muck-raking now? Angus Bluett, brother of Mrs Nightingale Junior, was the current owner. Joe Fletcher was the tenant. Angus was no more a farmer than Florrie was. Fletcher kept himself to himself and young Bluett never visited because he was having a high old time being a banker in Sydney. The Mayor's guess was that the greedy little bastard, aided by Stokes, meant to go after all the O'Connell land, because trouble-making Frank O'Connell was out of the picture.

The Mayor sighed again, this time for his principles. He so badly wanted to be a man of principle. The sigh contained a smattering of sympathy for little Miss O'Connell and that bit of his sigh conjured into his presence young Maggie herself, who opened the door, saw him on his knees and hurried to his side. 'You're not ill, are you, Mr Mayor? Have you fallen?' When he looked at her dear little face and heard the genuine concern in her sweet voice, unsullied by gross ambition or greed, he wondered if he could make her love him, whatever he did or didn't do regarding her land.

Chapter Twenty-two

Martin Duffy, so much more to Maggie's taste than the Mayor, was having a very early lunch in a sunny corner of Mrs Quirk's pub, writing his mother an amusing letter about the ladies' hopes for him, which he had every expectation of fulfilling. *Their problems aren't nearly as bad as they imagine. You'll be delighted to hear that I don't need money. I'm not sure I can repay you as yet but you know, dear Mother, that I will when I can.* He put down his pencil, content with the effort.

'Delicious rabbit,' he said to the tired young man behind the bar who, unlike the cheeky young woman, was disinclined to engage in small talk. 'Lovely food, thank you,' elicited only a nod. A direct question was required. 'The girl who was here yesterday . . .' produced a blank stare. 'Brown hair, brown eyes, this tall.' He lifted his hand to his chin. 'What's her name?'

'Norah. Proprietor's daughter.' He could have been saying, 'Horse. Won't gallop.'

'Oh,' replied Martin Duffy, 'I'm a proprietor's son. My mother runs a pub.'

'Then you're practically married,' said the tired young man, causing Martin Duffy to laugh in agreement.

'Now, who will sell me a stamp?' he asked, waving his letter in the air. The answer, it turned out, was the very same young woman, who appeared to be fully employed at the Post Office. 'Mail for Sydney,' he announced minutes later to Norah Quirk, who was very pleased to see him.

'Are you enjoying your stay?' she replied. 'It's very different from Cork. Or Dublin.' He agreed that it was, but about as cold. He asked when she'd last been to either place. The answer was never because she'd been born in Ballarat but she gathered he was from either one or both, which he said wasn't entirely correct. His people were from Kilcare. 'It must be your cousin who's from Cork or Dublin,' concluded Norah, a stickler for accuracy when it came to who was lying about what. And he said that was correct but as she was very quick to report to Theresa Fellows, 'He didn't have a clue. What a hoot!'

By the time he'd found his way back to Nightingales and located Archie Stokes, the grocer was very well aware that no one for a minute believed Mr Duffy to be Miss McCleary's cousin. That being the case, he was only too prepared to invite him into the office so they could become properly acquainted. 'Take the weight off your feet,' he advised, taking the weight off his own with a thump as he dropped into the manager's chair. 'Cup of something?'

'Just had my dinner, thanks,' Martin Duffy said.

Archie Stokes nodded, deducing without appearing to that the young Irishman had never served in any army anywhere, let alone one defending the King. It mattered not a scrap to him. He hadn't either. What interested him was the man's business. If he wasn't the housekeeper's cousin, who was he and why had he moved in to Mrs Worthington's when he could have had one of Mrs Quirk's excellent rooms? If he was a lodger then how long did he intend to lodge? That was the question. 'Always nice to see a visitor stay more than a day or two,' he said. 'Any plans while you're here?'

'Not so far,' smiled Martin. 'My cousin likes it here. She thought I might too.'

'And how are you finding us so far?' asked the grocer.

'So far, very pleasant.'

'Well your cousin's a boon to the Nightingale household, I can tell you that much,' Archie Stokes ventured. 'Poor Captain Nightingale isn't the man he was and poor Mrs Nightingale Junior tries to help but she's never been what you'd call an intelligent woman. That household would be lost without Miss McCleary and me, the whole town will tell you that. We're keeping their heads above water.'

'I'm pleased to hear it,' said Martin Duffy. 'My cousin is a very capable woman. I'd go so far as to call her a very clever woman.'

'And a fine housekeeper,' agreed the grocer. 'But unmarried. Odd that such a clever, good-looking woman remains unmarried. Maybe she's too clever. Or sour. Sometimes she wears a sour look. I mean no offence.'

'The war,' said Martin, standing. 'Terrible for the wedding business.'

Mr Stokes also rose, telling himself that the young man reeked of opportunity as powerfully as the Jenkins' family pigs reeked of ham. Not a cousin, certainly not a cousin, but very likely a lover and you couldn't go beyond secret love for opportunity.

'You'll be well looked after by Mrs Worthington.' He paused as if suddenly struck. 'Another clever woman but between you and me, not quite as clever as she thinks.' He opened the office door. 'Good-looking though. Very good-looking.' He winked. 'Watch out for that.'

He offered Martin Duffy a taste of Maisie Jenkins' excellent ham as he guided him from the store. 'Let me know if you ever need anything,' he said. 'I never turn my back on a man in need.' He laughed. 'Or a woman.' They shook hands and Martin Duffy left the palace of dreams imagining he had the measure of the man and, given time, would be able to wrap him around his little finger. He said as much to Louisa over their evening meal, rabbit casserole on toast.

'I met Mr Stokes today,' he said. 'Nice man.'

'Do you think so?'

'He spoke highly of you.' And when Louisa raised an eyebrow, 'Of course he did. Why wouldn't he? I believe we understood each other. Which must be a good thing, don't you agree, Mrs Worthington? It's a good start, don't you think? To know we can get along and work towards some kind of agreement?'

'Adelaide says he's a thief and so does Maggie O'Connell. He wants to buy all my horses for meat, which is disgusting.'

'But it would solve a problem, wouldn't it?'

Louisa put down her knife and fork. 'I don't think you understand my problem. The horses aren't the difficulty. I could shoot the horses. You could shoot the horses. I need someone to shoot the people sending them to me with menaces.'

'Well it won't come to that. Negotiation is the thing,' said Martin Duffy. 'Don't you think, Mrs Worthington?'

But Louisa didn't know what to think, apart from, *You have lovely eyes.* She said, 'Please, Martin. I thought we'd agreed. Call me Louisa.' She tossed her curls. She smiled at him. 'Where else did you spend your day?'

'Here and there,' he said, watching the bounce of the curls. 'I toured the town, I wrote to my mother, I had something to eat at Mrs Quirk's and after that I visited Mr Stokes to get the measure of the man.' He returned to the subject because it was hanging like a broken branch that might drop on his head any minute.

'And what did he measure?'

'He isn't small. He's wide and quite tall but not very deep. That's my estimation of him from my experience in pubs and boiling-down factories.'

'Which is limited,' Louisa teased.

'I think I will have a small rum,' he said.

'In any case,' Louisa said an hour or so later, 'I don't imagine anyone will deliver any more horses now you're here.' Because she was sitting dangerously close to him on the sofa and because they were both looking at the fire neither saw the expression in the other's eyes – one of longing, the other of alarm – and neither heard the note being pushed under the front door. It wasn't until they headed to their separate bedrooms that Louisa saw it and handed it to Martin Duffy because it was addressed to him. They both stared at it, unopened, in shock.

'They won't call you a whore,' Louisa said.

And of course Pearl hadn't because the note was from her and on the face of it as straightforward as could be, which wasn't very under the circumstances.

We head to the railway tomorrow immediately after breakfast, she'd written. *I have made arrangements to hire a buggy from Lambert's, as Mrs Nightingale's turns out not to be available.*

Chapter Twenty-three

Marcus had considered the housekeeper's request an outrage and said so in tones ringing enough to be heard in Pearl's room even though it had been less of a request than an offer made by his wife. Not only were they to be without a housekeeper who was costing them an arm and a leg, she wanted to take their sulky so she and her cousin could go gallivanting all over the countryside. And not any countryside, but along the hellish road that led to the railway, which was full of ditches deep enough for a man to drown in. He wouldn't hear of it, even if it hadn't rained. There would be so much dust. He'd just had the sulky cleaned, he said. Did she know how annoying it was to have a freshly cleaned sulky made dusty at once? This was the nub of the household's problem. Its head, when not drinking himself senseless, was bad tempered and intolerant. Occasionally he was tearful. Drunk or sober, he was a snob on his mother's side.

The loss of the sulky was a nuisance, Pearl had decided, but not the end of the world. Imagine the fuss if Martin Duffy crashed it, or ran over someone. Not for a minute did Pearl believe Adelaide's regret when she announced the news as if Pearl mightn't have heard it for herself. There had been more resentment than regret in the conveying, as if the outrage had had to be explained to her because she hadn't seen it for herself. 'You won't be late back, will you?' was all she said as Pearl left the house the next morning before Freddie had even been changed.

'I'll do my best,' Pearl replied, but in her heart she knew that whatever best she had in her would not be devoted to getting back early, it would be to holding her nerve while the hopeless boy went about business whose challenges she couldn't begin to anticipate.

She had no idea how long a hellish drive might take. She had no idea how long it might take for them to find anyone who might have come across an ex-soldier who, now she thought about it, probably looked like any other ex-soldier. If she could choose, they would be there and back by lunch and full of delight that they'd spotted Daniel at once, explained Beattie's wretched plight and received his immediate assurance, with barely a backward glance, let alone any awkward kissing, that he was on his way home. Or, failing that, that they'd immediately met a fellow who not only knew Daniel Flannagan but had seen him days before and could report he was homeward bound already.

Her next best hope, she decided as she walked ahead of Martin Duffy to collect the buggy Bert Lambert promised would get them safely there and back, was that she would sit in it while Martin Duffy drove to the railway and that she would stay sitting in it while he approached men going about their various businesses. He'd ask everyone he met if they were, or had come across, Daniel Flannagan and they would treat him civilly because his only obvious talent was for civility.

They were no more than five minutes from the town when it became very clear that even a fourth best hope, surviving the trip, was a slim one. Martin Duffy had little to no skill driving anything attached to a horse, and the horse in question, Betty, noticed within seconds. She jumped this way and that, unhappy from the off, threatening to head across country unless someone did something decisive with the reins. 'Whoa,' cried Martin Duffy to no avail. 'Hold up there,' and 'Come on, move, you stupid thing.'

It would have been a kindness not to notice, but Pearl's nerves were as frayed as Betty's and she found that her own profound wish was to bolt for home, ditching her useless passenger on the way. The more futile his efforts to keep Betty on the road, the more overwhelming was Pearl's need to punish him. How dare he be so pathetic when the very least she'd hoped for was not pathetic. How dare he look so petulant. How dare he not even manage to drive a cart. She'd had so little hope and all of it had been pinned on him.

'Dear God!' she cried, snatching the reins when they had travelled less than a mile. 'Give them here. And get ready to jump off and grab her if she bolts. I hope you're going to be more use once we get there.' She clicked Betty on and Betty did as she was bid more or less for the remaining three miles, sensing the new driver's lack of interest in any nonsense from anyone, man or beast, but especially man. The more Pearl dwelled on the inadequacy of her part-time husband, the shorter her temper grew so that it was all she could think about, even as vehicles of all sorts threw up dust that blinded her and clogged her nose and mouth. When Martin Duffy failed to appreciate the skill with which she was controlling the wayward horse and suggested he could lead her, she snarled, 'I doubt it.'

Unsurprisingly, Martin Duffy kept his lips buttoned and held on tight for the rest of the journey, prepared to jump but not at all confident, they both knew, of grabbing any reins. Good humour had just as readily deserted him. He too was glaring at the countryside and then at her, counting the moments – she could almost hear him – until he could pack up and head back to Sydney. *Well too bad*, she said to herself. But when eventually she brought Betty to a stop on the edge of the rumbling, squelching, noisy, shapeless, terrifying mess of mud and metal that was the railway in progress, when she clapped eyes on the tents announcing to all comers *Welcome to poverty and desperation*, and when she took stock of the line itself heaving with human shapes that grunted and cursed, she sighed in despair. How could she trust him to negotiate it when he was a blithering idiot? 'I'll go,' she said. 'Give me back the photograph and you look after the horse.' She could barely bring herself to look at him. But then he spoke so she was obliged to.

'That's enough now, Miss McCleary. Quite enough. You must stop being so angry because it's pointless. We're here to make enquiries and you can see for yourself, it's no place for a woman. Tell me what it is you need me to say and I'll say it.'

Pearl blew rage and disappointment from her diaphragm, allowing her shoulders to drop and her lungs to collapse even though accepting the offer felt more like defeat than relief. She studied his face, for stupidity, arrogance, reluctance or maybe competence but found only a smile. 'I need you to look for military men who might have come across him anywhere between here and Sydney, or possibly Ypres. He was at Ypres in '17. I know it's unlikely but he's been on the road for weeks and many of these men will have been as well. One of them, some, any of them, might have crossed his path. His name is Daniel

Flannagan and he started with the 19th, which was attached to the 5th brigade, but I'm not sure where they ended up.'

Martin Duffy jumped lightly from the cart. 'Looks? Height? Distinguishing marks?'

'Shorter than you by an inch or so, thicker set than you, lighter hair, brown eyes . . .' What *did* he look like? Could she even remember? 'Talks too much. People like him.'

'Accent?'

'Australian.'

'It's not much, is it?' said Martin Duffy. 'But I'll give it a go.' And then he was gone, a surprisingly graceful man, hatless, in a light jacket, wearing boots in no way qualified to tackle the mud. He darted among the untidy gangs of men and as Pearl watched his back she thought how mad she must be to trust Beattie's wellbeing to anyone so slight, let alone the fate of a fiancé probably as out of his mind as Captain Nightingale.

She steered Betty to the side of a rough hut that looked marginally more permanent than the tents and stationed herself behind it to wait for his return, remembering for no real reason Annie's admonition over something or other. 'It's an affliction. You are afflicted by silly ideas.' Then seeing the hurt on Pearl's face, she'd softened: 'We all have afflictions, even Jesus.' Pearl had asked what His was. Annie had replied, 'Talking too much.'

She waited and she waited, taking care to avoid the eyes of any man who dared to seek hers out but unable to avoid those of a burly fellow on horseback chiefly because he had only one of them. He dismounted when he saw her and attached his horse to the hitching post by the hut. 'You waiting for someone, miss?' he growled.

A criminal, Pearl thought, or a boxer. Neither, she saw at once. His bearing was military, his clothes neat and clean, there were medals on his chest. This was a man used to issuing orders and having them obeyed. 'My cousin,' she said. 'He had to deliver a message.'

'He should have delivered it to me.' As if to compensate for the failure of the useless thing behind the patch that took up half his face, his good eye rested twice as long as was comfortable on the object of his scrutiny. 'He's trespassing. So are you. You find him and remove him. Nothing and no one enters this site without going through me. Next time I'll have you arrested for your own safety.'

'The men look perfectly safe to me,' said Pearl.

'I'm not talking about the men,' said the soldier. He might have said more. He looked as if he wanted to say more but someone called, 'Sergeant?' from within the hut and he disappeared into it just as Martin Duffy reappeared at a trot.

'You took so long,' Pearl complained.

'That's how long these things take,' he replied. He hopped up next to her and they took off at a great clip because Betty wanted to be out of there even more than her passengers. 'I spoke to twenty men at least,' he reported. 'None of them was him. None of them knew him, no one had seen him and no one had heard of him. One fellow thought his mate might have met him but his mate's taken off. The difficulty you have, Miss McCleary, is that your fiancé doesn't want to be found. No one back there is going to give him away if they think it'll make trouble for him.'

'I'm trying to help him. We're trying to save him. Didn't you tell them that? Didn't you tell them his family was looking for him?'

'Half the men on the railway have families, debt collectors or policemen looking for them. We'll need a better story than that.'

'There isn't a better story than that,' said Pearl.

'There has to be,' said Martin. 'And if you'd just pull this stupid horse over for a minute, I think you should tell me what it is.' But she didn't want to. She'd told him all he needed to know.

The man was needed at home. He had a little sister, whose health was failing. What extra detail could possibly make any difference to a man who had no idea how to put a question in such a way that it produced an acceptable answer. She said nothing. She looked straight ahead.

'You have to trust me, Miss McCleary, or I'll be no use to you at all. If you want me to find your Daniel Flannagan I'll need all the help you can give me.' There was no arguing with it. She did have to trust him. Regardless of how inadequate his help might be, it was the only help on offer.

Pearl looked from the road to Martin Duffy then back to the road, which presented even fewer possibilities for a rewarding outcome than the quest she'd undertaken. She slowed Betty to a walk. When the slush eventually gave way to firmer ground and a small clearing appeared to the left of them, she pulled into it. 'Sandwich?' she offered. As she reached for the picnic hamper, she composed herself to overcome a lifetime of trusting no one but herself.

'He must be something for you to love him,' said Martin Duffy softly, and here trust deserted her. She wanted with her whole being to yell that she didn't love him, that he loved her and that he'd so swamped her with the weight of his love that she couldn't breathe or think and had only ever wanted to push him as far away as she could and now she'd be pleased if he was dead. But instead she said, 'He's a marvellous man.'

'How old?'

'Twenty-seven. No, twenty-six.'

'And his sister is called . . .'

'Beattie.'

'Does he love Beattie?'

'Of course he loves Beattie. We all love Beattie. You won't find a lovelier, gentler, kinder girl. But her heart was weakened by flu and we don't know how long she'll live.'

'Your Daniel doesn't sound like a very caring brother.'

Pearl frowned. Stupid Mr Duffy was forcing her to defend Daniel when she was in no mood to. But she would because Martin Duffy wasn't half the man Daniel was and frankly if she was angry with anyone right now it was with Martin Duffy. 'Of course he's caring,' she snapped. 'He tried to look after her when their mother died but she needed a proper home and he had to work and study. So, Mrs McGuire took over raising her. Mrs McGuire who interviewed you.'

'What kind of study?'

'Law. He wants to be a lawyer.' Here she might have gone on to say, *But he never will be one because he can't stick at anything.* But she didn't.

Martin Duffy rubbed his cheek. 'So, he has a good heart and he's trying to help the family of a soldier who died. Remind me why anyone would want to kill him?'

Pearl shrugged wearily. 'To get rid of him. That's all I know. Now let's go home.' They both sighed as Pearl took up the reins.

'It'd be easier if he minded his own business,' said Martin Duffy. 'Has anyone said that to him? It would be kinder to his family and better for us all if he just let bygones be bygones.'

And although Pearl in her heart agreed with him, she felt only fury that Martin Duffy should say it out loud.

Chapter Twenty-four

Adelaide had passed the day growing more furious with her housekeeper, silently congratulating her husband on putting his foot down about the trap when Miss McCleary, of whom she knew nothing, had no business even asking for it. Quite clearly she intended to place her own needs before everyone else's even though she was contributing no more to Mr Duffy's upkeep than anyone else and even though he was staying in desperate Louisa's house and Adelaide was sure she'd seen more horses being shunted into the overcrowded paddock that very lunchtime.

Salt had been rubbed into her wound. She'd heard from both Maisie Jenkins and Mrs Lambert that her housekeeper's cousin had been locked away with Mr Stokes yesterday, talking about heaven only knew what but rousing the curiosity of everyone. Had he mentioned this to her? Had the man to whom she was paying good money to sort out the mammoth problem of her thieving store manager shown her the courtesy of an immediate report? He hadn't. He'd run off with the housekeeper, whose ridiculous idea he'd been in the first place.

She would confront him. She would confront them both. No, she'd take him aside when the housekeeper wasn't around and she'd stake her claim to his attentions because surely hers were the most serious. If the Nightingale family went broke the whole town would go down with it, taking Louisa and the O'Connells with them. Miss McCleary would, of course, make her own arrangements since that was apparently what she meant to do anyway.

By tea time, Adelaide was standing by the front gate with Freddie on her hip, waiting for that same Miss McCleary to return because she was lonely and tired and desperate to discuss her concerns with the only person in whom she had any confidence. Her eyes were aching with the strain of peering through the Arch. Her brain was addled from the torment of wanting the woman home this instant so she could let her know who was boss around here. Her heart thumped with fear that she was drowned in a ditch, killed by the stupid cart she'd been forced to hire. It was almost a relief to see Louisa crossing the road so she could relieve herself of the agony. 'She should be home. Do you think Lambert's carts are safe?'

'You wouldn't get me out there in a month of Sundays,' Louisa replied.

'Have they delivered more horses? I'm sure I saw a few more being shunted through the back gate.'

'I couldn't give two hoots,' said Louisa. 'It's no longer my problem.' The thought might have startled Adelaide had not Pearl emerged finally, on her own, coated in dust, hair in disarray, and looking for all the world like a wife whose part-time husband had pushed her off the cart. 'I hope it went better than she looks.'

It hardly mattered to Adelaide whether it had or it hadn't. She had her rock back and now life would return to as normal as it had been yesterday. 'I wasn't sure what you wanted to cook,' she said as soon as Pearl was within hearing distance. 'I've put out some carrots. Freddie's been fretting for you all day and I really need to hear what Mr Duffy had to say about his meeting with Mr Stokes.'

'Give the woman a chance,' said Louisa, but Adelaide was already through the front door and holding it open for Pearl, who had time only to wave briefly at Louisa before it was closed, leaving Louisa alone in the road to check the paddock, agree it did look fuller and to decide that Adelaide's rudeness shouldn't go unchallenged. She waited just the single second before she knocked on the Nightingale door. When it was opened she said, 'Oh hello, Marcus. I just wanted to ask Miss McCleary if her cousin was coming home for his dinner.'

Marcus replied, 'Come in, come in, Louisa. I bet you'd like a drink to settle you.' And because there was no sign of Adelaide or Miss McCleary – or Martin Duffy on whom she'd been waiting with an impatience as urgent as Adelaide's – and because she thought she could do with a drink, and because she knew Marcus had taken a shine to her, Louisa smiled radiantly in reply. 'Just a small something, Marcus. I have a lodger who'll need feeding. Where are the others?'

'Where they usually are. With that boy of ours. He's running them ragged,' said Marcus. 'Into my office quick, before they come and nab you for themselves.'

They didn't even consider nabbing because they were being run ragged in the nursery soothing Freddie, who was screaming blue murder to celebrate the return of his best friend who should never have left him, and Pearl was singing at the top of her voice to divert him. Regardless of the distraction, Adelaide wanted immediate reassurance on the matter of Martin Duffy, who was clearly ignoring her needs in favour of everyone else's. 'I really don't think he is,' said Pearl, breaking between verses. 'It was my decision to take him to the railway.'

'But he's living with Louisa and they have miles of time to talk about her problems. Maggie was over there yesterday before you could say Jack Robinson, and you've had all day with him. Yesterday when he should have been seeing to my situation, he spent ages with Archie Stokes and not a word to me about the outcome. Not a single word. He should have come straight here from the shop and told me what Mr Stokes had to say on the matter of the missing money.'

Pearl stifled a groan. She wanted with all her heart to groan very loudly because that was preferable to screaming. 'That might be because he didn't mention the money to Mr Stokes. He's supposed to be my cousin, not a private investigator. He can't go wading in and making accusations on behalf of his cousin's employer when he hardly knows her, now can he?'

'I do think –' began Adelaide but Pearl would have none of it.

'But there's nothing,' she said firmly, 'nothing at all to worry about. If he's going to make any headway he needs to tread carefully.' She handed Freddie to Adelaide, who reluctantly undid the buttons of her blouse. 'Now I'll get dinner for us while you give Freddie his.'

If Pearl, on leaving the nursery, heard a laugh that was unmistakably Mrs Worthington's coming from the office, she ignored it. She was exhausted. The trip had been futile. The whole enterprise was ridiculous. She wished the idiot boy had never come and she wasn't entirely sure why she'd defended him so vehemently to Mrs Nightingale.

Less exhausted, she might have been comforted by the knowledge that Martin Duffy, after an hour at The Irish Rover, far from feeling he needed defending, believed he was doing well. He reported as much to Louisa, who listened with only slight interest since it didn't concern her. 'It didn't mean much at the time but now I think it could be important,' he said between mouthfuls of something that could have been potato pie or porridge. 'I talked to a man from Bega who hadn't heard of Miss McCleary's fiancé but he said there was someone on the coast who terrified the bejesus out of everyone who dealt with him. He said, if it's him he's after, forget it. How far is Pambula?'

'Pambula,' Louisa repeated vaguely. 'It's full of old people who want to die where they can hear the sea.'

'Friendly place?'

'I suppose so. Jimmy's parents had a holiday house there. His sister still has it. I never heard of anyone there who was terrifying. A name would help. More lapin? I think I might have a little more rum with mine.'

'There was no name. How long does it take to get there?'

'A day there, a day back. Rum for you? You might as well.' She smiled. She had small, even teeth and lips that curled sweetly. How could a man not be bewitched? But Martin Duffy replied, 'No thanks,' then he excused himself saying he needed to go to bed because it had been a long, hard day.

'The pub certainly takes it out of you,' was Louisa's dry reply.

Chapter Twenty-five

He was still in bed the next morning when Adelaide knocked on Louisa's door. 'Miss McCleary exhausted him yesterday,' Louisa reported. 'Are you going to the Mayberrys' Party For Peace?' She waved a newspaper in Adelaide's face.

'I didn't know they were having one. Aren't we having a Peace Ball?' Adelaide followed Louisa into the dining room, where the faintly charred smell of last night's meal lingered. 'You need to open a window, Louisa.'

'They've cancelled the ball in case it drew unsavoury elements.' Louisa read from the paper: '*That every other town is having a Peace Ball is no reason for Prospect to have one. The Mayor and his good lady wife will host a Candlelit Garden Party with Talks and Tableaux in the grounds of their magnificent home, which will do our soldiers returning and not returning proud.*'

Of course Adelaide hadn't read the paper. When did she have time to read a paper? 'Why isn't he up? It's after nine.'

Louisa didn't look up from the report she found so captivating. 'Tired? Lazy? Drank more than he should have before coming home for his dinner? I don't know, Adelaide. Can you believe the woman? She thanked the Ball Committee for their excellent work and then she sacked them. She's running the show on her own. Maybe she has another announcement to make to the women of the nation. Cup of tea? I've just made a pot.'

'Thank you,' said Adelaide. Her hesitation was tiny. She and Louisa hadn't sat down for a cup of tea together, just the two of them, since they'd both taken a shine to William Mayberry. It was in the spirit of this unusual togetherness that she asked Louisa how she was finding Maggie O'Connell, with whom they had also been thrown together. Odd they had nothing in common with her except access to the same stretch of road from their front doors and now a part-time husband.

'She's a spiky little thing, isn't she?' was Louisa's opinion. 'But you know her better than I do.'

'I don't. I've barely spoken to her in all the years we've been neighbours. Far too much water under the bridge. I always suspected she was spiky. Like her father.'

'I hadn't heard the father was spiky. Just unlucky to have crossed your father.'

'I'm not sure what you mean, Louisa. He tried to rob us.'

'Don't get cross, Adelaide. It's nothing to do with me. I never listen to local gossip. Martin asked me what I knew about the O'Connells and it was nothing much. Weren't her mother's side good farmers?'

Adelaide smiled, not with her eyes but with her teeth, which was better than nothing. 'The Careys took up their land the same time my grandfather took up ours and I think they did well. Mother was fond of Cissy. They got on famously until she married Frank O'Connell.'

'And what did you think of him?'

'Louisa, you know very well. Dishonest. Unreliable. Greedy.'

'Then he ran off with that awful red-haired girl, what's her name from the Post Office. And here he is. Good morning, Martin. Sleep well?'

'Who ran off with a redhead?' Martin took a cup and saucer from the sideboard and poured himself some tea. 'I love gossip. Who doesn't?' If he'd heard the slight on his fellow countryman he didn't show it, merely delight in the world around him.

Louisa thought how attractive a tousled head could be on a newly woken man late in the morning, and Adelaide surprised herself by deciding that as Irish traitors went, this one at least had some tact as well as a pleasant manner. 'Louisa apparently,' she said lightly. 'And how did you find the quality of Mr Stokes' gossip?'

'Well that was more in the way of him trying to find out as much about me as he could and me trying to decide why such a lovely old fella would want to bite the hand that fed him, namely yours. Could I trouble you for a slice of bread, Louisa?'

And where Louisa might have said to a less tousled head, *Help yourself if you can find any*, she said, 'Of course,' and went to the kitchen to bring in a loaf with some butter and jam, placing it on the table as if she'd paid for it.

'I was wondering, Mrs Nightingale, if I could have a look at the store's books so I can see exactly what's going on there. I can't promise to come up with anything but at least I can see what you're getting at.'

'Adelaide,' said Adelaide, since Louisa was clearly Louisa. 'Please call me Adelaide. Louisa, would you mind if I brought them over here? I'm not sure Marcus would understand the need for Martin to be looking at them.'

'Poor Marcus,' said Louisa. 'He doesn't understand much these days, does he? But I think he was happier when I left. Did he seem better to you?'

'When?' asked Adelaide, startled. 'Happier when? When did you come and go?'

'Last night before dinner,' replied Louisa. 'You were nowhere to be seen after you closed the door on me so suddenly. Martin was at the pub so your husband asked me to have a drink with him. I must say I found him in low spirits.'

'He didn't mention it. How funny. He must have forgotten.' Adelaide stood. 'I'll be back in an hour. I won't be interrupting anything, will I?'

This was how it always was with Louisa. Adelaide fumed as she crossed the road. One minute she was your friend, the next minute she was trampling all over your happiness with uncalled for announcements of her superiority in any way she could, whether it was her capacity for good cheer or the cut of her bodice.

The minute the door closed behind her, Louisa rolled her eyes at Martin Duffy. 'Funny old Adelaide. I'm not sure she's ever known how to handle the opposite sex.'

However you looked at it, it was an invitation for him to appreciate her own expertise on the subject.

You could argue it was an underhand tactic when these four respectable ladies were jockeying hard for the attention of their part-time husband, each having to draw on whatever charms they had at their disposal, not all of which were as obvious as Louisa's. But Norah Quirk could have told Louisa she was barking up the wrong tree.

If Martin Duffy was thinking that, tantalising though Louisa might very well be compared to Adelaide – compared to anyone, really – he knew trouble when he saw it. His landlady was trouble from top to her very dainty toe. He knew because he was trouble himself, as Norah Quirk was quick to report to anyone interested, which was everyone. It had taken just the four beers the night before for him to confide that it was the very thing that had driven him from Sydney.

'A beautiful woman,' she'd reported to her mother within minutes of him leaving the bar. 'With a husband she'd been keeping to herself and who didn't take kindly to him. I said to him, "Mrs Worthington is a widow so you're safe there. But it won't stop people talking."'

'And what did he say to that?'

'He said, "Let them talk. My cousin's arranged it, and she knows what's what."'

'You watch your step, Norah Quirk,' Mrs Quirk had warned. She didn't trust her daughter's eye for trouble.

'He's no one special, Mother,' Norah had said aloud, but to herself she'd admitted that trouble was the thing she loved most in the world.

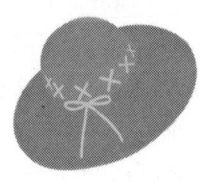

Chapter Twenty-six

You can't blame a town for taking such an interest. A good-looking stranger lodging inexplicably with its most beautiful widow is rich pickings. When his arrival precipitates unusual activity in the immediate locale of his lodgings, how can it not draw comment? 'Have you noticed how pally Mrs Nightingale is with Mrs Worthington all of a sudden?' Maisie Jenkins invited Theresa Fellows to address it on the steps of St Benedict's shortly after seeing Mrs Nightingale hurry across to her neighbour carrying what appeared to be a basketful of ledgers. 'I can't think what to make of it. What do you make of it?'

'I don't know. What do you?' Theresa Fellows was interested but wary. Maisie Jenkins was prone to wicked speculation about the comings and goings of others. Sometimes it was fun. Other times it wasn't. You never knew what she was going to do with your opinion when she interpreted it for the amusement of others.

'I'm making nothing of it. Just wondering. There's certainly more to it than meets the eye.' The two ladies stared down the road together, aware of but not seeing the town's activity as wind swept dust along the high street, driving everyone and the horses mad. If Theresa Fellows decided silence was the better part of survival, Mrs Jenkins was under no such constraint.

'It'll be the cousin who isn't a cousin. And if he isn't her cousin, we have a right to know why he's here. There's no work going. He can't have come all the way from Sydney to look for a job in a town with no jobs. What's Norah Quirk say?'

A direct question couldn't be comfortably shrugged off. 'Norah says he had to skedaddle because of a woman.'

'And doesn't he look the type!' Maisie Jenkins considered his type. 'Would you put a type like his into the same house as a young, good-looking, grieving widow?'

'Who's no better than she should be.' Even as she spoke Theresa regretted it. You tried to resist Maisie's evil train of thought, tried not to gossip – Father Kelly loathed gossip – but in the end you were drawn in.

Thankfully Mrs Jenkins appeared not to have heard. 'I would not,' she answered herself. 'What was he doing with the house-keeper out at the railway? That's something we should be asking ourselves.'

'Maybe he was looking for work out there.' It was a charitable suggestion. Theresa felt better for making it but Maisie Jenkins scoffed at it.

'That man has never done a day's heavy lifting in his life. He went out to talk to people. That's what I heard. She sat in the buggy and he went round talking to people. What about? That's what I want to know.' She appeared to know already. 'Some chap no one had ever heard of. Certainly not about work. So why's he here? Something's not right. We need to know what. The last thing we want in this town is Bolsheviks.' Mrs Jenkins' busy little lips folded in on themselves as she thought about Bolsheviks. 'Mrs Mayberry should be informed about subversives on the railway. We can't say she didn't warn us.'

'You can tell her at The Candlelit Party for Peace.'

'I very well might. She'll be making another announcement I shouldn't wonder.'

She did wonder though. Everyone did. They wondered how on earth the Mayor's wife had had the nerve to sack a hard-working committee who'd been planning a ball for months and had even asked her to represent Victory in the parade. No one wondered more than the Mayor himself.

'Why, Florrie? Why do anything so drastic? I'm the Mayor. Peace celebrations are for me to decide. The ball plans were going so well. Have you offended the committee? I'm sure you'll have offended them.'

'I didn't,' said his wife firmly. 'They still want to help with the food and so on. That's what a committee does, wherever the event is held.' They were in the garden, which was to have second billing to Mrs Mayberry at the event in question. She snipped a not-quite-dead rose from its moorings as her husband stood by helpless at the brutality. 'I explained that we wanted to give something back to the town and that our house and gardens were so much safer and better protected from intruders than the town hall.'

'But they're not. Not for a Peace Ball.'

'This isn't a Peace Ball. It's The Mayor and Mayoress's Candlelit Party for Peace, a delightful idea whether you think so or not. I don't care what you think. It's something I'm doing off my own bat because I have found my bat.' The Mayoress, who strictly speaking wasn't a Mayoress but the unimportant wife of a Mayor, considered her bat. 'It's my own and I intend to use it. To strike, to . . . hit a few sixes.' Oh, that was good. That was very good, she knew from the look on her husband's face. Oratory was so clearly her gift. 'The people expect more from me. They came to hear me at my assembly and now they know I'm their voice. They would like it heard across the land, and it will be. I will inform them in a speech I'm going give on the subject of How Things Will Be Around Here From Now On. I will be their saviour, their protector and their figurehead.' Snip went her horrible little shears.

'Dear God!' cried the Mayor as the words pierced his breast.

Maggie O'Connell, not ten yards away on the other side of French doors to the drawing room, coming late to the conversation, heard only the horror in his voice and wondered what his wife might have done to cause it. She peeped around the curtains but the Mayor had moved away and his wife had also moved away but in the opposite direction.

It was as diverting an exchange as she could ever hope to hear between her employers and very briefly she was diverted, but there is nothing more likely to distract an eavesdropper than the sound of her own name. Except in this case it was not the sound so much as the sight. There, as large as life on a sheaf of papers that clearly belonged in a different room entirely, were the words *BLUETT v O'CONNELL LAND DISPUTE (FINAL!)*.

What could a sneaky housemaid do except sit down and read the document concerning her family's fortunes from beginning to end? She read no less avidly than Maisie Jenkins spoke in Mr Stokes' office behind the smallgoods. Not on the subject of her most excellent hams, but about the goings-on of the ladies Beyond the Arch on whom she had been specially charged to spy.

Had any personage other than the shopkeeper himself asked her to do such a despicable thing, she would have reported it immediately to the very next twelve people she met in the street, and that personage would have been hounded from the shire. But Mr Stokes was a man whose character, in her eyes certainly, was above reproach. Not only did he admire her work with curing and smoking above all others, not only did he pay her handsomely for her hams and refuse all other offers from country women for miles around who imagined their work to be the equal of hers, he supplied her with a week's provisions free of charge. All he required in return was a cuddle now and then, which she was pleased to provide because he'd been alone so long and frankly the quality of cuddling in her own home was less than up to par. Lately, very lately, as well as the cuddling, she was required to partake on his behalf in a little light spying. 'They're in and out of each other's houses like mad little birds on a cuckoo clock,' she reported from his lap, on which he'd suggested she sit for convenience.

'Any further sign of the books?' asked the grocer, rearranging his legs under the weight.

'Not since this morning. Want me to keep watching?'

'Oh, most definitely,' said Mr Stokes. 'Just excuse me a minute, my dear. I just need to . . .' He gave her a shove from behind to extricate himself then he went to the door. 'Ginger,' he called and, when the boy appeared, he whispered something before turning back to her with a grin that revealed carnal intention as well as yellow teeth. 'Now what's that perfume you're wearing? It smells exactly like my favourite. Juicy Pink Sow.'

Chapter Twenty-seven

It was a shame from Mr Stokes' point of view that Mrs Jenkins was where she was. Had she been at her post, she might have heard Adelaide enquire of Louisa, as Louisa opened her front door to her, whether Martin had discovered anything interesting. She might have seen Louisa roll her eyes and heard her report, 'He doesn't seem to have a very good head for figures.'

'Are you unwell, Louisa?' Adelaide asked, pausing at the dining-room door to stare intently at her neighbour's pallor.

'What do you mean?'

'I mean are you ill? You look very pale.'

'I'm very well, thanks,' said Louisa and if there was bristling in the exchange, there was only sweet concern on Adelaide's face. She entered the dining room uneasily and her stomach sank at the sight of Martin Duffy with the ledgers open and next to them a sheet of paper, which he'd covered in dreadful columns of figures.

He got to his feet and pulled out a chair for her. 'Who'd be a bookkeeper?' he said. But he laughed to show he meant well and that all was well.

'Not me,' Adelaide replied as she took off her hat and gloves and put them on the table in front of her. 'Obviously. I know how to add up, but it takes me hours to get the same result twice.' The hat was straw and decorated with small white flowers, nothing special, but enough to distract Martin Duffy.

'Daisies,' he observed and in the observation Adelaide heard her own aversion to the ledgers and felt hope slide from her heart.

'They haven't defeated you as well, have they? Please tell me they haven't.'

'Of course they haven't,' said Martin Duffy.

'You can see my problem though, can't you?'

Martin Duffy confronted the ledgers and inhaled deeply. Adelaide wondered if there wasn't something stupid in his expression. Marcus was less good-looking, no denying it, but he was intelligent, or had been.

'The point, Mrs Nightingale, Adelaide,' Martin said, 'is that I can't see much difference between the docket totals and the takings. They seem to tally perfectly well.'

'Because they do,' said Adelaide. 'But then look.' She turned several pages of the ledger in front of him. 'Go to bank entries which Mr Stokes assumes I can't read and if you match them against the statements from the bank . . .' she flicked through several pages . . . 'they don't. When you add up the weekly takings and compare them to the bank deposits, there are pounds missing every week. Also,' she flicked back to the daily entries, 'look at the dockets.' Adelaide picked up a pile of dockets. 'Sometimes he charges different amounts for identical items on the very same day. A pound of sugar on one docket costs nine pence and on another costs a shilling. And there are items here I've never seen in the shop as well as all these items he only calls by initials. See here. Item A. And item C? From a supplier who crops up all the time called QM. I don't know any QM.'

'So how does Mr Stokes account for that?' asked Martin.

'He says market forces. He says all the money that's taken at the till goes into the bank so why am I fussing?'

'But it doesn't.'

'It doesn't. And he doesn't keep proper records of payments to the suppliers. He says it's the war. "You get things where you can and you pay what you must so you charge what you must always remembering the laws of supply and demand." That's what he says.'

Martin smiled at Adelaide's clever impersonation. 'And what are the laws of supply and demand?'

'I don't know.'

Adelaide and Martin Duffy exchanged a look of mutual sympathy, clueless people at war with ledgers cleverly manipulated to bamboozle the likes of them. When they finally removed their eyes from each other's gaze, which had proved surprisingly difficult, they fixed them on the table and when they eventually looked up, Martin said, 'You mustn't worry though, Mrs Nightingale, Adelaide. I might not be a bookkeeping genius but I know someone who is. Give me a week or two and we'll have a proper case against the blighter, you'll see.'

Despite all odds, Adelaide believed him and she felt the weight of many months leave her poor, tired shoulders. A week or two was nothing when the only alarm being raised was hers. She took Martin Duffy's hand and held rather than shook it. Any doubt concerning treachery died within his firm grasp, which might not have been calloused from hard manual labour but was steadfast and reliable as well as gentle and soothing.

Here was a man of principle prepared to do battle for her, not against her. 'Thank you,' she said and she left Louisa's house happier than she'd felt since the day Pearl McCleary had agreed to come and work for her.

The joy was short-lived. 'For God's sake, Adelaide,' her husband greeted her as she entered her own front door, 'where are the bloody ledgers? Stokes wants them.' It was all she could do to stop herself fleeing back across the road and into the arms of a man more interested in her welfare.

She'd have been disappointed if she had. Martin Duffy was that very minute putting on his jacket. 'Off to Maggie's,' he was saying to Louisa, who had emerged from her bedroom with cleverly rouged cheeks. 'I promised. She needs help with her hen house. That's all right by you, isn't it?'

It wasn't. Louisa was pouting prettily, if you like a pout. 'But I thought we could have some afternoon tea. The O'Connells aren't urgent.' And though she was extending a fragile arm, he managed to avoid it, so Adelaide would have found herself alone with a very cross Louisa and not a sweet and smiling substitute husband.

Maggie, on the other hand, was preparing herself for his passionate embrace. She was charmingly attired in a neatly fitted calf-length skirt and an enticingly scoop-necked lace blouse cleverly adapted from further items in her mother's trunk to resemble the height of fashion as displayed in the English *Women's Weekly*. 'Welcome to our humble home,' she said as she showed Martin into her newly spotless kitchen. 'I thought we could have tea and cake before I showed you the mess the boys made of the chook pen. It's not something a hungry man could tackle.'

Martin took from his jacket pocket the list Pearl McCleary had provided. 'The hen house – or chook pen,' he read. 'Some fencing. Your roof. Some painting. A hand with the boys. I'm not sure we have time for tea.'

'We do. Of course we do. And anyway, something else has come up that's more urgent. I made a sponge cake. The cake's not urgent. Well it is, because I baked it specially and I'd like you to try it. But this is more urgent.' As he took a chair in front of the cake, she handed him the folder marked *BLUETT v O'CONNELL LAND DISPUTE (FINAL!)* and announced with some pride, 'I stole it from the Mayor.'

Martin flinched. 'Was that wise?'

His disapproval rattled Maggie. 'I don't care if it was or wasn't. It's about my family and he has no business with it. I'll take it back tomorrow. He won't even know it's gone. I needed time to study it.' Her voice softened. 'I wanted you to study it.'

'Now?'

'Not now. There's pages and pages. You can take it home and give it back first thing in the morning. Not that I should have to give it back.' Her cheeks had grown hot from juggling annoyance and seduction. 'There are all sorts of drawings in here I don't understand as well as lists of laws and Acts and what have you. None of them have anything to do with the boxing I thought was the problem. They make no sense to me.' She reduced her tone to helpless.

'You've lost me,' said Martin Duffy, even more helpless as he flicked through the file. 'What's boxing if it's not in a ring?'

'It's mixing your own sheep with your neighbour's sheep so when you separate them you take a few that aren't yours. That's what Bluett accused Daddy of doing. That's why he shot him. But he wasn't boxing, because the land was ours.' Martin needed reminding of who shot whom. 'Adelaide's father was arrested for it and it went to court but they settled.' Maggie, spotting her beloved's incomprehension, decided the mood was all wrong for passion. 'Take it home and read it. Let's have cake now.'

'Good idea,' said Martin Duffy, only too delighted. 'A bit of cake, then I'll crack on with the hen house. The boys can give me a hand.'

But the boys were at Theresa Fellows'. They were the last thing a sister needed when her aim was to impress on the man of her dreams her great gifts as a homemaker, sensible person, elegant hostess, potential wife and excellent kisser. Maggie guessed she would be an excellent kisser. The boys would have shown her in a light that was none of those things. Her intention was to introduce them gradually to their future brother-in-law.

That thieving little Maggie O'Connell might even entertain such a hope would never have occurred to Maisie Jenkins as she stomped towards The Arch, disgruntled because the grocer's attentions, usually so ardent, had been distracted and short-lived. 'Why don't you,' he'd mused, possibly insisted, after a single desultory peck despite her tantalising aroma, 'wander along the road and see what's happening? No need to report back unless there's anything of interest. But on the off chance, you know. See if that cousin's hanging about.'

She had no intention of going as far as the O'Connells'. The O'Connells were only interesting because the deceitful girl had stolen a pie from under Mr Stokes' nose and Mrs Nightingale had, against all expectations, forgiven her. Maisie Jenkins, like everyone else in town, put it down to Mrs Nightingale's feebleness. A proper Nightingale would have sought justice. An older Bluett would have sought justice. The whole town was agreed on that.

Mrs Jenkins was lost in thought that had nothing to do with the O'Connells as she passed the Widow Worthington's, where there was no sign of the lodger. She crossed the road and peered into the Nightingales' house, where again she failed to spot him even though her glance was drawn towards an open window facing onto the street. Through it she heard Captain Nightingale declaring to his wife, 'Please, no more rabbit,' and all she concluded from that was that captain was not alone. As she turned back towards home to prepare tea for the husband who was so inferior in every way to Mr Stokes, she found herself in torment. Why had her love suddenly lost interest? Was it something she'd said or done or something she hadn't said or done?

It preoccupied her all the way back to her kitchen, when concern for the whereabouts of the housekeeper's cousin would have served her so much better. Not two minutes later, she might have learned something to make Mr Stokes' loins throb with gratitude. She'd have heard this from Captain Nightingale: 'Give me the ledgers, Adelaide. I'll take them to the shop myself.' Then this from Mrs Nightingale: 'No, I need them. I'm cross-checking.' Followed by this from the Captain: 'Don't be ridiculous. They're not in the office. Where are they? I'll get them myself.' And then she might have heard the sound of a crash as Captain Nightingale gave the door to Adelaide's bedroom such an almighty shove that it flew open, he flew in behind it, and in the flying collided headfirst with the bedstead and stunned himself. 'Miss McCleary, Miss McCleary,' she might have heard Mrs Nightingale call. 'Quickly. He could be dead.'

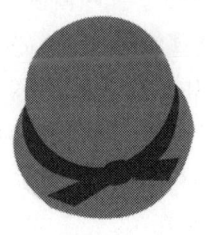

Chapter Twenty-eight

He wasn't dead. Of course he wasn't. Here was a man who'd survived unspeakable hardship. He was more than a match for a bedstead. But Pearl responded as if to a real emergency. She shoved the half-dressed baby at his mother and bent over the body, which was now on all fours and embracing life, and helped it to its feet. 'Thank you, Miss McCleary,' the Captain was gasping. 'Just a bit dizzy.'

Pearl guided him gently to the drawing room, prepared him a drink, and soon he was in his favourite chair with a double something in his hand inviting her to join him. The ledgers were for the time being forgotten, and as soon as she could, Adelaide told Pearl to scoot across to Louisa's to retrieve them and to place them somewhere in the office where they might easily have been overlooked.

'Who will join me?' the Captain called sadly.

Adelaide replied, 'I'll join you, darling. Just give me a minute to settle the baby.'

Pearl was not halfway across the road when she heard yet again, 'Miss McCleary, Miss McCleary,' as Norah Quirk tottered down the road towards her in a dress that revealed an alarming amount of calf. She was brandishing a letter like a fan as if the air somewhere to the right of her nose was pungent. Pearl waited. 'I thought I'd deliver it personally. It looks important.'

Miss Quirk handed over the letter and waited, imagining Pearl might read it and report its contents on the spot, or at least have the courtesy to explain its condition, which was dirty and crumpled. Its postmarks indicated it had been forwarded from Sydney but posted originally in Cooma, a good sixty miles away. 'Thank you,' Pearl said, putting the letter into her pocket. 'Nice evening for a walk anyway.'

'I was on my way home. I said, this probably can't wait until tomorrow.'

'Oh it probably could have,' said Pearl. 'Not much in my life can't wait until tomorrow.'

'Going for a nice walk yourself?'

'Just dropping over to Mrs Worthington.'

'To see your cousin. Nice man. I hope he finds work soon.'

Pearl moved away without comment, leaving Miss Quirk to turn back reluctantly towards the town. She paused at The Arch, remembering what she'd heard from Theresa Fellows who'd heard it from Maisie Jenkins, and she concealed herself behind a pillar. 'I had a premonition,' she later reported. Within seconds, it can't have been more than a minute, she'd seen the housekeeper go in then out of Mrs Worthington's, carrying the very large blue books Theresa Fellows had told her were of such interest to Mr Stokes.

Pearl, without giving Norah Quirk a second thought, pushed opened the Nightingale door, which had been left ajar, tiptoed into the office, dropped the ledgers onto the floor and pushed them under the desk. They were no concern of hers. Her concern was burning a hole in her pocket. Baby Freddie was whimpering and there was dinner to be put on the table but she headed straight to her room and, carefully closing the door behind her, took a deep breath to compose herself. The letter might have been dirty and crumpled but the script was Daniel's and even though she resented him with all her heart, she found herself trembling.

My darling Pearl, she read. *I am sending this to you at Annie's even though I know you are closer to me than you are to her. I'm begging you to stop looking for me. You are placing yourself in danger and not doing me much good either. I am in much hotter water than you could ever imagine and am in too deep to turn back. I beg you to go home. Beattie needs you. I will cherish you always, Daniel.*

Bloody idiot. Bloody, bloody idiot. Never knowing when to stop. Where was he? He should go home. Why didn't he go home? She had sworn to bring him home and she would.

'From an excellent family touched by tragedy,' Mother Declan had told Annie. 'The boy's a good scholar. But headstrong and stubborn.' Pearl stared at the letter so recently touched by him and at the dirty fingermarks she knew weren't his because he'd have found a way to wash his hands. He might have been feckless in the pursuit of what he thought was right, but he was always clean. He'd have given the letter to post to a person whose hands weren't washed. Someone who either didn't care to wash or wasn't used to washing or wasn't in a position to wash. Someone living rough.

'Miss McCleary, are you in there?' called Adelaide. 'I know we said rabbit but I think it needs to be something with cow in it.' Pearl stared at the letter. What kind of hot water? How deep in could he possibly be? 'Are you coming?' Adelaide put her head around the door. 'I think we can't have rabbit tonight or Marcus will leave home for good.'

When was a housekeeper allowed time to have thoughts of her own? Pearl left her room deciding to turn tomorrow's sausages into tonight's curry with the help of Captain White's curry paste, and she did this with good cheer even though she'd spent the morning making the most delicious rabbit rissoles. While she cooked, she weighed up options, discarding the unlikelys and concentrating on the possibles since there were no probables.

He must be on the railway or he must be near the railway or someone on the railway must know him. It would account for him knowing she was looking for him and for the dirt, which could easily be railway dirt. She would resist jumping to conclusions and wasting time and energy on fruitless enterprises, but she was decided. She'd go back to the railway with the next-to-useless blockhead and this time she wouldn't come away without proper information. If it meant leaving him in the cart while she accosted rough-looking strangers with no inclination to help her, then so be it.

The next-to-useless blockhead, meanwhile, was standing amid a pile of charred timbers and some less charred timbers wondering where to start. 'What have you got in the way of tools?' he was asking and Maggie was saying there was a load of stuff in the shearing shed and here she nodded to a decrepit outbuilding that gave no indication of containing anything useful or even salvageable.

'Want to look?' she asked doubtfully, but Martin Duffy said he would measure first then see what she had later. He paced the area that was required to cage the eight birds Maggie imagined she might manage and when he asked her roughly how many feet she thought it would convert to she said thirty feet by ten feet. 'That's what I thought,' he said. When he asked her to guess again how many posts she might need to build that size of run, she said at least a dozen and they would need to be eight feet high so two feet could be embedded and he told her he'd thought the very same himself.

'I'd also like a roof and some laying boxes,' she said and he told her that was precisely what he'd had mind and what were her feelings about methods of construction? When they found themselves to be in complete agreement as to how the thing could be built and held together, Martin Duffy said he might as well take a look in the shearing shed and Maggie said it wasn't locked so he could help himself.

He said, 'Aren't you coming with me?'

She shrugged. 'Not dressed for it.'

To another girl, he might have replied, *Then take your dress off*, but to Maggie, young and pretty and blushing, he said only, 'Leave it to me then.' It was laughable. They both knew it. Maggie watched from a distance as he pushed open the door and she bit her lip as he recoiled because that shed was heaving with mess of all sorts and God alone knew what wildlife. There was ancient timber in a hundred different shapes and sizes, posts, planks, beams. There was corrugated iron, tools of every size, shape and purpose, all rusting. There were hundreds of tins, piles of newspapers, half a dozen old trunks, sacks spilling stuff, and everything in a jumble that would require an army to sort. Frank O'Connell had given up once he'd been shot, a spent man, winning the argument but losing his spirit, restored only by the red-haired girl at the Post Office.

'Find anything?' Maggie called.

'Plenty,' he said as he strolled towards her. 'Here's what I'm going to do.' Overnight, after he'd read the document concerning her land, he'd draw a plan for the hen house and if she liked it, he would build it, one way or another. There was plenty in that shed that could be turned into something good enough for chooks. He spoke with such confidence that, once they'd parted company, Maggie chuckled. She knew he hadn't the faintest idea how to build anything and she loved him for it. They would learn to build together. They would restore and expand the home that would be theirs and the boys' and they would live in it and be happy ever after. The prospect of such a life, such a romance, such a breathtakingly lovely future was so transforming that Theresa Fellows commented on it when Maggie unexpectedly arrived fifteen minutes later to collect the boys even though they were, as Theresa Fellows also remarked, old enough and ugly enough to see themselves home as they'd done a thousand times.

'I felt like a walk,' Maggie said, which of course she had when the first hundred yards had been with her intended.

'You're looking very well on it,' Theresa Fellows told her, as well as noting privately, to be reported publicly later, that the astonishing outfit young Maggie was wearing was in no way suitable for the walk. It was all flimsy bits of this and that and hugging her figure so tightly it was a wonder she could put one foot after the other. 'I can't remember when I saw you last looking this well. You're quite grown up. If I didn't know better, I'd say –'

Maggie was spared what Mrs Fellows was going to say by the wayward boys tumbling past her, lashing out at each other and landing a painful blow on their hostess's plump right arm. This required so many demands of apology that the original thought was abandoned and Maggie hurried away before it could be recovered, saying she'd get the scamps out of there before more harm was done. If she stared longingly into the Worthington house as they passed, it was only briefly.

Louisa had closed the drawing-room curtains the minute her lodger had returned and now he was washing before joining her for dinner, an excellent sign, she was telling herself. A man who took trouble over his presentation clearly wanted to impress. She'd taken some trouble over her own presentation and was looking easily as fetching as a woman ten years younger. Not only that, she'd whipped up a quite miraculous meal of sardines on toast, which resembled nothing so much as sardines on toast and could only be improved by a few minutes gathering flavour while they enjoyed a pre-dinner drink.

'I wouldn't mind a beer,' Martin said when the drink was offered. But Louisa had no beer, only rum because rum was all Archie Stokes currently had under his counter. The gin that had sustained her through her very hard times had been a gift from Larry Murdoch, husband of the infinitely more memorable Baby Worthington, who'd barely spoken to her since the gift had been given. In fact had snubbed her completely the night of the Mayberry speech.

'We're lucky to have anything at all,' she remarked when Martin Duffy commented on the taste. 'I'm very fond of a drink before dinner and this rum is so much better than nothing, thank you, Mr Stokes.'

'Who supplies Mr Stokes?' Martin Duffy asked.

'How would I know? No one ever asks where he gets anything. We're just grateful he gets it so we can live better than most. Now, how did you get on with Adelaide? She seemed positively bouncing as she crossed the road.'

Chapter Twenty-nine

Louisa had every reason to close her curtains. Incessant nosy traffic was not only passing her house but entering it as and when it felt like it. Next morning it included Maisie Jenkins (passing, more than once), Maggie O'Connell (entering) and Miss McCleary (entering). It was the merest fluke it didn't also include Adelaide (entering), as she returned from town having delivered the ledgers first thing. She was about to look in on her neighbour when she spotted Maisie Jenkins plodding into view, so she didn't bother and it was just as well because Louisa was in no mood.

If the number of uncalled visits was outrageous, the neglect of the one person whose attention she craved was worse. It seemed to her that because he was her lodger, her problems were being ignored in favour of everyone else's. She was certainly not in the mood for Maggie turning up in yet another strange outfit claiming not only more time for the chook house – which, Louisa reminded herself bitterly, Maggie's own family had burned down – but for something that hadn't cropped up on any previous agenda and so had to be unconstitutional.

'I don't know what you mean,' she very nearly spat at her. 'What file?'

'My file. Martin was attending to it overnight.'

'What's in it?' They were at the dining table, sitting opposite each other like angry patients in a doctor's surgery, each insisting they had priority owing to the greater severity of their symptoms. They were waiting for Martin Duffy to rouse himself from his bed so he could cure their lives.

'I'm afraid it's confidential,' Maggie said.

'What do you mean *confidential*? Our arrangement doesn't stretch to secrets.' It was insulting, and even more insulting that Louisa was sure Maggie had given a tiny, insolent smile and here she was, not only pretending she hadn't smiled, she was changing the subject as if Louisa was too stupid to notice.

'I think Martin will be just what my boys need. You should see the way he's tackling the chook house. So calm and sensible.'

'Doesn't it make better sense for the boys to fix the chook house? They burned it down.'

Maggie raised her eyebrows as she had seen Louisa do, and replied in a tone Louisa might have used. 'I have more to do with my time than supervise them doing something none of us can manage. I have to go to work to support them and lately I've realised I have no clothes to speak of so I've been making myself some.'

'So I see,' said Louisa, and if Maggie saw Louisa's small spiteful smile, she said nothing because Martin Duffy had appeared in the doorway and everyone else in the room was invisible to her.

'Another pretty dress,' he said.

'It's just an old thing,' she replied truthfully. She dropped her voice to a whisper. 'I've come for the file.'

'I'll get it,' said Martin.

'We can discuss it later when you bring me the drawings,' Maggie continued to whisper. 'I'd like you to meet the boys.'

'For God's sake,' said Louisa. 'The man's not superhuman. And speak properly. Martin, get her stupid thing so she can leave because you and I have other business to see to.' Since matters could only have become more uncomfortable, it was just as well they were interrupted by Miss McCleary, who knocked loudly, was admitted by Martin and who marched into the room in such a determined manner that everyone was at once on their mettle.

Maisie Jenkins noted the look on her face, which she later described as bossy and cranky. *Cousin opened door*, she also noted. She failed to spot, at his elbow, Maggie, who'd followed him as he'd gone to fetch her file and was preparing to flee once she had it. Maggie, however, spotted Maisie Jenkins.

'Why is Mrs Jenkins watching the house?' she asked. Despite the arrival of Miss McCleary and the bulk of Mr Duffy blocking the doorway, she could make out the satisfaction on Mrs Jenkins' face as she imagined such excellent gossip restoring her to Mr Stokes' good books. 'She looks very pleased with herself.'

'Why don't you steer her back in the direction of town and find out?' Pearl suggested thoughtfully. 'She can't resist a chat.' So Maggie slipped from the house and in the urgency of the moment the file was forgotten. 'Now,' said Pearl to Martin Duffy once she'd gone although they were still in the hall. 'Down to business. Is Mrs Worthington home?'

Her firmness of intent could easily have been mistaken for cranky. Louisa certainly heard cranky in her tone and found irritation in her own heart for the uppity housekeeper. Who was she to demand they get down to business? 'Hello, Miss McCleary. You've called at a difficult time,' she said.

'Have I?' said Pearl in surprise. 'I'm sorry. Please don't let me hold you up. It's Mr Duffy I need to speak to urgently.'

'If it's urgent for him, then it's urgent for me too,' Louisa snapped. Martin and Pearl followed her cross little shape into the dining room, which would have smelled of sardines had not last night's meal been taken in the kitchen, which did smell of them. 'Everyone sit down,' she commanded. But Martin stopped short at the door.

'Maggie forgot her file,' he said in alarm. 'I'll have to go after her.' He headed back to his bedroom.

'She can get it later,' said Louisa. 'I really won't put up with any more O'Connell nonsense.' When Martin Duffy hesitated she insisted, 'I mean it.' So he returned to the dining room. 'Sit down, Miss McCleary.' She placed herself at the head of the table and she tapped on it as if she were calling the rabble to order.

'What file?' Pearl asked.

'*BLUETT V O'CONNELL LAND DISPUTE (FINAL!)*. She stole it from the Mayor,' Martin explained. 'He'll notice it's missing. I'm sorry, Louisa, she needs it.' He headed once more for the door. But Louisa's patience had abandoned her.

'Martin, sit down!' she shouted. He sat at once. 'It's not a priority. I'm a priority even though everyone else has pushed in ahead of me. It isn't fair.' Her voice continued to rise and now contained a tremor, which she directed at Pearl. 'Martin is living with me. I'm shouldering the whole responsibility for looking after him, so I should be given proper consideration and my problems should be properly recognised as being more serious than anyone else's. I've been very tolerant . . .' And here she burst into tears. Neither Pearl nor Martin, she saw though she had her head in her hands, looked surprised.

Martin half-rose again from his chair. 'We've upset her,' he said. Through her fingers Louisa saw the housekeeper restore him to sitting.

'She has a lot on her plate, that's all.' Pearl reached across to pat Louisa's shoulder but Louisa shrugged the gesture off. If she wanted anyone to pat her on the shoulder it wasn't Miss McCleary. But Miss McCleary seemed not to notice. 'It's what I came here to say. I've been thinking about the horses and what's to be done about them and I have a plan.' Annie McGuire, after a lifetime of dreading Pearl's planning, might have warned Louisa to watch out but Louisa needed no such warning.

'Spare me,' she said to herself, knowing she'd be expected to be grateful. She felt a bit sick, now she thought about it. She'd woken up feeling sick, just as she woke to every new day feeling sick, because despite Martin Duffy her problems hadn't gone away. It was the worry of the horses and the blackmail and the no money. It wasn't the gin or the rum, even though that's what Adelaide and Miss McCleary would say if she mentioned it. Pearl's plan turned out to be hopeless anyway. She'd thought of it herself already, of course she had. It was unworkable. There were two gates to man but only one of her. Martin Duffy could now cover the other gate but it was still impractical.

The suggestion was that two people should station themselves at the gates overnight and, as new horses were delivered, to scream blue murder drawing the whole neighbourhood to the property so the blackmailers would be caught red-handed. It was a joke. The whole neighbourhood was hardly a force to be reckoned with or even to have any faith in. 'Miss McCleary,' Louisa said sorrowfully. 'Do you honestly think Martin and I can stay up night after night, all night, in the cold, watching and waiting and that the horse people will wait while we scream, and hang about until Adelaide pops over to see what it's all about? Really? Do you?'

Miss McCleary didn't so much as blink at the sarcasm. 'I'll help you. We can all help you. We can take it in turns. I don't see how else we can unmask the blackmailers when you don't want to involve the police.'

'It's a sensible plan, Louisa,' said Martin. 'We don't need to shoot or arrest anyone. We just need to identify them so we know who they are and they know we know.'

'Exactly,' said the smug, increasingly odious Miss McCleary.

Chapter Thirty

Of course it was stupid. Pearl had no idea what anyone might sensibly do after the screaming because she hadn't given it enough thought. She'd unveiled the plan when it was barely formed to stop Louisa crying even though, she was quite prepared to admit to herself, it was skimpy.

Her urgent need was to keep everyone onside. She badly needed Louisa's cooperation with the master plan she'd been grappling with since receiving the letter from Daniel. Her intention had been to explain it to both Martin Duffy and Mrs Worthington in the first instance, and eventually Mrs Nightingale and Maggie, but she'd blurted the Worthington section too early. Now it had backfired and here she was in the street with Mrs Worthington no more inclined to be sympathetic to her cause than the one-eyed man at the railway had been.

It served her right. Annie would have said it served her right. She should have kept her lip buttoned until she was sure of what she wanted to say. It was a failing. An affliction. She should have been more aware of the others' desperation. It was equal to her own even if theirs didn't include a life at risk. She would have to be kinder if she wanted to put her needs first. She would have to be cleverer.

As she hurried up Hope Street with the file under her arm, possibilities of every sort were clamouring for space in her chatterbox of a head. She was no sooner through The Arch than they were interrupted by Martin Duffy at her side asking if she could spare him a few minutes because he needed her advice.

'I won't lie to you, Miss McCleary,' he said, regardless of what she could or couldn't spare. 'These problems you're asking me to tackle . . . I'm out of my depth. They're all so much more complicated than any of you seem to realise.' And there it was! Shoe dropped.

She'd advertised for a clever, brave, physically able man and Annie had selected the one man in the whole of Australia who was even less capable than Mrs Nightingale. Pearl drew a deep breath, stopped and turned. Yelling at him would be useless. Making him feel even sillier than he was would not improve matters. He was going to need reassurance and encouragement if he was going to be of use to anyone, most importantly her.

'Could we go somewhere we can speak in confidence?' he asked. And she replied, even though she was carrying Maggie's file that required urgent delivery, 'Yes, if you make it quick.' They hurried back towards the river and her favoured bench and, once seated, he invited her to take a look at the contents of the file she had in her lap. 'Tell me what you make of it. I'm no expert but even I can see there's all sorts of shenanigans in there.'

'Mr Duffy, I can't possibly look at it now. What kind of shenanigans? The result was perfectly straightforward, I thought. Mr Bluett shot Mr O'Connell. He had to pay compensation.'

'But the boundary dispute was never acknowledged in court as far as I can see and the papers that proved it aren't in here. It's more than I can take on. Maggie thinks I can help her but I can't even build her a chook house.'

Pearl considered his miserable expression and struggled for sympathy over impatience but found only self-interest. 'Anyone can build a chook house. I could build a chook house. I'll help you build the chook house, but in the meantime I need you to come to the railway with me again. I know we're close to him. I've had a letter.'

Martin Duffy put his head in his hands. 'She needs a good lawyer and Mrs Nightingale needs a good accountant. There is something up with the books but she needs an expert to prove it. She needs a proper audit.'

'I thought you were getting advice from an expert.'

'The advice was to get a proper audit.'

They contemplated the river, which was ambling lazily towards the sea, unaware it had a hundred miles to go and so quite content. How she wanted to amble and not care about the dreadful miles ahead. 'And your plan for the horses,' Martin Duffy said. 'Exactly what do you imagine we should do once we know who's delivering them?'

'I haven't decided,' Pearl admitted. 'Just knowing who's responsible is a good start.'

'I think she should sell the lot for meat to Mr Stokes. He's put in an offer.'

'And where would that leave her?' said Pearl.

'Out of debt and out of horses,' Martin Duffy replied.

'But not out of blackmailers. They'd still want their money. It's pointless.' Even as she spoke she thought maybe it wasn't. But Louisa's problem was not her problem. She was perfectly happy to help solve Louisa's problem. She just wasn't inclined to give it her full attention now because her own problem required her full attention.

This is what her head was trying to explain to her conscience, which knew very well that she had taken charge because being in charge suited her best and that being in charge involved responsibilities she couldn't ignore. 'Enough!' cried a voice from deep within her bones. 'I'm tired.' As if fatigue were a proper excuse for a bossy person to turn her back on responsibilities.

'You're in charge,' Martin Duffy reminded her. Then added, 'I might be a disappointment to you, Miss McCleary, but the truth is no one man could solve all the difficulties you have here.'

'Probably not, Mr Duffy, but the big advantage even a man like you has over the three of us is that you are listened to where we are not because we're women. Men listen to other men. It's as simple and as annoying as that. If we were men, I'm sure we could tackle our own problems without requiring your services. And even not being men, we could certainly build a chook house.'

How this went down with Mr Duffy wasn't immediately clear to Pearl and nor did she care. He jumped up from the bench and strode to the river, apparently to consider his position. It was the briefest of considerations. He'd no sooner reached the water's edge than he was back. 'If you want to terminate our arrangement, it's fine by me,' he said. But Pearl didn't want any such thing, now it was offered. She wanted him to come to the railway with her.

'For heaven's sake,' she said, summoning good humour. 'You've made great headway. If I'm impatient, it's just with the situation.' She stood. 'Mrs Nightingale will be wondering where I am. Will you take this to Maggie?' She held the file out to him but he didn't take it.

'You have a fine brain, Miss McCleary. I spotted it straight after I noticed your beautiful eyes. Couldn't you have a quick look at it first? She mightn't need a lawyer if you can make sense of it all.' And Pearl, despite herself, was flattered because she did have a better brain than his, and even if it was impudent of him to notice her eyes he wasn't the first man to do so.

'I'll look at it,' she agreed. 'And we'll go to the railway first thing tomorrow. Watch your step between now and then,' she called over her shoulder. 'Mrs Jenkins is keeping an eye on you.'

'Who's Mrs Jenkins?' he called after her but all she did was wave in response.

Mrs Jenkins, mistress of the hams, wife of a drunk, lover of the grocer, was put out. Having believed she'd struck gold in young Miss O'Connell's offer to walk with her as far as her turn-off, she'd realised too late that she should have been back at The Arch. 'I often call in on Mrs Worthington,' Maggie had explained innocently. 'I think she gets lonely.'

'Not any more,' Maisie Jenkins had pointed out with a sly nudge. 'What's his name again?'

'Martin Something,' said Maggie. 'But I'd better run, Mrs Jenkins. I'm late for work.' She'd pulled ahead of the wily cook and hurried through the town realising too late that she didn't have her file with her and that discovery of its loss could result in her ruin.

Her brain, like Pearl's, was quick and decisive, if not as honed by experience. Three possible courses of action occurred to her in rapid succession: report for work, take ill, go home and produce the file next day from under a cushion; turn back immediately, recover the file, arrive at work late and risk the wrath of

Mrs Mayberry for lack of punctuality; or go home at once, send message that she was ill, keep the file and never go back to work again because her husband Martin Duffy was taking her case to court where he would argue with all the vigour and cleverness of a city lawyer. The last of the options was by far the most appealing but the truth she couldn't avoid was that the romance was in its early stages and she wasn't sure how well versed in law her fiancé-to-be was.

She turned and ran as hard as her skirt allowed back to the Worthingtons', gasping only as she passed Maisie Jenkins still trundling towards the town. 'Can't stop. Forgot something!'

Chapter Thirty-one

Louisa's door was slightly open when Maggie arrived, so she entered without knocking. 'Mrs Worthington? Martin? Anyone home?' she called as she reached the kitchen. Mrs Worthington was most certainly at home. She was, however, in no position to answer because there she was, head thrown back, eyes closed, collapsed in the arms of Captain Nightingale, who was moaning, 'Louisa, ah, Louisa.'

'Sorry to disturb you, Mrs Worthington,' Maggie said anyway. 'I came back for my file.'

It meant nothing to Captain Nightingale, who whipped around wild-eyed. 'Fetch a doctor!' he barked.

The scene was compelling enough to justify questions if not comment but Maggie neither argued nor commented because this was Captain Nightingale, who had never addressed her civilly in the whole of her life. She said, 'Right you are,' but she didn't do as he'd asked. She hurried across the road to summon Miss McCleary, the one person she trusted to deal with a situation that was delicate, however you looked at it.

As luck would have it, the door wasn't opened by Miss McCleary but by Mrs Nightingale, impatiently waiting for her housekeeper who'd popped across the road for a minute and that had been half an hour ago. 'Why do you want her?'

'It's an emergency. Mrs Worthington has fainted and only Captain Nightingale is there to look after her.'

'What do you mean, Maggie? Why has she fainted? Where has she fainted? Captain Nightingale is in the study.'

'She's in her kitchen, I don't know why she fainted and it's definitely Captain Nightingale who caught her.'

'But where's Miss McCleary? And where's Martin Duffy? Miss McCleary went over to see him.'

'I don't know,' said Maggie again, in such a tone that the two women saw suspicion clouding the other's eyes but of what, neither was prepared to convey to their lips. Certainly Adelaide's husband should not have been in any position to catch a fainting tart of a woman who ought not to have been entertaining him on her own without first getting the permission of his wife. Certainly it was very odd that Miss McCleary and the part-time husband were both not where they ought to have been, and really had they been where they ought to have been, then the circumstance of the tart and the husband would never have arisen. Eyes can convey that many words between blinks. When Adelaide asked Maggie to stay and mind the baby while she ran across the road to see what she could do, both knew more or less what the other was thinking.

It was fortunate for Louisa that Pearl appeared from her rendezvous by the river just as Adelaide entered the Worthington gate. 'Where have you been?' Adelaide yelled at her. Definitely yelled, Pearl noticed. 'Louisa has collapsed. Lucky for her, Marcus was there when it happened.'

'What kind of collapsed?' asked Pearl, ignoring the question when the statement was so much less complicated. 'Has a doctor been called?'

'It's just happened,' said Adelaide. They hurried into the house and into Louisa's bedroom where Marcus had placed her on the bed and where she was returning to consciousness and wanting nothing more than to be alone.

To her horror, the house was now full of people demanding to know what was wrong with her. 'I fainted,' she murmured. 'The heat.'

'What heat? It's mild. Where's my husband?' Adelaide found concern just beyond reach.

'I was hot in the kitchen.' Louisa struggled to get to her feet as Marcus appeared carrying a cup of water.

'Oh there you are,' Adelaide said. 'You didn't say you were dropping in on Louisa. I would have come with you.'

'I don't need to account to you for my every move, now do I?' He was smiling. Adelaide heard no smile.

'I'm feeling much better now thank you,' Louisa said quickly. 'All I need is rest. I'll be right as rain on my own, I promise.'

Adelaide said, 'Well if you're sure.' She nudged her husband towards the door. 'You coming, Miss McCleary?'

'I think I should stay for a few minutes, if you can spare me,' Pearl said. 'Mrs Worthington's looking very pale.'

'But I've had to leave Maggie with the baby. I'm sure she'll be all right on her own, won't you, Louisa?' Adelaide was insistent, but her husband would have none of it.

'You stay, McCleary. The baby can be attended to by his mother for once.' It was no way for a loving husband to speak to a suspicious wife in front of neighbours and staff. Every female in the room knew it. He took Adelaide by her elbow and guided, possibly pulled, her from the house, leaving Pearl and Louisa to pretend nothing untoward had been said or heard. Louisa pretended for less than a minute.

'He's so moody,' she said, lying back on the bed.

'Are you still feeling ill?' Pearl asked. 'Can I get you tea?'

'Miss McCleary,' sighed Louisa. It was long, deep sigh of resignation. 'I think I can trust you. Well, I do trust you. I didn't faint. Sit down, why don't you?' Louisa patted the bed beside her. 'I fainted because the situation I was in was very difficult and it was the easiest way out of it.'

Pearl sat to receive the confidence that was coming whether she liked it or not, and she didn't much like it. It was a complication and she had no room in her head for another. She said, 'He does seem a bit out of sorts.'

Louisa laughed drily. 'That's one way of putting it. He wants me to love him. Obviously I can't and I wouldn't but I can understand it. Adelaide's hopeless with men. Always was. Always will be.'

'Oh,' said Pearl.

'Don't "oh" me, Miss McCleary. It sounds like a judgement. I'm sure you can handle men better than she can.' Louisa smiled in expectation of the confirmation but there was none. Just a silence, heavy with reproof. It was infuriating. Pearl knew it was infuriating and cast about for a diversion because Louisa was not only peevish and prickly, she was deathly pale for someone who had merely pretended to faint. 'Tell me about your fiancé,' she was insisting. 'I'm certain you manage him or you wouldn't be trying to find him.'

'I don't think I manage him at all. I'm not sure I manage anyone.'

'Don't be ridiculous,' Louisa scoffed. 'You manage the whole household over there. And you manage Maggie and me. Martin Duffy wouldn't be here if you hadn't arranged it. None of us would be doing what we are if you hadn't organised it.'

It might have been an insult since it was uttered without affection, or it might just have been a statement of the obvious. Either way, Pearl acknowledged to herself, this wasn't a comfortable situation. She might have been bound to Mrs Worthington by a contract that suited them for practical reasons but the last thing she wanted was a cosy chat about men. The cosiest feeling she had about Daniel was guilt. The cosiest feeling she had about men in general was that she couldn't imagine ever coming across one who might meet her exacting standards.

'Maybe your fiancé is sick of being managed by you and that's why he's taken off. Maybe you love him too much. That can happen with women like you who are prone to very strong feelings.'

'It's not true in this case.' Pearl swallowed hard to still the indignation rising in her chest. 'My fiancé is a lovable man with many good qualities but he's more at the mercy of strong feelings than I am.'

'Like my poor Jimmy. He loved me much more than I loved him,' said Louisa. 'That's why I married him. It didn't make us happy though.'

'Someone's knocking,' said Pearl getting to her feet. 'At the front door.'

'It's no one,' said Louisa. But it was. Someone was knocking hard and fast and Pearl rose to admit them but Louisa grabbed her arm and held it, like a child clinging to a departing mother. 'Please, please don't answer it,' she cried. 'I can't see a single other person today. I've had my fill. And this is a private conversation.

I feel this is a very private conversation.' So Pearl sat down again, the knocker went away and Louisa resumed where she'd left off.

'That's the terrible truth. I married Jimmy Worthington because he loved me so much and then we made each other miserable. Be careful, Miss McCleary. Unequal loving isn't a recipe for a good marriage.'

'Is there one?'

'Maybe not. I'm enjoying our part-time husband though, aren't you?' Louisa caught Pearl's pained expression. 'Not your type?'

'He's not here to be anyone's type.'

'Ha,' said Louisa. 'Tell that to young Maggie. Tell it to Adelaide. They're completely smitten. You must have noticed. He has his charms, Miss McCleary, even if they aren't apparent to you.'

'I'll be charmed when he's been of some use.' Pearl now did get to her feet, telling herself that colour was restored to the pretend patient's cheeks even if it wasn't entirely 'The baby will be wondering what's happened to me,' she said.

'The baby will be doing no such thing,' Louisa replied. 'I'd like you to stay. Please won't you stay a little longer? We've so much more in common than I thought we had. And you're very soothing company.'

But Pearl was growing agitated. Where was Martin Duffy? He should have come home when he'd left her. She hoped with all her might that he wasn't somewhere acting on his own judgement. She wished with all her might that she'd told him to do nothing without consulting her. She left without so much as a backwards glance, which was a shame because any glance at all might have taken in the troublesome file now sitting on the hall table where she'd placed it half an hour before.

Chapter Thirty-two

Martin Duffy was, indeed, acting on his own initiative, chatting to Archie Stokes without authorisation, under the impression he was doing all manner of good. 'She'll never sell the horses for meat,' he was reporting to the grocer. 'It goes against her grain.'

They were in the storeroom, to which Mr Stokes had led him the minute he'd asked for a quiet word. The grocer was listening attentively, less for information than for tone, for innuendo, for any suggestion of a little something that could be taken down and used if and when the time was right. 'She told you about the offer, did she? Made out of the goodness of my heart, I can assure you. There's nothing in it for me.'

'Of course not,' said Martin Duffy. 'Who was going to kill the horses?'

'A bloke I know. Out of town. Good butcher.'

'Does he kill your pigs?'

Mr Stokes, who was rearranging tins on shelves above his head, expelled air noisily through his nose, on guard, but not wishing to appear so. It wasn't as if the whole town didn't know who killed the pigs. Owen Jenkins killed the pigs because he was Maisie Jenkins' father-in-law. She grew the pigs and Owen Jenkins killed the pigs. All above board.

What alerted the grocer was the cousin connecting the pigs to the horses and the horses to him, which could give rise to all sorts of idle speculation, the least dangerous of which was that he'd sell the horse meat as some other kind of other meat in a product that rendered its flavour unrecognisable and that he might feed it to an unsuspecting township. Which he should have been able to do with no shame attached, given the horse was a perfectly edible meat product that should be used in times of deprivation and might have been anywhere else in the world except Prospect where horses were valued more highly than wives.

Mr Stokes nursed a quiet outrage at the idiocy of a town in which he was a favourite only because it suited him to be one. He hadn't been going to sell the bloody stuff locally anyway. It didn't matter, given the way things were working out. How quickly the grocer's brain worked. How clearly. Not unlike Pearl McCleary's, even though hers was female.

'Funny business,' said Martin Duffy.

'What? Horse meat?'

'No, the horses. Why Mrs Worthington has so many.'

'She not told you why?'

'Nope. She told you?'

'I've got a theory.' Mr Stokes groaned as he sank to his knees to pull a large box of tins from under the bottom shelf. 'You tell Mrs Worthington those horses are never going to be worth anything and my offer is the best she's going to get.'

'I will. I agree with you,' said Martin. 'It's a shame.'

The grocer heaved himself to his feet. 'It *is* a shame. A woman like that, sliding into poverty.'

'Oh, I don't think it'll come to poverty. She has her friends.'

'She has her enemies,' said the grocer. 'I'm not one of them. Tell her I'm at her service. Where Thomas at the bank might not be, I could be.' It was a risky overture, but he was nothing if he wasn't a gambling man and something told him that with this young fella in the mix, he couldn't lose.

'What are your terms?' Martin Duffy asked. 'I could pass them on to her to think about.'

'Step into the office and I'll see what we can do.'

And so it was that when Martin Duffy entered The Irish Rover ten minutes later, a rough and ready contract was burning a hole in his pocket. Louisa had only to sign it to banish every money worry she had, even if she wouldn't sell the horses. There'd be interest of course, and a reckoning, but not one she had to worry her distractingly pretty head about. He was delighted with himself. Good with money after all. *What an idiot*, Pearl would have thought.

Had she and Louisa considered the recipe for an unsuccessful marriage, they would surely have counted among its chief ingredients a difference of opinion over money. It worms its way into a marriage's foundations, giving rise to secrecy and suspicion as surely as damp gives rise to rot. Look at Mr Stokes stealing from the Nightingale household. Here was a wife reporting it to her husband but there was a husband telling her she was a fool.

Not that Adelaide considered her marriage unsuccessful. She'd never have allowed herself to be attached to any such thing. But she was sorely challenged, she couldn't deny that.

'Thanks, Maggie. You can go now,' she'd said briskly when she'd reclaimed the baby in the hallway where Maggie was waiting in her hat and coat. It hadn't occurred to her to ask why Maggie had been at Louisa's when she should have been at work. She had far too many ingredients on her marital plate, all of which needed to be weighed one against the other. Her disrespectful, possibly treacherous husband was chief among them.

Maggie didn't enquire after Mrs Worthington either. She was out of that house in a flash, dashing straight back across the road to collect the wretched file, but she'd found the Worthington front door well and truly closed and though she'd knocked until her fists hurt, no one had answered. With no alternative she'd gone to work without the file to be greeted on the doorstep by her employer wearing an experiment in Hair for Victory and a face like thunder. 'You are a disgrace. If I didn't need you urgently, I'd sack you on the spot,' she said.

It was remarkably similar to the sentiment Adelaide was planning to convey to her husband when she found the right words and tone. She had so little experience in fighting her corner. She sought inspiration from the spirit of her late mother, whose firmness of intent and ferocity of expression had been such a key ingredient in her parents' marriage. But she was not her mother. Instead of demanding to know what her husband had been doing in Louisa's kitchen, because she couldn't think of a single innocent reason for it, she said, 'We need to talk about money.' He was in the hall, ready to depart it seemed, but she was in his way.

'We certainly do not,' he said. 'You have your housekeeping. You get all the food we need from the shop. You want for nothing.' He tried to brush past her but she stood her ground.

'Marcus, I've been running the shop for years. You might have your head in the sand but I don't. There's something wrong with the bookkeeping.'

'Adelaide, you know nothing. Mr Stokes does the sourcing, the buying and the pricing and he oversees the selling. You pay the wages and you get yourself into a state over numbers you don't understand so he needs to correct them. Now let me pass.' And with that he closed a door in her face, both literally and figuratively, wounding her in every conceivable way.

Adelaide stood very still in the hallway before taking a shocked if figurative step backwards from the husband to whom she had plighted her troth. It was one thing to nurse, sympathise and make allowances for a man rendered unstable by the war. It was another thing altogether to continue loving a stranger who couldn't keep his contempt to himself, even in company. Her hurt was beyond consolation, a hard knot of despair she would carry forever. It would shape her marriage irretrievably; it would loosen the bonds she'd imagined were unbreakable.

Her thoughts turned inevitably to gentle Martin Duffy, who she knew even now was seeking expert help on her behalf and whom she trusted to be her ally regardless of her slight ability with sums. She wanted him to put his hand firmly in the small of her back as he had done when they'd last parted company. His touch had been so sure, so comforting, so manly that her spine had tingled.

Maggie's thoughts were headed in the same direction. Fear of discovery had been put aside because the Mayor was out and had left no angry directives about missing documents. His wife was concerned only for the Candlelit Garden Party for Peace. She would require Maggie for serving duties and her brothers for washing up but more urgently, she needed her to make adjustments to the Victory dress with which she would enthral her guests. She handed it over, a monster of a thing in red, white and blue built from all manner of fabric and bone. 'I wore it to the Federation Ball,' she said fondly. 'It's a wonderful piece. It will do beautifully once the hem is raised. I want some ankle showing but no calf.' She studied Maggie's hemline. 'That skirt's far too short. Please don't arrive again for work wearing anything so unattractive. Your mother is dead and I don't expect your father ever told you. Fashion should always be tempered by modesty. Men expect it.'

Maggie, now sitting quietly in the kitchen hemming, wearing an overall over her too-short hemline, smiled quietly to herself. Martin Duffy wasn't a man who expected modesty, she was pretty sure of that. He was a man who liked a bit of spirit and she intended to show him that she had plenty. She intended to be a spirited wife who would stand shoulder to shoulder with him, building, farming, raising children and sheep and ducks and a fortune so they could travel.

Chapter Thirty-three

Norah Quirk was equally sure of Martin Duffy's inclination for fun. Cheeky, devil-may-care Norah Quirk whose chief interests were flirting and gossip, who was fancy-free, the right age and up for anything. She was leaning towards him, exposing him to more velvety cleavage than was seemly for a Post Office clerk on a lunch break, though possibly not for a pub-owner's daughter. 'They're a boring lot down there. Never go anywhere or do anything. You ought to come to the Saturday dance or a bush picnic. Do you play tennis?' And he, with temptation in his eyes, was sighing if only he weren't so busy.

'Busy at what?' she asked and he replied that his cousin had him running all over the place. 'Well let me know when you want a break,' she said. 'Give me half an hour's notice and I'll join you.'

'I will,' he said. And he might have safely left it at that but he turned at the door to ask by the way did she know a good lawyer.

It was out of his mouth and into the clutches of Norah Quirk faster than a snake into a dead log.

She said, 'I'll ask Mum.' She thought, *Mr Stokes will love this.*

Pearl would have had a pink fit. As it was, her heart was already thumping because she remembered Maggie's file ten minutes after she'd passed it without seeing it and was gripped by the catastrophe about to envelop poor Maggie if it was still where she'd left it on Louisa's hall table. She picked up baby Freddie and said, 'You need a walk, you sleepyhead.'

Adelaide, overhearing her, declared briskly, 'I'll take him. There's washing and cleaning to be done here and I'm sure you haven't given a thought to dinner.' The housekeeper had forgotten her place so the spirit of Cordelia Bluett would remind her of it.

Pearl took stock. There was very little to take. She was in no position to argue with anyone from whom she intended to ask a favour as soon as the right time presented itself, so Maggie would have to bear the consequences. 'What do you think Captain Nightingale might like?' she replied. 'Mutton? Shoulder of mutton?' She couldn't have sounded more sedate. But in the endless mood-fuelled possibilities between what is said and what is heard, Adelaide found, *You've married a monster and look, you're trapped,* so she bristled.

'I know he seems hard to please, Miss McCleary, but he isn't. You thought he was grumpy earlier. He wasn't. He was concerned for Mrs Worthington. And in case you're wondering, he only dropped across to enquire after her health because I'd said how pale she's been lately. So, there you are. Mind your own business.' Her face was red. Her voice was flat.

'Well she seemed better when I left,' agreed Pearl evenly. 'I think she should see a doctor though.' And because she sounded unflustered, Adelaide's own fluster abated.

'Do you?' she said. 'Do you? She's such a funny person. I can never tell when she's acting. She acts so much of the time. Shoulder of mutton will do fine.' She packed the baby into his pram and took her misery with him to the river. She imagined finding Martin Duffy alone and thoughtful and she dallied in case he miraculously appeared, but Martin Duffy had finished his beer and headed home with his triumph.

The contract in his pocket was proof that he'd been about his business and that even a quiet beer with a pretty girl was in the interests of the job he'd been brought here to do. He found Louisa lying on the sofa with a rug tucked under her chin and a book on her lap. There was nothing to suggest she'd picked it up the minute she'd heard him turn in at the gate or that she'd hastily assembled her features into those of a woman who hadn't been counting the minutes until he returned, so he, unsuspecting, asked, 'Had a good morning?'

'Very pleasant, thank you,' she replied. 'I fainted into the arms of Adelaide's husband, she accused me of having an affair with him, he stormed off and she went with him, Miss McCleary stayed for ages boring me half to death about her fiancé who's obviously a complete fool, then she went home and I decided to bring myself in here because my bedroom was depressing and I wasn't sure how sick I was. I've given almost no thought at all to the hundreds of horses in my paddock because we're going to catch the devil who's delivering them in pitch darkness and then do something we haven't decided with him. I've given even less thought to the money I don't have because I have a lodger whose upkeep is my responsibility and he only turns up to be fed when it suits him.'

She was speaking very quickly and the pitch of her voice suggested a tantrum, or a fever. On the other hand, it might just have been the relief of a nervous wreck giving vent to the single person in the world she believed she could trust with her misfortune, however huge. Whatever it was, it spurred Martin Duffy to an action he might otherwise have taken a little time to introduce properly. He pulled the contract from his pocket in triumph. 'I've been to see Mr Stokes,' he announced. 'I told him there was no way you would consider selling the horses for meat and –'

'Why?' cried Louisa, tearful now. 'Why would you do that? Why would you? I've changed my mind. I wish you'd asked me if I was sure before you told that horrible man I was.' Martin Duffy dropped to the floor next to her because he knew from experience that his physical closeness soothed her. They often sat side by side when rum caused them to feel more than usually comfortable in each other's company despite such a short acquaintance.

'He knows things are hard for you and he wants to help,' he said gently.

'He does not,' said Louisa.

'He's offering you unlimited credit through the shop and all you need do is pay a token amount each month until you get yourself straight. You have collateral, he says. The house. He trusts you. And he says a woman like you won't remain a widow for long.'

Louisa wiped her eyes. 'What did you say to that?'

'I said he was right.'

'Did he put it in writing?' she asked. Martin handed her the agreement. 'And have you read it?'

'I have.'

'And if you were me, would you sign it?'

'I would. It's just for the time being. You won't be a landlady for the rest of your life.' Martin Duffy clambered to his feet. 'Now,' he said, 'I need to hop across the road and see Mrs Nightingale because I have news for her.'

'And when will you have time for me? Tomorrow?'

'Tomorrow it's Maggie. The day after, maybe. Right now it's Adelaide.'

'Watch out for her husband,' Louisa called after him and he laughed because it sounded like a joke. It wasn't.

Marcus had returned from his march into town on Lord alone knew what business. He answered the door and Martin Duffy, unable to ask for Mrs Nightingale, enquired instead for his cousin. 'She's busy,' snarled Captain Nightingale. 'Call on her when she's off duty.'

'And when might that be?'

'When my wife decides she doesn't need her, that's when.' He closed the door in Martin's face only to open it and ask of Martin's back, 'And who are you, anyway? What are you doing here? That's what we all want to know. Who are you?' He closed the door, leaving Martin to hover in case he opened it again to hear the answer. Had Pearl not heard the exchange and hurried out the back door, through the side gate to the front of the house and called 'Pssst,' he might have wandered back to Norah Quirk, whose troubles, if she had any, were no concern of his.

Pearl put a finger to her lips as he approached in case he bellowed a greeting. 'We can't go back to the railway first thing tomorrow,' she hissed. 'I haven't had a chance to ask Mrs Nightingale for time off or to book a trap. We'll leave at lunchtime.' Like Marcus, she wanted no response from him but hurried back the way she'd come, mission accomplished.

'I can't,' he called after her. 'I have other plans for tomorrow.'

Pearl stopped in her tracks. 'What plans? You're not paid to have other plans.'

'I've promised Maggie she can have me tomorrow. It's her turn.'

'It isn't,' she said. 'It's not for you to promise her anything. We're tackling the problems in order of urgency.'

'Miss McCleary,' said Martin unfazed. 'All your problems are urgent and you all think your own is the most. So in the interests of fairness and common sense, I'm deciding the order in which I tackle them. I know you're a fair person with bags of common sense but Maggie is getting overlooked. Have you had a chance to read that file of hers?'

'I left it at Mrs Worthington's on the hall table. Surely you saw it there and took it back to her.' Every syllable accused him of stupidity even though the mistake had been hers.

'Well I didn't and I haven't and it's not on the hall table now. Ah, Mrs Nightingale. The very woman.' And without so much as a *See you the day after tomorrow*, Martin Duffy strolled away from Pearl McCleary to greet Mrs Nightingale, pushing the pram wearily up from the river. 'Mrs Nightingale, Adelaide,' he called. 'I've had some advice about your bookkeeping.'

'Shhh,' hissed Adelaide in alarm. 'We can't talk here.'

'It will take just a minute,' whispered Martin Duffy. 'My contact says you need to get an audit. It's the only way you'll catch the bugger out.'

'I don't know what that means,' Adelaide whispered back.

'Meet me by the river, tomorrow morning at eleven.'

'I wish I could. But tomorrow is Maggie's day. She has a lot on her plate and I've hardly lifted a finger to help.'

'Maggie!' cried Adelaide. 'When did her problems become more important than mine?'

'Not more important,' said Martin Duffy. 'Yours are under control.' He spoke so charmingly that Adelaide could only agree. Because she didn't want him to leave without touching him if he wasn't able to touch her, she reached out and patted him, not on the shoulder as she'd intended, but on the back of his head because he was off and into Louisa's before he'd seen the need in her eyes.

'Have you seen a brown folder thing tied with pink tape?' he called the minute he was through the Worthington door. 'Miss McCleary says she left it on the hall table but it's not here now and it has to be somewhere.'

'Are you talking to me?' Louisa asked icily from the sofa on which she continued to languish. 'Can you spare me the time of day now you've lost something that might be useful to your precious Maggie?'

'Can I get you a cup of tea?' he replied. She was no longer tearful or smiling through tears. She was resentful, but distracted, which was both good and bad since it was by business that wasn't her own. The contents of the file were spread across the floor. 'Oh God! It's got to go back to the Mayor. She'll be in awful trouble.'

'She should have thought of that before she stole it.'

'It was hers to steal.'

'Then what's the fuss?' Louisa began to pick up the scattered sheets. 'Have you read it? It *is* odd. I mean, why on earth was my brother-in-law advising the O'Connells? Larry Murdoch isn't a lawyer. He used to be an accountant. And he hates the Irish, no offence.' She sifted the pages, searching for one in particular. 'Also, who does own the 400 acres on the border with Somerset Station? Frank O'Connell says here that he bought the land fair and square, but he couldn't prove it because the documents are missing.' Louisa yawned and stretched. 'It's a mystery. Now, you get tea and I'll put this back the way I found it. No one will ever know I've been snooping.'

And no one would have, had she not included among the papers an important one of her own, to whit the contract she had lazily signed from Archie Stokes. She discovered it was missing well after Martin Duffy had swallowed his tea and legged it across town to the Mayor's house where he dumped the folder into the overgrown hydrangeas, unaware of the bombshell it contained.

In his ignorance he might well have turned for home, to apply his overtaxed energies to, say, Louisa's difficulties, but he was, quite suddenly, overtaken by a plan at the heart of which he knew was genius. It involved him inveigling his way into the Mayberry household to further investigate the bewildering implications of Maggie's file, and it was so simple and brilliant that even the disapproving Miss McCleary would gasp at his cleverness. Bright as a button, he proceeded to the Mayberry front door and rang the bell.

Chapter Thirty-four

'Hello,' he said to Mrs Mayberry, who opened the door. 'My name is Martin Duffy and –'

'No thank you.' Mrs Mayberry closed the door on him before catching the briefest glimpse of a smile, which encouraged her to open it a fraction.

'I'm hoping you are Mrs Mayberry. I come with a recommendation from the Nightingale family.' She opened the door fully in order to stare at him.

'What kind of recommendation?' she asked.

'Catering. Catering is my trade. I wanted to offer my services for your very worthwhile garden party on Friday. Extra help, unpaid obviously, for such a good cause. Peace.' They considered each other, exaggerations forming on Martin Duffy's lips, delight gathering in Mrs Mayberry's eyes. 'I know it's odd, turning up unannounced, but Mrs Nightingale spoke so highly of you.'

Mrs Mayberry considered his reputable appearance and rapidly concluded that along with his pleasant manner and reasonable connections, it overrode his accent. She scanned his figure from top to bottom and, on the strength of what she saw, recalled she didn't mind the Irish. She wasn't one of those Anglicans who regarded them to a man as reprobates and thieving revolutionaries. She was against dangerous subversives – she would take up arms personally against dangerous subversives – but this young man looked normal by anyone's standards so she invited him into her house, an act she at once congratulated herself on. She was a woman of the people and this particular person, with his charming manner and fine looks, could only add quality to her event.

'Are you able to manage thtaff?' she enquired and wasn't surprised when Martin Duffy assured her he could. She invited him into the Mayor's study, where she described the vast hordes she was expecting, the enormous quantities of food being donated (mostly by the Nightingale family via Mr Stokes) and the gallons of punch the committee had agreed to make. She explained the number of tables and benches that would be arranged around the gardens and verandahs and she described the order of play, which would involve her emerging through the drawing-room doors to a fanfare of trumpets from two local soldiers who had been commissioned by her son, Lieutenant Mayberry, although he, personally, seemed to be held up in Sydney.

When Martin Duffy was eventually able to speak, he congratulated her on her wonderful gift for organisation and said it would be a pleasure to help. She nodded and led him into the kitchen, where Maggie had been sewing so long her shoulders were stooped and aching with the effort. The hem of that dress was many miles around. 'This is my maid. Her name is Maggie. She will be assisting you. She's quite competent.'

Maggie, peering around the mountain of frock that engulfed her, betrayed nothing of her shock and joy at the audacity of the man she loved. 'Pleased to meet you,' was all she said.

'This is Mr Liffey. I'm employing him to oversee the serving of food and drink on Friday. He's an experienced caterer so he'll be able to guide you. It's a godsend really, Mr Liffey . . .'

'Duffy,' Martin corrected her, but she blinked at the interruption and pressed on.

'. . . because I'm not sure who else in this town has city experience. I'm bringing in Norah, whose mother runs one of our hostelries, and another girl from the Post Office in Myrtle Grove. Both are experienced in waiting but you'll also have the services of the committee who, I'm afraid, are mostly elderly ladies and not really what I'm looking for in the way of efficiency and normal appearance.'

Not even a sneakier man than Martin Duffy could have found a way to signal to the girl he wasn't supposed to know that her precious file was dumped outside in the hydrangeas. When Mrs Mayberry showed him the door and waved him off, he had no choice but to keep going, so the file stayed where it was, under the bush and no one thought to tell Pearl McCleary. Not even Maggie, who was finally informed of its whereabouts when Martin joined her an hour later and walked her home. 'It's as safe there as anywhere else,' was her happy view of the matter.

Pearl, on the other hand, remained on tenterhooks well into the evening, though less from concern for Maggie than for herself. She cooked and served the shoulder of mutton, she cleared up after the meal, she asked if either Nightingale needed her further. Captain Nightingale didn't reply, which was unsurprising since he seemed to have decided the women in the house were invisible. Adelaide said no thank you, but would she please check on the baby before she went to bed.

Pearl said, of course, but one more thing, she was sorry to trouble them, she would work many days on the trot, but she would need to take the day after tomorrow off because she had urgent business. The Captain finally broke his silence. 'What?' he asked.

'It's my cousin's business,' said Pearl. 'It involves another trip to the railway.'

'No,' said Adelaide.

'The sheep bleats,' said her husband, leaving the table to drink himself to sleep or possibly death in the drawing room.

'If your answer is final,' Pearl said, 'then I'll hand in my notice, effective immediately.'

Again, Adelaide thought. *Always wanting to leave*. Perhaps she should fire her and be done. 'Why is it so urgent?' she asked instead.

'My fiancé has written. I know he's somewhere close.'

How difficult it was when Adelaide wanted only to be considered the good person the world believed she was and the good wife her husband believed she wasn't. Does a good wife risk a husband's wrath or does she show kindness to an insubordinate but well-intentioned housekeeper? She leaned back on her chair, closed her eyes and imagined life without Pearl. 'Go,' she said angrily. 'I'm sure you don't need me to remind you that you work for me and not the other way round.' Then she too left the table where her place was taken by a chill that Pearl decided was friendlier than it might have been.

She ate her own meal, cleared it up and then went to her room, where she sat on the bed and re-read the letter from Daniel. She read it, she put it in her lap, she stared into space where she found no answers. She too pondered the right thing to do. She asked herself how an honourable, sensible, decent fiancée would act in the face of such a thing. She asked herself who was most important. Daniel, Beattie, Annie or herself? That was what it boiled down to. Then it turned out not to be. What did it matter how well she behaved towards those she loved, or even whom she loved more? What mattered was what exactly she could do to alter a situation she so greatly risked making worse. She'd promised Beattie she'd find Daniel. Daniel was begging her not to find him. She closed her eyes to search for an answer but all that came to her with a sickening jolt was that Maggie's file was missing. She'd left it at Mrs Worthington's, Martin Duffy had said it wasn't there and he didn't have it.

She jumped to her feet. What kind of person had she become, so intent on her own concerns that she could forget completely the more urgent problems of others? She pulled her large shawl about her shoulders, she crept into the hall and she opened the front door quietly to look for signs of life in the house opposite. Seeing lights in the windows, she put the door on the latch and hurried across the road.

Who knows what caught her eye? It was less her eye, she thought later, than her ear. The horses at the far end of Louisa's paddock were restless, trotting up and down the fence calling to each other. She knew nothing of horses. What she saw at once was that their arrangement in the paddock was peculiar, that their behaviour was not what she was used to. It had been to watch for this very oddness that she'd suggested Martin Duffy and Louisa spend night after night outside in the cold.

She didn't bother alerting them. No time, she told herself. She let herself into the paddock and, crouching, she scampered to where the fence bordered the neglected garden so she could advance in the shadow of the overhanging trees to where she had a better view. Her heart was cantering. Anyone could hear it.

She paused where the treeline stopped and there was no more cover. Dozens of horses were gathered in the far left-hand corner of the paddock, many more than there had been that morning. She strained to hear above the neighing and the munching of the few animals closest to her. She ran along the top fence line, bent so low she was almost on all fours, hugging the shawl tightly to her body to contain any wayward garments that might catch the moonlight. She didn't ask herself what she intended to do when she confronted the half a dozen burly delivery men. She was no more than fifty yards from the main body of horses when she saw quite clearly that the northern gate was open, that a rider was guarding it to keep the resident horses where they were and that another was driving more through it. 'Oi!' she yelled loudly without giving it a thought. 'Oi, what do you think you're doing?'

The rider at the gate said, 'Jesus! Let's go.'

The rider herding the horses said, 'Close the gate, you fool.' But the fellow manning it had taken off, leaving the herder no choice but to take off after him. Half the horses in the paddock followed his lead, charging through the open gate in the same direction, back across the untended land that belonged to the nation and up onto the bush track that ran behind the town. Some headed in the opposite direction towards the river. Others, in a panic, ran back down the paddock and out the bottom gate Pearl hadn't closed on her way in. 'Cowards,' she called. 'Cowards! I know who you are.'

Maybe she should have screamed. Maybe it would have attracted someone's attention and she might not have found herself stranded in the paddock flapping her arms at horses bolting from her to the north, south and east, but it had all happened so quickly and so quietly that the fleeing horses were the only evidence of anything having happened at all. That anyone turned up out of nowhere was a miracle of timing. But someone did.

A lone horseman trotting down the lane from Somerset Station paused briefly to stare after the runaways heading into town before his attention was drawn to her forlorn figure yelling at nothing. He rode towards it, pulling up at the paddock gate.

'That's one way to get rid of 'em,' he said.

Pearl walked slowly towards him, not recognising him but drawn to the amusement no one else she knew would have summoned under the circumstances. The rider hopped off his horse as she reached the paddock gate.

'Mrs Worthington, is it?' he said. 'Joe Fletcher.' He put out his hand to shake hers. No fuss, she noted, just a frank stare and a normal handshake.

'Pearl McCleary,' she said. 'From the Nightingales' house.' She nodded in the direction of her bedroom. 'Someone was up at the other gate delivering more horses so I yelled at them and they took off.'

'Right,' said Joe Fletcher. 'Better get 'em back before they trample the town to death.'

'I don't see how I can manage that,' she said.

'You can't,' he replied. 'I can.' And without waiting to hear whether or not it was what she wanted, he was up on his horse and galloping so hard in the direction of the town that the clamour finally brought Louisa and Martin Duffy into the street wanting to know what was going on.

'What a mess,' she began. 'Oh God. I ruined it. It was a total failure.'

It wasn't how a furious Martin Duffy saw it. 'The only failure was you being so reckless,' he said sharply. 'You had no idea what you were up against. You should never have tackled them on your own.'

'Don't be so silly, Martin,' Louisa said. 'She's right as rain. It's not a mess. All the horses have gone. It's a marvel.' She laughed so oddly that Martin and Pearl looked everywhere but at each other. She laughed until she heard trotting hooves and saw twenty or thirty horses heading home through the Arch, urged along by a horseman who had no idea of their implication. She put her hand to her eyes and murmured, 'Please no. Make him take them back.'

Joe Fletcher had no intention of doing anything other than the thing he'd set out to do. Without so much as a nod in the direction of the three standing by the gate, he rounded the horses into the paddock, closed the gate behind him and addressed Pearl McCleary. 'I reckon I know where they're from. I'll need a day or two to check with my brother and I'll let you know.' And with that he was off, leaving Pearl to explain who he was and why she hadn't been able to identify any of the blackmailers in the dark. 'The only thing, but I couldn't swear to it, one of them might have been a woman.' She looked to Louisa. Martin Duffy looked to Louisa.

'What colour hair did she have?' Louisa asked sharply.

'No idea. She was wearing a hat.'

'What kind of hat?'

'A big one. Covered her face.'

'What else was she wearing?' But Pearl couldn't say. 'For heaven's sake! What did she sound like?'

'A man. But it wasn't a man. I saw her hands.'

'It will have been a man,' said Louisa. 'Now let's go inside. I need a drink.'

Since there was nothing more that could be done that night, or possibly ever, it was a sensible suggestion, but it didn't tempt Pearl. She said only that they should wait to see what Mr Fletcher's enquiries revealed. More urgently, she hoped Martin Duffy had found Maggie's file because that was why she had come out in the first place. She dreaded the trouble for

Maggie if he hadn't. He was able to tell her that not only had he, it was back where it belonged, which was moderately true. He had no time to explain his magnificent plan because Louisa was calling him from the front door. So Pearl went to bed easier of mind than she'd expected to be even if she had been accosted by Captain Nightingale on the way there saying, 'I am head of this house. You know that, don't you, McCleary.'

Chapter Thirty-five

Maggie, who'd gone to bed fuller of hope than she should have been, greeted the new day with less. Dawn, as it so often does, brought with it the dreadful anxiety of realities unchecked. She woke, she dressed quickly and she hurried through the town so early that only the baker and the priest were about their business.

Curiously, both the Mayor and his wife were awake. Neither had slept well. Mrs Mayberry's head was too full of the handsome, city-trained maître d'hotel who had appeared so fortuitously on her doorstep. He'd raised the social standard of her party so substantially it now perfectly accorded with the view she had of herself presiding over it. What was causing her anxiety at dawn was her failure to find out where the young man lived. They needed another consultation. She needed to ask him to act as master of ceremonies, introducing her in his pleasantly lilting

Irish voice so she could say a few words. She most definitely intended to say a few words.

The Mayor was agitated because his wife was being so damned secretive about the whole thing. The town might have been abuzz with the stupid party – they could hardly fail to be when she had notices of it in the paper and pinned to any bloody surface that could even slightly display one – but he felt overlooked. She was deliberately keeping him out of the picture. Whenever he asked how she imagined the event would unfold, she smiled that stupid new smile of hers and told him he should wait and see. She was certain he'd enjoy himself. Last night she'd said, 'And if you don't, it will be your own silly fault.'

'Are you awake?' he asked her now. He didn't care if she was or wasn't. He intended her to be, so he enquired loudly.

'Of course I'm awake,' she replied. 'My mind's racing. You won't believe who's coming.'

'I know who's coming. Everyone,' he said.

'Including the Murdochs and Mr Joe Fletcher from Somerset Station. I made a point of writing to them and they made a point of replying. They are fans of mine. Mrs Murdoch and Mr Fletcher both came to hear me speak and you would . . . What was that?'

'What?'

'A noise in the kitchen.'

'Rats?'

'Not rats. Someone's trying to get in.' And someone was, ineptly and noisily. Through their closed bedroom door came the unmistakable sound of a window being opened and with effort. 'Quick, George. Shoot first, ask questions later. I think I left my pearls in the dining room.'

The Mayor was in no hurry to confront any intruder even if he was after his wife's pearls, or for that matter any of the sensitive documents or large pile of cash locked in his safe. He searched for his dressing gown, struggled with its confounded arms, tied the ridiculous cord into a double bow, pushed open the bedroom door and paused. Someone was climbing through the kitchen window, puffing and scuffling and making small whimpering noises. His gun was in the dining-room cabinet. The dining room was across the hall next to the kitchen. Far easier to call out and forestall, he decided, than to confront. A call would allow whoever it was to escape but not give them time to steal anything more than breakfast. 'Somebody there?' he called mildly. And just as well.

Maggie answered. 'It's only me, Mr Mayberry. I've come for my purse. I didn't want to wake you.'

'There's a good girl,' he said. 'Very thoughtful. Mrs Mayberry and I need our beauty sleep. And what's that you have there?' Maggie was carrying the folder.

'I've no idea. I saw it in the hydrangeas when I was passing and thought I'd better bring it in.' She handed it to him.

The Mayor narrowed his gaze. Her name was plastered all over it yet she was saying she had no idea what it was. She looked as if she were telling the truth. On the other hand, a man was a fool if he didn't cover his back. Women were not to be trusted. 'How on earth did it get there?' he asked, sounding as innocent as she. 'It's not mine. This has come from a lawyer's office or some such. I'll make some enquiries. Now, do you have your purse?'

Maggie said, 'It's not where I thought it was. I'll have to go home and search the place again from top to bottom.' So the Mayor showed her out and she ran until she reached The Arch, where she slowed to an amble in case Martin Duffy emerged and found her sweating and panting as opposed to glowing and sighing. And so her day began, bumpily and anxiously, but it progressed beautifully, just as she'd hoped and, indeed, intended.

Martin Duffy didn't appear on her doorstep until well after nine, by which time the boys were at school and under pain of death to stay there all day or else. 'Else what?' Ed laughed. 'Your boyfriend will beat us? I don't think so.' Maggie didn't think so either but she said any lip and they'd be sorry, which she reported to Martin Duffy so he'd know that she considered him to be both manly and mild. It was all she wanted in a husband who was more handsome than he was handy and more friendly than he was effective.

Their day passed in such a romantic whirl of sorting bits of wood, hammering them, joining them up, attaching wire, congratulating themselves, laughing, sitting under a tree and staring at their handiwork, that there was no time for talk of the file other than Maggie's report that it was back with the Mayor. Before she knew it the boys were home and were, she was delighted to see, immediately charmed by both the new chook house and the builder. 'Can you shoot?' Ed asked. 'We can't.'

'Nope,' said Martin Duffy. 'But we could have a go. Where's your gun?' Maggie said they didn't have a gun and Martin Duffy said quite right and in any case, boys, he had something important to discuss with their sister so could they please buzz off for a couple of minutes. The boys sniggered, Maggie blushed and Martin, choosing not to notice either, waited until the door was shut and said, 'We haven't talked about your land. I read the file but only understood some of it. Mrs Worthington also read it and she understood more. You need a good lawyer. I'm trying to find one for you.'

'I know what's in the folder. I can't afford a lawyer. I wrote to Mr Murdoch and he said the documents I need are missing.'

Martin said if the Mayor had them, he intended to find them. He'd find a way on the night of the party or his name wasn't Martin Liffey. They laughed together until he added seriously, 'We'll still need legal advice. Leave it to me.'

How proud she was of him. How delighted he had said 'we'. How little faith she had in leaving anything to him now she'd seen him with a hammer. But before he left, he squeezed her waist, congratulated her on being an excellent cook, told the boys how lucky they were to have her and told Maggie herself she was a great girl. She'd make someone, which she took to mean him, a fine wife one day. How could she keep such joy to herself? She couldn't. When, half an hour later, she spotted Miss McCleary walking the bawling baby to the river she said, 'Mind if I come with you?'

'Of course not,' said Pearl. 'I could do with the company. I think Mrs Worthington has taken to her bed and Mrs Nightingale has spent the day locked in her study. Did you hear about the horses? People from all over the place have been returning them. As if she wants them back. Mr Fletcher is going to consult his brother about them. What's his brother do?'

Maggie shrugged. 'Still in the Army, I think. No, a policeman. Not sure. She should have sold the horses for meat. To be honest, Miss McCleary, no one feels very sorry for her and nor do I. If she's made terrible decisions in her life, then she has to learn from them. I hope I do. I hope,' she paused, 'Martin and I do.'

Pearl looked at her in fright. 'Maggie!' she said. 'This wasn't what we agreed.'

'It wasn't what *you* agreed,' said Maggie. 'I always said I wanted a husband. I don't want to share him with anyone. I love him with all my heart and I intend to marry him.'

'Does he know?'

'Of course he knows. He loves me too.'

'Has he said so?' If Pearl's face remained noncommittal, her voice was full of doubt.

'For heaven's sake, Miss McCleary. You have a fiancé so you shouldn't have to ask. I just know. That's all there is to it.'

'Maggie,' she said, 'the one thing I know is that love takes many different shapes and not all of them sit comfortably with each other.'

Chapter Thirty-six

Disturbing though they were, Pearl had no time to consider the implications of Maggie's heart's desire, but they stirred a memory that so coloured her dreams she woke the next morning with a looming sense of unease. The memory was of Daniel in his uniform, looking as unfit for war as it was possible to look, proposing when it was the last thing she'd wanted of him. 'War will make a man of me,' he'd joked. 'You'll see.' She'd wanted to love him but she couldn't.

As she washed, she considered herself in the mirror. A crabby-looking woman, lost for all her leading, floundering for all her planning. To banish her, she summoned the memory of a man on a horse who trotted towards her smiling. *That's one way to get rid of 'em.* She put the memory away and slammed the door on it.

Martin Duffy was sitting on the Worthingtons' fence waiting for her when she left the house ten minutes later. 'Quick,' she said, 'we're running late.'

'Good morning to you as well,' he replied. 'You look very . . . unusual.' She was wearing a dark skirt, sturdy boots, her enormous dark shawl and a hat that fitted tightly over her head, containing all her hair.

'You always look unusual,' she replied. But he didn't. He looked usual, as if he were on a day out into the countryside to collect nothing more challenging than wild flowers.

Lambert's had supplied a better standard of horse after Pearl's complaints about the last so the journey, even with Martin Duffy taking the reins, was less eventful. They spoke little because to speak would have involved swallowing gusts of dust, not to mention a long explanation of why she intended to do the questioning while he waited with the horse and cart prepared for a hasty getaway if they were to avoid arrest. The only words spoken were these: 'I think it's going to rain.' To which Pearl replied, 'Too bad.'

It wasn't until they were a quarter of a mile from the railway that she said, 'I don't want you to argue with me. I don't care if you don't like it. This is how it has to be if we're going to get anywhere.' It was more bravado than certainty. She knew it was bravado because it had the dull echo of no expectation.

She would sneak around the back of the works and accost men on the fringe. She would explain that they might already have spoken to her cousin when he had enquired after Daniel Flannagan a week ago but she was asking again in case anything had changed, in case her cousin hadn't given them the right information. Daniel was a shambling sort of man, with a light-hearted manner who was always very curious about other people and was currently on a mission to help a fellow soldier who couldn't help himself. For all his silliness, he was a stubborn blighter who wouldn't give up until he finished what he set out to do but he didn't know that his little sister was dying and that she needed him. This was the speech she'd prepared. It would sound better coming from a woman.

Martin Duffy did argue. He told her she was being not only foolhardy but insulting. He was perfectly able to question as many men as she liked, more able than she was. She was paying him to take on tasks that a woman couldn't and this was one of them. He was still arguing when she wrapped herself in the shawl and took off towards the mud and the slime and the cursing of men whose limbs were creaking under the weight of enormous pieces of timber.

Who knows whether those she approached would have treated her kindly, or laughed in her face, or pushed her to the ground and beaten her to death with a sleeper? She'd no sooner emerged onto open ground from the undergrowth that had concealed her progress from the cart when a heavy hand grasped her shoulder, causing her breath to stop and fear to halt her in her tracks. 'Where do you think you're going?' growled the one-eyed overseer as he spun her in the mud to face him. She could have run, she contemplated running, but he had a rifle over his shoulder and, one eye or not, she knew he'd aim straight.

'You,' he said. 'You're coming with me.' He took her arm and marched her to the hut, where a large wooden sign had been erected with the word SECURITY painted on it. He shoved her through the entrance. 'What did I tell you about trespass?'

'I wasn't trespassing,' said Pearl, 'I was making enquiries. I'd have asked permission if I could've found you.'

'I warned you before and I'm not warning you again.' He placed himself between Pearl and the door. 'Joe!' he called to no one she could see. 'Here a minute. I need you to escort a trespasser back to town.'

A man emerged through the flapping canvas that served as the hut's back wall, took one look at her and laughed. 'Hello,

Miss McCleary,' he said. 'What brings you out here, dressed like a woman on the run? Relax, Harry, this is Miss McCleary who works for the Nightingales. Miss McCleary, meet my brother, Sergeant Harry Fletcher of the Military Police. He's –'

'Joe,' warned the policeman. 'Enough. She's to go back to town. I'll let McDermott know what do with her in due course.'

Another woman, Louisa maybe, might have cried with joy at the sight of a body she associated, on the basis of very little, with kindness, calmness and protection but Pearl felt no such thing. All she felt was anger. 'Please tell your brother I don't care who he is. There's no need for Constable McDermott to do anything. I'm looking for a friend who's needed urgently at home.'

'Are you?' said Joe mildly. 'I've been discussing Mrs Worthington's horses. They're of interest to Harry. It was Miss McCleary who let them out.'

'I didn't let them out. They escaped.'

It hardly mattered to Sergeant Fletcher. 'Well now you're snooping. You've broken the law. Twice. You're leaving under escort.'

'Come off it, Harry. I can vouch for her.' Joe Fletcher had no more grounds for trusting her than she had to trust him, but there you are, they'd sized each other up amid a midnight stampede of skinny horses and each had reached conclusions about the other that had no basis in hard evidence. 'Tea?' he said. 'I bet you need a cuppa.'

'No tea,' said Pearl but the offer calmed her. She turned to Harry Fletcher with less rancour. 'I wouldn't be trespassing if I wasn't desperate. I'm sure you'd help a fellow soldier in trouble and my . . . friend is in great trouble.' Whether or not Harry Fletcher would have given her the time of day without the presence of his brother was doubtful. But Joe Fletcher urged them all to sit, so she sat and she told her story without elaboration or untoward emotion, dwelling on the noble nature of Daniel's mission and the danger he was in owing to the ignoble nature of the man who had stolen whatever it was he'd stolen. 'We know so little,' she concluded. 'I think he's bitten off more than he can chew.'

'You'd be surprised at exactly how much a soldier can chew,' Joe said thoughtfully.

His brother nodded. 'He sounds like an honourable man. Looking after the family of his dead mate. I don't know why you're interfering.'

'Because his sister is dying. She's sixteen, she's running out of strength and she hasn't seen him since he went to war.'

Harry Fletcher studied her in silence. Then he stood up. 'What's his name? I'll know if he's out there.'

'Daniel Flannagan.'

'Never heard of him.' He turned to his brother. 'You're right. The horses are Walers. Headed for the Middle East. Definitely never paid for, or not to anyone who cared to mention it.'

'Ex Army,' Joe Fletcher explained to Pearl. 'Who reported them stolen?' he asked his brother.

'No one. Same person who never reported the missing alcohol, tobacco or sugar.'

'Ah,' said Joe.

'But I'm getting closer,' said Harry. 'I know where the chain begins and where it breaks and now he's getting greedy it'll be easy enough to trace it to the bitter end.'

If Pearl wanted badly to ask closer to whom or what, if it was on the tip of her tongue to enquire after a crooked scheme that somehow had provided horses to Louisa's blackmailers, she checked herself. Instead she said, 'Maybe he isn't calling himself Daniel Flannagan anymore. He's five feet nine, brown hair, broad shoulders, a bit fat, good talker . . .' But the Fletchers had lost interest.

'Keep it under your hat, Joe. You too, Miss McCleary,' said Harry Fletcher. 'Not a word to anyone about what you've just heard. Joe says you're trustworthy and I'm taking his word for it. I'll ask around about your friend but my advice is to let him get on with whatever he's doing. A man's choices are his own to live with. Say your prayers for the sister.'

Martin Duffy sulked all the way home because Pearl wouldn't tell him what she'd discovered. It led him to believe it was nothing, which wasn't far from the truth. She knew no more about Daniel's whereabouts now than she had when they'd parted company an hour earlier. On the other hand, if she'd understood the Fletcher brothers correctly, the horses were part of a much bigger, much more complicated picture that anyone had ever imagined and Martin Duffy might, under usual circumstances, have felt entitled to be informed. But she'd been accused of snooping and she'd been sworn to secrecy so entitlement didn't count. She had her own problems, one of which was him.

'Don't toy with the affections of Maggie,' she said, startling him from his silence. 'She's very young and very innocent.'

'Why on earth would I? I think far too highly of her,' was his offended reply, followed by, 'You obviously don't think very highly of me.'

'Why should I think highly of you when you have such a low opinion of me.'

Had Pearl seen the hurt in her part-time husband's eyes and heard the miserable intake of breath, she might have been kinder, but maybe not. She was in no mood for kindness or even talking. Happily, the heavy cloud of resentment that hung over the cart all the way back to Prospect spared the need for any further conversation whatsoever.

Chapter Thirty-seven

It was a sorry state of affairs. The part-time husband and the woman who'd invented him were poles apart. Neither had the foggiest idea about which wife the other considered to be in most danger, nor from whom, let alone what was to be done about it. Such a failure of minds to meet is a shocker in a full-time marriage with just two spouses, but a disaster in a part-time one with five.

Martin and Pearl could have been more frank with each other on that trip home. Pearl might have explained the difficulty of her position regarding the information she'd received from the Fletchers and Martin might have alerted her to his independent activities about the town and their implications for all of them. But neither did.

This meant Pearl had no idea Martin had volunteered his services at the Mayberrys' party. It meant Martin had no idea that Sergeant Fletcher was getting closer to the unknown criminal stealing cigarettes, alcohol and luxury items as well as horses from the Army, or that Pearl's money was on the criminal's name being Archie Stokes. Yet again, they parted company at Lambert's with positively nothing to say to each other.

He was off and away with scarcely a wave of his hand the minute he'd helped her from the cart, so she walked home alone and let herself into the Nightingale house shortly after lunch to be greeted by Adelaide, whose mood was surprisingly benign. 'I've been thinking,' she remarked before Pearl had time to remove her hat, gloves and shawl, 'we should all go to the Peace Party as a family. What do you think? You can bring Freddie home as soon he starts to grizzle.'

'Why not?' Pearl agreed wearily. 'How has he been this morning?' She was tired, she was preoccupied, she was filthy. She was the housekeeper.

'Cranky,' said Adelaide. 'He wouldn't eat his lunch. Marcus will come to the party with us. He's been a much happier man today. And we'll take Mrs Worthington because she can't go on her own. You look very dusty. What a strange hat. Why don't you have a wash before you start dinner?' From which good-natured chatting Pearl was able to deduce that something pleasant must have happened. And it had.

Marcus, out of the blue, had behaved like a normal person. The stranger had vanished. The friendly, sensible husband had returned, not gone forever after all, just hiding. With no Miss McCleary in the house, he'd asked her for a cup of tea at ten clock, just as she was about to feed the baby, then he'd sat down to drink it with her. She had ignored the clock ticking past her fractious son's schedule. She had smiled at her husband to show she too could let bygones be bygones. She had told him all about the horses escaping just as fresh ones were being delivered, how Miss McCleary had challenged the people delivering them but they'd taken off and how Fletcher from Somerset Station had rounded them all up and put them back in the paddock. 'Poor Louisa,' she'd said. 'Last thing she wanted.' She'd told the story with amusing asides and clever imitations and Marcus had laughed.

'Odd business,' he'd remarked. 'But something I wanted to say to you, Adelaide. Stokes has come up with an excellent plan to stop you worrying about the books. An audit.'

She'd very nearly vomited. He must have overheard her speaking to Martin Duffy and now he was leading her into a trap that would end in a domestic horror that could only be imagined. 'What's an audit?' she'd asked and he'd smiled affectionately.

'What a duffer you are!' He'd patted her hand. 'The shop is far too much for you. I should never have lumbered you with it. An audit will put your mind at rest.'

'But what is it exactly? An audit.' She had a pretty shrewd idea, of course she did, but the question was genuine. Martin Duffy had had no time to explain it to her, what with his excursion to the railway with Miss McCleary today and his devotion to Maggie yesterday.

'It's a thorough examination of a company's books by a special accountant who goes through the figures with a fine-tooth comb. Stokes says Larry Murdoch might come out of retirement and do it for us as a favour.' She'd said it sounded like a wonderful idea. He'd said, 'Good,' and it had put the household on such an excellent footing that despite Freddie's whinging and carrying on, there had been no shouting or slamming of doors and Adelaide had been able to think about gentler things.

She'd thought about the silly Peace Party, first with amusement, then with delight. Everyone had come to terms with Mrs Mayberry's cavalier treatment of the Ball Committee so she could have the party in her own garden because, they remembered, her Address to The Nation had inspired them all and wasn't she the Mayor's wife, so didn't she have some authority? Anyway, a party was a party. A Peace Celebration was a Celebration of Peace, so who cared where the celebrating was done? That was the feeling abroad and Adelaide went along with it.

She'd taken herself and Freddie across the road to ask Louisa what she was wearing and Louisa had said she had no idea. She'd thought about not going but Jimmy was to be given an honourable mention, she'd been informed in writing by the committee.

'My black lace with the silk underskirts probably,' she'd said. 'I should wear mourning even if it is a party.'

'Do you think so? What did Jimmy like you in? That might be more fitting.' Adelaide had meant it well but it hadn't been received well.

'You don't know what you're talking about, Adelaide,' Louisa had snapped, and given her tone, Adelaide had decided Freddie had had enough and removed him from the scene. She'd spotted Maggie hurrying home through the Arch and had waited to ask her what she planned to wear but Maggie had informed her nothing special since she'd be on catering along with the boys, who'd be washing up.

'Shame,' Adelaide had said. 'Was Mr Duffy able to build your shed yesterday?'

'Chook house,' Maggie had corrected her. 'Yes, he was and now I have to run. Promised I'd make him some potato scones.'

It had jarred but not as much as it might have yesterday. Louisa was no cook. Adelaide had thought she might bake him a cake herself just to show him she could. Trawling through recipes had kept her happy all day and now, finally, Miss McCleary was home so she had someone congenial to talk to and take care of the baby.

'I hear Mr Fletcher was in top form when he rounded up the horses,' she said, putting aside her cookbooks. 'He's such a strange creature. We never see him even though he's just down the lane, because he works from dawn to dusk. My father would have loved him. What did you make of him?'

Pearl was peeling potatoes. 'We hardly spoke,' she said carefully. 'I didn't see him very clearly. He's a good horseman.'

'He's not bad looking, is he? Just grumpy and sullen.'

'He was friendly enough,' said Pearl. 'Given the time of night.'

'Well he'll be at the party. Mrs Mayberry's full of who's coming. She thinks Larry Murdoch and Mr Fletcher are the bees knees when they're two of the dullest men in creation. We can have fun though. Martin is bound to be fun.'

Chapter Thirty-eight

Martin was looking for fun that very minute, desperate for congenial company, but he was failing to find it. Mrs Quirk said, 'Norah's at the Post Office.' He hesitated no more than a minute before deciding that now was as good a time as any for him to trap Mr Stokes into confirming he was the crook Mrs Nightingale, Adelaide, and the ledgers said he was.

He didn't enter Nightingales through the main doors. He rounded the corner and wandered into the delivery bay where Mr Stokes was watching a small man heave the last of half a dozen sacks, each nearly as large as himself, onto a trolley. 'Mr Stokes. The very man,' he called amiably.

'The very man for what?' snarled the grocer. 'I sell nothing from the back door so don't even ask. Everyone in town knows I'm not a back-door man.'

'And I know that. I've never come across a more respectable establishment.'

'Finest in the state,' Archie Stokes muttered. 'Let me see that.' He lumbered towards the small man staggering under the weight on his back. He poked the load, creating a hole in it. 'It's damaged. Tell your boss it's damaged and I won't be paying for it.'

The small man dropped the sack. 'He won't like it,' he said. 'He'll say it left him in perfect condition.'

'You can tell the QM it wasn't perfect when it got to me and I don't like damaged goods. Don't like them and don't like the man who tries to palm them off onto me. Tell him that, Cocky Watson.' He towered over the small man.

'I'll take it back.' Cocky Watson couldn't have looked or sounded less cocky as he heaved the sack back onto his shoulder. He turned awkwardly but Mr Stokes gave him a shove, which sent him reeling so the sack fell to the ground and split further open, not a long way open, just open enough to spill a small trickle of sugar.

'I'm not asking you to take it back, Mr Watson. I'm telling you I'm not paying for it. See that split? Just give me the invoice and I'll make the necessary adjustment.' With that he deftly lifted the sack so the split was uppermost and no longer spilling and marched with it into the storeroom.

'Shoddy,' Martin Duffy said, following him.

'You're telling me,' agreed the grocer. 'Now what is it you want?' He dumped the sack, dusted himself off and smiled cagily. 'I bet I can guess.'

'Go on,' said Martin Duffy.

'Ham,' said the grocer.

'Not ham,' said Martin Duffy. 'Though yours is a fine ham.' He lowered his voice. 'Something a little stronger than milk to drink and possibly something to smoke.'

Archie Stokes headed back into the shop. 'Scarce, Mr Duffy. Very scarce.'

'It's why I came to you. My landlady says you're a man who can find his way round scarcity.'

'I've got my contacts,' agreed Mr Stokes, arranging the sack among other similar sacks. 'I've been lucky, and anyone will tell you, clever. I can sometimes help out a friend.'

The amateur sleuth coughed and, in doing so, overstepped a mark the grocer might have ignored. 'I'm looking for a bit more than I actually need, if you follow. Can you help me out there?'

Archie Stokes turned slowly. 'Now you're asking a lot.' He crossed the room, heavy footed, eyes like a pig's, clever, watchful. He placed his face so close to Martin Duffy's that Martin Duffy could smell the pig on him. 'I'll need to think about how friendly we are exactly. Give me a day or two,' he said. 'You might as well leave the way you came in.'

Martin Duffy watched the large retreating back for the briefest of seconds and as he turned to leave he heard the storeroom door slam as the grocer returned to the shop. The delivery bay was now empty of everything except the trolley loaded with the five sacks that were to be paid for. Not a soul in sight. The wretched driver with whom he'd hoped to have a discreet word had disappeared and so had his wagon.

He also missed the Mayor because the Mayor, also intent on a few words with Mr Stokes, changed his mind about looking for him in the delivery bay and chose instead to look for him in the shop. It was a decision he regretted at once. Sometimes the Mayor enjoyed the shop and the deference of other shoppers. Other times, he resented them. Today he wanted to say what he had to say to the grocer and go.

Martin Duffy passed the shop entrance on his way to visit Maggie O'Connell, who never whined or complained, just as the

Mayor called to Mrs Lambert, 'Mr Stokes about?' and Mr Stokes appeared from the storeroom, a little redder in the face than usual and a little less inclined to smooth the Mayor's feathers.

'Mr Stokes, a minute if you don't mind,' called the Mayor. He proceeded directly to the office expecting the grocer to follow him, which the grocer did without grace and only after deciding he might as well.

'And what can I do for you?' he said when the door was closed and they were seated. His smile was of a man who had no wish to do anything for anyone.

The Mayor fished about in his waistcoat pocket and removed a bit of paper, which he handed over. 'Yours, if I'm not mistaken.'

The grocer took the scrawled note of agreement between him and Mrs Worthington, recognised it at once but stared at it without comment. It was a turn up for the books, so he had no immediate response. 'What is it?' he finally asked blankly.

'It has your signature to it,' sighed the Mayor.

Mr Stokes held the paper closer to his face. 'Oh,' he said. 'This. Where did you come across this exactly?'

'In a file clearly marked *Bluett v O'Connell*, which I had on my desk as per our last conversation but which went missing. Our maid found it in a garden bed when she was breaking into our house to retrieve her purse or some such, and when I went to examine the contents of the folder to make sure nothing was missing, there it was. Something's up, Mr Stokes. I don't like it.'

Mr Stokes put the agreement on the desk in front of him and appeared to read from it but was actually reading only from his brain as it delivered possibilities and likelihoods. 'The folder was in your study. The maid found the folder, with her name on it, in the garden. There was no note in the folder when the folder was in your study. The note was intended for Mrs Worthington. The housekeeper's cousin was to deliver the note to her. She has signed it, so it was to be returned to me. It wasn't returned to me. It found its way into the folder. You didn't put it there. It stands to reason that Mrs Worthington has been in possession of the folder. Or the housekeeper's cousin has been in possession of it. Or the maid has been in possession of it, somehow come across the note and stolen it and placed it there and the folder never was in the garden bed. The maid is Maggie O'Connell, a known thief. The housekeeper's cousin has taken me for a fool. The folder concerns the enterprise you and I were discussing in total confidence. There is a connection between Mrs Worthington, the maid and the housekeeper's cousin as well as the enterprise. I don't like it either.'

'So what will we do?'

'We'll leave it to me,' said Mr Stokes. 'Now you'll have to excuse me, Mr Mayor,' he said, rising. 'It'll soon be closing time and I have work to do.'

What a day the grocer was having. He'd no sooner seen the Mayor to the door than Captain Nightingale was bearing down on him demanding a few minutes of his time exactly as the Mayor and Martin Duffy had done, as if he had minutes to dole out to all and sundry like scraps of ham for sampling.

'About this audit, Stokes,' he said with positively no acknowledgement of the need for discretion in a forum to which all and sundry had access. 'We need to tread carefully.'

'Like a cup of tea, Captain Nightingale?' he suggested softly, already treading carefully. 'Or something stronger?' Captain Nightingale never said no to something stronger and a Captain Nightingale a little the worse for wear was definitely more easily managed than a Captain Nightingale wearing well.

'Thank you, no, Stokes. This won't take long.' The Captain closed the door on the office and sat in the chair that Stokes usually occupied. 'Larry Murdoch,' he said. 'You know and I know the fellow's banned from practice. My wife, as far as I know, doesn't. I don't want my wife harbouring unhelpful suspicions. I think she's taking advice. I think she might have confided in someone and if that's the case, for the sake of our good name, we need to show that our books are not only as clean as a whistle but that the man who says they are as clean as a whistle is himself whistle-clean. Do you get me?'

Mr Stokes got him in an instant and leaned forward. 'Is she indeed? And from whom do you think she might be receiving this advice?'

'I've no idea. Possibly the housekeeper. There's something not quite right about her. Something a bit too big for her boots.'

'Or her cousin. It could be the housekeeper's cousin.'

Captain Nightingale was puzzled. 'Her cousin?' he repeated.

'Who's lodging with Mrs Worthington. A ladies' man, by all accounts. I hope you won't take this the wrong way and I only offer it out of loyalty to you and your mother.' Mr Stokes moistened his lips, preparing them for the treachery that was about to spill from them. 'Keep an eye on that one. He may be offering your wife something more than advice, and it occurs to me that she might be taking it.' Mr Stokes left no room for doubt. If he wisely didn't spell matters out in as many letters, his face conveyed the state of affairs even more effectively than anything an alphabet could offer.

'Christ,' said the Captain, slamming his fist on the desk. 'I knew it.' And with that, he stormed from the shop, kicking the display of tinned fruits as he went, back down Hope Street, meeting no gaze and returning no greeting. All he could see in the eye of his bruised and battered mind was a grotesquely painted wife naked on a bed in the arms of a man whose features he could barely remember. All thoughts of the rightness or wrongness of Larry Murdoch's audit had been vanquished, as intended.

Chapter Thirty-nine

Captain Nightingale strode not to his own home to confront the painted Jezebel. He turned in at Louisa Worthington's gate in the hope of finding the housekeeper's libidinous cousin in so he could punch him in the face before returning home to sack the housekeeper and deal with his wife. Not once, in the eight minutes it took him to get from his shop to Louisa's door, did his thoughts stray to logic or reason. Not once did he ask himself if he truly believed Adelaide was the kind of wife who would be anything other than loyal and upright.

'Louisa,' he said when she opened the door, 'may I come in? I'd like a word with your lodger.'

Louisa, in pale pink muslin scooped low to reveal the generous rise of her bosom, said, 'You may come in but the lodger isn't here. Will I do?' He hesitated. He looked at Louisa in bewilderment and she, spotting his confusion, opened the door wider to admit him. 'What is it, Marcus? You look dreadful. What's happened?'

Oh the dilemma for Louisa when he told her. His wife, he'd heard on the grapevine, was conducting some kind of dalliance with their housekeeper's cousin. An Irish good-for-nothing ne'er-do-well who was a nobody, a no one, not even a returned soldier with an excuse for . . . Well, an excuse. It was beyond outrage when he considered the love, the loyalty and the comfort he'd lavished on her. It was criminal. He was heartbroken. He would have revenge. How could she? What about their child, his son, his lovely innocent son? What about the sanctity of marriage? He'd been away a long time it was true, but only to defend her. What horrors had he not endured on her behalf? What lack of appreciation in return. It was too much to bear. And so on and so on, amid fury and tears and pacing and banging fists against hard surfaces.

She listened in silence then she suggested he sit for a minute to gather himself because really, these were very large accusations he was making and who on earth had made them in the first place? The grapevine was a very long one in Prospect and surely he knew how unreliable it was. She did not, however, contradict it. She simply asked him to consider it. She could have laughed in its face and told him it was the silliest thing she'd ever heard and could he hear himself, because honestly when was Adelaide supposed to have had time to conduct a dalliance and frankly when was the lodger? He was up to his eyes in the affairs of his part-time wives whose existence she clearly couldn't reveal but whose demands she could discuss in a general way. She raised no such objections. She offered him a drink, which he accepted.

It didn't suit her to defend Adelaide. It suited her to have Marcus look at her with longing and desperation and to tell her in great misery that now it was out, it hardly surprised him.

Ever since he'd come home he'd been asking himself if he'd made a terrible mistake in marrying a girl so, well, foolish, if he was honest, so easily led, so open to persuasion on every single little thing.

'Unlike you, Louisa. I should have married a woman with your spirit.'

Louisa smiled at him, thinking he was being a bit of a dill but even as she thought it, a plan occurred to her, the brilliance of which swept aside any drawbacks connected to inadequacy. It was a plan so neat that only its extreme wickedness stopped her from executing it immediately. Instead she said, 'Now, Marcus, you really have to be calm. Adelaide is a nice woman. She's large boned but she's not bad looking and she's easygoing. She's everything a man could want in a wife.'

'But is she loyal? How can I know if she's loyal?'

'You could ask her,' Louisa said innocently. 'That's what I think you should do. I think you should go straight home and ask her.' She took the glass from Marcus because he'd drained it in an instant and she showed him the door.

She stood in the hallway calculating, smiling to herself, but as she smiled an awful thought occurred to her. What if there were truth to the rumour? What if Adelaide was a dark horse? Not for a single second had she imagined that. The only idea along those lines she had ever entertained was that if Martin Duffy had eyes for any of them, it was for herself. But what if it were Adelaide? She laughed. Of course it wasn't, and her plan really was too clever.

Martin Duffy had not made it as far as Maggie O'Connell's. Mrs Mayberry, having accompanied her husband to the shops and parted company with him at Furlongs, the dress shop, had seen him from a distance and cried out with joy. She'd taken a good many very short steps at amazing speed to catch him up, the entire time calling, 'Mr Liffey, Mr Liffey, please stop, could someone please stop that man,' and Theresa Fellows, imagining him to have performed all sorts of mischief upon Mrs Mayberry's body, kicked him hard behind the knees and brought him crashing to the ground. Any gratitude she might have expected was slow in coming.

'For heaven's sake, Mithus Fellowths,' Mrs Mayberry had cried. 'I didn't ask you to kill him, just to stop him. Are you hurt, Mr Liffey?' When he'd assured her he wasn't and had forgiven Mrs Fellows for taking quite understandable matters into her own capable hands, he'd accepted an invitation to have a cup of tea at the Mayoral home. They had walked back up Hope Street together, deep in conversation, leaving Mrs Fellows to ask of Maisie Jenkins, who'd seen the whole thing, what she thought that was all about. Mrs Jenkins had said she would search herself but, having done so, came up with nothing except that this was a juicy titbit she would pass on to Mr Stokes with all speed.

Had either of them actually taken the trouble to eavesdrop they'd have heard nothing more sinister than the Mayor's wife expressing only very high hopes for the smooth running of her Peace Party. Not just its smooth running; its triumph. It must be a triumph. She was relying on Mr Liffey to help her make it so and he could do this by presenting her in the most dramatic and effective light as a representation of Peace On Earth. It went without saying, so she said it anyway, that the association between herself and Peace would benefit all their futures in the immediate and long term. 'My performance needs to be perfect. I want it to go like clockwork,' she explained as they skirted the park.

The nub of the meeting, which required very little input from Martin Duffy, was the order of service as she described it. Mrs Mayberry would, with her husband the Mayor, greet all guests as they arrived and she would welcome them into their grounds. Then while they mingled and chatted and drank punch and ate sandwiches, which he would supervise prior to the serving of the suckling pig, which would be after the speeches, she would hurry to the house to deck herself out in a costume that represented Victory and so Peace. At her signal he would take the dinner gong onto the verandah, sound it and the band would strike up 'Land of Hope and Glory'. She would emerge, the perfect embodiment of Everything She Stood For in a costume of her own design. He would march ahead of her, clearing a path through the throng until she reached the marquee from where she would address the assembly.

It took two cups of tea to tell him this, and Martin Duffy, having smiled only where manners allowed, informed her that he really did have a very clear understanding of her expectations. Then he rose to leave, saying he was expected at home for dinner. She asked where home was and when he explained he was lodging at Mrs Worthington's, she said, 'Poor woman. All alone. Unprovided for, so I understand. And unprotected. Happily, no children.'

Adelaide was nowhere to be found when her husband, as far from calm as it was possible to be, unlocked the front door with a trembling hand and stamped from room to room in search of her. Not finding her, so in extreme agitation, he ran back across the road and knocked on Louisa's door and she, half-expecting it, indeed having rehearsed it, opened it with a smile that might have been of sympathy but equally could have been delight.

'That was very quick, Marcus. I hope you were kind to her,' she said. But he didn't reply. He strode past her and into the drawing room where he helped himself to another rum and threw himself onto the sofa, where she joined him. She allowed her thigh to rest gently against his.

She said, 'Marcus, I know you like me and I want you to know that even though I am your wife's friend, I am also your friend. In fact, I sometimes feel I am more than your friend than I am hers.'

'Do you?' He clutched her hand. 'You are so lovely, Louisa. I know you understand me better than Adelaide does. You seem to, Louisa. I think you always have.'

'I think I always have. So when you turn to me in distress, you know I will always comfort you.' She stroked his hand. He dropped his head onto her shoulder. 'I comforted you the other night, didn't I, when you were so unhappy about things.' She couldn't remember what things but the things hardly counted, just the comfort.

'You did,' he said. 'You're so kind and sweet and gentle and clever. And you smell so nice.' She kissed the top of his head lightly. 'I'm so miserable,' he moaned.

'There,' she crooned. 'You needn't be. I could have made you happy, Marcus, if things had been different.'

'Life is cruel,' he said.

'But it doesn't have to be,' she said.

The Captain got to his feet, overwhelmed by the need for another drink. He waved the bottle in her direction, inviting her to join him and she said, 'Just a small one.' As he poured she said, 'Marcus, you remember the other night, after you took me in your arms . . .' He froze. Of course he froze. A war-damaged man smells danger at a million miles even if he doesn't know how best to avoid it. Louisa saw him freeze but decided the strength was with her given his madness and her own desperate need. 'I'm pregnant, Marcus,' she said.

'You can't be,' he gasped. He sat down heavily, so close to her that his thigh pinched hers.

'Well I am.'

'But who's the father?' Though her expression was regret with a hint of joy, mostly it was explicit. 'I can't be,' he whispered.

'You must be,' she said. 'You are the only . . . I know you were very confused, and perhaps it was wrong of us, but certainly we – it was a very brief encounter, but a lovely one.'

'But we didn't,' he cried. He put his hand to his brow. 'I know we didn't. I'd remember. Surely I'd have some memory . . .' But they both knew that he mightn't and that he hadn't a leg to stand on. 'Are you going to blackmail me?' he asked. 'Is this what you're doing? I don't know what you're doing, Louisa.' His voice was ever rising. 'I don't know what my wife is doing. But between you, you'll drive me mad.' He got to his feet and wheeled on her. 'You're not pregnant. How could you be? I want nothing to do with it.'

'Marcus,' she said, rising from the sofa to soothe him. 'Of course I'm not blackmailing you. I'm appealing to you.' She took his elbow but he shook it off. He glared at her, angrily and miserably, and then he fled, leaving the poor widow alone, unprotected and unprovided for, sipping rum, definitely pregnant as her body had only too clearly confirmed, and not at all sure that she'd played her brilliant hand correctly.

Captain Nightingale wasted no time. He went directly to his room, he packed a small bag, flinging garments into it willy-nilly. He scrawled a note for his wife containing no accusations of infidelity or any suggestion of extraordinary paternity, and he left the marital home, cadging a lift with Cocky Watson, who said, 'I'm only going as far as Myrtle Grove tonight, but I'll be pleased of the company. There must be trouble on the road. There's coppers everywhere looking for someone.'

Chapter Forty

A less bewildered husband might have spotted the need at this news to protect his household from the someone, but no such thought occurred to Marcus. He said, 'Myrtle Grove will do,' and chucked his small bag into the cart.

The rest of the town reacted with greater alarm. As the cart gathered pace, Norah Quirk heard from the girl on the exchange at Myrtle Grove that something was up but no one was quite sure what. She ran from the Post Office to announce the imminent arrival of bushrangers to everyone within earshot, and everyone within earshot hurried home to check their front doors for sturdiness.

Adelaide and Pearl heard nothing. Adelaide, in particular, was blissfully unaware of anything awful thundering across her horizon because the one she was admiring, as Cocky put mile after mile between her and her protector, was a glorious festival of pinks, purples, reds and oranges that reflected her spirits. There was no hint of trouble brewing. No runaway husband, no aspersions on her good name, no treacherous friend. Not even an inkling of a conspiracy between her husband and the shop manager to allay her fears about the books by further cooking them.

In the very short time between her apparently loving husband leaving their house in seemingly good order and him fleeing from it a broken and deranged man, Adelaide had embarked on the gentlest and pleasantest of walks with her baby and her housekeeper, whose company she was deciding she enjoyed more than most people's. She'd looked out of the window, seen the wondrous sky and suggested that since Captain Nightingale was clearly delayed at the shop they might as well take a stroll. Despite her very tiring day, Pearl agreed and in the briefest of heartbeats turned it to her advantage.

'Instead of going to the river, why don't we walk along the lane?' she suggested.

'Why not? If Mr Fletcher isn't as moody as he looks he won't mind his landlord's sister trespassing,' Adelaide said. They wandered at a leisurely pace along the dirt track towards her childhood home with Adelaide pointing out special landmarks and wondering at improvements the tenant had made to fencing.

She explained again how the land had been acquired in bits as parcels were released for auction, how the best bid won and how canny her grandfather had been in his acquisitions compared to Maggie's grandfather. 'We ended up with all this. And the O'Connells ended up with just that, and Frank O'Connell was very bitter. It's odd I'm on such easy terms with her now. She's a brave little thing. You have to hand it to her.'

The air was warm and comforting. The breeze allowed no suggestion of upset or disharmony, just softness and welcome, and Pearl listened to Adelaide burble about this and that with just the one ear. Nothing was needed in the way of a response apart from the occasional nod and exclamation of wonder, so she allowed her mind to drift to the garden party and what she might wear.

A more responsible fiancée might have applied herself to the missing Daniel, but she was sick of Daniel and whatever he was up to. The only advice she'd had, from Father Kelly and the Fletcher brothers, well-meaning men all of them, was to leave him to his own devices, and were it not for Beattie she thought she would. She still might. She'd decide after the party. Why shouldn't she go to a party? There was no direct connection between the possibility they might see Joe Fletcher on their walk, and her wardrobe, just a small sliding from one thought to the next.

She certainly didn't care one way or the other what either Fletcher thought of her. It would be fun though, she thought to herself, to see the surprise and admiration in Joe's eyes when he noticed that she looked, in her natural state, less like a rural housekeeper or woman on the run than a creature of style whose worldly air sat more comfortably on her. She didn't imagine he'd be especially impressed by a worldly air. But he had a way of studying her as if she were someone with notions above her station, and that amused her. She'd show him. She knew she could.

'Are the Fletchers from around here?' she asked idly.

'From Goulburn, I think. I've never shown that much interest.'

'But only one brother went to war?'

'No, both. Someone said Joe Fletcher was in Palestine. He doesn't talk about it. He doesn't talk about anything so who knows?'

At the sound of a horse galloping fast behind them they turned. 'Talk of the devil,' Adelaide said. 'This has to be him, doesn't it?' And it was, summoned by Pearl's thinking, which she told herself later was certainly not wishful.

He slowed as he grew closer and when he was alongside he stopped and tipped his hat. 'Miss McCleary,' he said.

'You know Mrs Nightingale,' Pearl reminded him.

'Of course.' He tipped his hat again. 'Enjoying the sunset?'

'Hope you don't mind,' Adelaide said. 'It's such a lovely time of day.'

'Don't mind at all. Pleased to see you back safe and sound, Miss McCleary.'

'Quite safe and sound thank you, Mr Fletcher,' said Pearl, explaining to Adelaide, 'I met Mr Fletcher at the railway. He was visiting his brother.'

'I thought your brother was still in the Army,' said Adelaide.

'He is. On special duties.'

'At the railway,' Pearl confirmed.

Joe Fletcher nodded. 'He took off just after you left, chasing someone or other he's been after for a while. Nothing to worry about but all the same, good to see you in one piece.'

'What someone or other?' Adelaide asked.

'Just a report. Better get cracking.' And with a brisk nudge of his horse, he did.

'See what I mean? Gruff,' said Adelaide without rancour. 'We'd better head back or Marcus will think we've been kidnapped.'

It took seconds for her to realise her husband was thinking no such thing. Pearl, lifting the sleeping baby from his pram, heard her cry from the kitchen. 'Oh no! Oh Marcus, no!' and as she put the baby into his cot and tucked him in, she waited. When there was no sound of angry footsteps or doors banging or anything crashing in the kitchen, she emerged to find Adelaide with her hand to her face from which all joy had fled and a note in her hand, which she passed to Pearl to read.

I can't go on, Adelaide, it said. *I need to think. Nothing is right. I'm making everyone miserable. You're better off without me.*

'I thought he'd turned a corner,' Adelaide whispered. 'He seemed so much better this morning.'

'Should we try to find him?' asked Pearl already deciding the quickest way would be to get the Fletcher brothers on his tracks. 'He can't have gone far.'

Adelaide rubbed her brow and took a long, quavering breath. She looked out into the kitchen garden for the briefest of minutes and then turned to Pearl with tightened lips and hardened eyes. 'No,' she said. 'I can't help him. He needs to help himself.'

This is how tough a heart can become when it's broken and healed, then broken and healed then broken.

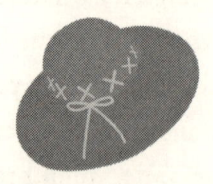

Chapter Forty-one

Louisa, it would be easy to argue, had been born with a toughened heart, but that wouldn't be fair. She'd have been born with the same capacity for tenderness as the next baby, but there's no doubt that she had acquired toughness earlier than most, that she'd developed more than the usual amount of mental sinew and gristle along the way because when the knocks came in adulthood, she braced. No amount of bracing comforted her next morning, however.

Martin Duffy hadn't required dinner the night before. He'd come home well after dark and gone straight to his room saying he'd had a long hard day and needed sleep. It was just as well. Had they sat together in perfect ease, she might have been inclined to tell him what she'd done and she was as sure as she could be that he wouldn't find it funny, whatever jokes she made about Marcus, morning sickness and insipid Adelaide.

In the cold light of the following day, the last thing she was finding it was funny. She was staring disaster in the face. How could she have been so foolish? How could she have taken such a stupid step against a neighbour who was famed for her goodness? It could only rebound on her, she realised, as dreadful clarity descended on her, and the only way out was to claim insanity brought on by pregnancy, panic and Marcus declaring his love for her.

She'd known for weeks that she was pregnant, for many more weeks than had elapsed since the night she'd suggested Marcus had made her so. It had been madness to imagine she could insist he was the father and to expect him not only to believe her but to leave his wife for her. Even if his wildest dream was to abandon Adelaide and his son for his more attractive and enticing neighbour, nothing on earth would have persuaded him to do such a terrible thing.

This truth was so unsettling it allowed her no rest. She jumped out of bed, she washed, she was sick in the basin, she washed again and she dressed. She would walk to clear her head and then she would call on Marcus and throw herself on his mercy. He would understand insanity, she told herself. Many men had come home from the war unhinged, everyone knew it, just as many women went mad with worry in the face of a disgraceful unplanned pregnancy. He would help her.

She let herself quietly from the house, pausing at her gate to look up and down the street in case anyone else was in it and saw, to her profound annoyance and horror, that Maisie Jenkins already was, hovering by the Arch, watching her. Spying. How dare she spy!

Louisa didn't walk to clear her head and calm her brain. She hurried, head down, straight across the road to bang on her neighbour's door, which was opened almost at once by Pearl

McCleary, who said, 'Mrs Worthington, what's wrong? It's so early. Are you ill again?'

'Mrs Jenkins is hiding in the Arch watching me,' Louisa said, scurrying into the house and away from the hideous gaze. 'What's she doing? She's always here, prowling up and down. Why are you dressed like that? Are you leaving?'

Pearl was indeed oddly dressed for a housekeeper who should have been going about her chores. She was wearing deep blue silk, off the shoulder and tight at the waist. While Adelaide and the baby slept, she'd fished out the single possible dress that might be suitable for a Candlelight for Peace Garden Party.

'Just seeing if this still fits,' she explained. 'Were you wanting to see Mrs Nightingale? She's had a difficult night. Or did you just come in here to hide?'

'I came to see Captain Nightingale but I expect he's asleep as well.'

'It is early,' Pearl agreed. 'If you give me a minute, I'll make you a cup of tea. Sit down. Will you be comfortable in the kitchen?'

It was ludicrous. There could be no comfort for Louisa anywhere in that house at that minute but there was even less outside. She sat in the kitchen uncomfortably and waited, praying that Adelaide wouldn't wake before her husband and that her husband, when he did wake up, would be kind and thoughtful and prepared to accept her heartfelt apology.

Pearl had no idea what explanation she could offer for Captain Nightingale's absence. She wasn't even sure she should admit he was absent. It seemed very odd that Louisa should be seeking him out at this time of the morning. 'Now, would you like breakfast or just tea?' she asked as she bustled back into the kitchen in clothes that made sense.

'No food. Definitely no food, thank you,' Louisa said. 'When does everyone get up around here? How long do you think I should wait? I probably should go because they won't be expecting me and it will be awkward.'

'You could leave a note. Why don't you write a note and if I give you a small covered basket to take home, Mrs Jenkins will think you just popped across to borrow something for breakfast. Poor thing must be bored to sobs to make us her hobby.' It was an excellent suggestion for which Louisa was grateful. Pearl showed her into the office and left her to it.

Any other day Louisa might have poked around looking for evidence of the life she thought she wanted, but not this morning. This morning she had to compose something that let everyone off the hook. She wrote, *Dear Marcus. Please put aside last night's conversation. The more I think about it, the more I realise I made a mistake and that you are in no way concerned in the matter. Please come and see me when you can so I can explain further. Affectionately, Louisa.*

She placed the note in an envelope and she sealed it. Had she known she had frightened him so profoundly that he'd departed the house and the neighbourhood for possibly ever, she'd never have left it. But the note was left and an hour later Adelaide opened it. She passed it to Pearl, saying, 'We'll go and see her together.'

It was innocent enough in itself. It might have been referring to a game of cards, or a lost hanky or gossip Louisa had passed on that she now regretted. But nothing about Louisa was innocent in Adelaide's eyes. Had the note not been penned at dawn the day after her husband had taken fright then flight, she might have viewed it more kindly. But there was steel in her heart as she confronted her nauseated neighbour, and even though Louisa attempted to smile through her illness and unease, nothing of the sort was returned. Not even from the housekeeper.

'Where's Martin?' Adelaide asked.

'Asleep,' Louisa assured her.

'Good,' said Adelaide. That was by way of greeting. She led the way to the dining room and when the three of them and the pram were comfortably arranged, she shut the door. She held out the note. 'What's this about?' she asked.

'It's between Marcus and me,' Louisa said.

'No it isn't, Louisa. Nothing is between you and Marcus. How dare you even suggest to me, his *wife*, that anything might be. I'm sick to death of you. You've treated me abominably before and I've forgiven you. But even now, when we both know each other's difficulties and agreed to face them together, you have met my husband in secret and conducted secret business with him. Well you might like to know, he's left the house and as far as I know he won't be coming back.'

'Oh God. Adelaide, what have you done?' gasped Louisa.

Adelaide laughed drily. 'No, Louisa, what have *you* done?'

'I'm pregnant,' admitted the woman who couldn't have looked more fallen, even if fallen is not how anyone with an ounce of compassion in their bones would have described her. She looked shrivelled and collapsed, tiny and unprotected, alone and unwanted. Unwanted and unneeded by anyone other than the tiny life inside her.

'Is Marcus the father?' Adelaide asked harshly. Louisa shook her head. 'Then who is?'

'I can't say.'

'Can't say or won't say?'

Louisa began to whimper.

Pearl said, 'Does he know you are having his baby and will he marry you?'

Louisa shook her head.

'It is Marcus, isn't it?' said Adelaide, cold and calm.

'No, it isn't, Adelaide, I promise. But I let him believe I thought he was even though we both know he can't be.'

'Why? Why would you do such a thing?'

Louisa shook her head again. 'Because I'm a bad person. I'm very sorry, Adelaide, I am so very, very sorry.' She was weeping copious sorry tears. 'I came to tell Marcus I was very sorry. Does he know that I'm sorry?' She sobbed into her hands but no one comforted her. 'This baby needs a father. I need a husband and I need one quickly.'

'Well you can't steal mine.' Adelaide stood and took the pram. 'Come on, Miss McCleary, I can't stay here a minute longer. Please don't try to pretend we are friends again, Louisa. We never were and we never will be.'

'No. Adelaide, please. I know it was bad. I know I'm bad but it was a moment of madness. I felt so desperate.' She was shouting.

Pearl said briskly, 'You must talk to the father of the child.'

'I can't,' Louisa called after them but the ladies' backs were already turned against her.

She'd have gone to her room and thrown herself onto her bed to die of misery and shame had Martin Duffy not emerged from his room asking if he were missing out on some fun. 'Just Adelaide and Miss McCleary,' said Louisa dully, gathering her composure so she sounded subdued rather than deranged. 'Being bossy. You need breakfast.' She smiled wanly as if there were no misery and shame. She offered eggs and ham and she prepared them as if they were married, this was their usual morning routine and the routine always included heaving at the sight of eggs.

It was a kind of miracle really. By taking deep breaths and indulging in the possibility, she suddenly saw the probability. The blissful, simple, natural solution to her terrible, terrible difficulty was staring her in the face and had been for weeks over so many happy drinks and meals. Oh God, the relief! She had been stupid but it would be all right. The idiots from over the road could all take a running jump.

Chapter Forty-two

Over the road, Adelaide threw off her hat and coat and slumped into a chair while Pearl put the baby into his cot with a rattle and a teething ring, which was all the company he was going to get until his mother could relieve the agony in her heart. 'Do you believe her? She's such a liar, she could be making it all up. She needs a husband, so she pretends she's pregnant.'

Pearl, putting the kettle on, sought only to soothe, not to delude. She agreed Mrs Worthington was unreliable but she believed she was telling the truth. She was pregnant so she needed a husband. The signs had been there for at least a month. 'So who could the father be?' Adelaide wanted to know. 'Who? Who has she seen and why won't she say? He's either married or won't have her, or both.' Pearl didn't know. 'I can't blame anyone for not taking her on. Why would anyone take on a tramp? She doesn't care what she does or says, provided it's in her interests.

Other people's interests can go to hell. It's how she's been as long as I've known her. I've got some sympathy for whoever's sending her those horses. She'll have driven them to it. I've a good mind to send her some myself.' Adelaide railed and ranted and accused until she'd run out of insults and the baby was crying so hard and furiously that there was no going on.

Pearl suggested she have a lie down while she took the baby for a walk, and Adelaide agreed even though she said, 'Don't patronise me, Miss McCleary. I'm not an invalid. I'm a woman who's been betrayed by a friend and abandoned by a husband.'

When she had the house to herself, Adelaide did not take to her bed. She squared her shoulders and took up a thinking position in the office, bolt upright at the desk staring at the blotting paper stony-faced. Now she'd had her say, she was less angry and she could be rational.

Had Marcus not been involved, she was persuading herself, she might have been more tolerant of Louisa's predicament. She wasn't the first woman in wartime to find herself pregnant to a man not her husband. There was the woman in Cooma who ended up living with the Chinese cook. But she was the first woman in wartime to decide the solution to her problem was to steal Marcus in order to stay respectable. She might not have succeeded, but one way or another she had deprived Adelaide of the man she had married for better and or worse. He'd taken off under the strain of it and she wasn't sure she wanted him back.

The man she had married until death parted them had come back from war a drunken bully who showed her little respect. She was no longer prepared to sweep under the carpet the assignations with Louisa he'd said were none of her business. They were and had always been her business and now she knew where she stood. She was as unprotected as Louisa and Maggie. He might even be dead. Perhaps he'd already killed himself. She told herself he wouldn't kill himself. But then she thought he might. Then she thought that if he did she would be free to marry again, and once that possibility occurred to her it took just the smallest tilt to the light to become something blissful. She saw clear as day a life with Martin Duffy, who was so at ease with himself, so honest and true, so kind and affectionate, so supportive and brave as well as handsome.

Pearl, striding along the river pathway even though the lane had tempted her, entertained no thoughts of marriage to anyone. She was thinking only of her own mother, newly arrived from Ireland who'd fallen for a man who'd turned his back on her, and her heart was breaking. Tears rolled down her face unchecked for her girl of a mother, for herself and for Louisa. She wanted to tell Louisa not to despair, to have her baby, to love her baby and if she couldn't raise it herself, to part with it with love. She would stand by her even if it meant not standing by Mrs Nightingale.

She carried this thought for the best part of a hundred yards and then realised she couldn't abandon Mrs Nightingale just when she'd been abandoned by her husband. Her position was in so many ways worse than Mrs Worthington's, whose plight could be tackled head on. If Mrs Worthington wasn't prepared to tackle it on her own account, Pearl would tackle it head on for her to honour her own mother, wherever she was. She formed a plan within seconds.

Annie McGuire would take in the abandoned widow until her baby was born and found a home. She would support her out of her own wage. In the meantime, she'd keep an eye on Mrs Nightingale until the storm blew over, which would surely not be long.

That settled to her satisfaction, Pearl wiped her face with her sleeve and decided that life would be better with the Captain out of the house and matters could be taken more firmly in hand. 'Good!' she remarked as she turned the pram and headed for home. If the plights of Daniel and Beattie Flannagan were completely absent from her calculations, it could only have been because the plight of the mother she'd never known had driven them from her aching heart.

Chapter Forty-three

Adelaide adjusted overnight to the absence of her husband. It felt more familiar, she explained to Pearl. Most of their marriage had been spent apart, when, despite the distance between them they had remained devoted to each other. Maybe they would always need distance between them, she confided. The distance felt normal. In the spirit of this normality, she threw herself at once into the matter at hand, no longer the horror of the ledgers but the Mayberry party, which held all the promise of dances before she married.

'Martin must come with us,' she said. 'Obviously.' But Martin couldn't go with them because he was attending as a lackey, a bombshell that had yet to be dropped on her. Unaware, she could easily imagine a delicate heart-stopping encounter in a sweet-scented arbour, so she fussed over her dress, she tried different hairstyles, she fished out dainty little shoes that hadn't been worn in years, she plastered her face in paste that would restore bloom and freshness and she allowed herself the glorious anticipation of a night to remember when she would be looking and sounding her best and she would charm the socks off a wonderful man she knew already was just as charmed by her.

Louisa was imagining an equally poignant encounter in a shady moonlit nook where she would confide her love and her very great interest in converting the part-time arrangement to full-time regardless of the interests of the other wives. Hers would be a simple but elegantly worded proposal, huskily delivered, and his delight would be her delight. He might not be everything she'd ever wanted in a husband but he had distinct advantages such as charm, kindness, good looks and a dreamy way of speaking which she knew could soothe her into old age. Possibly not old age. Possibly until she had enough money to escape abroad with her wonderfully handsome son who would escort her to the finest restaurants and hotels and health spas in the world where she would be mistaken for his sister.

Oddly, the part-time wife who'd unequivocally claimed first dibs on the part-time husband had positively no idea she had rivals. In the two days before the party she expected would change her life, Maggie had given very little thought to the others because no one had given her any reason to. No one had mentioned any missed periods, or morning sickness, or ghastly pallor or confirmed state of affairs and no one had mentioned any accusations of infidelity on the part of either Nightingale. Certainly there was no hint that the Captain had done a bunk. Not even the ever watchful Maisie Jenkins had seen him hop up alongside Cocky Watson, and since nothing had been seen or heard of that driver once he'd left town, no reports had trickled back. Maggie knew nothing because no one had told her because no one had thought it necessary.

It hardly mattered. She was busy. She hadn't been entirely truthful about her costume. She intended to serve food and drinks for no more than two hours and then she would change her clothes in Mrs Mayberry's bedroom and emerge belle of the ball. The world would be unable to take its eyes off her and Martin Duffy would know that she could be no man's but his.

Not only would her dress fall from her shoulders, sweep down her slender body and spread into a kind of mermaid's tail a good nine inches from the ground, her pretty strawberry blonde hair would be short and shiny, because even as Pearl was striding, Adelaide was musing and Louisa was flirting, Maggie was cutting a good two feet of tress from down her back, and what with the trimming from here then here then here to get a straight line, it was shorter than intended, barely grazing her chin, but wonderfully modern and carefree. She would be the smartest thing at the party, courtesy of Mrs Mayberry's magazines, talk of the town and imminent fiancée of the mystery man known mostly as The Housekeeper's Cousin.

The mystery man was as oblivious as Maggie to the dramas that had unfolded in Louisa's house and the one opposite. The closest he'd come to being told anything was Louisa casually remarking over early dinner that she sometimes thought Adelaide made goo-goo eyes at him, but when he'd stared at her in amazement and said, 'That's ridiculous. She's every inch a lady,' Louisa had let it go, observing simply that if he meant stuffy and dull, then she could be that, definitely.

Now he was to be found in his own room while Louisa busied herself with beautification in hers. He was making notes in the exercise book he'd divided into four so that he could keep track of his progress with the problems of each of his part-time wives. Under Adelaide he was pleased to note: *Progressing well. Audit in hand. Exposure imminent. Dishonesty confirmed to own satisfaction.* Under Pearl he'd noted: *Out of my hands. Can do no more. Breaks my heart.* Under Maggie: *Chook shed up, boys learning to throw before they can shoot, need to chase up lawyer.* Under Louisa he began to jot, *Money matters in hand,* when it occurred to him he had no idea where her signed agreement with Mr Stokes was.

He'd offered to deliver it but he hadn't seen it since the moment he'd given it to her. Maybe she'd changed her mind. He hoped she hadn't. He was pleased with his work on that score. He'd ask her in the morning. He put his book aside, closed his eyes and went to sleep.

In the Mayberry household, the Mayor had also decided to set aside the matter on the basis that, although it had implications for him, they were not as serious as the implications for Mr Stokes, and Mr Stokes, having been alerted, would sort things out. He'd informed Mr Stokes that the incriminating scrap of paper had been in the folder that had gone missing and now it was up to Mr Stokes to decide what to do about it. That's what he told himself as he rested his eyes in front of the fire in the small sitting room where his wife, with a mirror propped up on the table before her, companionably massaged cream into the lines of her neck. At least he'd had the forethought to remove the 'missing papers' from the folder while he examined it. At least they were safely locked away for him to dispose of as he saw fit.

The Mayor found himself more or less comfortable with the state of things. But he did wonder why the file had been at Mrs Worthington's. He didn't for a moment suspect the lovely widow, whom he knew from common report to be an arrogant, selfish young woman who never showed any interest in anyone or anything that didn't involve herself. He suspected her lodger, as did Mr Stokes. Mr Stokes would deal with him, and that would be the end of it. He didn't much care for Mr Stokes but

Mr Stokes had a decisive way of snuffing out trouble before it sprang into life. Then from nowhere came a brilliant idea that would restore both honour and sense to his life. He knew precisely how to deal with the missing papers. He could get rid of them and never be connected to them ever again while doing immense good.

'The very fortunate thing, George, is my acquisition of a young man from Sydney who has served in the finest establishments to oversee the service.'

'Mmm?' said her husband. Did he care? He did not. But he wanted – no, *needed* – to be on good terms with his wife for at least the next twenty-four hours because to not be on good terms with her in public could only hurt him. He needed nothing to hurt him at this point in the delicate negotiations over who was paying for the railway station when there were claims for stations being made by towns all over the country. 'What young man? A returned soldier, is he? Good thing. We must employ our fighting men where we can.'

'I don't think he's returned. I think he's visiting his cousin. A lovely young fellow. Irish but charming.'

'Name?' asked the Mayor, suddenly wide awake.

'Liffey,' said his wife. 'A Mr Liffey lodging with Mrs Worthington. He'll have the girls working like clockwork.'

'Did you tell Mr Stokes?'

'Why would I tell Mr Stokes?'

'Because he is catering.'

'He's only providing some of the food and some of the drink. The rest is being supplied by the committee, and the committee are delighted I have found Mr Liffey.'

It shut the Mayor up until morning when he was out of the house before breakfast and hotfooting it to Nightingales, where he found the grocer and informed him that the housekeepers' cousin had wormed his way into the event and would need to be monitored. To which Mr Stokes replied, 'Thank you, Mr Mayor, I thought as much,' and had at once despatched Ginger to The Irish Rover to ask Miss Norah Quirk to drop by at her earliest convenience.

And so Prospect's Peace Celebration began in the time-honoured tradition of community functions the world over: with anger, suspicion, resentment and the threat of violence.

Chapter Forty-four

Much to the dismay of Adelaide and Louisa, whose hopes were diminished (though not extinguished) by the realisation that their love trysts would be with the waiter, it was agreed that Martin Duffy would escort Maggie and the boys two hours before the party was to begin, as required by Mrs Mayberry. Pearl, Adelaide and the baby would escort Louisa, as required by common courtesy.

Iciness had given way to tolerance once Louisa had dropped a note to Adelaide begging forgiveness and understanding for her abominable behaviour. It had been brought on by the horror of her situation to which, Adelaide would be gratified to hear, she now saw a solution, which she was, for the time being, keeping to herself since the matter was such a private one.

'She must have spoken to the father. Or written to him,' Adelaide speculated and Pearl agreed since nothing else would really do. So when the Nightingale household, dressed to the nines, collected the head of the Worthington household, dressed just as effectively to the eights out of respect for her late husband, and after everyone had exclaimed to everyone how beautiful they all looked, though each was naturally most interested in comments directed at herself, the party joined the throng as the entire town drifted towards the Mayor's house, which had only the day before been named Tranquillity Park.

'We always conthidered it Tranquillity Park we juth never put the sign up,' Mrs Mayberry was explaining to the group she was greeting before she extended her hand to the Worthington/Nightingale party. 'It was one of the reasons we thought it would a good idea to have the Candlelight Garden Party for Peace here.' Mrs Mayberry was wearing a tiara. It was the only tiara in Prospect at that time.

She shook hands and nodded and smiled and urged them on with a deft flick of the wrist very much in the manner of royalty. She chose her words judiciously as a Member of Parliament might, though less as a woman of the people than as a leader of the people, which led her to impart some little wisdom or other to anyone she thought might benefit from it. To her social equals this was, 'I think we have made the world a better place.' To the hoi polloi it might be, 'Please don't pick any flowers or enter the house.' Or, 'All food and drink has been arranged on both the east and north verandahs.' The very lowly were advised, 'There are tents behind the kitchen garden for your convenience.'

There was indeed an impressive array of tents. The paddock behind the house had been annexed for the event and now was overtaken by a very large construction for the dancing and speech-making. From deep within it, the Prospect and District Military Band was playing marches in the spirit of Victory, very soon to be embodied, along with Peace, by the Mayor's wife. There really had been nothing to match it in the town's history, Mrs Mayberry announced every five minutes, and everyone thought she was probably right. The opening of the butter factory had involved far fewer tents. It was a great occasion and the people of the town were prepared to enjoy it to the full. They mingled and laughed and chatted and rediscovered each other in wonder even though they'd seen each other in the street just that morning.

'Adelaide,' roared Baby Worthington, a muscular blonde woman whose expensive clothes and weather-beaten face could have been fashionable though somehow were not, but whose small, shiny eyes suggested impishness of one sort or another. She clutched Adelaide to her chest in what might have been a wrestling move. 'How long is it since we've seen each other? I was saying to your mother-in-law, where's Adelaide got to? Haven't seen her in donkey's years. Is she dead?'

Adelaide detached herself and rubbed her front. 'We've been busy.' She nodded into the pram. 'And Marcus hasn't felt very sociable.' Baby scanned the scrum for sight of him but Adelaide said he wasn't with her. 'He sends his apologies. He's gone away for a few days – hello, Larry – to see his mother.'

'Hello, Adelaide,' said Larry Murdoch, a small, dapper man whose teeth were too large for his mouth. 'I thought Phyllis was on her way to America. Maybe not.' He leaned in to whisper confidentially, 'Not the time to discuss it but, just so you know, happy to do that audit to set your mind at rest.' He stepped back. 'Let's have a look at the son and heir.'

'He's sleeping,' said Pearl.

'This is Miss McCleary, our housekeeper,' said Adelaide. 'Louisa is somewhere around. Have you seen her already? I'm sure she'll be looking for you.'

Baby Worthington's expression soured. 'For my husband, possibly. She's a husband woman, isn't she, Larry?' Oblivious to the tumult this caused in Adelaide, Baby turned to Pearl, those beady little eyes alight with curiosity. 'The housekeeper with the cousin.' So frank was her inspection that Pearl dropped her gaze as a housekeeper might.

'I'll take Freddie for a stroll, I think,' she said. 'Very pleased to meet you,' and away she hurried, composing her features to betray nothing of her confusion, which had nothing to do with Martin Duffy being known as far afield as Upsand Downs, or Baby Worthington's witting or unwitting reference to the situation between Louisa and Marcus. It had everything to do with blinding comprehension. In flashes that came thick and fast, Pearl now understood the following. Baby Worthington's was the mannish voice of the rider delivering horses. Baby Worthington loathed Louisa. Baby Worthington was Louisa's blackmailer. Louisa knew already.

She found a seat in a far corner of the main garden under a tree decorated with streamers and Chinese lanterns to digest it all and as she stared into the crowd she asked herself the following. If Baby Worthington were the blackmailer, where did Archie Stokes fit in? Because it was surely Stokes the Fletcher brothers suspected.

He was no more than fifty yards away holding court by the pig on a spit. Everything about him said *Up to no good*, even the way he was chatting in lowered tones to Larry Murdoch. And what of Larry Murdoch, who'd done no more than smile in the face of his wife's insinuations about him and Louisa?

She watched as Mr Murdoch leaned towards Archie Stokes to hear him above the crowd and it seemed to her that both men were anxious, even angry. She saw Louisa, in her widow's black dress with its shiny scarlet trim, approach and she saw Larry Murdoch turn his back on her in order not to welcome her into his conversation. She watched as Louisa, without missing a beat, turned to Maggie and took from the tray she was carrying a glass of punch, then she watched her glide towards Martin Duffy, who was lingering in the most peculiar manner behind a hedge on the other side of the pig. Was he eavesdropping on the conversation between Mr Stokes and Mr Murdoch? They both turned abruptly to stare at him when Louisa called, 'Martin, is there anything stronger than this unspeakable punch?' Planning was impossible when no one was behaving as they should.

'There you are, Miss McCleary.' Joe Fletcher emerged smiling from the shadows behind her. 'A friendly face at last. Mind if I join you?' And if she'd intended to respond to his approach with all the composure of a woman who'd never been in love and never expected to be, but who was beautiful and amusing and sophisticated in case he hadn't noticed, her body forgot in the clamour of the moment.

She jumped to her feet, gave the pram a shove to make room for him and, in doing so, caught her dress in the pram's large wheels. When Mr Fletcher gallantly bent to free her, she also bent and rammed his head with hers causing him to sit abruptly, less gallantly. She also sat, hot and unamused, forget amusing. When she looked back into the crowd, she saw Martin Duffy winging his way through it, ducking and diving, looking to neither right nor left, hell bent, apparently, in his search for a decent drink for his landlady. As she followed his progress she saw him enter the house. On his heels was the girl she recognised from the Post Office as Norah Quirk, following him, but taking care not to be seen by him. 'Good heavens,' she said.

'No good heavens about it,' said Joe Fletcher. 'You may look like a slip of a thing with the grace of a dancer but that was clumsy.' When she didn't reply, he added, 'No need to be glum about it. I'm a bit of a clodhopper myself.'

'I know who's been delivering the horses to Mrs Worthington,' Pearl whispered urgently, any notions of impressing her company with wit gone for the night. 'Her sister-in-law. Mrs Murdoch from Upsand Downs.'

The smile that had softened his teasing vanished. 'Can you prove it?'

'I recognised her voice from the other night. It's as deep as a man's.'

'Drink, Miss McCleary?' Maggie asked, shoving her tray between them. 'Mr Fletcher?'

'Do you know Maggie O'Connell?' Pearl said. 'Of course you do. You're neighbours.'

'How are you, Miss O'Connell?'

'Have you seen Martin, Miss McCleary? Mrs Mayberry's looking for him.'

'In the house I think, Maggie.'

'Thank goodness. That's where he's supposed to be.' Which it both was and it wasn't. Adelaide would have liked him to be by her side even if he did look like a waiter. Louisa would have liked it less had he not been a waiter but still wished he were with her. He was where Mrs Mayberry wanted him to be very roughly.

Norah Quirk, following him not nearly as covertly as she imagined, hesitated when she reached the verandah. Mrs Mayberry had made the rules quite clear in her lecture to staff and sundry volunteers on How You Are To Comport Yourselves and What Your Duties Will Be Once Our Guests Arrive. Martin Duffy was in charge and he alone would have access to the main body of the house. Everyone else was kitchen only. So Norah hesitated, not sure whether she dreaded the wrath of Mrs Mayberry more than the disappointment of Mr Stokes. She said to Maggie O'Connell, who passed her on her way to reload her tray, 'What on earth have you done to your hair?'

'Cut it,' said Maggie.

'It looks . . .' Norah Quirk strove to be offensive without sounding it.

'Lovely,' said Martin Duffy, emerging through French doors from the Mayor's office where he had really no business to be even if he did have licence. 'Modern. Suits her.'

'Listen to you,' Norah Quirk said huffily. 'You're not supposed to be in there.'

'Mrs Mayberry's about to make her speech. I'm about to introduce her. You need to do a tray run before I get the band to strike up her march.'

'What room's that?' Norah asked Maggie as he hurried away.

'It's where Mrs Mayberry keeps her notes,' Maggie snapped. Then she disappeared into the crowd where all sorts of conversations and chance remarks were giving rise to amusement, amazement, boredom, indignation and hurt as they will do at any spirited gathering, Peace notwithstanding.

Norah Quirk, carrying a perfectly empty tray on her way to Mr Stokes, was waylaid by a young woman not much older than she was, who pulled her roughly into the shrubbery. 'Stop, Norah,' she hissed when Norah tried to break free. 'This is important. I haven't been able to sleep. You are not, I really mean it, Norah, not to repeat a word of what I said to you last night. I should never have mentioned it. You haven't told anyone already, have you?'

Norah shook the woman off. 'Don't be so silly, Lorna. I have to go. I need to see Mr Stokes.'

'Well, for God's sake, don't tell him.'

Whatever she did tell him caused Mr Stokes' face, large and pendulous, to contract with rage. 'See what I mean?' he observed to the Mayor, who had listened to the report.

The Mayor said, 'No trouble though, Mr Stokes, I want no trouble.' But it seemed to be brewing, whatever he wanted, as tiny incendiaries well beyond his control exploded in exchanges that were on the face of it innocent.

Larry Murdoch had struck up a conversation with Adelaide about her brother's intentions regarding Somerset Station. 'I want to buy it,' he was saying. 'I've every reason to believe he'd like to sell it to me.'

Louisa found herself buttonholed by Baby Worthington, who asked spitefully if she'd heard that William Mayberry was about to marry an heiress whose brother he'd served with in Syria, and Louisa was saying, 'Good luck to him,' even though her expression suggested that luck of any kind had deserted her.

Theresa Fellows was asking Maisie Jenkins if she had any idea what Lorna Stutt was doing in Prospect when she was supposed to be in Broken Hill with Frank O'Connell, and Maisie Jenkins was saying wasn't she back on the telegraph in Myrtle Grove?

Joe Fletcher was explaining to Pearl McCleary that his brother had indeed captured suspects on the Myrtle Grove Road and that they'd thrown great light on his Prospect enquiries. 'He'll be interested in your theory though, by Jove. Now what about a drink?'

Maggie O'Connell was speaking to no one. As she studied her reflection anxiously in the office window she saw on the Mayor's desk the *BLUETT V O'CONNELL LAND DISPUTE (FINAL!)* file with contents spilling from it in a way she knew for certain the Mayor would never have left it. She would have tidied it to save Martin Duffy's skin had not the Mayor's wife called her loudly to adjust her headdress.

It was both a relief and a nuisance to all of the above that Martin Duffy at this very moment gave a nod to the bandleader then hurried back to the verandah, where he sounded the dinner gong three times as instructed. The crowd duly fell silent, however urgent the remark on their lips, and where Martin Duffy should have called, 'We welcome Victory and the Peace she has brought to our land,' Ed O'Connell did instead. As Martin Duffy disappeared back into the house, the lad's wonderfully piping voice carried about the grounds and was so innocent and pure in its tone and intention that everyone cheered, so Mrs Mayberry forgot to be furious.

She appeared as if on wheels through the drawing-room doors, resplendent in a dress made from a flag emblazoned with the words King and Country and wearing on her head the best part of an olive tree, which Maggie had attached to her hair with wire. What wild acclamations. What clapping and whooping. The band played 'Land of Hope and Glory' as the citizens of Prospect marched behind her into the main tent where she mounted the podium and held up her hand for silence.

'People of Prothpect,' she began. 'Welcome.'

'Yes, welcome,' called the Mayor, from the back of the tent. 'I will of course be addressing you when my lovely lady wife has said a few words.' He waved to his people, who turned their backs on him, and annoyed by the insult and by his wife's unusual speech patterns, he allowed his attention to roam. He'd placed himself next to Mr and Mrs Murdoch, infinitely superior, he thought, to Mr Joe Fletcher, tenant of Somerset Station, whose standing with his wife was lost on him. Mr Joe Fletcher, he saw, had joined Mrs Nightingale and her housekeeper, natural enough when they were neighbours. He steered clear of Mrs Nightingale, out of deference to Mr Stokes who had no time for her. He valued Mr Stokes' opinion in as much as it was wise not to contradict it, either in word or deed. Mr Stokes, he noted, was not in the tent. He'd remained with his pig, turning it, basting it, lavishing love on it.

'And so it is with great pride, people of Prothpect, that I thank our brave men on your behalf and welcome them back into the fold of our community whoothe Christian values, so beloved of us all, they have defended against the heathens and the Bolsheviks.' A small murmur arose among the citizenry, expressing less concern for the accuracy, than approval that the theme so well explored in her last speech was being revisited by this wonderful local icon on such a momentous occasion. 'And now I have something of great import to ask of you. I would ask you, on this night of nights, to thupport me in my own battle against the self-same enemy. I intend to carry my battle, which is your battle,' she raised her arm as Victory did, 'to Parlia–'

Blast and rats! Her plea for their encouragement, and votes when the time came, so patently the true point of the evening, so beautifully poised on the tip of her tongue, was overtaken by a breathtaking scream, tentative at first then shrill and persistent, so terrifying at its conclusion that men at the back of the tent turned as one and ran towards it. They were followed by their womenfolk, whose intention was to bear witness or give succour, make tea or whatever else was required under the circumstances.

Mr Stokes was there before anyone, dragging Martin Duffy though the French doors while little Norah Quirk was to be seen leaning against the verandah balustrade, clutching her chest with one hand and her brow with the other. 'He assaulted me!' she cried to them all. 'I found him stealing from the Mayor then he tried to . . . to . . .' She was lost for words.

Pearl McCleary had left the baby with its mother in order to run towards the scream and, like everyone else, pulled up in horror at the scene before her. 'I did no such thing,' Martin Duffy protested. 'I would never do such thing. I don't know why she's saying that. I stole nothing. I didn't touch her.'

'I hope you're not calling Miss Quirk a liar, you young scoundrel,' Mr Stokes bawled, but whatever Martin Duffy replied was lost to the town as he was surrounded by Mr Murdoch,

Mr Stokes, the Mayor and Joe Fletcher. Mainly they wanted to hear what Norah Quirk had to say, which was less lost as she had managed to compose herself pretty smartly.

She'd found Martin Duffy in the Mayor's office stealing from the safe. She'd only gone into the office, which was out of bounds to her, because she'd heard a noise, like a safe cracking, and when Mr Duffy saw he'd been discovered, he'd jumped to his feet and taken her in his arms then forced himself upon her. The look on his face! The fear in her heart! As her tale grew longer and increasingly vivid and the crowd more restless, her mother took her by the arm and, attended by Maisie Jenkins and Theresa Fellows, assisted her into the kitchen. The menfolk bustled her assailant back into the Mayor's office while they decided what to do with him.

Everyone else was left to their own devices. Should the merriment continue given the plight of the wretched girl? They decided that it should, because, when you boiled it down, the speeches were dull, there was a pig on a spit, they'd already drunk quite a lot and they were here for the dancing. But when is dancing more fun than fighting and arguing and making your opinions heard above everyone else's?

Chapter Forty-five

Mrs Mayberry wanted to continue her speech but few of her guests could be persuaded to return to the tent even when the band struck up their favourite melodies. They gathered around the verandahs drinking, thanks to the committee stepping into the breach with the pouring. Before long, sides had drawn up – several sides, not just one against the other, all of them against each other.

The man was a Bolshevik, a bushranger, a common Irish thief. No one had ever trusted him. He hadn't fought, had he, what was he doing here anyway, and what had he been doing in the office when he should only have been in the kitchen? Others said no, he was allowed out of the kitchen. He'd been, inexplicably, in charge of the whole proceedings. Norah Quirk, equally, had been brave, foolhardy, too pleased with herself and terrified, poor thing. Or, she was talking through her hat and had made the whole thing up and was a known fibber, did everyone remember what she'd said about that blind boy who'd gone to war? No one could because they'd drunk too much.

What it boiled down to was evidence. Had anyone checked the safe for missing items? This was precisely what Joe Fletcher was insisting the Mayor do because, first things first, if there was no attempted theft then Miss Quirk must have been mistaken and the whole sorry incident just a misunderstanding.

The Mayor, in the presence of Martin Duffy, Joe Fletcher, Larry Murdoch and Archie Stokes, approached his safe, which was uncracked as far as anyone could tell, certainly not swinging open and empty of its contents. The Mayor knew for certain it was as he left it but he assumed the expression of a rich man worried for his fortune. He asked if the company could all turn their backs while he used the combination to open it. Archie Stokes gave him the slightest of winks and the barest of smiles.

How heavy was the weight of expectation on the Mayor. The battle between his best interests and his conscience was normally a battle of little consequence but tonight there were witnesses. He must be seen to be doing the right thing in front of the town's citizenry, especially Mr Joe Fletcher, whose brother was reportedly something secret to do with law and order. On the other hand, Mr Stokes was depending on him to ruin the Irishman whose foolish curiosity had taken him into territory that locals had long recognised was forbidden to trespassers. He was decided. 'Hang on a minute,' he cried. 'What's this?' He turned to announce his findings to the witnesses and realised that one of them, Mr Joe Fletcher, damn it, hadn't looked away as requested. What had he seen? What had he not seen? 'Absolutely as I left it,' he said.

'Are you sure, Mr Mayor?' barked the grocer.

The Mayor avoided his glare. 'Quite sure.'

'And is everything else as you left it?'

The Mayor saw quite plainly that the *BLUETT V O'CONNELL LAND DISPUTE (FINAL!)* folder had been disturbed but now was not the time to draw attention to it. 'Looks all right to me.'

'So a misunderstanding,' said Mr Fletcher.

'Apart from his assault on Miss Quirk,' said Mr Stokes.

'Quite,' said Mr Fletcher, and he might have suggested that she be brought in to show exactly how and where she'd been assaulted by a man who hadn't been stealing anything had not Maggie O'Connell decided that her beloved needed public defending and she was the very woman to do it. Miss Quirk had felt well enough to emerge from the kitchen with a smile on her face, which so rattled Maggie that she grabbed her by the arm and yelled into that silly face, 'You are a liar!'

'Didn't I tell you?' announced a large proportion of the population. 'A love triangle.' It was going to end in tears, mark their words. But it was worse than that. Young Maggie O'Connell was red in the face and shaking Norah Quirk, demanding she admit that nothing she'd said was true, that there had been no attempted theft and no assault on her body. 'I heard. I heard what happened,' Maggie shouted. She'd been on her way into the kitchen and she'd heard, plain as day, Norah Quirk ask Martin Duffy to kiss her and Martin Duffy tell Norah Quirk they had work to do and so they'd better get on with it.

The passion of her harangue brought Archie Stokes from the Mayor's office with a smirk on his face. He hovered directly in the eye line of Miss Norah Quirk, who at the faintest of nods from him began to sob. 'He pushed me to the floor,' she gasped tearfully. 'He did, Mum. Mr Stokes, he did push me.' Her mother said firmly, 'It sounds like a misunderstanding.' But

Maisie Jenkins, reading the grocer's eye, said shame on her for a mother. She demanded to know who this Mr Liffey was in the first place. He'd come into town from nowhere purporting to be the cousin of a woman no one knew the first thing about and there was nothing to say he wasn't a thief and a Bolshevik.

Louisa laughed out loud. 'I will say it.' She stepped into the light. She placed herself squarely beside Maggie O'Connell, on whose arm she rested her hand. Maggie released her grip on Norah Quirk but not her position three inches from the accuser's head. Louisa turned to the throng. In her best Hampshire voice, she announced she had never heard anything so preposterous in the whole of her life. Mr Duffy was Miss McCleary's cousin and Miss McCleary had arrived in the neighbourhood with impeccable references.

If neither observation were true exactly, it didn't matter because it suited the lovely widow to believe it for the time being. What was undoubtedly true was that Martin Duffy had acted with all the propriety of a neighbour's housekeeper's cousin and Miss McCleary could not have been a more responsible, well-regarded housekeeper. 'Mr Duffy has been my lodger for the best part of a month and I know him to be well mannered, intelligent, helpful, considerate and kind.'

'Yes, but how is he in the bedroom?' asked a lair, a joker, a wise-cracker, all in good fun, which was the spirit of the occasion but so far beyond the pale that a loud gasp swept like an outraged breeze across the lawns. It tossed high into the air any vestiges of laughter that might have been lurking. A few people chuckled but only briefly. It might have been what everyone thought, or wanted to think, it might even have been quite funny when Louisa Worthington was so stuck up, but it was outrageous to cast such aspersions on the widow of a man who had died for them.

'How dare you?' demanded Adelaide Nightingale, taking her place beside Louisa and Maggie. 'How dare you say anything so vile to the widow of a war hero? Miss McCleary is my housekeeper and I have met her cousin on numerous occasions. He's an honest, trustworthy and decent man, and a good many of you could learn from his example.'

'Ask the housekeeper if he's her cousin. Ask her,' said Norah Quirk. 'She doesn't even know where he's from.'

It was ugly. Could it get any uglier? It could. Maggie O'Connell administered a quick slap to Norah Quirk's face to spare Pearl McCleary from lying. Norah Quirk emitted such a howl of rage and anguish that Archie Stokes hurled himself onto Maggie O'Connell and pinned her arms behind her back. Martin Duffy was on him before Joe Fletcher could lift a restraining hand. He gave Mr Stokes an almighty push from behind, which had positively no impact on the grocer. 'Let her go!' he yelled. 'Let her go or I'll see you in jail for assault.'

The grocer roared with laughter. 'There isn't a judge between here and Timbuktu who'd listen to you.'

It was a desperate shame that Mrs Mayberry chose just then to stagger from the tent through the crowd with her olive tree askew, pale and tearful but striving for dignity. 'Stop it!' she cried. 'Stop it. I order you all to take your hands off each other and behave.' She turned to Martin Duffy. 'I don't know who you are, Mr Liffey, but if you are a Bolshevik then you will be found out and hounded from the district. As for you,' her wave took in pretty well everyone, 'I won't have anyone insulting respectable women like Mrs Worthington and Mrs Nightingale in my house.'

Archie Stokes inclined his head in the direction of Norah Quirk, who raised her voice in triumph. 'They aren't respectable,' she announced. 'And nor is he.' She pointed at Martin

Duffy. 'Mrs Worthington advertised for him. He is her part-time husband. He has four part-time wives: Mrs Nightingale, Mrs Worthington, Maggie O'Connell and his own cousin, Miss McCleary.'

The intake of breath was enough to deprive all the plants in that garden of life-giving oxygen. 'Trollops!' someone shouted. 'Whores!' cried another. The ladies, ashen and disbelieving, huddled together, speechless. Martin Duffy and Joe Fletcher took up positions in front of them but the crowd, which might have moved on them, was diverted by a voice that came from nowhere.

'Norah, you made that up!' shouted Lorna Stutt. 'You know that's a lie. I told you it was a lie yesterday. You can all take it from me that Norah Quirk is a liar.'

For a few seconds it was unclear just who had spoken because it seemed to come from the shrubbery. Maggie O'Connell broke away from her co-part-time wives and took one or two steps towards the crowd so she could peer into the darkness for a closer look at the woman so boldly bearing witness to her own testimony. 'You!' she gasped. 'You! Where's my father? Where is he?'

Lorna Stutt, formerly the redhead from the Post Office in Prospect, looked startled. 'What are you talking about?'

Maisie Jenkins stepped in. 'You know very well what she's talking about. You ran away with Frank O'Connell to Broken Hill.'

'I did not,' cried Miss Stutt in disbelief. 'I went to Broken Hill. I didn't like it. I came back to work at Myrtle Grove. Who said I ran away with him?'

All eyes turned to Norah Quirk, who smiled foolishly. 'It was a joke. What does it matter? These women advertised for a part-time husband.' But it was too late. Everyone knew Norah Quirk and everyone now knew she wasn't just a fibber but a liar.

Adelaide, Maggie and Pearl held their tongues now that their reputations were reprieved but Louisa, believing she was onto a winning streak owing to the quite strong drink she had enjoyed, addressed the party. 'All women need husbands of some sort, to protect and provide for us, don't we, Mrs Mayberry? You said so yourself and you gave us no choice. Not all of us have men to protect, provide, defend or speak up for us when we should be able to speak for ourselves. So what were we to do, Mrs Mayberry? We found a voice. We advertised for one and we found one. It's true that Martin Duffy has come to our aid and that four of us have shared him to tackle men's work because we could not. But I intend to convert him to a full-time husband and to make an honest fellow of him.'

If there was horror on the faces of her three co-wives, it was no greater than the collective amazement of the crowd, but Mrs Mayberry swatted it in an instant. 'And that is the message I will be taking to Parliament. Fellows must be full-time and honest. There is no room for part-time commitment in marriage if we are to defend ourselves against the . . .'

Popularity is a fickle thing. Perhaps it was the olive tree or the backbiting of the thoroughly peeved committee who were sick of being elbowed as they poured. Perhaps it was annoyance at her poor timing. Either way, the Mayor's wife's moment had come and her moment had gone as the crowd's roar drowned her out.

The Mayor, more experienced at spotting a drift, strode to her side. He said, 'Well that's quite enough excitement before we eat. Mr Stokes, if you wouldn't mind carving the pig, I think everyone would like some tucker.'

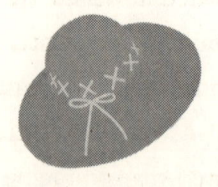

Chapter Forty-six

The residents from Beyond The Arch had no stomach for tucker. Archie Stokes fumed that none of them had been taken into custody and he threatened to arrest Martin Duffy himself, but Joe Fletcher would have none of it. He personally would escort the party from Beyond The Arch home and if anyone felt like stopping them, they'd have to deal with him first. No one felt like putting him to the test. He was tenant of the largest station in the district, his fearsome one-eyed brother was something or other to do with the law and he was carrying a whip and a gun. So they departed amid murmurs that were both delighted and disgusted, hounded from polite society when only hours before they had been its very epitome.

They made a sorry bunch: four ladies, one pushing a pram and another carrying a dress (unworn) on a coat hanger; two boys too tired even to shove each other; one waiter disinclined to fall into step with any of the ladies; and a man on horseback, riding to the side of them, acknowledging no one, intent on avoiding all gazes and attempts at conversation at which there was only one. 'What's your horse called?' Ed asked.

'Go To Blazes,' was the answer, which Ed thought was rude.

They reached the turn-off to Somerset Station without incident. Joe Fletcher fished a whistle from his pocket and tossed it to Martin Duffy. 'Blow three short, three long, three short and I'll hear you.' Then he took off, leaving the rest of the party to examine each other in dismay, because surely one or all of them had betrayed another and now their lives were in ruins. They each turned towards their homes without relish, in need of comfort, reassurance and friendship; a captain, anyway, to steer their crazily storm-tossed ship.

Maggie, whose landscape now included a father whose whereabouts were a mystery, clutched Pearl's arm but Pearl could offer her no hope. All of hers had died, extinguished by the certainty that the shame she had brought upon the ladies was too much to bear. Not only had she failed Beattie, her foolish planning without thinking had brought ruin to them all, and where she had a different life many miles away, theirs was here.

Yet as they huddled wretchedly in the street between Louisa's and Adelaide's, they looked to her for guidance because that's what they did. She led. They followed. She had rolled into town and led them all astray, as it turned out. She said, 'I'm to blame for all of this and I don't know how to help.'

'Don't be silly,' said Louisa, who imagined her own future to be miles rosier than it had been before Pearl's arrival. 'You'll think of something.' And because it was their general expectation, despite the horror they all felt for the damage each had done to the other, when Adelaide suggested they all go inside, by which she meant into her husbandless house, they agreed.

The boys were given bread and butter though they whinged and carried on about missing the pig and they were instructed to stay in the kitchen and amuse each other but to touch nothing. Their elders and betters trooped into the drawing room, where for a full minute they sat in shell-shocked silence.

Would a military doctor have counselled immediate return to the fray? Is it always right to address the implications of a battle when the bullets are still flying? Suddenly, as if someone had given the order to open fire, a hideous lethal exchange burst upon the tiny squadron and wounds were inflicted of the nastiest kind. Lying, stupid, thoughtless, selfish, insane. Think of an insult and its cartridge would have been on that floor somewhere. Only Pearl sat in silence, speechless from remorse, wanting to flee but knowing that to flee would result only in greater remorse. As suddenly as it started the barrage stopped and all eyes turned to her because she hadn't spoken and she had a duty to do so. They waited. She waited, praying for words to enter her mouth that would convey an immaculately conceived plan to save them all. A few came but none with a plan.

'There will be repercussions,' she said. 'I don't know what but there will be.' The sound of her voice encouraged at least one coherent thought because it was familiar. 'We must face the facts and respond calmly and quickly.'

Louisa looked as if she were going to speak but Martin did ahead of her. 'Any ideas?'

Pearl forced herself to address what she knew to be true. 'I'm sorry, Mr Duffy. I know you were acting with the best of intentions but the town will always suspect you of something. Theft at least.'

'I was looking for the contract Louisa signed with Mr Stokes. I thought it might have got lost in Maggie's file while we had it.'

'Which contract? What file?' Adelaide asked.

'A contract offering her an unlimited account at Nightingales that need be repaid only when she could afford it. Mr Stokes said you suggested it.'

'That's ridiculous. I'd never suggest such a contract.'

Pearl held up her hand. 'Did you find it, Mr Duffy?'

'No.'

'The Mayor said nothing was missing so apart from everyone suspecting you, there might not be any other consequences from that but there will be from the advertisement. We can't deny we placed it. It's in the paper and someone is sure to find it.'

'You were an idiot to admit it, Louisa,' Adelaide snapped. 'Such an idiot.'

'Have you all forgotten that I proposed to Martin?' Louisa replied. She was smiling at him as if she already had his ring on her finger. 'It solves the problem once and for all. Martin came to work for me. We fell in love. We'll get married and there we are, all respectable again.'

'Thank you, Louisa,' said Martin Duffy quietly. 'It was a very kind offer. I'm grateful to you all for your loyalty.'

'I wasn't being loyal,' said Louisa.

'You're not going to marry her, are you?' Maggie demanded of her one true love. 'You can't.'

'Of course not,' said Martin Duffy.

'Why of course not?' Louisa continued to smile. 'I wasn't joking. I mean it. I really do want to marry you, Martin.'

Martin Duffy stared at her in astonishment. He smiled back. His smile faded. He looked in anguish from Maggie to Adelaide and finally to Pearl. 'Thank you very much, Louisa, but I can't. It was part of the agreement. There were to be no romantic attachments.'

'Noooo!' howled Maggie. 'I never agreed to that. I told you, Miss McCleary. I never did. You all did. But I didn't and I have formed an attachment. I love you, Martin, and I know you have feelings for me. Don't pretend you haven't. We knew from the minute we met.' Her pleading eyes took hold of his and insisted they stay on her, insisted they see what she had seen and understood what she had always understood. 'Please!' she cried. 'You know how attached I am to you. My life is nothing without you.'

Adelaide said gently, 'I think we've all formed attachments to you, Martin. Even me and I already have a husband.' Her own large grey eyes full of meaning, as an afterthought, she added, 'Who has abandoned me.'

'I haven't,' said Pearl. 'And none of you should have.' Her voice was returning, despite its reluctance. 'You knew the terms. This was a business arrangement and no silly emotions were to come into it. If that's what's happened here, thank heavens he's going.'

'Going?' repeated Louisa, Adelaide, Maggie and Martin Duffy.

'Of course he has to go. He has to go because he's made an enemy of Archie Stokes, and Mr Stokes is determined to destroy him and us into the bargain. It's as plain as day. Surely you all saw it. He was working Norah Quirk and Maisie Jenkins like puppets.'

'I'd like to speak to Martin in private,' said Louisa.

'So would I,' cried Maggie.

'Mr Duffy?' Pearl couldn't help him.

Mr Duffy rubbed his eyes. 'Oh God,' he said. 'This is so difficult. Speaking in private won't help, Louisa. And, Maggie, you know how much I care for you. But even if it made all the sense in the world, I can't marry either of you. I love someone else.'

'I don't believe you!' Maggie yelled. 'Who do you love?'

Martin Duffy shook his head. He addressed Louisa, 'I'm sorry, Louisa. If I misled you I am very sorry. I should have stayed at the pub.'

'With Norah Quirk,' bawled Maggie, whose rage and hurt and fatigue were overwhelming her.

'Another pub. I should have stayed somewhere else.'

Louisa was on her feet, swooping up the remains of her pride. 'If you're going to go, Mr Duffy, please collect your things and leave right now. I don't want you under my roof a minute longer.' She turned to Pearl. 'And you can drop dead as well. Nothing has gone right since you took over. You're a menace and a bore and –'

'That's enough, Louisa,' said Adelaide, also getting to her feet. 'Your problems are of your own making, you know they are.'

'And they're none of your business.' Louisa was in the hall.

Martin Duffy was also on his feet. 'I'll see you home,' he offered.

'Don't you listen?' she replied. 'I never want to see you again.'

The door slammed in his face and the boys in the kitchen, relieved that the night was finally ending, appeared in the drawing room. 'We leaving now, Maggie?' they asked. But Maggie didn't want to leave. To leave now would be to walk away from the hope that had sustained her for so long. She had been going to marry Martin Duffy even when he'd hovered as a dim outline, waiting to take shape. Now he was living and breathing and within her grasp, how could she let him go?

'I can't,' she sobbed. 'I can't.' And suddenly she was sobbing so hard that the boys could only stare at her. They stood, arms by their sides, faces aghast, hopeless, helpless.

'What have you done?' cried Al. 'What have you done to my sister?' Who there could explain to the luckless brothers that their sister's dreams were shattered and not all the king's soldiers or all the king's men could put them together again?

Martin Duffy knelt before her. He took her hands in his. He said, 'Maggie, I wish you wouldn't cry. Please, please don't cry. I'm not worth it, I really am not. I would make a terrible husband. I was bad part-time. Think how dreadful I'd be full-time.'

But Maggie pulled back her hands. She buried her face in them. She wanted to stop crying, she so badly did, but how do you stop sorrow this bottomless? Her father was not in Broken Hill. Her father had vanished. And now Martin Duffy would vanish and she'd again be all alone with no hope of a husband or a father or anyone to share her heavy load.

'I promise you this though, Maggie. I will be your friend always and I will be there should ever you need me. I can't be your husband, but I will be your protector for as long as you need one. However it can best be managed.'

At which point, Maggie stopped crying but Adelaide's eyes began to stream, and her breath to choke, because she understood the sorrow. The words were those she herself had wanted to hear her from the part-time husband she knew was about to be banished.

She was his secret love. She was as certain as an unprotected woman could be.

Chapter Forty-seven

The rest of the night passed in misery for the residents Beyond The Arch. Martin Duffy walked Maggie and her brothers home with very little said between them. 'I hit a bird today,' Alec reported. 'With a cricket ball.'

'Did you mean to?' asked Martin Duffy.

'No.'

'When everything dies down, I'll come back to see you.'

Once the lamps had been lit and the young O'Connells were as safe in their own home as they could expect to be, Martin Duffy walked slowly back to the Nightingales', hesitating only briefly outside Louisa's, from which no light shone. Pearl let him in and directed him to the tiny box room, which smelled of damp, and to the hastily found mattress, which also smelled of damp. A dismal hush descended on all the households because no one could bear to say another word to anyone despite the misery of their thoughts and the horror of their options.

A very few hours later, as dawn broke, the Nightingale front door opened and Martin Duffy crept through it. He crossed the road and let himself into the Worthington house, tiptoeing to his room where he hastily shoved belongings into the suitcase he'd kept under the bed. He took a last look around the room and he left. As he pulled the front door behind him Louisa called, 'You're going.'

He replied, 'I am.' And that was that. All his part-time wives bid farewell.

He didn't leave through the town. He headed in the opposite direction along the road that would take him to the coast, and he might well have been walking for days had not Joe Fletcher, up with the lark, come across him and offered him a lift on his cart laden with feed. They travelled quickly along tracks that were hardly tracks at all until they met the main road within walking distance of Myrtle Grove and there they parted company.

'Thanks,' said Martin Duffy, shaking the hand of Joe Fletcher. 'You're right. She's a woman in a million.' A couple of hours later, eating the sandwiches Pearl had packed for him, he opened the letter she'd included in his lunch bag.

Dear Mr Duffy, it said. *I am sorry to have sent you away but I know you understand there was no alternative. Please accept an additional week's salary and my thanks for the help you have given us. I appreciate that the tasks were enormous and that you did your best. I have one more favour to ask. Could you please call on Annie McGuire at 94 Limerick Street, Bondi and give her the enclosed letter.*

'Oh, Miss McCleary,' he sighed, hearing her bossy voice in every line. 'I'll miss you.' His flibbertigibbet heart lurched disconcertingly, causing him to place his hand on it, to stop it from lurching again. But it would lurch and thump. The more he held the letter to his face to smell her soap on it, the worse it was. *Dear God*, he thought. It was she he loved. He hadn't had anyone precisely in mind the night before when he'd admitted an attachment that precluded all others, but there it was, blindingly obvious now there was distance between them. Miss McCleary was magnificent. She had been from the very first day they met. She was infuriatingly, alarmingly sure of herself, and she was always just beyond reach. It was everything he found attractive in a woman. She had confided in him and trusted him and in the end, he reckoned, respected him. He congratulated himself on loving her. He would deliver this letter as if his life depended on it. If he imagined her hearing him and staring sadly into the mid distance because he was gone and she was bereft, he'd have been way off beam.

Pearl might not have been any happier than he was, but once she'd seen him off, the fact that she had met Martin Duffy at all became just another cause for regret. She busied herself in the kitchen, numbing the terrible anxiety that gripped her innards. Very little had come from the facing of facts, apart from his banishment, and now she had to come to terms with the hopelessness that was left.

Mrs Worthington remained pregnant, husbandless, penniless and afflicted by dozens of horses. Maggie was as unremittingly on her own with the same boys to raise and the same injustice concerning her land, still without a father but with no way of knowing where he was. Mrs Nightingale still had Mr Stokes to contend with and a husband unaccounted for, though that struck Pearl as a very small blessing.

As for herself, she was no closer to finding Daniel Flannagan than she had been when she'd arrived and Beattie's heart was no closer to finding peace. Everyone was worse off than they'd been before Martin Duffy had arrived, and she was responsible for Martin Duffy. Annie would have said, *You made that mess, you clean it up.* And so she must, whether she felt like it or not.

Before anything else, she must see Mrs Worthington. Even in the cold light of day, marriage to Martin Duffy seemed to Pearl to be the worst solution imaginable to her problem. Martin Duffy was no more husband material for Mrs Worthington than he was a horseman. He might have made a husband for Maggie – it had been heartbreaking to see what hopes Maggie had pinned on him – but he hadn't wanted her any more than he'd wanted Mrs Worthington. He'd behaved both sensibly and honourably, but she was relieved he was gone.

'Where are you going so early?' Adelaide asked, emerging from her bedroom carrying baby Freddie.

'To see Mrs Worthington.' She was putting on her hat.

'What will you say?'

'I don't know.'

'Take her some eggs,' said Adelaide.

For a good two minutes it seemed that Louisa wouldn't come to the door but just as Pearl had decided she should make her way to the back of the house to break in, she called, 'Go away. I've got nothing to say to you.'

'I will go away, Mrs Worthington, but please hear me out first. I have a plan that might interest you.'

'Nothing you can say will interest me.'

'Then at least take the eggs I have for you.'

'I'd choke on them.'

'Please, can we talk inside? You never know who's listening and what I want to say isn't for public consumption.'

Louisa opened the door wide enough to allow Pearl in. She led her through the house and into the backyard, where there was a small table with two chairs. 'This secret enough?' she said.

'I can't imagine what business we have that the whole world doesn't know already.'

'They don't know you're having a baby,' Pearl said bluntly. 'That's what I want to talk to you about. I'm sorry things didn't work out the way you'd hoped with Mr Duffy. But it would have been a mistake.'

'And who are you to judge?' Louisa's face was the colour of soot. Her expression was ashes. 'You've never been married so you haven't the faintest idea.'

'And I might never have the faintest idea,' Pearl agreed. 'But you need help and I want to offer mine.'

'In that case, get rid of the baby, find me a husband, and give me a thousand pounds and a ticket to England. You can get rid of the stupid horses. You can burn my house down. You can let it be known that I never had any intention of marrying the man no one ever believed was your cousin and you can wipe the last month from my life so I can do it again without you or Martin Duffy in it.'

Pearl said without smiling, 'Which first?'

'Suit yourself.'

'What about this? I can arrange for you to go to Sydney and stay with Annie McGuire, who is the kindest woman on earth. She'll look after you until you have the baby and she'll help you decide what to do with the child once it's born.'

It wasn't what Louisa wanted to hear. Louisa didn't want to hear that she was having a baby. She didn't want to look into the next six months and see in it a misshapen body and a life inside her. She wanted to slap Pearl McCleary across the face for reminding her, and then she didn't. Then she wanted with all her heart for Pearl McCleary to fix it for her. She stared into the bedraggled flower beds and the trees that shielded her from the horror of the horses but not the horror of the rest of her life.

'Who is Annie McGuire?'

'The woman who raised me.'

'And why would she help me?'

'Because I've asked her to.'

'Already? Without consulting me?'

'You don't have to go. But if you don't go, what will you do?'

Louisa dropped her gaze. 'There's a woman in Stony Creek,' she said so quietly that Pearl might not have been intended to hear.

'There's always a woman. But is that what you want? The woman in Stony Creek could kill you as well as the baby. This way is better. You can just pack up and go. Annie could pass you off as her niece.'

'Oh, Miss McCleary. I'm from Hampshire. Why would I be her niece? At least Martin sounded as if he might be your cousin.'

'Then you could be a pregnant widow from the country who's come to her for peace and quiet.'

Louisa stared into the unkempt garden, striving to picture possibilities she might be able to accept. 'I could just pack a few things and go, couldn't I?'

'The sooner the better.'

'People might think that Martin and I have eloped. That would show them.'

'They might. It would.'

'It means no more Mr Stokes.'

'It does.'

'And no point in Baby Worthington delivering more horses.' Louisa smiled at last. Her sigh was long and steady.

In her expression, Pearl saw nothing more sinister than relief. 'How long have you known it was Mrs Murdoch?' she asked.

'A while. When you said she spoke like a man, I knew. Knowing made no difference. She was never going to stop. She hates me.'

'Why?'

Louisa shrugged. 'Jealous. She thinks her husband is in love with me.'

'And is he?'

'I'm certainly not in love with him.'

The many questions Pearl could have asked lingered for a minute, as Louisa considered the ground at her feet, then drifted away. What would she do with the answers once she had them? 'Another reason to go,' was all she said. And so it was decided.

A similar decision under similar circumstances was being reached regarding the immediate future of Miss Norah Quirk. 'You're going, my girl, whether you like it or not,' her mother was saying. 'I don't know what you agreed with Archie Stokes but nothing was worth the disgrace you've brought on our family. We are respected hoteliers. You'll stay in Ballarat until I send for you.'

'But Mr Stokes was right,' the sulky girl protested. 'Martin Duffy was trying to steal something. And those women did advertise.'

'None of it was your business,' said her mother. 'Now get up and get dressed. I've packed your bag. I want you on your way the minute you've eaten. Mr Wang will take you to the coach.'

'What about the Post Office? They're expecting me.'

'I'll tell them not to. Now get up!'

Within the hour, the troublesome daughter, wrapped in a blanket and wearing a very wide-brimmed hat tied with a scarf, was sitting up next to the driver from the brewery and she was carted out of town to obscurity. After such a night, why wouldn't cutting and running be the order of the day?

On the other hand, surely it wasn't the intention of Archibald Stokes who, for so long, had held the town in the palm of his hand? But it had been in the wind. Oh yes. The wind had most definitely changed direction with the arrival of the housekeeper's cousin. Mr Stokes had, every morning and every night since he'd clapped eyes on the blighter, held up a finger to test the wind's direction. Well before dawn on the morning after the night before, he detected a gale so hostile that cutting and running was most definitely the proper thing to do.

Wally Mason, a potato farmer from beyond Stony Creek, had pitched up as he usually did, before dawn, with unusual news. Cocky Watson, the very man whose shoddy sacks Stokes had been confiscating throughout the war, had been arrested on the road to Myrtle Grove on suspicion of dealing in goods stolen from the Australian Army Ordnance Corps. 'Arrested. Who arrested him?' Mr Stokes had asked in alarm. 'No one's told me about any arrest.'

'Not one of the usual coppers,' Wally had reported. 'Someone on army business. So are we agreed? Twenty quid the lot?'

'Twenty quid?' bawled Mr Stokes from habit. 'Forget it.' But there'd been no time to haggle, or any point. He'd told thieving Wally Mason to give his bill to Mrs Lambert, who'd settle it at the end of the month, take it or leave it, then he'd hurried to his office, locked the door and sat at his desk to think. The loss of Cocky Watson was the last straw. It was time to go, no doubt about it. He'd listened to that wind howling all night long.

The town hadn't turned against young Duffy. It had turned against Norah Quirk. The Mayor had turned against him because Joe Fletcher's presence had terrified the life out of him. And who was Mr Fletcher, he would like to know, turning up when he never turned up?

Now here was Cocky Watson arrested, and the last person he could trust not to blow the whistle was Cocky Watson, a coot of a bloke always grizzling about something. The quartermaster had warned him he was pushing his luck and maybe he had. Maybe he had given it one shove too many.

'Time to go, Archie m'lad,' the grocer said to himself. 'But first things first.'

Chapter Forty-eight

'Mrs Worthington has decided to go to Sydney until she has the baby,' Pearl reported to Adelaide as she removed her hat and checked the kitchen fire in one swift movement. 'She can stay with Annie McGuire. I've written to her. Mr Duffy will deliver the letter as soon as he gets to Sydney.'

'One less thing to worry about,' Adelaide replied. But she hadn't spent an undue amount of the night worrying about her neighbour. Without the faintest idea what to do about her, she'd decided quite quickly to do nothing. She had enough on her own plate and her intention now was to work on what was in front of her. She may well have woken with the same dread she'd taken to bed, but by the time she was dressed, she was sure of one thing: it would not defeat her. She would entertain no more foolish hopes for Martin Duffy. He might love her as he'd acknowledged the night before and she might love him a little bit but she couldn't seriously imagine a future with him. Not in Prospect, and she'd never leave Prospect. She had no great sense of loss. Not for him or Marcus. Instead she found herself embracing a sense of purpose. Marcus had left her to it, and now he was gone she would act on her own judgement.

'Put your hat back on, Miss McCleary. I'm off to sack Mr Stokes but I'd like you by my side.' And where, as recently as a week ago, she might have dithered this way and that arguing with herself and Miss McCleary all the way up the high street about the wisdom of what she was doing and the manner in which it could best be managed, today she rehearsed only what might happen if things turned ugly, which was to pick up the nearest heavy tin and throw it. But they didn't.

The shop had yet to open so it was empty of bodies apart from Mrs Lambert's, which was tired and listless after hours pouring on behalf of the committee.

'Mr Stokes about?' asked Adelaide. Mrs Lambert nodded towards the office door. 'Would you mind the baby for a minute? Miss McCleary and I have business with him.'

Mrs Lambert took the pram with pleasure. But the office door was locked. Adelaide used her own key to unlock it, and in doing so startled the living daylights out of her manager, who'd imagined he had all the time in the world to make his getaway. He was shoving ledgers into a baker's basket, which he quickly covered with his jacket.

'Ah, Mrs Nightingale and Miss McCleary. What a night that was, eh? That Miss Quirk has an imagination on her, doesn't she?'

'I've come to sack you, Mr Stokes. I'm not giving you notice. I'm ordering you to place that basket on the floor, move away from it and its contents and leave the premises now or I'll call the police and have you arrested for theft.'

The grocer opened his arms in a gesture of innocence and astonishment. 'Mrs Nightingale . . .' he began. But this wasn't any Mrs Nightingale he recognised. This was a Mrs Nightingale, he decided later, who might well have advertised for a part-time husband to take the place of an existing husband clearly of no further use to her.

'Go,' she said.

So he changed tack. 'You can't sack me, Mrs Nightingale, because I've resigned. There's a letter here already composed and addressed to you. I have no wish to work for the likes of you. This shop will collapse without me, and do you know what I say to that? Good riddance.' With that, he scuttled out of the office through the storeroom to the delivery bay, leaving Pearl and Adelaide to contemplate the mess he'd made of the desk and the filing cabinets.

'Mr Stokes is no longer with us,' Adelaide informed Mrs Lambert and Ginger, who'd turned up late and was now cleaning the windows. 'But it will be business as usual. I'll be running the place from now on.' Mrs Lambert, pushing the pram back and forth, said that was fine by her but what should they do about cash for the till. Mr Stokes had cleaned it out before they'd arrived as well as all the money from the safe.

In the Mayor's house, affairs could not have been more different from the morning before. There was no balance of power being fought over, no acid repartee about whose service was more important to the nation, no sense of doom looming over the Mayor or his hopes for the railway. Mrs Mayberry was a broken woman.

Despite her impeccable planning, despite the majesty of the occasion, despite its civic importance, despite the significance of her rallying cry to a better future with her somewhere near the helm, the party on which she had pinned so many hopes had been a catastrophe. It would be remembered only as the night Norah Quirk and Maggie O'Connell had fallen out over an Irish tinker, and the awful disgrace of Mrs Nightingale and Mrs Worthington, who'd apparently advertised for a man everyone agreed had been a gigolo. 'You must sack Miss O'Connell the minute she walks in the door,' was the only feeble instruction Florrie could issue.

'Of course,' said George. He could afford to be generous because he was perfectly comfortable with the night before. He'd displayed integrity and statesmanlike diplomacy. In fact he felt quite buoyed by the way things had turned out.

In the end, there had been as much eating and drinking and laughing and dancing as there should have been at a celebration whether it was for peace in our time or a win at the races. There had been a scene or two, but no bones broken, nothing had been stolen and Mr Stokes, it now seemed to him, had been put in his place though he wasn't sure by whom. His private plan was to extricate himself from Mr Stokes as quickly as he could. It was one thing to share the occasional useful confidence and to accept the odd useful bottle or leg of something but asking him to resurrect the stolen-land business had been one presumption too many and his vindictiveness towards the ladies Beyond The Arch had been unsavoury in the extreme.

'I don't believe there was any such advertisement,' he said to poor, limp Florrie, a misjudged remark because it somehow caused her to rally.

'Don't mention those women to me. They are prostitutes, all of them. I intend to form a committee to denounce them. They are everything I abhor.'

If this wasn't exactly what she'd said the night before, it counted for little. His wife was a woman of strong conviction and high moral standards. The Mayor saw a gleam of intention creep across his wife's sorrowful demeanour and took steps to smite it. 'I would watch and wait, my dear. See what everyone else thinks before you do anything decisive. It might be a good idea if we went to visit William in Sydney for a few weeks. What do you reckon?'

'I'm afraid you're fired again,' he said to Maggie when he found her minutes later in the kitchen contemplating the very large pile of washing up the boys had failed to tackle in the chaos. 'My wife won't tolerate your presence in this house a minute longer. You brought dishonour upon it and dishonour can't be tolerated.' He was speaking loudly because the marital bedroom door was open and he knew his wife was listening for any suggestion of disloyalty.

'Suits me,' said Maggie. 'It's all yours.' She collected her belongings, including the folder with her name on it, which she'd already removed from the Mayor's office, and three magazines containing her favourite stories. What did it matter? She was already an outcast. If she held her head high as she walked through the town, looking at no one, hearing nothing, it was only pride, the little she had left. Her poor head ached as it had never ached. Smashed dreams racketed about in it as noisy as the wheels of an out-of-control cart. They crashed into sorrow and rejection; they bounced over rage and defiance. She would lock up the house that was now beyond hope; she'd take the boys to the city to find a life that could be no worse than the one they had here. But first she'd settle a score or two. She wouldn't leave without saying what needed to be, and now could be, said because there would be no feelings to spare or comeuppances to reckon with.

In she bustled to Nightingales. 'What are you staring at?' she demanded of Ginger, whose expression, had she bothered to decipher it, was not of glee but of concern. Into the office she barged, where she found not Mr Stokes but Pearl bouncing the baby on her hip and Adelaide bent over the desk, staring at a page of figures that might have represented something in Egyptian.

'Hello, Maggie. You're good at sums. I can't make head or tail of this,' said Adelaide. 'Mr Stokes has done a bunk with the contents of the safe and everything in the till. I'm trying to work out how much he's taken.'

'Shh,' said Pearl to the baby. 'Mrs Lambert, can you get me a rusk?'

Of course Maggie was good at sums. She was especially good at calculating what should be and what wasn't. Within a very short space of time, no more than a few hours, which passed in a heartbeat, she was able to compare one set of books to another set of books and calculate the amount missing. She was also able to explain the inconsistencies, which were as obvious to her as the sixpence missing from the change Archie Stokes had given her for her cheese. By lunchtime, she'd handed to Adelaide a page of numbers arranged in neat columns all ending in totals. The piece of her mind she'd intended for Norah Quirk once she'd dealt with Mr Stokes was all used up in the joy of arithmetic calculations, which was just as well because Norah Quirk was halfway to the border.

News of Miss Quirk's flight was delivered by Theresa Fellows, who also reported that Lorna Stutt was to be comfortably restored to her proper position at the Post Office. The job at Myrtle Grove had only ever been temporary; she'd been marking time there only until Miss Quirk could be given the heave-ho.

Everyone would have laughed and laughed had the situation not been totally eclipsed by the news that Mr Stokes had cleaned out the safe and done a bunk from Nightingales. No one could believe it. 'The bloody bugger!' said Maisie Jenkins tearfully on hearing that the love of her life had taken to the hills. 'Where does that leave me?' She spoke for the town, whose mood swiftly changed from hungover to disbelief, rapidly escalating to fury at a grave injustice.

The extraordinary night had given birth to a dark, dark day. No one would miss Norah Quirk. But for the loss of Mr Stokes someone needed to be held accountable, and that someone was Mrs Nightingale Junior along with her sidekicks the unsmiling housekeeper and the fiery Maggie O'Connell, a known thief. Look at them skulking together in the office that only yesterday had been his. Look at them rejoicing like witches over a cauldron. They had seen him off only because he had revealed them to be creatures of the moral swamp they clearly were. Well, they would be made to pay. They certainly would. They would be *made to pay*. Archie Stokes had been a hero all war long and now he was a saint. If he'd taken money from the till as reported, it would have been due to him. The man was a saint before morning tea, and by morning tea the town had agreed to a woman not to shop at Nightingales until justice was done for that poor man.

That they were the objects of such anger and derision simply did not occur to Adelaide, Pearl and Maggie even though the shop was as astonishingly empty of customers when they emerged from the office to close its doors at noon as it had been all morning. 'Everyone's sleeping it off,' Maggie decided and the others agreed. If Mrs Lambert and Ginger had other thoughts they kept them to themselves, because that's where they had kept them under the reign of Mr Stokes.

The ladies walked home together oblivious to any whispering and back-turning because they had so much to discuss: firstly how to proceed with the case against Mr Stokes, which was mounting with every document Maggie uncovered, and secondly how to manage the running and maintaining of a thriving business when the only experience any of them had was Adelaide's. Maggie said she would be proud and delighted to take on any work Mrs Nightingale wanted to offer her and Adelaide was only too happy to oblige. 'You have an excellent head for numbers and I'm sure if you put your mind to it you could deal with some of the suppliers. Miss McCleary and I will be on hand to help you.' It might not have been what Pearl had in mind for herself but she was as silent as Mrs Lambert and Ginger.

Chapter Forty-nine

In their ignorance, it seemed to the ladies that afternoon that the awful fog of futility and despondency that had surrounded them for so many weeks was lifting. A way forward could be glimpsed for all of them. Pearl and Adelaide called on Louisa and it was agreed that on Monday she would take Mr Lambert's taxi to Cooma and the train to Sydney where she would wait at The Cumberland in Phillip Street until Annie McGuire came to collect her. All bills would be paid for by Adelaide. 'I would do the same for you,' Louisa said by way of thanks. Adelaide said she knew she would, though she knew she wouldn't and, another day, she might have agonised.

There was no need for agonising today. Adelaide was finding independence a very pleasant thing. She could make decisions without deference to public opinion, or anyone's opinion, and so she could be generous. With Pearl and Maggie by her side, she felt no fear of the basket of ledgers. They would no longer be a burden. They would serve her as evidence. Nightingales would make a fresh start without Mr Stokes, Marcus or his mother to interfere. There would be a new set of ledgers, drawn up and overseen by Maggie O'Connell whose genius had been a wonder to behold. *She'll get over him*, Adelaide had told herself of Maggie's broken heart as she'd watched her tot column after column aided only by a pencil. *I'll work her to the bone to make her forget.*

If Maggie herself was unable to trust in the happy future Adelaide saw for her, she was at least grateful for occasional pain-free moments it offered. Leaden sorrow continued to engulf her when she raised her head from anything engrossing. She mourned the loss of Martin Duffy's easy laugh, his affectionate gaze, his gentle touch, his reassurance, his friendship, his company, the life together she believed he'd agreed to. But she found herself comforted by the value placed on a skill she'd taken for granted as a critical tool for survival. She might still be unprotected but with a job at Nightingales, should there ever be a job at Nightingales, she could provide for the boys and they would eat well and often. She told them as much as they sat down to some excellent ham that Saturday lunchtime and they hugged her.

Pearl and Adelaide also viewed possibilities over a late lunch together. Pearl said their best hope for justice was with Harry Fletcher, brother of Joe, who was a law-enforcement officer with the Army. What kind of law was he enforcing, Adelaide wanted to know, but Pearl, honour bound, could only shake her head. 'He arrested some bushrangers,' she said. 'Joe Fletcher told me.'

'Then Joe Fletcher should tell his brother to arrest Archie Stokes because he's worse than a bushranger. I mean it, Miss McCleary. We have the evidence. Go and ask him. Take the sulky. It's a long walk along the lane. Quickly, go.' It was as clear an instruction as she'd ever given.

Pearl didn't take the sulky. She took a note. Her plan was to leave it and disappear before she was spotted. She had no confidence that Joe Fletcher would receive her with anything other than scorn, and the closer she got to the homestead, the more certain she was that he'd despise her. She'd been denounced before his very eyes as a woman without morals or scruples. Her intention was to tell Adelaide she'd found the place empty. The note said all that needed to be said. Mr Stokes had taken money from the shop and fled. He'd also tried to take the ledgers that incriminated him. She and Adelaide had caught him red-handed. As she turned the corner to the front of the house, her heart sank.

There was Go To Blazes hitched to the post by the verandah. Pearl told herself she could still take off without having to see him. She was on her knees, cramming the note through the very small gap under the door when it opened and she fell through it. 'There's a knocker,' said Joe Fletcher. 'Look.'

He helped her to her feet but she kept her eyes firmly fixed on the ground as she handed him the note. 'What is it?' he asked. Was that scorn? Loathing? How could she tell?

'A note.'

'What does it say?'

'It says Mr Stokes has taken off with the contents of the shop's safe.' Finally she met his gaze but it was just the gaze of a man receiving old news.

'Want a cup of tea?' he asked. She didn't. They stood together on the verandah looking out into the distance rather than at each other. Smoke curled from the chimney of a tumbledown shack halfway up the hill many paddocks away. 'Harry reckoned he'd take off when he'd heard about the arrests,' Joe Fletcher said.

'Shouldn't someone go after him?'

Joe Fletcher paused, weighing up her trustworthiness, she guessed. 'They'll know where he is, don't you worry about that.' He dropped into one of the two large chairs strategically placed to view the sunset and gave her arm a tug obliging her to sit in the other. 'He was the last link. Using men posing as bushrangers to hold up deliveries to the Army.'

'Surely the Army could have stopped him. They're the Army.'

'The Army was in on it. Not the whole Army. Just a dishonest quartermaster working for a mastermind yet to be unmasked.' Joe Fletcher grinned. 'Exciting, isn't it? Stokes is just a middleman, a very greedy middleman. Now that's as much as I can tell you.'

'Do you know who the mastermind is? You do!'

Joe Fletcher laughed. 'I can tell you no more.'

'You can't stop me asking. Louisa's horses are Army horses. So why's Mrs Murdoch delivering them? Is she working for Archie Stokes or for the mastermind?'

Joe Fletcher raised his eyebrows. 'You any closer to finding your missing friend?' Pearl shook her head. 'Have you tried advertising?' And where this might have been better said with a laugh, there was no laugh.

Pearl felt herself redden, first with shame, then with annoyance. A deep flush. 'Maybe I will,' she said sharply and in a fit of pique she regretted at once, she jumped up from the chair, hurried down the verandah steps and took off as fast as a housekeeper could while maintaining her balance and her dignity.

Joe Fletcher laughed at last. He said, 'You can't run all the way home. I'll drop you at the gate.' But she didn't stop, no matter how silly she told herself she must look. She couldn't. He unhitched his horse, caught up to her, swept her into his arms and up into the saddle, then he swung himself up in front of her.

They galloped down the lane to the side gate and as he helped her from the horse, his hand lingered very slightly about her waist. He said, 'Miss McCleary, I've trusted you with information my brother would shoot another man for blabbing. So keep it to yourself and keep your wits about you. You're too clever by half and I won't be the first one round here to have noticed.' She didn't watch him ride away. She hurried through the back door and directly to her room, wanting peace and privacy and time to recover from her extreme agitation at everything.

Adelaide waited no more than five minutes before banging on the door. 'What did he say?'

'He said I should advertise for Daniel.'

'About Mr Stokes?' Pearl opened the door and joined Adelaide in the kitchen.

'He said his brother knew Mr Stokes would run. He has someone watching him.'

'Do you trust him?'

'Of course I trust him.'

This was lucky. By the next morning, none of the ex-part-time wives trusted anyone very much, not even themselves. Each, in her own way, was juggling with an unfamiliar self who might also prove to be untrustworthy, so in their unease, the best they could do was stick together. Pearl and Adelaide called first on Maggie, then on Louisa.

They found Maggie supervising the boys' homework while preparing clothes for a job that didn't require an overall. 'Theresa Fellows has let me know she can't take Ed and Al any more after school,' she reported dully.

'They can come to the shop,' Adelaide said. 'I'll give them pocket money for sweeping.'

Louisa opened the door to them but didn't ask them in. She said she needed no help. They'd already done enough. She had private matters to attend to so they left, rebuffed but relieved because there was nothing to be said that wouldn't result in someone's hurt feelings.

On her own Louisa wandered from room to room looking for a hopeful future among the ruins of a messy past. She stared without seeing into the room she'd shared with her husband for just long enough to know the marriage would only ever have been temporary. She entered the room still smelling of her lodger, where she smoothed the blankets, sniffed the pillow, then jumped up quickly, prodded by the treacherous longing that was to blame for the state she was now in.

The kitchen, once so bare, was as stocked as it needed to be for an affluent landlady with a paying guest. The pantry spoke only of lost hope. She stared out into the overgrown garden where the falling-down lean-to remained unattended to by the man employed to put her life to rights.

It was enough to make a woman give up on men altogether. It crossed her mind to give all the unneeded food to Maggie. She thought she could sort through her wardrobe and possibly give her some of the dresses she certainly wouldn't be taking to Sydney as well. But these thoughts were idle and she soon forgot them. She spared no thought at all to the future of the baby inside her. She gave no thought to the horses. She gave no thought to her sister-in-law or her sister-in-law's husband, even though Larry Murdoch had taken her aside in a Mayberry arbour to assure her that the feelings he'd always had for her were as strong as ever. Ugh!

All Louisa could think was she'd wear her pink-and-white with the three-quarter sleeves on her journey because she intended to arrive in style. The hotel would admire style whereas Miss McCleary's pretend mother, she was one hundred per cent sure, would not.

She wondered how on earth she'd survive in a pokey house in Bondi with strangers so distant from her in every respect. They were ungrateful thoughts, she knew it, but they were hers not to be shared. What she would share was a brave face and no complaints because these would be her lot. If she were thankful at all, it was that her lot could be endured well away from the judging eyes of anyone she knew even slightly.

Chapter Fifty

On the first business day of their new lives, all the ladies were on the move well before the town was properly awake. Pearl and Adelaide saw Louisa into Bert Lambert's cab, then they, the baby and Maggie with her brothers made their way quickly up Hope Street in tight formation despite the empty streets. They reached the palace from which the prince had fled, passing only Mrs Jenkins sweeping the church steps, and they entered it through the delivery bay, which was empty of deliveries and of anyone attempting to deliver.

'That's funny,' said Adelaide. 'Mr Benjamin should be here from across the border. He always delivers first thing on a Monday. Was it my imagination or did Mrs Jenkins turn her back on us? Maybe she didn't see us.'

'She saw us,' said Maggie.

There was, however, seeing and looking right through, and that's what the town was doing when avoiding completely, which was preferable, was impossible. Loyal Mrs Lambert arrived as usual at half-past seven to prepare the counters for opening at half-past eight, but there was no sign of Ginger who, Mrs Lambert said, must be sick. By half-past nine, not one customer had entered the shop and there was no pretending it was the plague or an accident or everyone waking up and thinking it was Sunday.

Their reputations, which might have been questionable on Saturday, by Monday were in ruins. After Mass on Sunday, Lorna Stutt, who wanted only to be liked, had admitted in confidence to Theresa Fellows that the story of the advertisement had come from her, but not in the first place. She'd heard of it from the girl on the telegraph in Cooma, so who was to say whether it was true or not. Of course it was true, Theresa Fellows said. There hadn't been a body who'd heard it on Friday night who hadn't told themselves there was no smoke without fire, except possibly Mrs Quirk who had learned many years ago not to trust her daughter.

Given the very clear light in which the ladies were now viewed, the town agreed that nothing was beyond them. Had anyone had seen Captain Nightingale lately? He hadn't gone to his mother because his mother was on the high seas. Did anyone else think this was suspicious? Did anyone trust the housekeeper? Had anyone seen her smile? Who was she anyway? Arriving here out of the blue.

It seemed not to matter that young Mrs Nightingale had been a firm favourite in her youth and that, in her youth, if anyone had had a mean word to say about her they'd have been slapped down hard. Overnight, the sweet, slightly silly, large-boned but very popular Adelaide Bluett that was, had become the bullying, possibly murderous, wife of a deranged hero. She'd taken advantage of his illness to dismiss out of hand the store manager whose fierce loyalty to the family was famous throughout the shire. She had counted for nothing his extraordinary success during the war in providing the town with a showpiece from which they had all taken heart.

'Who does she think she is?' was the rallying cry. They would show her, and they did. They found they could make do with Merrivale the butcher, Andrews the baker and by swapping what they had from their kitchen gardens, home cows and chooks. As for suppliers, it seemed only those who hadn't been alerted in time turned up. The few local vegetable growers, dairies, butter and cheese makers who appeared at the door skedaddled the minute they'd been paid. 'Shut the shop,' Pearl advised at close of business on Monday. 'Put a notice on the door. Closed all week for stock-taking.'

The shutters were pulled down, Mrs Lambert was advised to take her holiday pay, to let Ginger know he should collect his, and for both to come back the following Monday. 'Let's get on with it,' said Pearl. They would stock-take down to the very last grain of sugar. They would itemise every article on every shelf in the shop, the storeroom and the delivery bay and they would match it to the entries in the ledgers. It was a huge task. There were so many shelves. And who knew what was in the small shed at the far end of the yard to which no one could find the key?

The three of them worked together. Pearl and Adelaide took it in turns to mind the baby and count items while the other made notes. In the office, Maggie painstakingly produced columns of figures gleaned from every last ledger, folder, exercise book, bulging envelope, brown paper bag and box full of cryptic notes. They all told a story, she was certain. She ducked in and out of the office to scan the shelves, biting her pencil, shaking her head, so absorbed that she might have been a bookkeeper all her life. 'The problem is,' she reported, 'I can't find receipts for half the stock I can see. I've no idea who he paid or how much he paid them. It must be here somewhere.'

Pearl might have saved her the trouble of looking, knowing what she knew, but when it all boiled down, what inside information did she have except the man was buying stuff that appeared to be, but wasn't, stolen from the Army by bushrangers who weren't bushrangers. Who was she to say there'd be no evidence in writing anywhere in that office?

'Mrs Nightingale, Miss McCleary, come quickly,' Maggie cried mid-afternoon. 'Look at this.' She carried a small box labelled *J Worthington* into the shop and laid its contents out on the shiny mahogany counter. She opened it with care and removed the first document, the contract Louisa had signed so foolishly and so recently. 'Strewth, Mrs Nightingale, look at the interest he was going to charge. Why on earth did she sign it?'

'Mr Duffy advised her to,' Pearl said.

Maggie paled. 'Don't tell me he was working for Mr Stokes.'

'Not a chance. He was as useless at sums as . . . I'm sorry, Mrs Nightingale . . . Mrs Nightingale. He thought he was getting her out of trouble.'

'Here's a contract for the horses. It's signed by Lieutenant Worthington, 9th March, 1918.' Maggie handed it to Adelaide.

'A month before he was killed.'

Adelaide handed it to Pearl who said, 'It's the key to everything.'

In many respects it was. Jimmy Worthington, it seemed, confronted by his own regiment's need for horses to replace those killed at the Front, had spotted a way to make money for his impoverished wife back home. He would bypass the usual channels. He knew about horses, he knew what was needed, and someone, it seemed, knew where to find them. The lieutenant couldn't pay until the horses were safely delivered but he would put up his house as security. That was the contract he signed, for 200 battle-fit Walers to be shipped as agreed. There was his signature. The scrawled autograph beneath it bore no resemblance to the name Archie Stokes. In fact it bore no resemblance to anything other than a scrawl but it vouched for the war worthiness of the animals and a delivery date.

Maggie took the contract into the light and stared at it. 'Let me have a closer look,' she said. She stared and she stared. Then she put her hand to her mouth. She passed the document to Pearl. 'It's clear enough when you get the first few letters. Jimmy Worthington did the deal with his own sister. She's the blackmailer.'

It was a bad time one way or another for Larry Murdoch to bang on the shop doors and demand admittance. 'You don't usually close for stock-taking,' he said when Pearl admitted him. 'Everything all right, Adelaide? Marcus home yet?'

'Marcus has gone to Melbourne. Remember?' How calm she was. Not even slightly fazed by a man with a smile as friendly as the blade of a breadknife. 'He needed to get away. His nerves aren't as good as they used to be.' How brave she was with Pearl and Maggie standing shoulder to shoulder with her, no longer tiptoeing nervously around the subject of her husband's weakened health and frail temper. Not even slightly betraying the knowledge she had of his treacherous wife. 'Now what can we do for you?'

'The audit.' Larry Murdoch produced a large envelope with a flourish. 'You'll be delighted with it. Not a penny out of place. Not a tin unaccounted for. Everything as it should be.'

'Which ledgers were you working from, Mr Murdoch?' Maggie asked.

'Well if it's any of your business, young lady, those provided by the shop manager. That's how it usually works.'

'Thank you, Larry,' said Adelaide. 'I'll read it with pleasure. Please give my regards to Baby. It was lovely to see her looking so well.'

'And what's going on here?' asked Mr Murdoch, eagle-eyed suddenly and reaching for the pile of documents on the counter. 'Having a clear out?'

'Exactly,' said Adelaide, sweeping everything beyond his reach and onto the floor. 'Maggie's about to gather up the lot and put it in the bonfire we're going to have out the back.'

'Good thing too,' said Larry Murdoch. 'Now where's Mr Stokes? On holiday as well?'

'He's left,' said Adelaide. 'He resigned. Didn't you know? You must be the last person to hear. He's been gone two days.' As she was speaking she was walking him to the door, which she opened to edge him out.

'Two days?' Larry Murdoch repeated. 'Two days? I can't believe my wife didn't know. Surely she knew.'

'I don't know what Baby knows or doesn't know,' said Adelaide. 'All I know is he's gone and we're stock-taking.' It sounded more defiant than it should have. She closed the door behind him and leaned against it looking from Pearl to Maggie with the same anxious gaze they had fixed on her.

'He's up to his eyes in it,' said Maggie. 'He and his wife are in it together with Mr Stokes. Whoever QM is, he's not a bona fide supplier. I'd better hide some of this paperwork in case they come back to get it. He didn't believe for a single minute that we'd burn anything.'

'We'll give it to the Fletchers,' said Adelaide. 'Don't you think, Miss McCleary? Can you run in those shoes?'

'Maybe you should go,' said Pearl. 'I always go.'

'Of course you always go. You know how to explain things.' Adelaide was standing no nonsense. 'Maggie and I will be all right here. The boys should be in from school any minute. Off you go.'

So Pearl went, knowing that she could explain things well and that any explanation would need to be calm and concise because matters were urgent and action needed to be taken. There could be no blushing or stammering or sulking or carrying on like a silly young thing, just the telling of cold hard facts. 'Lock yourselves in,' she said as she arranged her hat to best effect. 'Just to be on the safe side.'

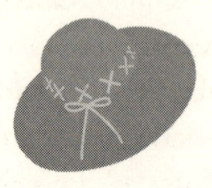

Chapter Fifty-one

It was to be on the safe side that Maggie decided to separate the most critical pieces of evidence against Mr Stokes and place them into a large shopping bag to be removed from the shop for safe-keeping. There were the papers from the file marked *J Worthington*, assorted ledger notes for mysterious deliveries, most especially those labelled QM, sheets of Maggie's own calculations with red circles to mark discrepancies, Mr Murdoch's audit and, dropped in at the last minute, the file marked *BLUETT V O'CONNELL LAND DISPUTE (FINAL!)*. 'Don't let go of it,' she said, handing the bag to Pearl. 'Don't stop for anyone.'

Pearl found Joe Fletcher in his yard, unloading timber fencing from the cart. He put down his load as she approached. 'You again?'

'Evidence,' she said, patting the shopping bag. 'The Murdochs are in it up to their eyeballs. Mr Murdoch came to the shop.

He's . . .' But before she could say exactly what Mr Murdoch was, Joe Fletcher interrupted.

'You need to tell Harry,' he said. They took the cart, jolting fast along the very bumpy track from the homestead to the shack in the distance whose chimney was now blasting smoke at a furious rate. 'Be prepared for a shock,' was all he said.

He hurried ahead of her, calling, 'Harry! Here's Miss McCleary. Murdoch's on the move.'

Harry Fletcher didn't greet Pearl. He rose quickly from a table in the far corner of the small dark room filling the entire space. 'When did you last see him?' He looked to Pearl for an answer.

'Half an hour ago. He came to the shop. He didn't know Mr Stokes had gone. He came to give Mrs Nightingale his audit. It's a load of baloney. And we've found the contract that proves Mrs Murdoch is Louisa's blackmailer.' She handed him the shopping bag, which he placed on the table.

'What's all this?' he asked.

'Ledgers, letters, a key, some folders . . . proof that Stokes was robbing the shop blind and Larry Murdoch knew. Proof that Archie Stokes knew Mrs Murdoch was blackmailing Mrs Worthington –'

'I think we'll grab 'em all now,' Harry Fletcher said to his brother. He reached for his hat.

'Not without me,' said Captain Nightingale, emerging from a room beyond. 'Hello, Miss McCleary.'

'Captain Nightingale,' said Pearl in alarm. 'Not in Melbourne. In good health, I hope.' She might have said, *Not dead? Not drunk? Any saner than you left us?* But she was the housekeeper, not his wife, and the man appeared more composed than she might have expected.

'Not in Melbourne. Held up on the way. And better than I was, thanks to these men.' His nod included a third figure, who appeared in the doorway and paused, causing Pearl to grip the back of the chair closest to her.

'It's all right, Pearl,' said Daniel Flannagan, limping towards her. 'I'm not a ghost.'

If all colour had left her face, if her mouth had dried and her body chilled, Pearl struggled to disguise it. Daniel was not the man she'd described to Martin Duffy. He might still have been in the order of five feet nine inches but he was thin and his face was grey and the look in his eye was careworn. He might have been a ghost.

It seemed, for a fraction of a second, that he might try to embrace her but the coolness of her greeting seemed to stop him in his tracks. 'You shouldn't be here,' she said. 'You need to be with Beattie. She's ill.'

'I know,' he said quietly. 'Harry has told me. I'll go home as soon as I've finished here.'

'And when will that be?'

'No time soon unless we get a move on,' said Harry Fletcher, heading to the door.

She should have kissed her fiancé, on the cheek at least. She should have hugged him and said she was pleased to see him. But she couldn't, paralysed as she was by the shock of seeing him in the flesh in the presence of another's flesh she believed she valued more. She chose instead to act as if this were a man who meant nothing more to her than the next returned soldier and whose appearance safe, if not precisely sound, was a matter of relief more than unbridled joy. Her head was as full of questions and recriminations and concern as it should have been, but her tongue had no access to them. She said to the Fletchers, 'I'm coming back into town with you.'

'No, Pearl, please don't go,' said Daniel. 'This is men's business. Stay here. We have a lot to say to each other.'

'We have, Daniel. But not now, I have my own business to attend to. It's neither men's nor women's.'

If the Fletcher brothers, or even Captain Nightingale, felt inclined to offer an opinion, they didn't. They looked everywhere but at Daniel and Pearl, and Pearl, in any case, was halfway out the door. 'If everyone's ready, I most certainly am. I need to get back the shop quickly. I will see you soon, Daniel. I'm pleased to have found you.' They were on their way before Daniel even had time to ask after Beattie.

The sad truth was that Pearl's thoughts were less with Beattie, Annie or Daniel than they were with Maggie and Adelaide. She had no real reason to fear for them – nothing in his manner suggested Larry Murdoch was a violent man – but fear she did.

Chapter Fifty-two

At the shop, Maggie and Adelaide were less fearful but jumpy nonetheless. The shop's front doors were locked and the shutters were down but everything was under control, with the possible exception of Ed O'Connell's hunger, which was constant.

While Maggie continued to sort and file records and Adelaide continued to itemise the contents of the shelves, Ed prowled. He looked for food from behind the counter, in the storeroom and for any scraps that other people might have left behind, but Maggie would say only, 'Ed, I've given you bread and butter. You can wait until we get home for your dinner. This is not our food to take as we like.'

No one noticed him wander into the delivery yard. No one heard his intake of breath at the sight of a figure in a dark coat with a hat pulled low, letting himself into the shed to which there was no key. Even Ed knew there was no key because he'd looked for it. Mrs Nightingale had told him no one had the key and the shed was probably empty. But the figure had a key and this figure, although not the build of Mr Stokes, was easily as big a wrong'un as Mr Stokes. Ed deduced this much in a heartbeat.

Thinking of nothing but justice, he called out, 'Hey, what are you doing there? This is private property.'

At which point, Baby Worthington turned and raised a rifle, which she pointed straight at his head.

Since Ed's experience of shooting was aiming and missing, he underestimated the nature of the threat and headed back into the delivery bay yelling, 'Take cover, everyone! There's a man out here with a gun!' And he might have slammed the door on Baby Worthington had she not fired, causing him to hurl himself into the delivery bay.

Adelaide, who'd been in the storeroom when he called, grabbed his arm and dragged him into the shop and then into the office where Maggie was placing herself between little Freddie and danger, yelling at Al to get in here quick. She thought he had. She thought he was under the desk with Ed so she pulled the office door closed and locked it.

'Open this door, Adelaide,' called Baby Worthington. 'There's no need to be frightened. I just need to talk to you.'

'Don't open it,' called stupid Al from his hiding place, not under the desk but ten feet from danger under the smallgoods counter. 'He's got a gun and it's aimed right at you.'

'Now it's aimed right at you, sonny,' said Baby Worthington. 'So get on your feet and walk out here where I can see you. Hear that, Adelaide? My gun is pointing at the boy so open the door.' In the silence that fell Maggie's mouth opened to give vent to horror but Adelaide put her finger to her lips. Baby's tone subsided into wheedling. 'I just need to collect a couple of items Mr Stokes left behind which he says are personal.'

'You don't need a gun for that, Baby,' called Adelaide.

'No, I don't. I thought the boy was a burglar. I've put the gun down.'

'He hasn't,' reported Al, believing himself too young to die.

'Baby, what on earth has Mr Stokes got to do with you?' asked Adelaide. 'What's it matter to you what he has or hasn't left?'

'Not much,' agreed Baby laughing drily. 'Except Mr Stokes dislikes you almost as much as I do and hatred is a powerful bond.'

'I don't hate you, Baby. I never have. I thought we were friends. We were very good friends, remember?' There was silence.

'Baby?'

'I remember, Adelaide. I loved you once. You know that. I told you I loved you. Now I hate you.' Another silence. 'To be honest, I don't care for anyone Beyond The Arch. That's the point, Adelaide. That is the point. Now open the door and give me the key. If you're going to be locked in, I'll be the one doing the locking.'

'Ow,' yelled Al. 'Ow.'

'Let the boy go, for God's sake,' called Adelaide. 'He's got nothing to do with you, me or Mr Stokes.'

'She's pulling my hair. She hasn't shot me,' called Al. But then the gun did go off and Al fell silent.

'Open the door!' ordered Baby Worthington.

So Adelaide did and Maggie rushed through it to take her rash young brother into her arms because all that had shut him up was fright.

How odd it should have come to this. Who was to blame? Everyone and no one, you could argue. Love is offered, love is rejected, love grows, love dies, husbands go or don't go to war, husbands fail to be the heroes or not the heroes their wives hoped they might be, parents prefer a son to a daughter. You could argue that, but not very well. Baby Worthington was to blame. She might have been full of pain but her intention was to inflict even more.

She lined up her hostages against the tinned goods, she pulled up a stool, and she spat venomous fury at them all one at a time, starting with Adelaide, who'd firstly spurned her love and secondly married Marcus Nightingale to whom she was so clearly unsuited. It had obliged her to marry Larry Murdoch, the clown. Did Adelaide have any idea of the pain that had caused? Of course she didn't. But she was about to find out.

She'd had her revenge and she was about to have more. 'See all this?' She waved her arms over her head embracing in her gesture the entire shop, its rafters and its contents. 'It's made me a fortune.' She'd been running Nightingales for years by remote control with the help of the greedy Mr Stokes. She'd been stocking it with stolen goods cunningly appropriated from Army supplies and all along the plan had been to pull the plug on it when the time was right. The time appeared to be now. The shop's reputation, the family's reputation, so painstakingly built during the war, would be as worthless as the naked shelves, and they would be naked, Adelaide. Stark naked. Baby Worthington hooted at the horror on the faces arrayed opposite her.

And where was Louisa? Deceitful, grasping, ugly Louisa who'd always looked down on her. Baby was grateful to Louisa. Louisa had been so whining and pathetic. Without Louisa it would never has been as easy to trap her Jimmy into a debt she'd known he would never repay. Now she'd get the house. It was the house she'd wanted all along. Louisa was welcome to Larry. She wished he had run off with her then she'd have been rid of them both.

On and on she went, sometimes on the verge of tears, sometimes laughing like a hyena, and all the while she was waving the gun about or training it at one or another of them.

'And look at you, Miss O'Connell, with your books and your figures, thinking you can outsmart me. You'll be smirking on the other side of your face when you have nowhere to live. What, didn't you know?' She had Maggie's property firmly within her grasp. It would be hers any day now, along with Somerset Station, because she had the paperwork. Of course it wasn't missing. It never had been. It was hers. Her husband had some uses and sliding court papers into unmarked folders was one of them. He'd been paid good money to make them disappear and the Mayor had been happy to turn a blind eye.

Was she raving? Maybe, but her cunning was plain as day. The extent of her plotting took their breath away. She wanted them all to be homeless for reasons that were barely coherent. Louisa had been so stuck up, Adelaide had been so spiteful, Maggie had been so . . . Catholic.

Al, who'd long ago stopped listening, was imagining what might happen if he charged. He had no idea what he was charging, man or woman – man, he was pretty sure – but he reckoned if he threw himself at his legs, he'd send him sprawling. He wasn't so big. On the other hand, help would arrive any minute. Someone would come. Miss McCleary had gone to get them.

But the someones, the Fletchers in particular, were miles away, staring up into a tree at the entrance to Upsand Downs Station, where young Ginger, in the employment of Sergeant Fletcher since Saturday, was describing the state of play.

'Mrs Murdoch's gone but Mr Stokes and Mr Murdoch are in the house. Listen to them.' In a wide open space surrounded by low hills, shouting of any sort can be heard for miles. This shouting was ugly and threatening, though who was getting the better of it was impossible to tell. What was clear was that Mr Murdoch had had no idea Mr Stokes was on the premises but more importantly, he didn't want him there. Without further comment, the Fletcher brothers dismounted. Walking their horses in opposite directions, they each took a wide arc around the property so one could approach from the front, the other from the rear. 'Here we go,' said Ginger to himself.

Pearl and Marcus were all the help that was on its way to the beleaguered shop. They'd taken Joe Fletcher's cart and left it outside the pub, where Captain Nightingale, believing something had to be said, confided his remorse. 'Who'd have thought it of Mr Stokes? He'll soon be under lock and key.' Pearl wondered at his calm, then worried about it. She had no faith in it. As they neared the shop he said, 'We'll go round the back,' and he led the way only to stop abruptly at the gates.

Baby Worthington's horse was hitched to the post by the delivery bay. The door to the shed that was always locked was swinging in the wind, its contents on display, enough guns to arm a regiment. 'Holy God,' he said. 'Look at that! How did that get there, Miss McCleary?'

'I'll go for the police,' said Pearl.

'That's Baby Worthington's horse,' he replied. 'Do you ride?'

'I can run. It won't take me a minute.'

'We don't need the police. We need the Fletchers.'

The Captain stared towards the shop, as silent as the grave, then back to Pearl as solemn as a headstone. 'What do you think she's up to, McCleary? Should I take her on?'

It was no question for a Captain fresh from battle, calm or not, to ask an employee for whom he'd previously shown little respect. He looked sane enough, but was he? It wasn't the time to put his capacity for clear-thinking or decisive action to the test, Pearl decided.

'Don't take her on,' she said. 'She's not going to kill anyone, is she? You go for the Fletchers. I'll keep watch. If the worst comes to the worst, I can go out into the street and yell blue murder.' How could anyone have known how mad Baby was?

The horse protested loudly at the unexpected weight of the Captain on his back but he took off in a flash of mane and tail and Pearl, alone in the yard, asked herself what exactly she intended to watch for and what she was supposed to do when she saw it?

The answer was right in front of her. She knew at once what she could do. The only window onto the yard was the very small one in the storeroom off the delivery bay. It was so covered in grime there was no seeing through it from either side so there was no need for her to conceal herself. She carefully removed from the shed the closest rifle with absolutely no idea what to do with it other than aim.

'Drop it!' roared Baby Worthington from the back door. 'Drop it, or this poor lad will lose the use of a foot.'

'Which foot?' asked the poor lad. 'I kick with my left.'

'Turn slowly,' said Baby Worthington. 'Drop the gun.'

The heroic thing might have been not to drop the gun but to turn quickly and blow her head off. But this isn't what Pearl did because she'd never fired a gun in her life and the head she blew off might just as easily have been Al's or her own. She dropped the gun. She turned slowly. 'Nice to see you again too, Mrs Murdoch,' she said, then she calmly strolled past her to put her arm around Al O'Connell and guide him to the shop. 'We're both here, Maggie. Don't worry,' she called because Maggie was screaming for Al and demanding to be released from the office so she could take his place in the gun's sights.

'Shut up!' yelled Baby. She unlocked the office and ordered everyone from it, except little Freddie who was sleeping and on whose tiny peaceful body she lay her rifle. 'I want the Worthington papers, the ledgers and the QM file. Where are they?'

'Burned,' said Maggie, who now had a boy under each arm, grasping them to her so three small ashen O'Connell faces were in a line like a ghastly painting of innocents in torment.

'We told Larry we were going to have a bonfire and we did,' said Adelaide, edging into the room to make a grab for the pram.

'I don't believe you,' said Baby. 'Get back, Adelaide. All of you stand back.' She stared at the piles of papers Maggie had created, neat little testimonies to the scope of Mr Stokes' dishonesty.

'If you can't produce them, I'm going to have to light my own bonfire.'

'Obviously we can't produce them if we've burned them,' said Pearl reasonably. 'Can I make tea? Shouldn't we all have a cup of tea so we can resolve this in a rational manner?'

Baby laughed hoarsely. 'Once a housekeeper, always a housekeeper.' With her eyes firmly fixed on her hostages, she took paper from the desk, set it alight from the lamp and applied the flame to the tallest files.

'My baby!' screamed Adelaide, stirring something in the crazed head of Mrs Murdoch, who thought about it for a minute then shoved the pram through the office door and into the body of the shop. She followed, closing and locking the door behind her. 'Into the storeroom,' she ordered, herding them in with rough nudges from her rifle. 'You can stay in there until the burning is done and I'm long gone.'

'The fire will take over the shop,' said Adelaide. 'We'll burn to death.'

'With any luck, 'said Baby. 'But I doubt it. You're the kind of woman someone always saves.' She counted them in, then she locked the storeroom door. They heard her prowling about the shop and within a very few minutes they heard her leave through the delivery bay, pulling its bolts noisily into place as she left.

'We're going to die,' sobbed Ed.

'We're not,' said Al.

'We most certainly are not,' agreed Pearl. 'This is what we're going to do.'

Four sets of eyes turned to her in expectation as she formed and discarded plans so rapidly she scarcely recognised them as they came and went. She was on the verge of suggesting they all throw their weight at the storeroom door when something combustible from among the tins did the job for her. It chose that very moment to unleash such power that the door blew off its hinges, revealing the hell beyond. Flames of every colour and size were licking along the shelves seeking nourishment from the packets and jars and bottles, which instantly saw the fun and exploded for the thrill of it.

'Get back. Get back!' Pearl grabbed sacks from a pile under the tinned goods and tossed them towards the others. 'Cover yourselves. Keep low to the floor. Mrs Nightingale, is there anything in here to dampen them?' She didn't wait for the response. Ignoring her own advice, she entered the inferno, grabbed the stool from which Baby had so recently unleashed her insanity and returned to smash the very small dirty window through which no body, unless it belonged to a small and wiry boy, could escape.

Ed, being the smaller and more wiry twin, was lifted and pushed through the inadequate opening. For a horrible minute, with his shoulders half in and half out, he appeared to stick, so he was given an almighty shove, which plummeted him to the ground, several feet below.

He gathered his senses, got to his feet then positioned himself beneath the window as instructed. He stood, as still as a rock with his arms stretched in front of him despite his completely useless ball skills, waiting to catch a very much smaller boy dropped by its mother into his skinny arms. Freddie was no lightweight, whatever the clinic nurse said about his erratic eating. The impact knocked young Ed to his knees and though the catch wasn't clean, it was taken and the baby, on arrival, yelled his head off. 'Run, Eddie, run and get help!' cried Maggie.

'He'll get it wrong,' wailed Al. 'He always does.' But he wouldn't go after him. 'You need me around,' he informed his sister. 'I'm staying.'

Ed didn't get it wrong. Within minutes shouts could be heard from the delivery bay and, at the sight of Maggie's face at the very small window, cheers.

'They'll have us out of here in a jiffy,' said Pearl. 'Everyone keep low to the ground.'

'Look, the flames are less and the office is open,' said Maggie. 'I know where the QM file is,' and before the others could grab her, she was back into the shop and weaving between fallen, burning beams.

'Watch out!' cried Pearl, spotting the danger before Maggie did. The shelves behind her were teetering, rocking, creaking, preparing to fall.

'Maggieee!' screamed her brother. But Pearl launched herself at the slip of a thing, turning her shoulder so taking the brunt of the merchandise tumbling onto them, and together they pitched away from the shelves towards the flour sacks where smaller but crazier blazes licked at their skirts. Pearl, one arm dangling uselessly by her side, wrapped the other around Maggie and dragged her towards the delivery bay where Adelaide was clinging to young Al, whose last hope of a reasonable upbringing appeared to be on fire. 'We need to roll them,' she said.

They smothered Pearl and Maggie in stinky, scratchy hessian and then they prepared to die because the flames had only been taking a breather and now the shop was truly alight and the partition between them flimsy as paper.

Outside the whole town seemed to be shouting. 'Push, push, push,' it cried. 'Push the bugger in. Come on, lads, all your might.' And suddenly the bugger gave up the ghost, and Father Kelly led Prospect's most able-bodied men to their rescue.

Chapter Fifty-three

Within hours, it hardly mattered that as recently as three days ago there had been a Bolshevik Irish part-time husband installed in the house of the town's most beautiful widow of a war hero, or that he was enjoyed not only by her but by three other ladies whose respectability had been trampled by notoriety at a peace party. The fire put everything into perspective, an act of God if ever there was one because God was angry with the town. Certainly He was angry with Mr Stokes, whose perfidy was acknowledged almost at once.

The miracle was, there had been so few injuries. Young Ed O'Connell had a bruised chest where the baby's head had crashed into it. His brave and pretty sister, whose cleverness with figures, someone said, had exposed the evil grocer, sustained burns to her hair, dress and shoes and scorches to the skin on her hands. Miss McCleary, equally brave, though not as clever as she looked, had a broken arm from Maggie O'Connell falling on top of her. She also had more serious burns to her ankles where her skirt had smouldered. But how much worse might it have been.

The fire truck had made unexpectedly fast work of the flames so there was little damage to the buildings either side of Nightingales, but as for the monument to all that was right with the town, it was now a stinking, blackened carcass of a thing oozing spirals of savoury with a hint of spice smoke across the township. As night fell, the people of the town could only stare in wonder at their loss. When Mrs Jenkins declared it wouldn't be the same without Mr Stokes, she was ignored. The smouldering wreck was a testament to his evil ways. It had had to go because of everything it represented. If the town felt complicit, it was only for a minute.

As with most non-fatal calamities, hope's appearance was pretty well immediate and, having been invoked by Father Kelly, so too was the word of God. This meant that God was probably less furious than a bit put out. It was generally accepted that Mr Stokes' customers could be held neither accountable nor responsible, and they agreed almost as wholeheartedly that Mrs Nightingale Junior had done her level best to bring him to justice and hadn't they always admired and respected her even when she was a new mother and mad-looking? They remembered that Stokes, always a thief apparently, hadn't been kind and helpful to everyone. He'd had a mean streak, hounding the poor for payments and racking up interest when they were late, even if he could provide unlike any other shopkeeper in the state. 'Cooking the books all those years. That poor woman,' said Theresa Fellows.

His evil, however, was nothing compared to the Murdochs', in whose employ he'd been all along. They had been the masterminds. 'Not him! *Her*!' Maisie Jenkins informed everyone because she'd heard it from Mrs Lambert who'd heard it from Ginger who'd been on the spot when Mr Murdoch and Archie Stokes were apprehended. Ginger had the whole story, tangled though it was, and how proud he was to tell it, which he did many times that night.

He'd been working alongside the gallant and wily Sergeant Harry Fletcher (brother of the tenant of Somerset Station), who'd been commissioned by the Army to track down stolen goods. They'd very soon suspected Mr Stokes, but it had taken them a little longer to connect him first to Larry Murdoch and then to his wife. But they had, and this was why Ginger had spent the best part of three days up a tree keeping watch on the comings and goings at Upsand Downs Station. The minute they'd connected Baby Worthington to the rogue soldier known as the Quartermaster, whom Harry Fletcher already had under lock and key, they knew they had their man. Woman.

The brothers had arrested Murdoch and Stokes in a brilliantly staged raid which had caught them by surprise. It had been wonderful to watch. He'd have missed it had it not been for the arrival of Captain Nightingale. Now there was a man. He'd been up the tree wondering what was going on inside the homestead, when the Captain had come galloping underneath as if his life depended on it.

'Stop! Stop!' Ginger had called because he had no way of knowing the man's business with the Murdochs, any more than the Captain could know that the Fletcher brothers were in the process of arresting felons. The Captain had stopped and, when informed of the situation, had considered what to do for the best, then he'd asked Ginger how brave he reckoned he was and Ginger had replied, 'Brave enough.'

The Captain had replied, 'Same goes for me.' Then he'd said, 'You need to get a message to the Sergeant. Tell him that

Mrs Murdoch is at the shop with my wife and son. There are guns on the premises. Miss McCleary is keeping watch. I'm on my way back.' And as he'd taken off to save them, Ginger had done exactly as asked, arming himself with a bit of tree, which, as it turned out, had not been required. Stokes was already handcuffed and Murdoch, having tried to run, was brought down in the dairy by Sergeant Fletcher, even though he only had one eye, in the best tackle Ginger had ever seen off a football pitch. When he'd finally been given permission to speak and had passed on to the Fletchers the Captain's message, Joe Fletcher had yelled, 'Shit!' then taken off like a bat out of hell.

The story was greeted with wonder and delight and many questions, including what had happened to the Captain and Joe Fletcher then, because they definitely weren't at the shop when the door came down and nor, as everyone knew, was Mrs Murdoch. Ginger didn't know and was alarmed to hear as much. There was talk of a search party but by the time volunteers had come forward and the womenfolk had given sensible instructions about the best routes to take, the need was gone.

As darkness fell on Hope Street two horses appeared trotting side by side carrying all three of the missing persons. Captain Nightingale was on Phantom, Baby Worthington's famous horse. On the other was Joe Fletcher, and sitting ahead of him, the dreadful Mrs Murdoch blindfolded, handcuffed and dressed like a man. A spectacle if ever there was one.

According to Constable McDermott, into whose cell they delivered her, and whose version of events was demanded by everyone who'd gathered outside the police station, Mr Fletcher had caught up with Captain Nightingale within minutes. They'd continued into town but when they'd turned Dead Tree Corner they'd seen her, beating the living daylights out of Slowcoach, the Lambert horse no one had noticed was missing owing to him always being kept in the far paddock because he was useless. She'd spotted Joe Fletcher and Captain Nightingale just as they'd spotted her and they'd had to chase the blinking woman for miles with her firing at them over her shoulder from the ex-Army rifle she was carrying. Despite Slowcoach's age, they'd had a hell of a job outflanking her. That they'd caught her at all was more good luck than good management. The poor animal had stumbled in a rabbit hole and she'd fallen off. 'Now excuse me,' the Constable said, 'I have prisoners to attend to.'

Late into that night, the town hummed with the same degree of excitement and inebriation that had signalled as special the candlelit peace party in the garden or whatever the ridiculous thing had been called. Several of the key players from that happy event were missing – Mr Liffey, Miss Quirk and Mrs Worthington had vanished off the face of the earth – but those creatures of doubtful virtue had been replaced by heroes, which was fitting because they rose, it seemed, from the ashes to restore faith in the town's essential goodness. Most obviously good, aside from Mrs Nightingale, were Sergeant Harry Fletcher, Joe Fletcher and Captain Nightingale, who, thank God, hadn't been murdered by his wife and whose stupid idea had that been anyway?

Bewilderingly there appeared to be a fourth hero no one had ever met or heard of, even by distant reputation. A fellow called Flannagan, another Irishman who was not the new part-time husband (ha ha ha!) but a returned soldier. The Fletcher brothers held him in very high regard, it seemed, even though Sergeant Harry Fletcher had shot him in the leg. 'He's a bushranger,' Theresa Fellows said to her husband. 'That's why Sergeant Fletcher shot him.'

'You're talking through your hat,' said her husband but, regardless of the late hour, he hotfooted it from outside the Arts and Crafts Club, where someone had set up a tea stall, to the pub to see what everyone else made of it.

They made nothing of it. They were confused enough already. Bert Lambert said, who cared? There was an even more important hero to salute and they should all raise their glasses. 'Ed O'Connell,' he said and everyone agreed, 'Ed O'Connell.' That young scamp had run from the back of the shop with a baby in his arms to raise the alarm, when all that had been visible from the front was a bit of smoke.

'The little bugger was screaming his head off. "Fire! Fire! There are people burning to death!"' That was how history recorded it. Less recorded was that he'd been blamed for lighting it by Maisie Jenkins, who'd snatched the baby from his arms and given him the shaking of his life. He had, however, shoved her large stomach and cried at the top of his lungs, 'My brother and sister are burning to death. If you don't save them, I will!' And he'd run back towards the shop just as its windows were blown out. Poor little Ed. Victim, villain, hero in less than six hours, not to mention orphan.

Chapter Fifty-four

Maggie insisted on taking the boys home after they'd all been examined by Doctor Pinkerton at the community hospital. He'd wanted to observe them overnight but she said, 'We'll be better at home.' She fed them on the chicken casserole she'd made for Martin Duffy, and together they climbed into the very big bed that had been their parents' and there they slept fitfully because they were sore all over, their nerves were raw and three in a bed was one too many.

Doctor Pinkerton would not hear of Pearl going anywhere. Her painful burns were treated, her arm was placed in protective custody but more worrying, he said, was the pace of her racing heart. 'You've strained it. You need bed rest. No visitors.'

Daniel Flannagan and Joe Fletcher both called to enquire after her but both were turned away because of her heart.

It was true. It was a mess. Her arm ached, her burns throbbed and her head contained so many thoughts, it would certainly explode if she added more. But her heart just didn't know which way to turn. Its choices were dread, hope and longing. Complicating them was love for the man who would certainly despise her for not having been truthful about the man she didn't love, and concern for the man she didn't love who would despise her for the same reason.

Adelaide could have reassured her. Of all the party that night, she was the only one who knew exactly where she stood in regard to the man professing his love for her. He'd marched into that hospital, taken her in his arms and whispered, 'I will never doubt you again.' He'd given the baby a pat on the head.

She had taken a step out of his arms and had looked at him long and hard before saying, 'Thank you, Marcus,' she said. 'I'm not sure that I will never doubt you again.'

There's enduring love, Adelaide might have told Pearl, and there's the love that can take only so much. Whack it too often too long and it bends out of shape so that what's left is no longer recognisable as the thing it had seemed to be. This isn't to say it can't turn into something else that might become worthwhile, but adjustments need to be made. 'You still have a home,' Adelaide said to her husband by way of consolation. 'I'm just not sure we still have a marriage.'

How decisive she had become. How clear thinking. They left the hospital together, and together they waved to the well wishers who'd gathered outside and who remarked how wonderful they looked together. But once they were alone, once their front door closed on them, the shadow of what had been took all manner of shapes until Marcus said, 'I need you, Adelaide.' She replied that she couldn't live with such anger as he'd shown since he'd been back. He said he knew. He hated his anger. He asked if they could pick up the pieces and she said she wasn't sure. First he needed to fill in those that were missing. 'You just took off,' she said.

He told his story simply. He didn't touch on the fear, self-loathing, anger, night terrors or the kindness of the Fletcher brothers and Daniel Flannagan because he was ashamed of them. All he provided was the sequence of events.

He and Cocky Watson had been ten, maybe twelve miles along the road towards Myrtle Grove when a man waving an ex-Army rifle had leapt in front of them yelling at them to stop. Cocky was all for running him down but Marcus knew a returned soldier out of his mind when he saw one. He'd asked for a lift to Myrtle Grove. An educated fellow, Marcus had guessed. When Cocky had grumbled to the soldier that he didn't need a gun to get a lift, he'd apologised. He'd bought the rifle from a bloke he'd met on the road and he'd been grateful for it. You never knew who you were hailing down, he'd said, and he was right there. He'd introduced himself: Lance Corporal Daniel Flannagan, lately of the 19th but formerly of the 5th. He'd gone to sleep the minute they'd moved off.

What had roused him was Sergeant Fletcher coming from nowhere, galloping alongside at breakneck pace and ordering them to stop in the name of the law. Flannagan had jumped from the cart and run. Fletcher had had no hesitation in shooting him and bringing him down. Cocky had taken advantage of the distraction to urge the horses on. 'Stop!' Fletcher had bellowed. 'Bring that cart to a halt.' Marcus had grabbed the reins and, in the process, pushed Cocky from the cart. Cocky had tried to run, so, Marcus, seeing Fletcher occupied with Flannagan, had given chase himself and easily caught him. Fletcher had loaded both fugitives back onto the cart and Marcus had driven them to Myrtle Grove with Harry Fletcher riding alongside.

'Weren't you terrified?' asked Adelaide.

'No,' said Marcus.

The funny thing was that all Fletcher did was take a statement from Cocky and then he'd let him go saying he had what he needed from him for the time being. Confirmation that would hold good in a court of law.

'What happened to the shot soldier?' Adelaide wanted to know.

'A doctor patched him up. And here's a thing,' said Marcus to his stranger of a wife. 'Flannagan was with Frank O'Connell when he died in France. Not in Broken Hill after all. In Ypres fighting for his country and dying for his country. A hero, Flannagan says. Took a bullet for him.'

Tears filled Captain Nightingale's eyes. His soft-hearted wife patted his arm. He patted the hand patting his arm. 'Are we going to be all right, Ade?' he asked.

'I hope so,' she said.

Chapter Fifty-five

Daniel Flannagan was the source of much conjecture in the days that followed. He'd been shot in the leg but not in France. He'd been captured by Sergeant Fletcher but in error. He was staying with Joe Fletcher, which meant he was an investigator of some sort. Constable McDermott confirmed it. 'Sort of,' he said. He appeared to know Miss McCleary but was not her cousin, though some insisted he was the cousin who'd been expected but he'd been waylaid by the pretend cousin Liffey, who had reported him to the police for a crime he had not committed. Had Norah Quirk been in town the story might have been even wilder.

Daniel himself kept his head down as he dealt with one thing at a time. He telephoned Beattie to say he was alive, in good health, good spirits but no danger, that he'd seen Pearl and they would both be home soon. He said no more because there was no more to be said. Pearl was in the best possible hands, but twenty-four hours after the fire, he still hadn't seen her.

His most urgent need was to fulfil the promise he'd made to Frank O'Connell. With the help of the Fletchers and the folder Maggie had included in the documents Pearl had taken to them, his hunt for the dead man's family had finally come to an end. It had been even more tortuous than the dying Frank had suggested.

Frank O'Donnell as Daniel had known him to be. Why he'd enlisted as O'Donnell and not O'Connell was anyone's guess. It might have been deliberate, it might have been a mistake, but either way, it was all he'd known of the man, apart from the fact that he came from Prospect, he had children and they had been cruelly wronged. The package he'd pressed into Daniel's hands had been addressed simply to My Children. It could be delivered only if justice had been done and their birthright restored to them. Not before. They had suffered too much disappointment in their lives already for them to learn their father was dead and the land he had lost would never be theirs.

It was Father Kelly who'd told him there was no Frank O'Donnell in Prospect. There was a Frank O'Connell, but Frank O'Connell hadn't been seen for three years and was said to be in Broken Hill. His children continued to live in the family home but the father was gone, for good apparently. Daniel had made his way from Prospect to Broken Hill but found no evidence of a Frank O'Connell or a Frank O'Donnell ever having been there. He'd been on the road back to Father Kelly when he'd shared a campfire with men claiming with a laugh to be bushrangers, who turned out not to be bushrangers but who, after a large amount of rum, boasted of stealing supplies from the Army for a rogue trader in Prospect.

The coincidence had been too great to ignore. It had been a small step in his imagination from rogue trader to fiend without a conscience but regardless of that, it had been safer than not under the circumstances to throw in his lot with the thieves. He'd stayed with them long enough to confirm that his imagination had been spot on. Archie Stokes, the middleman, had a fearsome boss. Harry Fletcher had laughed when Daniel had explained it to him, but the leads he'd been able to provide had been invaluable. In the long run, they'd led to Baby Worthington.

The morning after the fire, he made his way to the O'Connell house, where he found Maggie and her brothers pale and shaken and as nervous as kittens. The horror of the day before had taken its toll. 'Who are you?' asked Ed, still fully expecting to be arrested for burning the shop down even though everyone knew that Mrs Murdoch had. Maggie appeared in the doorway behind him.

'You must be Maggie,' said Daniel. 'I'm Daniel Flannagan. I fought alongside your father in Ypres.'

'Ypres,' repeated Maggie dumbly. 'When did he go there? He never said he was going there. Where is he now?' But she knew already. She saw it in Daniel Flannagan's eyes. She put her hand to her mouth because sobs were rising in her throat.

'Dad's dead, Dad's dead!' screamed Ed. 'Al, Dad's dead.' He ran back into the house, whimpering like a kicked puppy, then he ran back to the door again. 'How would you know? Why do you know? We don't know you. Go away. Go away.' But Maggie was asking Daniel in and closing the door behind him so their grief could be contained, even if it was grief for a father they'd long ago decided wasn't worth the bother. Maggie made a grab for Ed to hug him but he kicked her away and ran to his room, where he crawled under the bed.

'He needs to think,' said Maggie. 'I need to think. Al?' she called. 'Where are you?' But he was under the bed as well. She made tea mechanically, moving from sideboard to stove to cupboard to table in deepest, darkest sorrow. She sat at the table and waved to Daniel to sit as well. 'How did he die?' she asked.

'He died thinking of you,' Daniel said. It wasn't what he'd have said a week ago. But he now believed it to be true. Tears trickled from Maggie's eyes and down her nose.

'He should have let us know,' she said.

'He should have,' Daniel agreed. 'But he couldn't.' He handed her the package. A letter fell from it. She opened it and read it then she called to the boys to come and hear it because it would bring them comfort. She read it through gushing tears.

Darling children, it said. *I am sorry not to be coming back to you. I hope you will forgive me. I wanted to make it up to you for so many failures and disappointments, so much weakness and so much folly. I don't know who will bring you this package but whoever it is will get you back the land I lost and which is rightfully yours. Be brave and honest. Your affectionate, Dad.*

'What does he mean, Maggie?' asked Ed, wiping his nose on his sleeve.

'How will you do that, Mr Flannagan?' Maggie asked. 'My father couldn't manage it and I haven't been able to.'

Daniel shifted in his seat but said without hesitating, 'I can prove you own the land your father says is yours.'

'You need the papers to prove it.'

'I have them.'

'How could you?'

'They were given to me by Joe Fletcher,' said Daniel.

'Where did he get them?'

'They were posted to him by someone who knew where to send them. I know they're the ones you need because they're clearly marked as official proof of ownership. The person who sent them wanted them to be returned to you because an injustice had been done that needed correcting.' He could tell her no more because he knew no more. The Mayor hadn't wanted to admit his treachery, just to be shot of it. 'Someone stole the papers for reasons that aren't clear, kept them, then regretted it. You now have proof that the 400 acres your father said were yours, *are* yours.' And that was it, in a nutshell.

Frank O'Connell, Daniel was able to show, had spotted the anomaly in the land registry and had used all of his wife's money to buy the unclaimed 400 acres. The sale papers were tendered to the court but had gone missing, and Larry Murdoch had signed a statement saying to the best of his knowledge there had never been any sale to the O'Connells, who had been his clients for many years. That was the history as he understood it. There was possibly more to be made of the documents in the file. 'I'd like to study it properly. May I keep it?'

'No,' Maggie said. 'I'll keep it, thanks. If you want to read it, you can read it here.'

Chapter Fifty-six

As the days passed, the town began to reflect and it very soon decided in the privacy of its porches, kitchens, church steps or wherever else it congregated, that if Adelaide Nightingale, Louisa Worthington, Maggie O'Connell and Pearl McCleary hadn't advertised for a part-time husband, Nightingales would never have burned down. If Pearl McCleary hadn't turned up when she did, they would still be privy to its loveliness. It felt sullied by the loss. Of course this wasn't what it had agreed on the night of the fire but this is what it decided with hindsight.

The four respectable ladies didn't care one way or the other. They gathered the remnants of their pasts about them and extracted what they needed to proceed to the next bit because whatever the next bit held, it was far removed from where the last bit had begun. Maggie, for instance, now a woman of property, found herself adjusting to this new view of herself. She had land but she had no money. She devoted her days to deciding how best to turn one into the other. She spent pleasant hours with Daniel Flannagan examining all her possibilities, as delightful a pastime as she'd had since rebuilding the chook house.

Louisa was comfortable in Sydney. Her house in Prospect was boarded up under the supervision of Captain Nightingale, who'd been encouraged by his wife to set aside lingering resentment. The horses, for so many months a feature of life Beyond The Arch, had been removed by Sergeant Fletcher and returned to the Army. Adelaide had sweetly written to assure her she wasn't to worry because her neighbours would keep an eye on things for her and she had replied, saying thank you, could Adelaide please go to her bedroom and pack her green floral blouse, her grey skirt with the black trim, the cream crepe blouse and her pretty black shoes with the red strap, which she now realised she should have brought with her because Sydney demanded a different wardrobe from Prospect.

Louisa wrote propped up on the dear little day bed Annie McGuire had arranged for her in the sunroom and here she spent many happy hours. Beattie, so much happier and healthier since she'd spoken to her brother, waited on her hand and foot even though Annie had taken the child aside more times than she could count to tell her that Mrs Worthington wasn't sick, just having a baby and really she should do more things for herself because once the baby was born, she'd only have herself to rely on.

This thought seemed not remotely to trouble Louisa, pretty as a picture with her hair curling sweetly about her forehead and cheeks, which were fuller now she no longer threw up the contents of everything she put into her stomach before lunch. Quite honestly, she confided in Adelaide, she hadn't been this contented in years. She loved corresponding. There was always so much to tell even from this tiny house in Bondi. Did Adelaide know that the Mayberrys were in Sydney? They were staying for a month so she'd had to see them because she'd been spending time occasionally with William, who was now something important in the Ministry of Defence. He appeared not to be engaged to anyone despite what Baby had said. Horrible Baby, as Louisa had known all along, but out of her mind, which explained everything. She was going to have lunch with all the Mayberrys at the weekend. Why not? He was the Mayor, even if his wife was the silliest thing on two legs, and there wasn't even the faintest hint of a bump that she needed to hide.

To Pearl she wrote, yes thank you very much, she was quite comfortable in the room that had once been hers though the wallpaper was awful, wasn't it? Mrs McGuire was kind and thoughtful and Beattie a complete sweetheart now she was no longer Princess Gloomy. When, incidentally, did Daniel intend to return to Sydney? Soon? She couldn't wait to meet him. By the way, Martin Duffy was here only yesterday and locked in the front room with Mrs McGuire for ages. How funny, she wrote, that she might have married him. He was such a boy. Not her type at all.

Adelaide was almost as content. She continued to maintain some distance from her husband because trust takes time to recover. But she had forged strong bonds with Maggie and Pearl, whom she continued to call Miss McCleary, and she looked to the future with confidence. 'When the shop is up and running, we'll ask young Maggie to manage it for us. What do you think?' Adelaide said to Pearl, who was writing to Louisa. 'I truly believe she has the makings of a manager in her.' Adelaide once again looked with kindness on the whole world because this was her habit and so she was the joy she had always been to everyone who knew her.

Chapter Fifty-seven

Pearl's left arm was still out of action, her burns were still covered but her calm was restored, to all intents and purposes. Intents and purposes are the same as appearances. Pearl wasn't calm. Her injuries were enough to prevent her from tackling any household duties other than singing to the baby and so she wrote to Louisa and to Annie and to Beattie and then she found she was so agitated she wanted to scream. Nothing in her future had been resolved.

There was no question of her leaving Prospect even if the reason for her being there had been found alive and well and Beattie delighted to have him so. To begin with she was unable to travel and even if she could travel, where would she go, now that Louisa was occupying her room. There was also the matter of Adelaide, desperate for her to stay on in the household as something. 'I know you're not a housekeeper. Is Freddie too young for a governess? Or you could be my companion.' But the truth was, if Pearl left Prospect, she would be walking away from the only man in the world who had ever filled her sleeping and waking moments with longing.

'He's so much more handsome than you let me think he was. And so attentive. Will you marry in Sydney?' If Adelaide broached the subject of Daniel Flannagan once a day she broached it a dozen times, but all Pearl wanted was to shout from the rooftops that she couldn't imagine anything worse. He was a good man, he was clever and he seemed to have found common sense in France. One day he might make a fine lawyer but he wasn't for her. The thought of him kissing her made her feel sick. Nothing about his body drew her to him and if deceit was a sin of the flesh she had committed when she accepted his proposal of marriage, then a sinner she certainly was.

He visited every day and every day she steeled herself to say they had no future together, but there he was, so loving, so gentle, so steeped in the business of the O'Connell land that she hadn't the heart. He had gone to war to prove to her he was a man, he said. 'Just like Frank O'Connell, who couldn't face his children alive or dead unless he'd found them justice.' Then, as if that caused a comparison to enter his head as it had to hers, he added, 'Joe Fletcher seemed very surprised to hear we were engaged.'

'Why did you tell him?' she asked.

'Why wouldn't I tell him? I'm proud of you. Who wouldn't be proud of a wife who risked everything for you?'

Joe Fletcher sent his respects via his brother Harry, who called in on his way to Goulburn, where he would deliver his report on the suspicion, investigation, pursuit and arrest of Archibald Brian Stokes, Frances Elizabeth Murdoch née Worthington and Laurence Linus Murdoch. He said in passing that he couldn't have managed without Daniel and what a good bloke he was. He hoped he would be invited to the wedding. If this was Pearl's chance to say there would be no wedding, not to Daniel anyway, she missed it. She didn't miss it by accident. She rejected it.

She had great respect for Sergeant Fletcher and she knew he had time for her. He was in wonder at the bravery of advertising for a part-time husband, a post he now freely admitted to having applied for. He'd been tipped off by the girl on the telegraph at Cooma who'd been asked to keep an eye out for anything odd in the way of messages from anywhere in the district. 'I thought it might have been a code,' he said.

'It was in a way,' Pearl replied.

'Yes,' he said. He was a man of few words. Had she confided her reluctance to commit herself to a life with Daniel, he would have said, *Oh*. Sergeant Fletcher had only scorn for Martin Duffy. 'Goose of a man,' he said.

This goose wrote to Pearl a letter so ludicrously deluded she could scarcely bring herself to read it to the end. He admitted to having consulted with Annie McGuire, who had encouraged him to write by hinting Pearl had doubts about Daniel Flannagan. It was a confession Annie had tried to retract the minute it was uttered, but it had given him hope.

'I said I couldn't marry Louisa or be more than a friend to Maggie because I loved someone else. I know you won't be surprised to hear that it's you. Well you might be. I was shocked to realise it myself. I am not a man given to commitment as a rule but you are exceptional. I love you with all my heart.'

Surely such a letter deserved a considered reply. But Pearl was so disgusted with her failure to address either Daniel or Joe, that her reply to poor Martin was franker, blunter — well, crueller — than it ever needed to be. She couldn't even entertain the idea (she wrote to him). *Sorry Mr Duffy* (not even Martin) *but it's too silly for words. I know you'll agree in a week or two.* She was sorry she couldn't return his feelings and she really was alarmed to learn he was harbouring them even if the harbouring had surfaced only lately. Had she even the slightest inkling, she'd have told him at once to forget them. It was a horrible letter to receive and when Martin read it, he thought he might never recover. It took him days to decide he should invite the girl in the fruit shop to the flicks.

That he might be suffering at all did not even vaguely occur to Pearl. The part-time husband had claimed such a very small place in her affections that she could hardly imagine she had the place in his that he claimed she did. She put him out of her head because she had more important things to worry about. But no matter how much she fretted, still she didn't speak her mind to Daniel. In an agony of conscience, she told herself that maybe she could marry a man who so badly wanted to marry her and that she could make the best of it.

It was an argument that cut no ice with Maggie O'Connell, who saw through the shillyshallying and half-truths. She visited Pearl often, and, shrewd little piece that she was, had known at once there was something playing on the housekeeper's mind beyond boredom and a sore arm. So well versed was she in matters of the heart as described in serials such as *Oh Bitter Love* and *Deception,* that she remarked point blank, 'You don't want to marry him, do you? You can't marry a man you don't love. You know that, don't you?'

They were looking out across the Nightingales' orchard, where lemons were still on the trees and oranges were only now beginning to ripen. 'I do love him but he isn't the man for me,' Pearl eventually admitted.

'In that case,' said Maggie, 'you should set him free because he will be the man for someone else.' If she smiled to herself, good luck to her. Like Louisa, Maggie was beginning to see that alongside other men, Martin Duffy was a charming boy. Alongside Daniel Flannagan, he was a bit stupid. Daniel was a man who would protect and provide. Did she say as much to Pearl? She did not. And nor did Pearl mention Martin Duffy's declaration of love to her. But Pearl, on being advised that it was selfish not to speak, spoke, at last, very softly, on the bench by the river with the baby in the pram for moral support.

She said, 'Daniel.'

He said, 'I know.'

She said, 'Do you?' And he nodded.

'Too much time has passed,' he said. 'And I think you might love someone else.' He kissed her on the cheek (not revolting), held her hand for the briefest of minutes (soothing) and said he would love her always, and then he left.

Joe Fletcher arrived at the Nightingale back door via the gate in the lane the very next morning, when Adelaide and Marcus were out inspecting the progress of the shop with Maggie. He was delivering eggs, he said, because he'd heard the Nightingale hens had stopped laying. 'Morning, Miss McCleary,' he said lazily. 'Want me to make us a cup of tea?'

'I can manage,' she said but he insisted she shouldn't try, and in this slight exchange by the stove they brushed against each other, which so electrified their limbs they fused, as bodies do when a very strong current shoots from one to the other. He asked if he could kiss her, and she said he could.

Over tea he asked her advice. 'I've been offered Somerset Station. Young Mr Bluett wants to sell now he knows the O'Connells own a chunk of it. He doesn't want the fuss. He wants to get shot of it. And I might buy it. Just not sure.'

'Not sure of what?' she asked.

'You,' he said.

'You can be sure of me,' she replied, so he lifted her gently off her feet and kissed her for a very long time.

Epilogue

Three months have passed and all the ladies whose need for a part-time husband had caused them to confront what they wanted from a full-time one have taken stock and reached conclusions in as much as anything can be concluded in a lifetime.

The engagement of Miss Pearl McCleary, beloved ward of Mrs John McGuire of Sydney, to Trooper Joseph Fletcher (12th Light Horse Regiment), formerly of Dalgetty, son of the late Mr Ernest Fletcher and the late Mrs Ernest G Fletcher, much loved brother of Sergeant Harold Fletcher (12th Light Horse Regiment), was announced in the *Sydney Morning Herald* and *The Prospect Gazette*.

Mr and Mrs Marcus Nightingale were delighted to tell only their nearest and dearest that they were expecting a brother or sister for Freddie and that Nightingales, Famous Purveyor of Fine Food, would be open for business within the month. Its restoration had been miraculously fast because men from the railway, whose progress had been halted through lack of money and no Mayor with any energy to push it on, had moved into the town to supply the labour.

Maggie O'Connell, a single woman with a promising career, wondered if she were in love with Daniel Flannagan or Ginger Albright, who had visited every day since the fire and made it plain that he'd admired her all his life. Certainly he was a boy like Martin Duffy when compared to Daniel, who was a man, but look at him, working his heart out on the property, sifting through the disgusting shed in a way Martin could never have done and Daniel probably would never think to do.

Back in Sydney, Mrs Louisa Worthington wondered what kind of an idiot would let a man like Daniel Flannagan slip through her fingers. He'd already worked out she was entitled to her late husband's share of Upsand Downs, left to Jimmy on the death of his parents but taken by Baby Worthington who said it was owed to her along with the holiday house in Pambula to compensate for all the money their parents had lavished on Jimmy but not her. The very great joy of Daniel was that he knew she was pregnant and passed no judgement at all on her. He wouldn't mind who the father was, which would be a great help since she wasn't sure herself.

The Mayor and his wife returned to Prospect once he judged enough time had passed. 'The town will be back on its feet in no time,' he observed in the coach on the way home. 'I'm still Mayor, and you are still my wife.' If she didn't respond to the gentle dig in the ribs that accompanied this remark it can only be because the honour was somehow less than he thought it was.

After three months, did anyone spare a thought for the discarded part-time husband, now the amour of Mrs Elsie Patterson of Manly, other than to find him wanting compared to others? Now and then. He wrote to Maggie proposing the visit he'd promised young Al – or was it Ed – but she said they were actually very busy at the moment though she was pleased he'd kept his promise. The truth was that he'd served his purpose and now was surplus to requirements. His purpose, as things panned out, had been not to do what the ladies couldn't, but to show the ladies what they might achieve on their own.

Acknowledgements

I would like to thank my agent, Fiona Inglis of Curtis Brown Australia, for her loyalty, patience and encouragement, and Beverley Cousins at Penguin Random House for her clever and tactful editorial suggestions. I would also like to acknowledge the town of Bombala for its late railway, whose arrival inspired the landscape for this novel but whose population, neither current nor historic, are not in any way represented here; Carol Badewitz, who generously lent me her books on the town's history for guidance; the gallant Walers, 130,000 of which left Australia to serve in the First World War, though none returned; and the ladies of Nethercote, whose conversation led me to wonder what good could possibly come of a part-time husband.